HEARTS AFIRE

Blaine M. Yorgason

Book One: At All Hazards
Book Two: Fort on the Firing Line

BLAINE M. YORGASON

HEARTS AFIRE

B O O K   T W O

Fort on the Firing Line

SHADOW MOUNTAIN®

Library of Congress Cataloging-in-Publication Data

Yorgason, Blaine M., 1942–
    Fort on the firing line / Blaine M. Yorgason.
      p.   cm. — (Hearts afire ; bk. 2)
    Includes bibliographical references.
    ISBN 1-57345-525-3 (hardbound)
      1. San Juan County (Utah)—History—Fiction. I. Title.
  II. Series: Yorgason, Blaine M., 1942–   Hearts afire ; bk. 2.
  PS3575.O57F67   1999
  813'.54—dc21   99-11704
                                           CIP

Printed in the United States of America   72082-6464

10   9   8   7   6   5   4   3   2   1

For Karl and LaRue Barton,
dear friends who have never said no
when I asked for their help

CONTENTS

PREFACE

————◦—◦—◦————

Since the publication of *Hearts Afire, Book One: At All Hazards,* it has become obvious that the cast of characters involved in the settlement of the San Juan country is so diverse and extensive as to be almost mind-numbing. Hoping to ease that malady (which I also suffered during the writing), I have prepared a list of the main characters in this second volume, indicating whether or not they were historical and telling a little about them. You can refer to this list as you read the story.

Billy, Eliza, and Willy Foreman: Fictional. Their experiences are based on the journals and records of the actual San Juan settlers.

Mary and Kumen Jones, Bishop Jens Nielson, Annie Lyman, and Lemuel Redd. Actual historical characters, as are all others mentioned as part of the citizenry of Bluff Fort.

Thales Haskel. Historical character, Indian missionary, and interpreter assigned with his third wife, Margaret (Maggie), to assist the peace missionaries. He was charged by Elder Erastus Snow with bringing to a stop the thievery of the Navajos and Pahutes.

Posey. A historical character who was a young teenager when the Saints came through Hole-in-the-Rock. He quickly developed an antagonistic attitude toward the settlers, trying to humiliate or harm several of them, especially women, during the first few years. Despite periods when he became friendly and helpful, Posey nevertheless made continual efforts throughout his life to kill the Latter-day Saints. Severely rebuked by Thales Haskel, he was never able to do so.

Scotty, Old Chee, Poke, Mike, Too-rah, and so on. The Utes and Pahutes in this story are all historical characters who were involved in the incidents portrayed.

Natanii nééz, or Frank. A historical character, the tall Navajo was one of the craftiest thieves the Mormon settlers had to deal with. Finally Thales Haskel pronounced a curse on him, as described, and when it took effect he came to Haskel pleading for relief just as the story portrays.

Hádapa. A fictional name for a historical Navajo woman who came to raid but saw a starving Mormon child and took pity on it, thereafter making daily trips to bring fresh goat's milk until the child was healthy again. She became extremely close to the Mormon settlers in the process. Because we do not know her identity, or that of the wife of Natanii nééz, who struggled with the consequences of her husband's activities just as the character in the story struggles, I have chosen to combine the two into one character, creating Hádapa. I was never able to identify the starving child.

Dah nishuánt, Bitseel, Tsabekiss, Hoskanini, Hoskanini Begay, and others. All the Navajos are historical characters. Once again, I've tried to present them with as much historical accuracy as possible.

Bill Ball. A historical character who was the foreman of the LC Ranch, Bill befriended the Saints and did all he could to make their lives a little better.

Sugar Bob Hazelton. A fictitious character, he is actually a composite of four or five shadowy lawbreakers who left with their misdeeds neither their names nor the good feelings of the settlers toward them.

Curly Jenkins. A fictitious character, he is also a composite—this time of several cowhands and adventurers who wandered into San Juan County, often befriended the Saints, and left behind the respect and admiration of the settlers.

Alfred and Isadore Wilson. Historical characters, these young men were involved with their prominent father in the cattle industry in Southeast Utah, no doubt interacting with Spud Hudson, Bill Ball, and others. They were slain in the Pinhook battle as described.

Henry W. and James (Jimmy) Heaton. Historical characters, these young men from the mining town of Rico, Colorado, were not miners but appear to have been involved in the cattle industry in the

Four Corners area, trailing beef to feed the miners. Jimmy, who seems to have been as likeable as the book portrays, perished in the Pinhook battle as described.

The Rico Posse. Historical characters who were all members of the actual posse that chased down the Ute/Pahute horse raiders and were then killed in Pinhook Draw. There is no historical evidence that they were part of the same railroad tie-cutting crew as Dick Butt and George Ipson.

Dick May. Historical character who was robbed and killed by the Utes in the spring of 1881.

Tom and Bill McCarty and Matt Warner (Willard Christiansen). Historical characters, the careers of these outlaws were just getting started at the time of our story. The McCartys were also affluent ranchers on the southern end of the LaSal Mountains, and it is not known why they sold their ranch to the Pittsburgh Land and Cattle Company (in 1885, for $35,000) and turned completely to crime. Later, Bill was killed in a robbery attempt in Delta, Utah, and Tom and Matt teamed up with Butch Cassidy (Robert LeRoy Parker), the men gaining notoriety as the Invincible Three. Together they formed the nucleus of what became known by the late 1880s as the Wild Bunch.

The story that follows is a work of historical fiction. Whether the characters were fictional or real, and whether the incidents portrayed were fictional or real, everything has been rendered fictitious through circumstances, interactions, and dialogue that are solely my creation. That having been said, the major historical events portrayed in the following story did happen, either on the dates given in the story or as close to those dates as I was able to determine. The story begins on Monday, March 28, 1881, and ends Wednesday, May 18, 1881, not quite two months later. I was astounded by all that happened in that not-quite seven weeks of history, and I was forced to leave out a great deal simply so the story might be made manageable.

The Navajo story in chapter 16 is adapted from stories told by Tom Ration and printed in *Stories of Traditional Navajo Life and Culture* (Tsaile, Ariz.: Navajo Community College Press, 1977).

This book is written chronologically, each chapter comprising one day in the lives of one or more of the four major groups of San

Juan inhabitants—the Mormon settlers, the Navajos, the Utes and Pahutes, and the ranchers and cowboys. Initially this format may seem a little confusing, but I could think of no other way to accurately represent what was occurring almost daily with each of these groups that would affect one or more of the others.

From what follows, it should be obvious that all of these inhabitants were literally living on the firing line of the San Juan frontier, where life-threatening danger was ever present and survival was never guaranteed. This seems to have been especially so for the Latter-day Saint settlers, for whom the year 1881 was particularly difficult and in fact became pivotal for testing and trying their faith. I have done my best to portray that in the following story, *Hearts Afire, Book Two: Fort on the Firing Line,* as well as in *Hearts Afire, Book Three: Curly Bill's Christmas,* which will finish the year 1881 and will follow shortly.

PROLOGUE

○—○—○

Sunday, September 26, 1880

Bluff Fort

It was hot! Despite the lateness of the season it felt like August, and Elder Erastus Snow found himself wondering how these settlers he had called to settle the San Juan more than a year before could manage to work in such oppressive heat. And that wasn't all that was oppressive, he thought as he ignored the disapproving glance of Elder Brigham Young, Jr., and shrugged out of his coat. For a fact these few Saints were being oppressed on every hand, and the elderly apostle found his heart going out to them.

Beneath the cottonwood bowery a slight breeze stirred, and Elder Snow couldn't help but notice the relief on the faces of the eighty or so people who had gathered to hear his reply to their petition for release. A few more than eighty people, he thought, out of more than two hundred who had come through Hole-in-the-Rock the previous winter to establish a peace mission in this last true wilderness in the territory. That was all who had stayed with the community, all who had decided to make the mission call a permanent part of their lives. Of course, a few more had settled on Montezuma Creek, and Captain Silas Smith had taken several additional families on to the San Louis Valley of Colorado—families who were technically still a part of the peace mission. But it was these people seated before him, Elder Snow knew, who would be called upon to bear the brunt of the terrible opposition they were already encountering. If they chose to stay, they were the ones who would man the little fort

1

they were building; they were the ones who would hold the firing line secure for the remainder of the territory.

These eighty people were to bring peace to this formidable country with its intractable inhabitants, and more than half of that pitifully small number were women and children—

—◦—◦—◦—

"President Lyman, thank you for that wonderful introduction." Pausing to take another deep breath, Elder Snow squinted his burning eyes against the glare of sun on sand and rock. Even beneath this leafy bowery, the brightness was intense, and coupled with the heat, it seemed almost more than a human could bear. "Brothers and sisters," he continued, "Platte Lyman is going to make an excellent stake president, and we encourage you to do all you can to support him."

Pausing to wipe his forehead, Elder Snow wished for a moment that he had borrowed one of Sister Eliza Foreman's woven fans, which were seeing action throughout the congregation. He looked down to where she was taking care of her baby, who seemed quite fussy that morning. It was nothing short of a miracle that the older woman had given birth at all, and Erastus Snow was pleased for her and her husband, Billy, just as he was pleased for the good things in the lives of all the others. If only his news for them could have been different—

"The brethren in Salt Lake have considered, very prayerfully, I might add, your petition for release from this mission. Certainly that would seem the logical decision to make, for the opposition you face in this country seems formidable. But contrary to the logic of man, it appears that the Lord desires you to stay. Of course each of you is free to choose, and no one who leaves will be thought less of. But for those who decide to continue their mission, I'm authorized to promise that in a coming day the Lord will reward you for your faithfulness.

"Now because I feel so keenly your disappointment at this news, and because many of you are too young to have experienced these things, perhaps it might be helpful if I rehearsed for you a little of why you were called to this place. Brother Haskel, if you have anything to add, please feel free to interrupt me at any point."

From the rear of the congregation, almost all of whom were seated on blankets or canvas tarps on the ground, Thales Haskel nodded. Drawing a deep breath, the elderly apostle plunged ahead.

"On that day in 1847 when Orson Pratt and I first entered the Valley of the Salt Lake, it appeared to us that we were utterly alone. In fact we may have been, but whether we were or not, that valley and every other valley in the territory already had other inhabitants who soon became alarmed at our ever-increasing numbers. Through that long, cold winter these inhabitants—Ute, Pahute and Shoshone—drew their scanty rabbit-skin robes around themselves and nursed the little fires in their *wickiups* while they talked of the new adobe fort and its determined builders. Already they knew of our desires for friendship, but friendly or not, we had settled in their country, and if more of us came, they were going to lose more of their country to us. Believe me when I tell you that many of them knew and understood this fact clearly.

"In 1848 we sent explorers for hundreds of miles in every direction searching for suitable sites for new communities, and by that next winter we had two new communities surrounded by forts—in Sanpete and Utah valleys. Especially alarmed by the fort in Utah Valley, the Utes attacked, losing so many lives in the fight that within days the survivors were pleading for peace.

"By 1851 we had spread 300 miles to the south, into a fort at Parowan, and nearly that far north, into a fort in the Limhi Valley. Chief Walker of the Utes, seeing the strength of our forts and the dogged determination of our people, met with Brigham Young and encouraged further settlement, declaring that he wanted his people to learn the ways of the Mormons.

"Of course his intentions were to fight fire with fire, knowledge with knowledge, education with education. If he could get his people onto an equal footing with ours, he reasoned, then the crushing tide of our growth could be stopped. What Chief Walker didn't understand was that God had ordained this territory as the promised land of the Latter-day Saints, just as surely as the ancient land of Canaan had been ordained for the Israelites, and the best hope for Walker's people was not to oppose us but to join us. Walker's peaceful resolutions lasted until 1853 when, alarmed at our amazing numbers, he led an all-out war that lasted two years and forced us to abandon a few of our more distant forts.

"Yet even as the Walker War came to an end in 1855, the settlers in the southern end of the territory were becoming more and more aware of a tribe of Indians off to the southeast who were natural robbers, considering it folly to make peace with any people having valuable substance of which they could be despoiled.

"These robbers, the Navajos, struck always where they were least expected, and they'd made such careful preparation for retreat that they were always far away before their raids were discovered. Elusive and wary as coyotes, they weren't striking in reprisal for wrongs they had suffered or because their country was being invaded. In long and well-planned expeditions from their homeland, they were intent on taking horses, sheep, cattle—anything they could use or sell.

"While this tribe from the southeast wore their plundering trails deeper every month, the suffering settlers along the border appealed to their leaders for wisdom and a way to survive. Walker and his braves had been pacified, and comparative peace restored to the settlements to the north and west, but this Navajo menace seemed only to be getting into better position for greater activity. The Latter-day Saints had offered peace to the Utes and sued for peace before taking up arms against them. The only logical thing now was to send messengers into the distant Navajo country, inviting them to trade and live together in peace and harmony. These messengers were also to visit the Hopi, a friendly and industrious people whom the Navajos hated and plundered.

"Unfortunately, the Navajo considered his best neighbor to be the one he could plunder most easily. Jacob Hamblin, a great lover of the Indians and an ardent advocate for peace, took with him Brother Thales Haskel here, Ira Hatch, George A. Smith, Jr., and others, and made the long journey into the country of the Navajo, where they toiled from place to place seeking a hearing. But when the Navajo observed these Mormons consorting with the Hopi, who themselves were always cringing from war and pleading for peace, they concluded that the two were no doubt alike, timorous and fearful. Why be friendly with any people of whom they were not afraid, they asked themselves? Especially when they could so easily enrich themselves from such people.

"Haughty and vain in their declaration that they had no fear of white men who had failed miserably for generations to conquer them, the Navajos spurned and rejected these offers of peace. This attitude culminated in an attack on the missionaries, during which two warriors craftily disarmed the innocent and unsuspecting George A. Smith, Jr., who was only a lad of fifteen, after which they cruelly shot him with both bullets and arrows and left him to die.

"That was the contemptuous answer of the Navajos to the peace offer of a neighbor who wanted to be their friend instead of their prey. They had never been humbled; they felt perfectly secure in their remote deserts and mountains while they devoured weaker or more peaceable people on every side, and they didn't for a moment consider the cost of the suffering their raids created.

"The plunderers followed Hamblin's trail homeward and descended again from the forests of the Buckskin Mountains to raid the herds of the weary Latter-day Saints. Like creatures that live and work in the night, they skulked under cover and in shadow by day, ever watchful for advantage. Wo to the herder who had slackened his vigilance or who suffered himself to be found helpless and alone, for these robbers planned death for all who dared to pursue them with their spoil.

"But calamity, fearsome and tremendous, was about to strike in their homeland, terrifying and scattering them in all directions. Never had the Navajos been defeated by their enemies. For three hundred years they had defied the Spaniards, the Mexicans, the Pueblo Indians, and most recently the representatives of the United States, with whom they had signed no fewer than six treaties, each of which meant nothing more to them than the paper on which it had been written. Like birds of prey who despoil weaker creatures, they had been preying on all around them, with never an intention of stopping.

"However profitable the Utah field was proving to be, the beaten trails of the Navajo to the southeast were still too inviting and too rich in yield to forsake. From that direction they brought home crops, livestock, children, women. All the promises they had made in those six treaties to refrain from their raiding meant nothing to them. It was a rich industry, and they intended to pursue it forever.

"But from that plundered southeast arose a bitter cry from bereaved parents, outraged husbands, and desolated homes. The call of agony reached to our nation's capital demanding justice, and even though the nation was in the midst of the Civil War, the president of the United States ordered a detachment of troops to the distant home of the Navajo. But this time the soldiers came not just with a treaty but with fixed determination to back it. Desperate with its own dangers, the government had ordered the situation to be handled with firmness, and those soldiers were prepared to carry out their orders.

"Kit Carson was given command of this force, and he would have made peaceful settlement if the Navajo leaders had allowed it. They would not, and so he began rounding up the people as if they were cattle, driving them in herds to Fort Sumner, known also as *Bosque Redondo* or the Grove, in New Mexico. With light cannon mounted on the backs of mules, he compelled them to go or die. He chopped down their orchards, burned their *hogans,* killed or took their livestock, and spoiled their fields.

"Consternation and terror spread before him as the Navajo fled headlong, crawling into dens or gulches, climbing mountains and crossing rivers—anywhere to dodge Carson's grapeshot and keep out of his terrible roundup. Destitute of food and blankets, they rushed away with their women and their children, preferring starvation to capture.

"In spite of their efforts to escape, Carson still took twelve thousand Navajos away on what they called their 'Big Walk,' leaving the country stripped and silent. Into that vacuum swept the Pahutes—the one group of people in the country more to be feared than the Navajo.

"Unprincipled and lawless, these marauding bands of renegade Utes and others who had settled along the San Juan, and so become known as *Pah* or Water Utes, believed in eating *all* their bread by the sweat of other men. While the Navajos were at least industrious, these people were inveterate idlers, having no possessions for which the Navajos would be lured over among them. Always in poverty from indolence, as free and ready as a wildcat to fight, these chesty warriors had tormented the Navajos for generations. With never anything worth the hazard, nothing to lose and everything to gain, they happily stole from the stealers.

"Native to the most impregnable region of barriers that nature has made in the precipitous southwest, the renegades could sally safely out from their defenses to rob or torment the Navajos, and if pursued too closely they could disappear completely. Once among their defenses, it was death to follow them, and the Navajos knew it. More implacable as fighters, more persistent as thieves, more cunning and cruel than the Navajos could ever think of being, these Pahutes were a constant thorn in the side, and they grew even more troublesome after Kit Carson's big roundup.

"With haunted eyes and pinched faces, the starving Navajos who had avoided the roundup had only one remaining recourse. The Pahutes had nothing they could steal, and they dared not steal from the Mexicans or the Americans. In fact, they dared look to no other direction for their livelihood than the Mormon settlements across the timbered Buckskin Mountains to the northwest. Hence the desperation with which they descended from the tall timber in 1863, to skulk and await opportunity with the lives of themselves and their loved ones hanging in the balance.

"The raids of these hunger-crazed people became worse in 1864 and worse still in 1865, while in the rest of the territory the Ute leader Black Hawk took his people on a deadly warpath against the Mormons from 1865 until 1867, causing death and terror in the remote settlements of Utah that will never be fully comprehended. Nor will it ever be told about the braves who fell fighting for what they believed to be their rights, or the sorrow of those who waited in vain for their return.

"But Black Hawk and his people were to discover again, as they had in the Walker War, that they were not prepared to fight against a people so numerous and so well organized. It was with relief that Black Hawk put his thumbprint to a treaty of peace in 1867, and except for sporadic instances of violence, that was the end of Indian troubles throughout the settlements. Except, of course, for the Navajo War, which had been going on without letup for seventeen years here in the southern end of the territory, and which was only growing worse.

"Without warning the thousands of Navajos who had been held in humiliating captivity at Fort Sumner were released to return to their desolated homeland. Starving and destitute, they did, to eagerly join with their fellows on their frantic raids against the Mormons— the only people they still felt safe in raiding. Hoards of them set forth with stealthy step to find horses, sheep, cattle, anything that would help ease the ravages of hunger. It was for them to steal or die, and some of them were to die for stealing, leaving the survivors to seek revenge for those who fell in the fight.

"The Berry family they killed at Short Creek; Dr. Whitmore and his herder Mackentire they butchered at Pipe Springs. And everywhere they raided, taking, according to Ammon Tenny, over a million dollars worth of livestock from impoverished southern Utah in one year alone. It was becoming unbearable, yet no one knew how to bring this war to a peaceful conclusion. Like wolves sniffing at their prey, the Navajos waited eagerly to pounce on anything they could devour. Not in the summertime only, but driven by necessity they came in the cold of winter, forcing the Mormon sentinels to maintain their vigil whatever the weather, whatever the cost, growing in desperation to meet the desperation of their enemy, for they too had loved ones waiting and praying for their success.

"Through 1869 and into the 1870s the raids continued, the Navajos joining occasionally with the Pahutes to give each of them greater strength. And Jacob Hamblin, Thales Haskel, and the other missionaries wore out and even offered their lives going from place to place trying to stop the trouble and bring peace to this far-flung frontier. Yet all was for nothing, because the Pahutes and certain of the Navajos had no more desire for peace than did many of the whites, non-Mormon and even a few of the Mormons, who fought them.

"Yet with dogged determination Elder Hamblin and his brethren kept on, knowing that love and kindness are the most potent, the most enduring of all forces that change the lives of men for the better; that the methods of conquest that had reduced or exterminated Indian tribes from the Atlantic seaboard to the Rocky Mountains are the very thing against which the human heart will revolt with its last palpitation. But even though they made a friend here and another there, the terrible raids against the southern settlements by the Navajos, and more recently the Pahutes, have continued to this day."

"Brother Snow, may I add something?"

"Of course, Brother Haskel. Speak up."

Slowly the thin old Indian missionary and interpreter rose to his feet, his keen eyes glancing over the small congregation. "Besides these two implacable tribes of Indians," he said quietly, "with their impregnable walls and gulches behind them to shelter them, this country is becoming known as the surest and safest retreat from the arm of the law in all the United States. Desperate fugitives have fled to it from many states and territories, and they are still coming. Its precipitous terrain is bidding fair to fill up with the kind of men who are consumed with the lust to hurt and to kill. If these lean-brained human rattlesnakes, these fugitives from justice, are allowed to establish themselves in the rocks by these irritable tribes, they will bring trouble more sure and deadly than the killing of the three Kacheenebegay brothers in Grass Valley a few years ago. They might start this trouble at any time, possibly right away, and its deadly red flame would quickly be fanned beyond all control."

"Brother Haskel is absolutely right," Elder Snow continued as the other sank slowly back into his seat. "The combination of these three deadly elements has formed a grave situation calling for wise diplomacy. The problem is of sufficient proportions to engage the attention of the general government, yet it concerns no one so much as our own impoverished people—no one else has been under such great necessity of framing immediate measures against it. Furthermore, it appears that the Mormons are the only ones determined to do anything about it.

"The Church leaders met in solemn council to consider, and the thing they decided to do to head off the impending disaster here on the San Juan seems altogether weak and out of proportion to the problem. Their announcement was surprising; it was in keeping with nothing but the ethics of the peculiar conquest that is accomplished by the appeal of soul to soul. It took little account of the conventional notion of danger, the strength of arms, the defense made possible by

superior numbers. The plan they proposed to stem this tide of violence and wickedness was to plant a little colony of faithful Latter-
day Saints in the very heart of the incipient danger, right on the turbulent border between the Navajos and the Pahutes, and squarely on
the trail of the fugitive-desperado wolfpack from all over the West.
Of course, brothers and sisters, we are referring to you.

"You had no way of knowing, when you planted your colony of
Bluff here on these bottomlands this past spring, that in all of creation this very place you chose is the only river ford and crossroads
for all these troubled peoples. Do you suppose that was an accident?
Or do you suppose that God would have allowed this community to
be established anywhere else? Of course not! Your mission is to
bring peace to this country, and this dangerous spot is the best place
for it to happen.

"But there is more. Besides the precarious problem of saving
yourselves and your families from the wrath and rapacity of these
three recalcitrant peoples, and setting forth for them a Christlike
example of love and peace, your broader purpose is to save the rest
of Utah from further Indian troubles by making yourselves a buffer
between the old settlements and the mischief that might be incubat-
ing against them. You are to neutralize what might otherwise develop
into another territory-wide war. These are the reasons you are here.

"For our people here in Utah, the fort has always been the indis-
pensable protection to each new step farther into the wilderness, and
for more than thirty years the extending zone of these protections has
radiated out from that first adobe fort in Salt Lake City like ripples
in a pool of still water. This fort-zone and its firing line was destined
to mature and cease to be a factor in the north and the west, but in
the south and east it has continued to be necessary, and it is focusing
at last in this one faraway corner of wilderness—San Juan County.
Here you will truly man a fort on the firing line, your mission to protect us all from the ravages of these misguided peoples.

"However, you are few in number and have nothing in the way
of military defense, so you will be compelled to depend on the hand
of Providence and the faithfulness with which you can yield the
agencies of peace. Build your fort as quickly as possible, and house
yourselves and your livestock within it. Avoid the use of force or vio-

lence against any of these peoples unless you are compelled to do otherwise, and the Lord will protect each of you against the same. Be humble and prayerful, and seek always the Spirit of the Lord in all your communications—with each other as well as with your enemies—and the word of the Lord is that you will come off victorious.

"In the name of the Lord Jesus Christ I say it. Amen."

PART ONE

THE GRIM MONSTER

1

Monday, March 28, 1881

Bluff Fort

Eliza Foreman was straining milk through a patch of cheesecloth when she first heard the distant wail. She was still outside her tiny log cabin, having come only moments before from the corral, and all afternoon and evening she had been savoring the warm spring air. But now—

Drawing erect, she turned toward the south and stared off into the early evening darkness, her heart suddenly hammering with fear. The distant sound was a long-drawn, sighing wail that was definitely coming closer. "Mary," she called anxiously to her young neighbor in the uncompleted fort, "do you hear that?"

Mary Jones had also stopped gathering wood chips for kindling, and she, too, was standing motionless. "I hear it," she breathed into the still air. "Oh, glory, Eliza, it's another blow, and it's coming fast!"

Dumping the kindling chips from her apron, Mary ran toward Eliza's cabin. "Get your window closed, Eliza. I'll get little Willy's milk inside for you."

Grasping her crutch, Eliza hobbled to the cabin's single window, which opened outward on an upper, leather hinge. With a swipe of her crutch she knocked free the stick that had been holding the window open, and then she swung through the open doorway behind her friend.

"I . . . hope Annie has little Willy inside with her," she said as she fastened the window and hurriedly began stuffing rags into some of the larger holes between the logs where the mud chinking had fallen out. "She hasn't been here long enough to experience one of these San Juan blows."

"No," Mary agreed as she banked up the fire and began draping stained factory muslin over the shelves holding Eliza's prized china and crystal. "But Jody's wife Nellie has been here as long as we have, Eliza, and she'll tell Annie and Adelia what's coming."

"Still, I wish Willy was here with me. I truly do!"

"If wishes were fishes," Mary said with a sly grin, "then we'd all be swimming in the San Juan." Pausing to catch her breath after straining and covering the pitifully small amount of warm milk they had taken from both their cows, Mary gathered her skirts beneath her and plopped onto the bed. "As long as we're wishing, though, I wish Kumen and Billy were here too! But they aren't, and there's nothing we can do about it but fret."

Outside the tiny cabin the wailing wind had dropped down off the sandstone bluffs or abutments to the south. Now it was shrieking through the just-budding cottonwoods on both sides of the river, and with fearsome fury it slammed abruptly into the fort and the rows of cabins that formed it. Like a cold wave it rushed by, sucking sparks up the mud and willow chimney, rattling and tearing at whatever was not fastened down, kicking sand through the unchinked cracks between the logs and the openings around the poorly fitting door, and terrifying the cattle and horses in the nearby corral. Then it was past, the cooled air was suddenly calm again, and instantly Mary was back on her feet.

"Before the real storm hits, I'll go get little Willy, and—"

"No, you won't," Eliza declared as she pulled open the door. "You haven't done a thing to ready your own home, so you go see to your own needs, Mary, and I'll get Willy."

"Are you sure?"

Eliza smiled. "Dear Mary, despite my crutch I can get across this fort nearly as fast as you can, and you know it."

With a smile Mary thought of the times she'd seen her tall, ungainly friend moving along with that crutch. Despite the loss of her toes and parts of her feet in the snows of Wyoming so many years before, Eliza Foreman could skedaddle right along when she wanted to, leaving the much shorter Mary Jones hard pressed to keep up. "That may be so," she admitted as she apprehensively looked out the window, "but I'm not expecting my second child!"

"Oh, pshaw! I'm not even showing yet. Fact is, I'm not even certain I'm expecting. If Billy hadn't been home that first week of January, I'd know I wasn't. But whether I'm expecting or not, stop worrying about me and shoo! If I need you, I'll give a holler through the walls."

Mary smiled grimly. "Better holler loud, then. Hear that roar coming? This is going to be a big one, Eliza—maybe even bigger than the blow last fall before Elder Snow's visit. And this one's going to be cold, too. Here, don't forget your shawl."

With a smile of gratitude Eliza grasped the shawl, ducked through the low doorway, and hurried across the commons. Behind her she heard Mary shutting the door, and she was almost to the cabin that Annie Lyman was sharing with her sister-in-law Nellie and her mother-in-law, Eliza Partridge Lyman, when the real storm came roaring across the river and slammed into the pathetically incomplete fort on the San Juan.

"Oh, bother," she muttered as she covered her nose and mouth against the thick cloud of sand. "Maybe this one will at least bring a little rain. The Lord knows we need it—"

———◦–◦–◦———

It wasn't just being alone that frightened her, Eliza thought as she sat huddled on the bed several hours later, a quilt pulled tightly around her. No, when necessary she could deal with being alone. After all, she'd been alone nearly thirty of her forty-six years and managed quite well. So being alone wasn't so bad. It was the nights when she was alone here on the San Juan that terrified her, especially when it was storming and she couldn't see her hand in front of her face and so had no way of knowing who or what might be lurking nearby.

Outside her cabin the storm raged, a terrible fury of dry, cold air that blasted sand against everything it could reach. Occasionally blowing up from the Navajo reservation to the south, these nighttime storms were usually accompanied by dry lightning and thunder, violent celestial displays that, unfortunately, brought little relief to the drought-stricken land.

In spite of the frightful din, Eliza could hear the sand striking the small windowpanes and whispering around the corners of the cabin. Sand was blowing into the cabin in a thousand places, too, forming little wind-rows on each side of the door and blanketing everything within the small room. Normally it would have been too dark to see this, but sparks were still flying up the chimney, flames were licking at the log in the fireplace, and the dim light was enough.

Laying her head against the rough-hewn logs behind her, Eliza gazed at the tiny room she and Willy called home. Roughly ten by twelve feet, the cabin was one of several built in a row with occasionally adjoining side-walls and roof. Because it was made of twisted cottonwood logs that had been nearly impossible to work with, Eliza and the other women had diligently tried the previous fall to chink or fill all the gaping spaces between the logs with mud and dry grass. On the interior walls such chinking had been largely effective, but on the back and front where the elements had free rein, the chinking was forever coming loose or washing out, and Eliza couldn't get over the feeling of being perpetually exposed to the whole vicious world.

The roof above her was made of earth heaped on top of every naturally growing thing in the country, or so it had seemed to her when it was being built. Cedar logs were laid side by side overhead, and those had been covered with willow poles and wands, cattails, grass and brush—anything and everything they could gather that might hold the sandy soil and prevent it from falling through. All of it had been used, including some of the cattail mats she had woven as demonstrations for the children. And still the roof was only partially effective against the elements. In hot, sunny weather it provided a wonderful cooling shade, but the constant winds and the millions of insects with which the country abounded caused the dirt to continually sift downward into the room, leaving a perpetual blanket of soil over everything that was only rivaled by the wind-carried sand. During occasional rains or the thaw after their brief winter snow the roof had also leaked water, so that at least in Eliza's home the only place that remained dry was the corner where Billy had put their bed. Eliza had no idea why water didn't drip there, but she was grateful even for small favors and tried not to complain about the rest of it.

However, the previous fall she had also hung as a ceiling two layers of factory—cotton muslin Billy had brought by the bolt when they'd left Cedar City a year and a half earlier. Except for when the wind blew hard, the muslin had mostly stopped the sifting and falling earth. But the few rains had soiled the fabric terribly, and now it looked perfectly awful.

The floor, such as it was, consisted of packed earth covered by the extra canvas tarp Billy had brought from Cedar City the year before—the tarp that had provided the shelter of an evening for her table, chairs, and the fine furnishings she'd forced Billy to drag out at each stop on the long and grueling trail. Though she felt guilty about it now and had apologized to Billy again and again, he only laughed and told her he'd have done even more if she'd asked. But that was like him, she thought tenderly as she stared into the near-darkness, always giving of himself even when it was more than hard.

Oh, glory be! If only he were home—

Across the commons Charlie Walton had tuned up his fiddle and was playing for all he was worth, apparently keeping time with the storm. The song was "Bonaparte's Retreat," and the worse the tumult and more furious the wind, the harder Charlie seemed to play. Sometimes the gusts were so ferocious that the sound of the fiddle was lost, and Eliza held her breath, certain her cabin's roof and everything else in the fort would be torn loose and carried away. But then the gusts would subside and the raging strains of "Bonaparte's Retreat" would assail her ears again, forcing her to watch in her mind's eye those poor, suffering soldiers staggering along in the snow, sacrificing to one man's unholy ambition.

If only her Billy had come home from Colorado with Charlie the week before! If only she hadn't been left alone through the winter to face the terror and constant danger of this awful country—

The single log in the fireplace, her last log, flared as another gust of wind sucked sparks upward, and Eliza wished for the hundredth time that she'd carried in more wood before the storm began. Somehow the flames comforted her, for though she was warm enough under the quilts beside her sleeping son, the flickering light helped drive away many of her fears.

"Be careful taking little Willy home," Annie Lyman had

whispered urgently so many hours before. "The banshees are out tonight, Eliza, so hurry home and don't look out the window once you get there." Of course Eliza didn't believe in ghosts and haunts, but on a horrid night like this, one could certainly begin to wonder.

There seemed to be hundreds of noises outside the cabin—boards rattling, horses neighing, cattle lowing, dogs barking, the whispering of drifting sand, the moaning of the wind as it passed between logs and under eaves, and, of course, the endless sawing of Charlie Walton's fiddle.

Why did he have to play like that, Eliza wondered, especially on a night of such frightful noises as this? The wind was shrieking and howling and roaring all at once, and surely a body didn't need more noise to add to it.

A distant crack and boom announced the fall of one of the large cottonwood trees along the river, another terrible gust of wind rattled Eliza's window and nerves, and abruptly she shuddered, her mind going to the horrors of the previous year. Never had there been enough food, and the water from both the San Juan and Platte Lyman's well here in the fort had turned out so bad they'd had to settle it with ashes for two days before they could stand to use it. The horrible ditch had proven absolutely unable to carry irrigation water from the river to their fields, virtually all their crops had withered and failed in the unrelenting heat, and Billy and most of the other men had been forced to spend the winter away in Colorado, doing anything they could to hold body and soul together. And that, of course, had meant she and most of the other women had also suffered alone.

In her mind Eliza was suddenly seeing the cast of unsavory characters by whom she felt surrounded and threatened, a seemingly endless procession of white desperados from goodness-only-knew-where who passed almost weekly through the fort on their way from nowhere to nowhere else, appraising not just the women with their lust-filled eyes but also the livestock and even the miserable belongings of the poverty-stricken settlers. Many of these outlaws, Eliza knew, were secretly committing depredations of various kinds against the Saints, and that none had so far resorted to physical violence was nothing short of miraculous.

And then there were the Indians, Navajos and Pahutes alike, who seemed to be waiting in the background for a chance to steal or were brazenly doing it and defying the Saints to do anything about it. In her mind Eliza could especially see the sneering faces of the two Pahute boys who had become her personal trial of faith. Though not violent, at least so far, Eliza could nonetheless read in Scotty's and especially Posey's eyes the mocking disdain they had for her, for Billy, for their tiny son, and for all the rest of the settlement. It was terrible to have them fling open the door and enter her cabin without so much as a by-your-leave, demanding food, and it was even worse to know they were stealing from her whatever they could get their hands on.

Such depredations could only lead to worse things, Eliza was certain, and so over the past year her heart had grown smaller and smaller with fear—not only toward the two Pahute boys but also the other Indians in the area. She was terrified for herself and Billy, and she was even more afraid for Willy. And no matter how hard she'd prayed, her fear had simply grown worse.

But for Eliza, far and away the most frightening thing of all about being alone was Willy's obviously declining health. No one seemed to know exactly what was wrong with the child, but that didn't mean something wasn't. Back in December he'd grown listless and fussy, and Maggie Haskel, the settlement's only midwife, had suggested that Eliza's milk wasn't giving the baby enough nourishment.

Immediately she'd stopped nursing and started the boy on cow's milk, and for a few weeks it seemed the problem had been solved. But then in January, shortly after Billy had gone back to Colorado, Willy's appetite had all but disappeared again. Soon his weight was dropping, he was growing listless, and even his fussy times were growing less and less frequent. Now—and Billy didn't know of this, for she hadn't wanted to alarm him—the child was obviously in a state of starvation. Eliza had seen starvation before, in the snows of Wyoming back in '56, and so the signs were obvious. Bony arms and legs, hollow-looking eyes, swollen elbow and knee joints, swollen abdomen—the poor child seemed to be dying from malnutrition. And no matter how many different cows they tried using the milk from, and no matter how hard she coaxed and cajoled her son into eating the thin gruel she prepared daily for him, nothing seemed to be doing any good at all.

Sniffing back sudden tears, Eliza reached out and tenderly caressed her son's cheek. He was such a miracle, such an amazingly perfect little human being. Not yet even a year old, and in spite of his weakness he was walking already, or at least he was toddling here and there when he had the strength to do it. When he felt well he was an absolute chatterbox, too, and could very clearly say the word *Papa.* But it was his giggle that Eliza loved best of all, an infectious little laugh that seemed to light up the world with its pure joy. Eliza gloried in his laugh, and through the day she did all she could to bring it out, tickling him, teasing him, making silly faces even when she knew he wasn't feeling well.

But it was Billy who could really get the boy laughing—Billy with his tender ways and almost infinite patience and love. Oh, glory, if only he were home to help her know what to do—

In the dim light from the fireplace Eliza gazed fearfully at the tousled, white-blond hair and drawn countenance of her son. The way the thunder was crashing, it was a wonder the baby was still asleep. But thank goodness—or the Lord above, for she had certainly prayed for it—he slumbered on.

Despite his large, hollow-looking eyes and pinched cheeks, he still looked so perfect, so wonderful, so amazingly like his father. The blueness of his eyes; his square forehead and cute little nose; his long, sensitive fingers—these features looked exactly like Billy's. And the way he smiled, and even the way he wrinkled his nose when things displeased him, these were things Billy did that the baby couldn't possibly have learned. No, Willy was his father's son—his father's posterity that both he and she had been promised so many years before.

With a sigh of despair, Eliza laid her head back and closed her eyes. As if it weren't enough dealing with her fears and the terror of Willy's sickness, she was now expecting another child, which would only make matters worse. Besides, at forty-six years of age, she was simply insane to be having another child! How could the Lord expect any woman who felt as old and worn down as she was, and struggling as she was just to keep little Willy alive, to go through another childbirth and start raising a second child? Especially in this horrid, desperate country where every stranger, every problem, brought new terror to her heart. It didn't make sense, it just didn't!

She'd meant to write Billy about these miseries of hers—many times. In fact, she thought constantly about writing him. But when he'd been home in January he had seemed so consumed with worry over providing them a living that she'd felt unable to burden him further. And so she'd turned to the Lord, praying day in and day out for comfort as well as guidance. And though there had been times when she knew perfectly well that she was being comforted, she still had no earthly idea what to do about Willy. Neither did she know how to rid her heart of the fear of the Indians and outlaws that literally seemed to paralyze her whenever she even thought of them.

At some point in the midst of her worries and fears Eliza dozed off, and it was the chiming of Billy's Regulator clock on the far wall—the clock that had been a gift to him from Brigham Young—that awakened her. Three in the morning. It was pitch dark in the room, and instinctively her hand went to her son, checking his breathing, caressing his cheek, her fingers unconsciously keeping time with the ticking of the clock.

Eliza dozed again, and when she awakened at quarter of four she realized that the wind had lessened and that Charlie was no longer sawing out the fearsome "Bonaparte's Retreat" on his precious fiddle. Now he was playing "Annie Laurie," one of her favorites, and Eliza almost smiled into the darkness as she began swaying to the sweet strains.

Suddenly the single window of the cabin, as well as the cracks in and around the door and every single open chink within view, glared an impossibly brilliant white, illuminating with ghostly clarity everything within the cabin. In practically the same instant there followed a deafening crash of thunder that rumbled and rolled as if it would never end, hurting Eliza's ears and shaking the very wall she was leaning against, and bringing a blurry-eyed and suddenly tearful little boy groping for the protective arms of his mother.

Bluff Bench

When the storm was at its worst and the lightning was almost constant, Natanii nééz, the tall Navajo who was now using the *bela-cani* name of Frank, began to move. He didn't hurry, but neither did he go particularly slowly. Instead he simply walked, quietly but confidently, toward the large herd of horses. In his hands he carried a braided rawhide rope, but other than that he carried nothing, not even a knife.

In a small swale beneath a juniper tree a fire sputtered and glowed, and the tall Navajo ignored it as he passed by. He wasn't really interested in the *belacani* guards, for he had no desire to take their foolish lives. And neither did he fear them, for though they had corralled the horses close by, the two or three young men were either huddled under blankets or staring into the flames of their fire and so would be blind to his movements.

This *náá ádinii,* being a blind person, which almost all *belacani* did to themselves near a fire at night, never ceased to amaze the tall Navajo. To him it meant that they were *táadoo hazhóó baa ntsáháskézi,* without forethought, something no man of the *Diné* would wish to be accused of. But it also meant, and Frank smiled thinly as he thought of it, that they were *bitaashbaah,* a people meant to be raided. And he, Natanii nééz, was pleased that he could be a part of that raiding.

Now he was close to the horses in the rope corral, and he moved a little more slowly. Partly this was so that his movements wouldn't startle the animals, and partly it was so that he could locate the big black that he had determined to make his own.

He didn't fear that the horses would snort with suspicion when they scented him, for Frank had long ago been taught by his father the great secret of how to avoid that. Two days earlier he had stripped himself of the *belacani* clothing being worn by most of the *Diné* since their days at *Bosque Redondo,* leaving only a breechcloth and his knee-high moccasins. He'd also taken his long hair from the traditional bun, letting it hang freely around his shoulders. And finally he'd stopped eating, knowing it would take two days for the odors of his food to be taken from his body.

Natanii nééz had come to this place in the dark of that first night, and he'd had spent much time since then rubbing his body with the grasses and brush that were to be found on the Bluff Bench, as well as with the earth upon which all creatures lived. Now there was no man-scent about him whatsoever, but instead he smelled like the country in which these horses were accustomed to living.

Now the tall Navajo could easily walk among the animals without fear of their betrayal to the *belacani* youth who sat guard nearby. This pleased the warrior immensely and was the main reason he was raiding from this herd rather than simply taking strays that had wandered away. To Frank this was a sign of his own greatness—nothing more, nothing less. And soon, he knew, his daring raids would be well-told stories in the *hogans* of the People.

Still smiling at the thought, Natanii nééz stepped over the rope that had been run as a temporary corral. And then he was among the *belacani* mormonee horses, running his hands gently over the bodies of those he passed by, looking for the big black gelding he had been watching for the past two days. At length he found the animal, spoke quietly to it in the language of the night, and secured his rope about its neck. Carefully then, and slowly, he led the big horse to the edge of the herd.

Stepping on the rope that enclosed the animals he pushed it to the ground, and only as he was leading the black across it did he realize that another horse was following behind. In the darkness Frank couldn't tell the color of the animal, but his practiced hands knew in an instant that it was a small mare with tight withers and a well-formed head. Pleased, he allowed the mare to follow after, and as he led the two animals quietly across the Bluff Bench and away from the herd and the youthful *belacani* mormonee at the small fire, Frank felt *hózhó*—he felt perfect balance in his life.

This was the way a man of the *Diné* should live! *Aoo,* yes! And with the wise but dangerously arrogant Peokon gone, he thought, it now fell to Natanii nééz to show this way of beauty to the People.

2

Tuesday, March 29, 1881

Bluff Fort

"Well, Eliza, was I right about that storm?"

Looking up from her perch on the three-legged milking stool, Eliza smiled ruefully. "More than I would have wished, Mary. Charlie Walton's fiddling only made it worse, too. Like Annie said when I went to get Willy, it was a night for haunts and banshees."

"What in the world are banshees?"

"Female spirits, or so they say. Folks in England and Ireland believe they wait outside houses on nights like this last one, bringing death to whoever looks out and sees them. They howl like the wind, and believe me, last night was perfect for them!"

"I'll say!" Looking upward, Mary gazed at the still-overcast sky. "And to think that all these clouds haven't given us a drop of rain. Well, it isn't because we haven't been praying. I for one have never prayed harder for anything in my life."

"Is that because after a year and a half you've finally grown tired of gruel porridge, stringy beef, dandelion greens, and pigweed?"

Mary laughed. "Don't forget those smelly fish from the river, and the wonderful bread we get whenever Platte brings a wagonload of flour from Durango."

Eliza nodded. "The bread is good, I admit, but I wish we hadn't run out of molasses last winter. I can hardly bear the lard we spread on it."

"Horrid stuff!" Mary said, pulling a face. "I hope this summer we can find some berries somewhere and make preserves. Anyway, Eliza, I'm more tired than I can say of feeling like I'm always on the ragged edge of starvation. If we don't get some decent rain, or if we can't tame the river and get that fool ditch to hold water this year—well, I for one will be ready to return to the settlements and give this country back to the Indians and the outlaws. They deserve it!"

"Mercy, Mary," Eliza teased. "You'd say that even when your father is the bishop here? And is always preaching his 'sticky-to-ity' doctrine?"

"I would, and I'd mean it!" Again Mary glanced upward. "Maybe the rain's still coming."

"I'm not getting my hopes up!" Furiously Eliza stripped the last of the milk from her cow while her mind dwelt on the grim monster that was their community ditch. The year before, within hours of their arrival on the bottomlands where they were now building their fort, work had begun on the surveying and digging. Entering the San Juan far upstream from the tiny settlement, the ditch had been designed to carry enough water to irrigate all the ground around the fort that they could possibly cultivate.

The trouble was, not only had the ditch been surveyed improperly, but no one had even begun to understand the capricious nature of the river they were attempting to tap. The riverbed was filled with quicksand, making treacherous all efforts to work on it, and the water itself carried so much sediment that it filled the ditch with sand and silt so rapidly that the teams and scrapers couldn't keep up with it. In other words, as Kumen Jones put it, water from the San Juan was "too thick to drink, too thin to plow."

Worse yet, the level of water in the river couldn't be counted on, rising and falling dramatically depending upon forces far upstream that the hapless settlers couldn't possibly prepare for. The previous spring they'd laid out the ditch and worked with all diligence to get it dug. Yet by the time it was ready for use, the water level had fallen so severely that the ditch remained high and dry with the already sprouting crops withering in the unrelenting heat.

Frantically the men had dug an extension to the ditch while the women and children had hand-carried water to tiny portions of their struggling crops, trying desperately to grow a little food. Then had come the discovery of the too-hasty survey and the need for another major adjustment. Next had come the sediment problem, the newest ditch either washing out or filling with silt and sand so fast that hardly any of the fields received more than a cursory amount of water.

With men and teams exhausted from clearing and farming a new country as well as fighting a losing battle with the ditch, the starving members of the community had watched in horror one morning the previous June as the river had suddenly risen, in the space of just hours, until it was over the banks and flooding the very land they had all been struggling to cultivate.

A day later there had been no ditch, no irrigated fields, and no crops, withered or otherwise. Instead the entire bottomland had been covered with a fresh layer of mud and sand, meaning that if they were to stay without starving to death, every one of the settlers would have to start over again.

Some had done so, and Jens Nielson, who'd been called as bishop to preside over the people, had actually raised a small crop of grain and vegetables. No one else had enjoyed such success, however, and by late summer families who had suffered so much hunger during the previous winter's journey were still going hungry and were starting to move along. Some had continued eastward into Colorado and New Mexico, while others had either returned over their terrible road through the Hole-in-the-Rock or had swung northward along part of old Father Escalante's trail, crossing the Colorado River and then making their way westward through the mountains and back to their original homes in western Utah.

Either way more than half of the company had departed, leaving a terrible burden upon the remainder of providing sustenance and of somehow coping with the constant drain on their limited resources from the Indians and occasional white desperados who more and more seemed to infest their country.

These were not happy thoughts, happy memories, and so Eliza was constantly forcing her mind to think of other, more positive things. Some days, however, that just didn't seem possible—

"I'll say this," she declared abruptly. "Rain or not, I've a layer of sand a quarter of an inch deep over everything in my home, mine and

Willy's hair included! Time to haul out the washtub for another bath in that awful water Platte's well delivers, and I suppose that despite my exhaustion I'll be brushing my hair for at least an hour tonight!"

Mary Jones laughed as she tied her cow to the fence behind Eliza. "Well, at least we're all in the same boat. Can you taste the sand that's still in the air?"

"Is that why my teeth keep feeling gritty?" Eliza shook her head. "I swan, Mary, but I'm afraid I agree with you. I believe the Brethren are inspired, but at the same time I can't help but wonder if there's truly supposed to be a Mormon settlement here on the San Juan."

As Eliza finished her milking chores, took up her crutch, and pulled herself to her feet, Mary deftly took Eliza's stool and settled herself near the udder of her cow. From a coop nearby a rooster began crowing, a little late, Eliza thought; some dogs took up the chorus, and just then the sun topped the hills to the east, illuminating the dust that remained thick in the air. In could be such a beautiful country, yet how could a civilized person appreciate such niceties when surrounded by so much evil, so much to fear? It was—

"Since we're talking about this settlement," Mary abruptly declared as she paused in her milking, "I'll tell you something else. I don't know exactly what it is, Eliza, but I feel certain that something awful is about to happen to us. Every time I think about it, I feel as though the pressure's building in a huge boiling kettle, getting ready to blow the lid off. I . . . keep thinking that something terrible is going to happen to Kumen—" Mary's worried look turned tearful, and angrily she swiped at her eyes. "Mercy, Eliza! What could it be?"

"I . . . don't know," Eliza breathed as she fearfully placed her hand on her tummy. "Oh, Mary, I do hope you're wrong!"

"So do I, but I'll wager I'm not. As Pap Redd might have put it, sooner or later something awful is going to splash over us like dirty water out of a too-full washtub. You mark my words—"

———◦—◦—◦———

"I don't know how they got out, Pa. Maybe in the storm they got scared and jumped the rope. Or maybe it was Indians. But it's hard to imagine any self-respecting Indian out in a storm like that."

Silently Bishop Jens Nielson looked at his son Joseph, who had been given responsibility for the Bluff community horse herd. "Vell, Yoseph," he said in his thick Danish accent, "tell me again vhich vones are missing?"

"Black Diamond, Pa; him and that little bay mare of Hy Perkins."

"Und de rope vas not down?"

Joseph shook his head. "There were tracks, though. At least I think they were tracks—heading toward the river. But the drifting sand was bad on the bench, Pa, so they may not have been tracks at all."

"Black Diamond, iss it?" Bishop Nielson stood and hobbled to the window of the cabin. "Yoseph, ve need dat horse, und ve need him bad! He's de best pulling horse ve haff, und vith fields ready for plowing und de ditch still in need of scraping, ve must haff him."

"All right, Pa, I'll look again."

Soberly Bishop Nielson turned and looked at his son. "I feel in my heart, Yoseph, dat de Navajo haff him. But I do not vant to accuse until I am sure. So look careful, und make sure he iss not yust in de villows or some grassy ravine. Iff he iss not to be found, den ve vill send Brudder Haskel onto de reservation again."

Joseph smiled. "Well, with all the times Haskel's gone there after one thing or another that's been stolen, it ain't like he don't know the way." And chuckling without humor, he clapped his hat on his head and exited the tiny cabin.

———◇—◇—◇———

"Eliza, Navajos in the fort! Two women. They've gone into Rachel Perkins's cabin!"

Her heart hammering, Eliza looked at Jane Walton, who had poked her head inside Eliza's door with the news. It was a way the women of the fort tried to protect each other during the absence of most of the men—a hurriedly passed word whenever an Indian of either tribe showed up within the fort. All who could would then gather, quietly and unobtrusively, until the Indian or Indians were literally surrounded by the Mormon women.

"I . . . I've just got Willy into the washtub," Eliza stammered from where she was kneeling on the canvas-covered floor holding her son in the laboriously heated warm water.

"That's fine, dear." Jane Walton smiled. "There's quite a crowd of women gathering already, and Kumen Jones and Lem Redd rode in a little bit ago from Colorado, so they and my Charlie are all available. But when you're finished give a look-see anyway. The two women don't look particularly warlike, but if they're still there, you can join us anyway."

Closing the door, Jane was gone, and for a moment Eliza fought to regain control of herself. "Oh, Willy," she breathed as she struggled to overcome her terror—the pounding within her chest that was driving away her very breath, "why am I so frightened of those people? They haven't hurt me. They haven't hurt a single one of us. Yet every time I see an Indian, or even hear of one being nearby, I get so frozen up with fear—Oh, Willy darling, if one of them ever tried to hurt you—"

Leaving the thought unfinished, Eliza began scrubbing the frail little child. But while he giggled and splashed, Eliza's mind wouldn't stop worrying about the two Navajo women. What did they want, she wondered, and why had they picked Rachel Perkins's cabin? Oh, glory! If only the brethren could take the time to finish the fort. If only they didn't always consider other things more important.

Still, she thought as she struggled to wash Willy's face, at least the two women had gone to Rachel's home and not hers! Thank the Lord for small favors—

———o—o—o———

Eliza's head came up with a start, her grimy cleaning rag motionless in her hand, and then frantically she stared at the door. She had heard someone there, perhaps those two Navajo women, or even worse, those awful Pahute boys—

The noise came again, briefly, and with a sigh of relief Eliza plopped herself into her rocker. It was nothing more than the wind, which was picking up again now that evening was coming on, blowing a crossboard on the outside of the door that had worked loose the night before. She had meant to fix it, but it took so much time and energy just keeping things clean for her and little Willy that she had forgotten. Thank goodness the banging wasn't loud enough to awaken the child, who was finally asleep after being an absolute terror since his bath.

Suffering from malnutrition, he was growing weaker by the day. The Lyman women seemed particularly concerned, and they had commented on it a little earlier when they'd passed by. But why Willy was starving, Eliza truly didn't know. He seemed to be losing what little appetite he had, and now that she thought of it, he was definitely sleeping more deeply, and for longer periods of time.

Oh, glory, if only Billy were there to help her know what to do—

Well, she thought as she gripped her crutch and dragged her aching body upright, it was getting late, and she still had cream to churn, so she'd better get on with her cleaning. Of course, she reminded herself with a wry smile, she needn't be so nit-picky about it, either. In this awful country, what did it matter how things looked? Everything was the color of the earth anyway—rattlesnakes, lizards, horned toads, Indians, homes, clothing, her and Willy's hands and faces—everything!

With a heavy sigh Eliza dipped her rag into the water bucket beside the door and began trying again to clean the place up. Only by keeping busy, she knew, could she keep the terrors of the country from paralyzing her with fear and dread. Only by forcing her mind to be still could she begin to pretend that life was good—

Yellowjacket Canyon

"This here cave makes a man thankful for small favors, doesn't it?"

Watching the firelight flicker off the roof of the shallow cave, Billy had to agree with his friend Dick Butt. A shelter during a storm like the one they were experiencing, any kind of a shelter, was something to be thankful for. And this cave in the sandstone cliff, a shallow depression not more than thirty feet deep and mostly less than half that high, had been sheltering people for a long time. Ancient ruins of the sort they'd first seen in Castle Wash, during their trip out from Hole-in-the-Rock, were still standing in one end of the cave. Certainly hundreds of years old, they contained pieces of pottery and arrow tips if little else, and the cave roof was still blackened with the soot of ancient fires. During the past year the San Juan settlers had found numerous such caves and ruins, usually hidden in out-of-the-way canyons and draws, though of a truth none of the caves had seemed so opportune a find as this one.

During the regular flashes of lightning, Billy could see the rain coming down in torrents, slashing diagonally past the cave's mouth and filling the wash below them with a brief but frenzied stream. Thank the Lord the ancient builders had known enough to climb a little, Billy thought. It wouldn't be pleasant dealing in the dark with flash floods like the one he knew was already building below.

For better than a week he, Dick Butt, and George Ipson had been cutting logs for railroad ties in Yellowjacket Canyon in western Colorado. In fact, the three of them, and several other crews of men, from Bluff and elsewhere, had spent the entire winter cutting ties—chopping, trimming, planing, hauling to the railhead—earning much-needed cash with which to purchase supplies they'd failed to grow for themselves the previous summer. Since October, Billy had been home from Colorado only once, for a precious week in January, and it was beyond imagination how lonely he was for Eliza and his little Willy. Sighing, he looked again at the rain slashing down beyond the mouth of the cave. With all his heart Billy hoped it had been raining just as hard back in Bluff, for word from the fort was that it was already hot, the infamous irrigation ditch was still not carrying water, and already the early crops were dry and withering. Rain would give everyone a little respite, providing them at least a few more precious days for the men to gather back home and re-dig the ditch. But if it wasn't raining at home, Billy thought with an empty feeling, then this summer season might become just as dismal as the previous one. And few of the colonists, he was certain, could face the thought of another year of starvation and poverty—

"Does the roof of your cabin back at Bluff work pretty well, Billy?" George Ipson asked as he fed more sticks into the fire.

"It leaks some," Billy admitted. "Except for right over the bed. I put some of Eliza's cattail mats there to hold the soil, and they do work wonders. If this storm extends all the way to Bluff, I'd imagine that's right where Eliza and little Willy are holding out."

"Do you really think it extends that far?"

"I hope so," Billy breathed fervently. "For Eliza's and little Willy's sakes, not to mention all the rest of us!"

"You think you'll be all right traveling home alone, Billy?" Dick Butt was obviously worried. "I know your contract's up with this load, but if you stay an extra week, the three of us can ride home together."

Touched by his friend's concern, Billy smiled into the darkness. "I know Platte's counseled us not to travel that country alone, Dick, but I don't think I can take another week away from my family."

"You prayed about it?"

"As a matter of fact, I have. The feeling I get is to leave as soon as we get back with this load—that all will be well. So I reckon I'll be traveling alone, and I'll leave my safety in the hands of the Lord. But you have to know, boys, that I can't wait to see Eliza. And glory! How I miss my little Willy!"

"Well, Willy's a fine-looking boy," Dick Butt declared, still sounding dissatisfied with Billy's decision. "I hope one day to have a son like him myself."

"You at least have the prospect of a wife," George Ipson groused, thankful for the change of subject. "Me, I don't see anything in my future except more bachelorhood."

"Maybe you need to make a trip back to the settlements to do a little courting."

George glanced over at Billy. "Don't think I haven't considered it. What about you, Dick? When are you and Julie tying the knot?"

For a moment Dick Butt was silent, thinking of Bishop Nielson's daughter, the lovely Julia. He'd been pleading with her to marry him for a long time, but she was set on nothing less than a marriage in the new temple in St. George, and he'd not been able to dissuade her. Not that he necessarily wanted anything less; he just thought they could be married in Bluff by Julie's father and then get to the temple when they could.

"I don't rightly know," he finally replied. "Whenever we can take the time to get back to St. George, I reckon."

"Maybe a few of you young lovebirds should travel together," Billy suggested. "Mons and Olivia Larson told me there's so many young folks from the Arizona settlements heading back to the temple in St. George that they're calling their route the Honeymoon Trail. They're chaperoned going west and honeymoon returning east."

"I heard of that trail," George Ipson stated. "The honeymoon part sounds like a mighty nice deal, but I sure wouldn't need much of a chaperon going west."

"Well, George, I think you would," Dick Butt teased. "The way you get turned around in these trees and gullies hereabouts, you'd need two or three chaperons just to get you there."

"That's the truth," Billy chuckled. "And maybe two or three more plus your new wife to get you home again."

"Now see here! Just because this country's too thick with trees or too deep with gulches for a man to keep his bearings doesn't mean I'm always lost. Way I recollect, Dick, Billy had to get us both out of that tangle two, three days ago."

Dick grinned. "I just didn't want you to get your feelings hurt, George. That's why I played along with being lost."

"Yeah, sure you did. And you were just playing along when I had to get the mules to drag that cottonwood log off where it had you pinned, too."

"No," Dick Butt replied while both he and Billy recalled the dangerous accident, "that was sure-enough trouble, George, and I'm right grateful you were close by. I'd hate to think where I'd be if you hadn't been there."

The man's sincerity stopped the bantering, and for a few moments the cave echoed only the noise of the storm—that and the occasional snap from the fire as a pocket of pitch in one of the logs was ignited by the licking flames. The cave was a comfortable place, Billy thought, with deep sand where their bedrolls were spread, warmth where the walls reflected the heat from the fire, and of course dryness. There was even a tiny seep or spring at the back of the cave where they'd been able to fill their canteens. It took a while because the water did little more than drip, but over the course of a night they could collect enough water for all of them.

Billy's thoughts returned to Bluff, and to his beloved wife and little son. How he hoped they were all right! How he prayed that the Lord would protect them from the dangers that seemed always to be lurking around the next corner, the next bend in the trail. Of course, so far the Indians, both Navajo and Pahute, had shown no disposition to cruelty or murder, but all seemed quite friendly as they mingled from day to day among the Mormon settlers. Yes, they were a thieving bunch, both tribes, taking anything that wasn't tied or nailed down. But somehow their thievery seemed more like a game, a way for them to show their superiority over the settlers. Unfortunately, it was no game to the Mormons, who needed every animal they had either for food or farming, and who had no way of replacing the precious little trinkets and mementos the Indians were so fond of taking.

Billy thought then of some of the Navajos who had come to the fort: tall and handsome Navajo Frank, old man Hoskanini and his son Hoskanini Begay, nervous Tsabekiss and his son Bitseel, a man he knew simply as Whiskers, and a headman someone said was named Kigaly or Kigalia. Of course, there were others whose names Billy didn't know, and he found it of more than passing interest that he hadn't yet met any of the Navajo women. In fact, in the entire year of their settlement, he'd seen only one or two, and these kept strictly to themselves and had little to say to anyone.

The Pahutes seemed more gregarious than the Navajo, and men, women, and mostly naked little children were always turning up in or near the fort. Old Peeagament and his elderly wife Peeats came often, as did their two grandsons Paddy and John. Another grandson, named Grasshopper, was of a mean disposition, and Billy and the others had learned to avoid him.

Moencopi Mike and his squaw; Old Chee and his two squaws, their sons Posey and the huge Scotty, whom somebody said had taken his name from a horse-wrangler named Johnny Scott who worked for a small-time rancher known only as old Dorrity; Tobuck-ne-ab, who had taken the name of a local cowboy and become Mancos Jim; Sanop and his two sons; Tuvagutts and his young friend Pahute Bob; and the four sons and youngest daughter of an old man named Norgwinups, who were called Hatch, Poke, Bishop, Teegre, and sweet little Too-rah; all these and many others lingered about the tiny fort for days at a time, pilfering, stealing, begging, demanding. Then in a morning they would all be gone, and no one would have the slightest notion of where or when they had gone, or of what new deviltry or mischief they might be about.

To Billy, it was almost as if—

"What do you suppose the folks were like who lived here in this cave?" Dick Butt suddenly asked.

"For one thing," George Ipson replied, "they were almighty short."

Billy chuckled. "Like me?"

"Yeah, only maybe even smaller. The doors in these ruins weren't made for very big people."

"I think they were an almighty frightened people, too," Dick said.

Surprised, for he'd never considered such a thing, Billy questioned the man.

"Look where they built these homes." Dick pointed off into the shadows. "You ever seen a cave house that wasn't high up and as out of sight as possible? These folks were afraid of somebody, and I reckon this was their way of protecting themselves."

"Sort of like the fort Elder Snow told us to build?"

"Yeah, Billy, that's right."

"President Young gave it as his opinion that the Hopi down in Arizona were the literal descendants of the people of Ammon in the Book of Mormon." Billy's voice was quiet, thoughtful.

"And?" Dick Butt questioned when Billy paused.

"Well, Thales Haskel says the Hopi villages are built just like these old ruins, only out on some high mesas instead of in caves. So I was thinking that maybe these folks were the ancestors of the Hopi. You know, with a bunch of generations between them. And then if you add a bunch more generations before these folks, maybe you'd come to the people of Ammon. And since the people of Ammon buried their weapons of war and became a people of peace, maybe these folks kept the same beliefs, hiding out like this so they could practice peace in a country filled with war-minded Lamanites."

"In other words," George Ipson concluded, "you're thinking that maybe these old people didn't fort up out of fear so much as out of an effort to practice their religion?"

"That's a good way to put it."

"That's a whole lot of maybes," Dick Butt said. "But it does make sense. In fact, I think that's the real reason we've been told to fort up. I don't think any of us are terribly afraid of our neighborhood Indians, at least not yet, so the fort can't be for that. The way I've been figuring it, the fort may be more to give us a little breathing room, a little peace where we can relax and practice our religion the way we believe. Goodness knows our Lamanitish brethren don't give us much breathing room now!"

"Amen!"

Billy smiled into the darkness as his two timber-cutting companions grew silent. Then he twisted onto his side and maneuvered his hips until a hollow for them had been dug in the sandy floor of the cave. Then he sighed with as much contentment as he could muster. Interesting, he thought, how once evening prayers were taken care of, conversations seemed to twist and turn until they ended up in the right places. The previous fall, both George and Dick had been reluctant to support the bishop and others in using some of their hard-cut logs for what they had long thought of as a useless fort. But now—

Lightning struck nearby and a rolling clap of thunder immediately followed. Billy drifted off to sleep listening to it but thinking of Eliza and little Willy, praying in his heart that they would be watched over and protected while he was forced to be away.

3

<hr>

Wednesday, March 30, 1881

Bluff Fort

According to Billy's Regulator clock, it was 2:30 in the morning. Willy was sleeping peacefully, yet Eliza's head was pounding so fearfully that she couldn't even hope for sleep. Like almost all her sick headaches, this one was centered behind one of her eyes—her left one this time—and was radiating upward and back from there. The pain was fierce, destroying almost all her ability to think or to function in a reasonable way, and Eliza feared it was leading to nausea, though as yet it hadn't progressed to that point. Still it was sufficient to drive all hope of sleep from her mind, leaving her desperate to somehow occupy her hands so the pain would seem less intense.

Recently Bishop Nielson had made a trade with a Navajo woman for a great deal of wool, sheared from her flock of long-haired sheep. Now it was washed and combed, and Eliza and several others in the fort had agreed to spin it into yarn so that Kirsten Nielson, the bishop's wife, could weave it into a fabric known as "homespun" on her small loom.

And so now Eliza sat before her spinning wheel, her foot pumping the pedal steadily, her hands only minimally busy, and her mind wandering where it would to give her something to think about besides her headache. On the left side of the wheel the distaff was loaded with the long woolen fibers, and as she pumped the wheel to spin it, the fibers—a few at a time—were pulled free of the distaff. Passing through her left hand, the fibers were twisted or "spun" into a continuous length of yarn or thread that was then wound on a spinning wooden spindle or bobbin that was turned by the pulley action of the wheel. It was a simple process, really, and required little more than the steady pumping of the pedal to keep things going. Yet before the invention of the spinning wheel the whole process had been done by hand, spinning the fibers into yarn between the fingers, and Eliza found herself feeling thankful that her task was not so difficult.

Beyond the spinning wheel, the logs in the fireplace settled, sending a shower of sparks up the chimney, and Eliza thought briefly of adding more wood to the fire. Yet she was sufficiently warm, and the fire was giving off more than enough light to spin by, and so she didn't stop. Neither did her mind, which in spite of her headache was worrying the issue of her fear as a dog might worry a bone.

Oh, mercy, she thought as the soft, woolen fibers passed through her fingers, coating them with the natural lanolin of the wool. Why did she have to feel so afraid all the time? What was there about this San Juan country that inspired in her so much fear? What was it—

"Eliza, are you all right?"

Mary's soft voice from outside her door startled Eliza, but recovering quickly she arose, lifted the latch, and invited her young friend inside.

"Mary," she said as she offered her heavily robed neighbor her rocker and then returned to her wheel, "what in the world are you doing out at this time of night? Especially now that Kumen's home from Colorado."

The young woman frowned teasingly. "I'm out because of you. Believe it or not, Eliza, through both log walls I heard your spinning wheel going, and so I got to worrying about why you weren't asleep. Since Kumen's sawing logs to beat the band, I thought I'd check. Is it the morning sickness?"

Eliza shook her head. "I haven't had any of that, at least not yet."

"But . . . you were sick every day for weeks with Willy."

Remembering back, Eliza nodded her agreement.

"Well," Mary smiled brightly, "that likely means you'll be having a girl. Sick with boys before birth, sick with girls after. At least that's what Ma always told me. So what's wrong if it isn't morning sickness?"

"I have another sick headache," Eliza responded with disgust. "Sometimes I get so tired of them I want to scream!"

"Too much worrying?"

Eliza sighed. "I suppose so. That's what folks seem to think, anyway."

Mary's look was sympathetic. "What is it that you're worrying about this time? Billy? Little Willy? The new baby? Yourself? Indians? Outlaws? The river? The ditch? Quicksand? Bad water? Storms? Drought? Insects? Heat? Scorpions in your shoes? Rattlesnakes under your bed? Failed crops? Starvation? A calamitous future? Which of those are you worried about tonight, my dear? Or have you perhaps discovered something new and refreshingly different to worry about?"

Eliza couldn't help but giggle. "You make our lives here sound positively awful."

"That's probably because they are. Truthfully, Eliza, I've never felt so worthless and out of control, and I don't know a sister in this community who doesn't feel the same. So which is it?"

"All of them, I suppose, including feeling worthless and out of control. This country does provide quite a litany of worries, doesn't it."

"The country be darned!" Mary adjusted her robe to better cover her legs. "We're every one of us quite adept at providing ourselves with all the worries a body could ever need—me included."

"You?" Eliza was surprised. "If you ever worry, Mary, you don't act it. You can make a joke out of anything, and usually do."

"And that means I'm not worried? You get sick headaches, Eliza, and I'm so troubled that I laugh in public and cry myself to sleep every blessed night!"

"About all the things you just mentioned?"

Soberly Mary shook her head. "Not really. Oh, most of those things bother me, I suppose. I worry most about Kumen's safety. But what really troubles me is that, no matter how hard I've tried, or how diligent I've been with my faith and prayers, I haven't been able to give Kumen a baby. If I . . . can't do that for him, Eliza, then what good am I? I . . . I'm afraid something is terribly wrong with me, and I'll never give . . . birth—"

And abruptly Mary Jones was weeping.

Yellowjacket Canyon

"Hello the camp! Can we come in?"

Standing and looking out into the gray gloom of the rainy morning, Billy could see the dim forms of two mounted men. Both were wearing wide hats and dark slickers, however, so he could make out little else about them.

"You see more than two, Billy?" Dick Butt's voice was quiet.

"I don't."

"Me neither. Go ahead and invite them in, and I'll stay here in the ruin with the horses until we know if they're friendly."

"Ride on in," Billy called out in response. "There's room here for your horses, too, happen you want them in out of the wet."

Without another word the two men rode up the steep incline and into the cave, where they were forced by the low roof to dismount. Without a word, and ignoring Billy completely, both men immediately saw to their horses, removing their saddles and bridles and rubbing the animals down with burlap from one of their saddlebags. That done, both animals were given nose-bags filled with oats from a bag one of the horses had been carrying, and only when that was done did the men turn toward Billy and the fire.

"Howdy," the one said amiably as he removed his Stetson and slapped it against his chaps to remove the water. "Looks like a mighty comfy camp you got here."

"It's dry enough," Billy replied, noting that the cowboy who had spoken was hardly more than a boy. "The sand's soft, too, if a feller needs a little shut-eye. My name's Billy Foreman."

"Mine's James Heaton," the young man replied, stepping forward and extending his hand, "though everyone but my ma calls me Jimmy. This is my big brother, Henry W. Most folks call him Henry W."

Smiling at the young man's slight humor, Billy shook hands with each of the men. "Howdy, boys. Welcome to the fire."

"Thank you. Is that Arbuckle Triple X you've got in that pot?"

"Nope. Scorched water. But she is hot, and the taste isn't bad, either."

"Scorched water?"

Billy grinned. "Yeah. Mormon coffee, made from roasted parsnips. Help yourselves if you're interested."

The two looked at each other questioningly, and then with a shrug young Jimmy Heaton pulled two tin cups from his saddlebags, handed one to his brother, took up the large pot, and filled each to the brim. "Bottoms up," he said wryly, and then both brothers took careful sips.

"Well," Henry W. Heaton said as he eyed the liquid in his cup, "she's at least healthy, even if she ain't Arbuckle. Parsnips, huh? I never heard of such a thing."

"Nor me," Jimmy said with an infectious grin. "But for not being coffee the taste ain't half bad, by gum, and the warm is even better. Billy Foreman, this does hit the spot. Thank you."

"You alone here, Billy?" Henry asked.

Since all three bedrolls were still nearby, and since the three cups and plates used earlier hadn't yet been put away, Billy knew the question was rhetorical and might more aptly have been phrased, "Where are the other two of you?"

"Nope," he replied easily. "Are there any more of you?"

Henry W. Heaton grinned knowingly. "Nary a one, so you can tell that feller back there in the ruin to put away his rifle and stop worrying. Jimmy and me is friendly, and we both intend staying that way."

Billy nodded. "Glad to hear it. Boys, this is Willard George William Butt, otherwise known as Dick. Dick, these are the Heaton brothers, Henry W. and Jimmy."

"Howdy, boys." Dick Butt strode to the fire and stopped, surveying the two. "Our other man is George Ipson, who'll be along directly, I reckon. Happen, that is, he ain't got hisself lost again."

"If he has," Jimmy Heaton declared emphatically, "I don't hardly blame him. This is the most cross-grained, disjointed country a body ever did see. Twice yesterday we lost the trail, and we ain't seen it at all since it started raining. You boys on it?"

Billy chuckled. "Not unless you count the tracks our wagons made when we drove them in here."

"We're cutting ties for the railroad being built by Otto Mears," Dick added. "If there's a trail hereabouts, none of us have spotted it yet. Where was you figuring on following this trail to, once you found it again?"

"A spread called the LC, located on some creek called Recapture over on the San Juan. Pa's ordered a bunch of cows from a feller name of Bill Ball to feed the miners back in Rico, and me and Henry W. are to take delivery and get 'em back to him pronto. We was told this trail had good water, so we thought we'd follow it out just to get the lay of the land in our minds."

"Well," George Ipson said as he stepped under the sandstone overhang and up to the fire, slapping the rain from his own hat as he did so, "you sure did find the water, all right."

"Yeah," Henry W. replied sourly, "but we was sort of expecting it to be on the ground. Ties for the D&RG, you say? Has it already reached Durango?"

"Not yet. But the tracks are past Antonito and moving right along. We're out here on account of Mr. Mears figures cedar ties will last longer than pine."

"He's a far-thinking man, all right. But it's a long freight from here to Durango, isn't it?"

"Not for us." Billy picked up the tin plates and began scouring them with wood ash and sand. "There's a tie lot down country a piece, just west of Cortez, where trimmers are squaring these ties and stacking them for freighting."

"Yeah, and Mears is probably using Dave Wood for the freighting, too."

Dick Butt nodded. "The wagons say 'David Wood Freighting' on their sideboards, all right. You fellers heard of him, have you?"

"Heard of him! That man's got freight outfits all over the western slope, and some east of there as well. Folks say there ain't a thing on this green earth he can't pack into or out of this country. Some of his freight outfits carry tons of mining equipment up mountains so steep a goat couldn't follow. One stamp mill he freighted up Otto Mears's impassable toll road and down into Telluride weighed 100,000 pounds and made some men rich and busted others, just from betting for and against him."

"Sounds about right," Billy said. "The feller we've met is named George Clive, though the other teamsters just call him Wagon Boss.

But I don't think there's a man alive who can pack a load so high and so tight as Mr. Clive."

"Except for Dave Wood," Henry W. stated firmly.

"Yeah, and he's a young squirt, too," Jimmy added emphatically. "Not even married yet, or at least that was the last we heard. So you fellers are Mormons, are you?"

"Officially we're members of The Church of Jesus Christ of Latter-day Saints. But there are plenty of folks who call us Mormons." Billy adjusted his spectacles. "Some don't mind the name, some do."

"You?"

Billy smiled. "Far as I know, none of us mind."

Henry W. nodded. "We heard there was a whole passel of you folks come into the country—on the river next to the Navajo reservation. Folks claim you're taking up with the Injuns."

George Ipson laughed sarcastically. "More accurately, they're taking up with us. I don't think any of us owns an animal or anything else that ain't been stolen by one tribe or the other at least once in the last year. Way I see it, those two tribes would've starved plumb to death if we hadn't come along to become their unofficial larder."

"Yeah," Jimmy Heaton agreed, "they're mighty handy with the midnight rope and ride system. If you fellers are Mormons, how many wives do you have?"

"Thirty six," Dick Butt stated instantly, not batting an eye. "And when I get back to the fort I'm figuring on marrying nine more."

Young Jimmy Heaton was astounded. "Nine all to once? Whooeee! Why, that'll give you forty-five wives, mister! I can't hardly imagine such a thing!"

"And he's just a piker," George Ipson threw in. "There's men back at the fort with close to a hundred wives each, and by harvest I figure to have sixty myself."

Jimmy Heaton was so dumbfounded his mouth was hanging open, and it was all Billy could do to keep from laughing.

"You ever heard about how Mormons have horns, Jimmy?" Dick Butt was enjoying this, and it showed. "Well, as you can tell by looking at us, that's an absolute fact. We even have to have our hats made special just to accommodate them. Take a look at my hat here, if'n you don't believe me."

"I heard about them horns," Jimmy said seriously as he reached for Dick Butt's hat. "Fact is, I even saw a picture of 'em onct, in a newspaper or magazine or something. Okay, let's see here . . . Say, there ain't no place for horns! This hat ain't no different than mine!"

"It isn't? Are you sure?"

"I ain't blind, Dick Butt! I can see—" Only then did young Jimmy Heaton become aware of the almost silent laughter of his older brother—that, and the twinkles in the eyes of the three Mormons. "Well, I'll be a dad-gummed, clod-kickin' idjit! You boys've been funning me right along, and like a rattle-brained nitwit I took it all in. Are you even Mormons?"

"Yes, Jimmy, we're all three Latter-day Saints." Billy winked at the young man. "But none of us have horns that I've ever seen, and between the three of us there's only one wife waiting back at Bluff, and she's waiting for me."

"One?"

Billy nodded. "One, and she's mighty purty! Fact is, these two yahoos would like to have wives too, but Dick hasn't been able to talk Julie Nielson into it yet, and George Ipson here can't even figure out who to ask."

"No foolin'?" Jimmy finally noticed that his older brother was putting together some flour, salt, water, and baking soda for breakfast biscuits, so he hurriedly busied himself as well. "Well, I know who to ask," he said as he fished out a large skillet and set it on the coals. "Thing is, I run plumb out of nerve ever time I come onto doing it. Miss Sally's so doggone purty she makes my head swim and my mouth go dry as cotton, and when she sings I get so filled up inside I think for sure I must be dying. No fooling, boys, that gal can sing just like a canary, only purtier. Ain't that so, Henry W."

"She can sing, all right," Henry W. acknowledged.

"Thing is, I just ain't come onto the right way of popping the question."

"Miss Sally sounds like a sweet little gal," Billy said. "Is she about your age, Jimmy?"

"No, she's a little older'n me—four or five years, maybe. But I don't think that's a bad thing. Do you?"

"Not me. My Eliza's older'n me by considerable more than somewhat, and I've never been troubled by it yet. How old are you, Jimmy?"

"Me?" The young man was slicing sidemeat into the pan. "Going on sixteen. But I've been doing a man's work for three years now, and I reckon I'm as ready for marriage as I'm going to get."

"What he don't reckon," Henry W. said with a wry grin, "is what Pa'll do to him if he ever gets up the gumption to try it. Pa figures Jimmy is still a kid, and I'd hate to be the one tells him he ain't."

"Yeah," Jimmy admitted, "Pa does get some riled. I figure, though, that this little trip over to the LC will be just the ticket. Pa'll figure out I'm finally all growed up, and then Miss Sally'n me can do 'er up good and proper. If only Henry W. and me can find that durn ranch—"

"I know about where it is," Billy said as he walked over to look out into the rain. "Fact is, we all do, since it's just a little upcountry from Bluff."

"No foolin'? Can you maybe draw us a map?"

Billy turned around with a grin. "I can do better than that, Jimmy. As soon as we can get our two loads of ties out of here and back to the railroad, my contract with them is over and I'll be heading home. You want to travel with me, I'd truly enjoy the company."

"You fellers aren't going with him?" Henry W. was looking at Dick Butt and George Ipson.

"No," George replied. "We started a week after Billy, so our contracts still have a week to go. We've been some worried about sending Billy off alone, though, it being so long since he's seen his wife and little son. Man who's been away as long as he has tends to lose his good judgment and get foolish and careless. But if you boys was to agree to ride along with him—"

"We'll do it!" Jimmy Heaton was beaming. "We'll even help you get your ties to the railhead." Quickly he turned his attention to Billy. "So, your wife really is older than you? That's great! How'd you do it, Billy? I mean, how did you get up the nerve to ask her to marry you—"

Bluff Fort

"Morning, Mary. Are you feeling any better?"

Sheepishly Mary Jones looked up from the stump where she was sitting while she buttoned her shoes. "Wasn't that something! I came over to comfort you and ended up bawling my eyes out."

Eliza smiled. "We were both just feeling sorry for ourselves. To my way of thinking, that's the lowest state to which a woman's mind can fall, and I've made up my mind to stop it."

"Good for you. Then I'll do the same."

"Of course, I've made up my mind to stop it in the past," Eliza admitted candidly, "and then I've gone along and forgotten my resolution. Sooner or later, though, I always come back to it, for I believe it's a truly sensible thing to learn. It's true if we're alone or our husbands are beside us, if we're wearing silk or homespun, or if we live in a cottonwood cabin or a palace."

Mary nodded as she finished doing up the last of her high-topped shoes' numerous buttons. "I think you're right. I also think you're wonderful for reminding me of it. Kumen can go now with Thales, and I will absolutely refuse to feel sorry for myself about it."

"Kumen's leaving again already?"

"He is. Bishop Nielson gave him the order this morning. So while the rest of us are trying to get the corn planted and that miserable ditch re-dug for the umpteenth time, he'll be gone with Thales Haskel and Ben Perkins to see if they can recover Black Diamond as well as the baby booties one of those two Navajo women apparently stole yesterday from Rachel Perkins. I told him I didn't think the booties seemed worth it, and he said he was inclined to agree. But Brother Haskel says we have to keep proving our point—that we have as much right to be here as anyone else, and that folks who steal from us aren't going to get away with it."

"Seems like the thieves are, though—getting away with it, I mean."

Mary nodded. "It does, at that. Is your headache better this morning?"

"Much, thank you." Eliza smiled wryly. "Now if I can just keep it away—"

"Yes, that's the trick, all right. How's Willy doing?"

Eliza's face immediately clouded with worry. "He didn't even wake up when I came back from doing chores, so I don't know. He's nothing but skin and bones, Mary, and he's sleeping more and more, almost like he's a newborn again. I wish I knew what to do."

"What do you feel from prayer?"

Eliza sighed. "I don't know, Mary. Billy seems able to get answers any time he asks. But me? Anymore, all I feel is confusion. Truthfully, I don't know which way to turn."

"Well, you could take Willy to Pa for a blessing. Or Kumen would be glad to do it once he comes back from the reservation. Or I suppose you can even wait for Billy to do it. Do you have any idea when Billy's coming home from Colorado?"

Eliza nodded. "Next week, he said in his last letter. But so many things can change that. Well, Mary," she declared brightly, abruptly changing the subject, "you have a marvelous time in the fields today. I'll be thinking of you."

"Ah," Mary grinned knowingly, "it's your week with the children, isn't it. I'd forgotten."

"Well, the little ones. Mary Ann Perkins has the older children." Eliza sighed again. "Of a truth I'd rather trade her, or else be planting corn. I'd even rather work on that awful ditch! With my awkwardness I'm so nervous around these little ones, so afraid of doing something wrong or allowing them to get hurt in some way, that I hardly dare to breathe."

Mary Jones giggled. "Now you know how those of us feel who've never had children of our own. That's what makes this United Order business we're living so wonderful. We all get to enjoy a little of everything, no matter what. So enjoy! And remember, dear, no more feeling sorry for ourselves! We've agreed."

Still chuckling, Mary picked up her hoe and started toward one of the fort's corner gates. Eliza, after seeing that Willy continued to sleep, plopped herself down on the split log bench in front of her cabin. "Oh, dear Lord," she breathed as she awaited her small and difficult charges, "I won't feel sorry for myself. I just won't! So, please help me to see the good in all of this—"

———◇–◇–◇———

"Heap hungry! Me want eat!"

Startled and then instantly terrified, Eliza spun from the bed, where she'd been leaning over little Lena Decker, changing a diaper. It was early afternoon, and the only sounds in the cabin had been the ticking of the clock and the ever-present buzzing of flies. Even within the fort there were no sounds, for all were either in the fields or strung out along the five miles of ditch, trying to ready it for water. Mary Ann had gone to goodness only knew where with the older children, thus removing their constant chatter, and four of Eliza's babies, including her own little Willy, were already deep into their afternoon naps. But now—

Grabbing the side of the table to catch her balance, Eliza stared at the two Pahute youths who had somehow stepped through the doorway of her cabin without her being aware, and who were now glaring menacingly. It was the shorter one, Posey, who had spoken, and though in the months since she'd last seen him he had grown and changed, the same hatred burned in his dark eyes, the same loathing filled his ever-deepening voice.

"*Ungh!*" the young man suddenly growled, pointing with his old rifle at Eliza's breast while he hit his own chest with his free hand. "Me Posey, him Scotty. Heap hungry! You squaw, you gettum *te-shut-cup,* you gettum bread! We eat!"

"I . . . I don't have any more bread," Eliza stammered, telling the terrifying Pahute the truth. "I g-gave the last of the bread to the children—"

Apparently understanding Eliza, and no doubt seeing the terror in her eyes, the young Pahute warrior grew even bolder, more insistent. Shouting in both Pahute and guttural English, he strode to the table, threw it onto its side, and then with a spin pushed the muzzle of his rifle into the belly of the child whose diaper Eliza had just changed.

"Me heap hungry! Me wantum eat!" Posey was now shouting so loudly that even little Willy had awakened, and to add to Eliza's horror, all the babies were suddenly crying with fear. Yet she had no idea what she should do—

"Squaw gettum bread heap hurry, or me kill—"

When or how Thales Haskel came into the room Eliza had no idea. All she knew was that in the middle of Posey's threat he was spun about, his rifle was jerked from his hand, and then with a solid kick to his backside he was sent stumbling toward the door.

Striding after him the tall old Indian missionary and interpreter ignored both Eliza and the wide-eyed Scotty as he pushed Posey out over the log doorsill. "Fool!" Thales snarled in perfect Pahute as he spun the startled youth about and drew him close. "*Katz-te-suah!* You call yourself Posey the great warrior, but like a fool with no mind, all you dare fight are squaws and papooses. You who call yourself Posey, hear my words, and remember them. These are mormonee squaws and papooses! These are friends of the great God *Shin-op.* You hurt one of these, even one, and you will wish many days that you were *e-i,* dead!"

In disgust Thales Haskel threw Posey's old rifle into the dust of the commons, after which he spat contemptuously upon it. "It is good that *Shin-op* is also your friend," he then thundered directly into the face of the cowering Pahute. "You may thirst all you wish after the blood of the mormonee, but for so long as you draw breath, you will never be allowed to take the life of even one. Your big guns will be no good against them! That gun there in the dust is no good against them! No, and it never will be! But as you desire for the mormonee, so shall your squaw one day die! So shall you one day die! These are the words of Jehovah, he whom you call *Shin op,* and they will be fulfilled!"

Spinning the young warrior about, Thales gave him another swift kick to send him on his way. And then he glared balefully as Scotty wordlessly left the cabin and trotted after his humiliated elder brother.

"Th-Thank you," Eliza stammered as the two young men disappeared through one of the fort's open gates. She was trembling visibly, and it was a wonder that her crutch was holding her upright. "I . . . I thought he was going to k-kill—"

Tenderly Thales Haskel reached out and took Eliza by the hand. "Sister Foreman, things are all right. Nobody got hurt, and nobody's going to get hurt. And those two young yahoos won't be back for a spell, either; you can count on that. I'm just sorry it took me so long

51

to get here. Only I didn't see 'em sneak into the fort, being busy getting ready to leave and all, so I reckon what happened was at least partly my fault."

Thales smiled. "Now go on inside, set yourself down, and take a couple of good, deep breaths. I'll round up two or three sisters afore the boys and me ride out, and by dark you should be feeling first rate again. By the by, you did good telling Posey the truth thataway— about the bread, I mean. Way it seems, a person lies to an Indian can't be protected by the Lord's Spirit, no matter why he does it."

Numbly Eliza nodded, bade the old man farewell, and then stumbled back into the room with the still-frightened children. Taking up little Willy and Lena Decker, who had been so horribly threatened, she sank into the rocker and then did as she had been directed—took two deep breaths. As she buried her face in Willy's blanket, the tears finally started, and the terrified and thoroughly defeated Eliza began, at last, to sob.

4

Thursday, March 31, 1881

Bluff Fort

"River's rising!" There was excitement in Joshua Stevens's voice as he galloped his horse into the fort with the first pink blush of dawn, and it was lost on no one. "Up and at it, everybody! The river's rising fast, and there'll soon be water in the ditch!"

"Water's rising!" Francis Webster shouted enthusiastically from near the corrals, taking up the refrain, and within moments the entire population of the fort was astir. For the first time the Saints began to feel hope for their crops.

"Eliza, did you hear?"

Groggily Eliza pulled her head from her pillow, slid out from her bedding, and swung her feet to the floor. Little Willy's sleep remained undisturbed, and as she gazed for an instant at his pale, pinched face, Eliza felt relief. Surely it was good for him to sleep, she thought. Sleep was good for anyone who was sick, no matter what their illness.

"Eliza, are you awake?"

"I'm awake, Mary," she mumbled as she shrugged into her housecoat, took up her crutch, and pulled herself to her feet. "I'm awake, so please don't awaken my baby."

It had been a long night, and what little sleep Eliza had found had been filled with distorted dreams of the Indian youth who had threatened the Decker baby and destroyed her own fragile peace of mind. Again and again her memory had replayed the incident of the afternoon before, seeing the hatred and contempt in Posey's eyes, seeing the empty cupboard where no bread remained, hearing her own pathetic stammering as she tried to explain that she had no food to give him, seeing Posey thrust the muzzle of his rifle into the soft stomach of the infant girl, and hearing the metallic click as he pulled back the hammer.

To Eliza it didn't matter that Thales Haskel had arrived at that moment and defused the explosive situation, disarming Posey and thoroughly humiliating him. All that mattered was that once again she had failed! Frightened beyond belief, she had responded poorly—no, pathetically—and her cowardly incompetence had almost cost the life of little Lena!

"Eliza?"

Swinging open her door, Eliza glared through hollow eyes at her young friend. "I'm awake, Mary, and I know the water's rising. Now, what more do you want of me?"

Stunned as much by the tone of Eliza's voice as by her haunted appearance, Mary stepped back. "Why, I . . . I thought—" And suddenly she understood. "It's that awful Posey, isn't it. And what he almost did. Oh, my dear friend, I should have spent the night with you!"

"What good would that have done?" Eliza's voice was harsh, for her anger at herself, and her despair, were spilling over everything around her. "Could you have stopped my nightmares, Mary? Or my memories? Could you have undone what happened, or given me the wits to handle it? Could you?"

"Eliza, that awful boy surprised you! You had no time to prepare. Besides, he was threatening little Lena with his rifle, for pity's sake. What on earth could you have done about that?"

"I could have thrust myself between his gun and the baby! I could have brought him into your cabin and given him a loaf of your bread!" Abruptly Eliza's voice lost its anger and grew tired, discouraged. "I could have at least screamed, Mary, distracting him and maybe bringing help a little sooner."

"Dear Eliza, you mustn't do this to yourself."

Her expression bleak, Eliza turned back into the room to hide her sudden tears. "Do what? Force myself to look at the truth? We're supposed to be on a peace mission to those people, and yet all I feel is fear and hatred. I . . . I loathe them, Mary, I absolutely loathe them! That's part of why I have no right being here. And now, not only am I not contributing, but I'm also a burden! I nearly cost a life yesterday, and for all I know it's me that's causing little Willy's illness. Oh, Mary, don't you see?"

And with that she finally broke into sobs.

—o—o—o—

"Pa, I'm concerned for Eliza. That boy Posey put a terrible fright into her yesterday, and I hate to see her left alone again today with the children."

Bishop Jens Nielson, over six and a half feet tall and still strong as an ox despite his fifty-nine years and the terrible crippling his feet had received in the snows of Wyoming when he had been part of the Willey Handcart Company, looked up at his eldest daughter.

"Ya, Mary," he replied slowly, his Danish accent still heavy despite his years in America. "I haff bin vorried, too. Ve vere not doing our duty yesterday, none off us. Ve should haff seen dose Pahute boys und gone to her aid. It vas goot dat Thales had not yet taken Kumen and Lemuel und gone onto the reservation after de horse und dose booties. Oddervise ve may haff had terrible bloodshed, und our mission vould haff bin over."

"Mary Jones nodded. "It may be over for Eliza anyway. I've never seen her so low. Pa, do you have any idea when Billy's coming back?"

"Ya, Brudder Lyman tolt me dat Billy's contract vith de railroad iss already up. I imagine he vill be back early next veek."

Mary shook her head. "That's not soon enough, Pa. She needs somebody right now, all day and all night. Not only does it look like little Willy may be dying, but she's grown so terrified of the Indians that she can't even sleep any more, let alone think normally. Is there any way I can stay with her today?"

Bishop Nielson looked down at the list of daily assignments he had been making. "I yust don't tink so, Mary. Dat river iss rising too quickly, und ve vill haff vater in de ditch before noon. Und ve haff more dan two miles of ditch dat are not even cleaned out from de flooding in February."

Pausing, the bishop looked again at his list. "You are strong, Mary, und vith Kumen gone, I need you driving your team und scraper. For a fact, your team iss de best ve haff left, und it iss already harnessed and vaiting. No, Mary, I can't spare even vone soul, for ve are so few, und de vork iss so—Vait! Somebody tolt me Annie Lyman iss not feeling herself today—stomach troubles from de alkali in de vater, I tink dey said, und she needs to rest. I vill ask Annie to spend de day resting in company vith Eliza und de little vones. Dat vay de poor voman vill not haff to be alone vith de children und her fears, und you can be free to do your vork. Ya?"

Leaning down, Mary kissed her father's cheek where he shaved it just above his beard. "You're wonderful, Pa! And don't worry. We'll get that ditch finished in time."

"Ya, ve vill." The old man's expression was suddenly bleak. "Now, if only dat fool river vill finally begin to cooperate—"

Sand Island

"Ho, my brother, it is in my mind to ask what you are thinking."

For a moment Posey remained silent, ignoring his larger but younger brother. He had said little since the day before, not even to his mother, who had also questioned his silence. Instead he had remained quiet, his agitated thoughts in the land of anger where they had compelled his tongue to be still.

What had happened to him was not right! No, not to the eldest son of Old Chee, not to a warrior and the son of a warrior! The old white mormonee who spoke in the tongue of the Pahutes had shamed him—yes, and worse, had shamed him in the presence of his younger brother. So, too, had the tall, ugly white woman shamed him! Such a thing must not happen to a warrior such as himself, especially when he was destined for such great things!

And so for hours he had sat in silence either in the *wickiup* of his mother or upon the old cottonwood log, his heart growing harder and his finger growing more feverish as it caressed the trigger of his old rifle. *Wagh!* It would be a good thing to use his big gun against those foolish mormonee. It would be especially good to use it against them in the presence of his brother.

All about him in the budding cottonwoods a flock of blackbirds chirped and warbled with the joy of the spring morning, and nearby the muddy waters of the San Juan rumbled angrily. The water was high and rising, digging at the sandy banks of the island where he and Scotty were hidden, eating away large chunks of sand only to redeposit it elsewhere. But knowing the strength of the pony he rode, Posey paid the threat of the water no mind. Neither did he pay attention to the worrying of his brother, who was very strong but did not have a mind for deep thoughts. So now Posey schemed, plotting way after way that he could lure the two mormonee, those who had shamed him, into the sights of his big gun—

"My brother, do you not hear me?"

"Of a certainty I hear you!" Posey snapped. "You jabber more than these birds."

Ignoring the insult, Scotty pressed on. "It is in my mind to know the nature of your deep thoughts, my brother."

"There is nothing in your mind!" Posey was angry even at his brother, though he had no idea why that would be so. "But if you must know, I am considering ways of *puck-ki*, of killing with this rifle those two foolish mormonee who shamed me."

Scotty was aghast. "But . . . my brother, did you not hear the words of that old mormonee, the one who is called Haskel? Did you not hear his words of power? He told you that your big gun is no good, that *Shin-op* would not allow you to kill the mormonee. I myself heard him speak those things."

Angrily Posey leaped from his log. "I heard those words, too, and they are the words of a fool! This big gun no good? It is in my mind to shoot a hole through your own belly so you can see who has power—that old mormonee or the warrior called Posey."

With a snarl Posey raised the old rifle and pointed it at his brother, who instinctively cowered back, his eyes wide and staring. Still snarling, Posey raised the muzzle a little higher, sighted briefly, and then fired.

Yelping in fear as the smoke from the gunpowder engulfed him, Scotty grabbed his middle and then looked downward, expecting to see his hands bathed in blood. When he found none he looked up in wonder, and that was when he realized that Posey was walking away.

"My big gun is no good?" Posey chuckled as he walked to a fallen blackbird, which he picked up by the long tailfeathers. "If it is no good, my brother, then by what power did I *co-que,* did I shoot this bird? Do you see, now, who is the fool?"

Numbly Scotty made the sign that he saw.

"It is good." Tossing the bird into the churning water, Posey strode back to his log. "Now leave me so I can think through how best to kill those mormonee—"

"Your bullets seem to have eyes of their own, my son."

Spinning in surprise, both Posey and Scotty were startled to see their father, Old Chee, standing in the trees behind them. How long he had been there they did not know. What they did know was that once again this one whom they both considered to be an old man had proven his skill as a warrior of the People.

"Did you aim before you pulled the trigger, or did your bullet find that bird by itself?"

Made proud because of the rare praise, Posey became humble. "It was a small thing, my father. Your shots are much more true."

Old Chee smiled. This one, he was thinking, would be a great warrior. Very soon. "Come," he said then as he turned back through the trees. "Mike of the big mouth has already taken his woman and son and crossed the river, so it is time that we take our *wickiups* and follow after him to the Shining Mountains."

In amazement the two brothers looked at each other. Somehow both of them had forgotten this wondrous journey that was taken each spring, a journey of many days when the Pahutes left their big river and rode to the Shining Mountains, the old—and some said still the true—homeland of the People.

"*Wagh!*" Posey breathed as he took up the rope of his pony and strode after his father, his anger temporarily forgotten. "This is the season, my brother, when we will show those other warriors that we have become true men. Yes, and we will show the *nan-zitch,* the young maidens, that our ponies are the fastest of them all!"

"*Nan-zitch,*" Scotty breathed, having no understanding at all of why his brother thought so often of the young women of the People.

"I wish nothing to do with them! They look only for evil things to say."

Posey laughed. "Ahh, so you also remember the one called Too-rah, the *nan-zitch* who called us those evil names. Well, brother, if that one is at the encampment where the races are held, I myself will ride a pony past her face so rapidly that she will see nothing but dust. *Oh-ah,* yes, and she will see that since she last saw me, I have become a man!"

"As have I," Scotty said as he followed after his brother. "Perhaps, since we have both become men, you and I will be allowed to ride along on any big raids that may be held after the races. That would be a good thing."

"Ride along?" Posey snorted with derision as he entered the encampment with his pony in tow. "Perhaps I will lead a big raid of my own, my brother! Yes, with this fine rifle I will put many meri-cats and many mormonee under the grass! Yes, and I will show all of those who cower in the Shining Mountains what it means to be a warrior of the People—a warrior and a great chief!"

And as Scotty watched in awe, Posey threw himself onto his pony, gave a wild whoop, and rode defiantly into the turbulent water of the river, not waiting at all to help his mother with her packhorses, or even for his warrior father to go first. Truly, Scotty thought as he turned to help his own mother pack, this brother of his would one day become a great chief—

The Jump

"Water's in the ditch!" Hanson Bayles's voice rang out between the stone bluffs of the San Juan River gorge, echoing and carrying for miles. "Here she comes, folks! The river's up and the water's in the ditch, so get yourselves ready!"

As the scattered members of the Bluff community, male and female, old and young alike, took up their shovels in preparation for keeping the water in their recalcitrant ditch and somehow getting it to travel the five miles to their not-quite-planted fields, Charlie Walton stood gazing nervously at the headgate they had taken to calling the Jump.

"I don't know, Hans," he shouted, shaking his head in concern. "I think we've got problems here—big problems. That river's rising way too fast to suit me."

Twenty-three-year-old Hanson Bayles soberly examined the murky water swirling against and through the open headgate. For a time then he stared up the river, his head turned to the side as though he were listening. Finally he turned his attention back to the new headgate, which was now wide open to the raging stream.

"Yeah, Charlie," he declared, his voice raised above the roar of the water, "she is. I don't know why I didn't notice it before. And look at all the silt coming through the headgate! I've never seen it this bad."

"Nor have I. You thinking what I am?"

"Probably. Looks to me like we don't have a prayer of keeping the water in the ditch, not with that much silt. She'll fill in no time flat, and I don't care how many shovels and teams and scrapers we have fighting it."

Hanson shook his head. "There's something else, Charlie. This is an angry river we've got here—angry enough to chew up banks and islands all the way upriver to wherever the storms were that have caused this flood. Thing is, look how she's digging and clawing at this bank where we've built the headgate. If she gets much higher we'll lose the entire bank, plus the gate and a good chunk of our ditch."

"Yeah. Then the river will shift to somewhere else, and we'll be left high and dry, with a silt-filled ditch to boot." Charlie Walton shook his head with discouragement. "I don't know, Hans. Doesn't seem like we're ever going to tame this demon of a river."

"It'll starve us all to death! You keep a watch here, Charlie. I'm riding back to the fort to give the bishop the bad news."

"Better hurry," Charlie Walton grinned wryly, "or it won't be news by the time you get there!"

Bluff Fort

"Eliza, I don't know how you did it, facing that terrible Pahute boy. I'd have fainted dead away just from the fear of him."

Eliza, trying to get food into the five oldest of the children she was assigned to watch, didn't look up. "I did nothing," she said quietly, her voice sounding dead, "except nearly get an innocent little child killed."

"Well, at least you didn't faint. That's surely what I would have done!"

Annie Maude Clark Lyman, a petite, dark-haired Englishwoman who was the plural wife of Platte Lyman, was lying on the bed doing her best to endure the severe cramping that had disabled her. Platte had brought her through the Hole-in-the-Rock the previous winter along with his first wife, Adelia, and her two children; his mother, Eliza Partridge Lyman; and other members of his family—all of them arriving at the fort on January 1, 1881. Almost immediately Annie and Eliza had been drawn to each other, at first because they were both from England, but then because they simply liked each other. They seemed to think alike about many things, and Eliza's only struggle with the younger woman was that she tended to idolize Eliza, much as she was doing now.

"Hello, Willy my boy," Annie said as the child toddled to the side of the bed and tried to climb up beside her. "Do you want to lie down beside Auntie Annie for your afternoon nap? Well, come on up, then. There's plenty of room for both of us."

"Auntie," Willy repeated, at the same time trying to climb onto the bed again. "Auntie."

"Why, Willy, you say that plain as day. When did you learn to do that?"

"He's becoming a great imitator," Eliza said as she moved across the room and lifted Willy to the bed. "Now, close your eyes and go to sleep. There. That's a good little boy."

Reaching over, Annie Lyman tousled the boy's hair. "That's a dandy, wee boy. Always be obedient to your mother, and you'll always be smiled upon by the Lord. My own mother told me that, and most of the time I believe she was right."

"Why, Annie!"

Quickly the woman smiled. "I'm only funning, Eliza. There, look how quickly the child has gone to sleep. I wonder why he doesn't do that when I'm tending him?"

"Because he's too busy getting into trouble with little Albert. It's a wonder how he can do so much when he's so thin and frail."

Annie nodded, her eyes not leaving the child at her side. "He is looking peaked, all right. Does Maggie Haskel have any idea what's wrong with him?"

"He's starving to death," Eliza replied bitterly. "No matter how much I try to stuff into him, no matter how many different cows Mary and I milk trying for a more nourishing formula, it does no good. Willy is slowly dying, and I'm powerless to stop it."

Annie said nothing, only gently caressed the child's hair, and the uncomfortable silence lengthened.

"Brother Lyman hasn't returned from Colorado yet?" Eliza finally asked.

"No, nor any of the others who went with him. Adelia thought they'd be back today, but so far there's been no sign of any of them. It's too bad, because the bishop could certainly use their help on that ditch."

"It'd do precious little good," Eliza murmured, her voice filled with discouragement. "Earlier when I was outdoors I overheard Charlie Walton talking to the bishop. He said the river was flooding upstream and was precious close to washing away the headgate we built last summer at the Jump. I shouldn't be surprised if by tonight we'd lost the whole five miles of ditch and maybe our fields as well. Then we'll have to start all over again—just like both times we started over again last year!"

"It's a trial living in this country, isn't it!" Reaching down, Annie pulled her skirt and petticoats up as far as the ruffles of her bloomers. "Just look at my poor legs, Eliza. There isn't a spot that hasn't been bitten by those awful sand fleas, and now my arms and face are providing three square meals a day for swarms of no-see-ums that I can't even fight because they're so tiny."

"Their bites aren't tiny, though!"

Annie chuckled bitterly. "I'll say not. How do you put up with it, Eliza? How do you endure living in this horrid country?"

"How do you endure it?" Eliza countered.

"By prayer, I suppose, though I'm more than willing to admit to the difficulty of it in spite of my prayers. The hardest part for me is the loneliness, the rarity of seeing Brother Lyman, my husband. For instance," and now the woman sighed, "even if he returns tonight, I shouldn't be surprised if I didn't see him until the morrow."

"Truly?"

"Truly. This business of living the Principle is the most difficult thing I've ever done!"

Knowing that the woman was speaking of the principle of plural marriage, Eliza remained silent. At least, she was thinking as she saw the sudden tears start down Annie's cheeks, that was one trial she hadn't been called upon to bear.

"I knew it would be difficult when I agreed to it," Annie continued, speaking almost more to herself than to Eliza, "but merciful heavens, Eliza, I didn't think it would be like this! Of course, I didn't know then that I'd bear no children—"

Tenderly Eliza looked at her friend. "Had you known that, would you have turned Brother Lyman down?"

"I . . . I don't know. Probably not. But being alone makes it so hard. Did you know that sweet little Evelyn and even baby Albert call Adelia Deelie-Ma or Ma-Deelie? Oh, Eliza! How I ache for a child to call me Annie-Ma instead of Aunt Annie, or to reach out and put his arms around my neck the way little Willy does with you! I know Brother Lyman would visit me more often if I could only give him a child. But I can't, and I . . . I don't blame him for spending most of his time with Adelia and her little ones."

"Adelia treats you well, doesn't she?"

"Yes, of course. Oh, I know having a sister wife is difficult for her, too. She told me once that having me married to her husband is like being shut up in a prison with a big problem and being compelled to meet it with no chance of retreat. Believe me, Eliza, it feels the same with me. And I ache for her, I truly do. Besides Evelyn and little Albert, Adelia and Brother Lyman have lost three children, all buried back in Oak City where Brother Lyman was the bishop. Those deaths have taken a great toll on her, and leaving them behind in their lonely graves and then coming into this horrid country have made it even worse. And between his Church calling and his travels to earn a living, Brother Lyman leaves that poor woman alone nearly as much as he does me.

"The thing is, Eliza, I'm starting to wonder if my decision to marry him wasn't a mistake—and not just because of the personal things. I loathe this dry, harsh land and the terrible people who inhabit it! And I . . . I just don't know what I should do about it."

Eliza almost laughed, the situation seemed so humorous. "And you're asking me what to do? Glory be, Annie! Except for living as a plural wife, which I don't think will ever be my trial, I'm little different from you. I detest this place, I'm terrified of the Indians, and some nights, like last night, I sit up all night weeping and praying. Billy tells me again and again to inquire of the Lord how I should deal with my fears, but I get nothing by way of answers, and absolutely nothing seems to change!"

"You pray to get answers?"

Eliza smiled ruefully. "Well, I try. What about you? What has the Lord made known to you about your problems?"

"Why, nothing whatsoever." Annie was completely perplexed. "I haven't even asked for such a thing. The Lord doesn't speak to me in that way. I simply pray and hope for positive results."

"Do you ever feel the Holy Ghost?"

"I . . . I don't know, Eliza. I have good feelings about certain things, I suppose. That's certainly why I married Brother Lyman. At the time, I felt good about doing it. But as for the Lord speaking to me, or giving me revelation in some other form, why, that's never happened in my entire life. I haven't expected it to happen, for like you I am only a woman, and not a prophet or anyone else of importance. Is that what you mean?"

Eliza smiled. "Yes, partly. But Billy is of the opinion that every one of us, no matter our mortal station, has the right to go before the Lord and obtain personal revelation—not about huge, earth-shattering events but about the little things in our own lives that cause us joy or terror or grief. Again and again he has told me this, and he has shown me numerous scriptures and statements made by the Prophet Joseph that seem to confirm it."

"Written statements by Joseph Smith? How does he have access to such statements? Mother Lyman is always telling us little things that Brother Joseph said, but outside of her memory and perhaps her journals, she has nothing of his that was written down. She feels badly about it, too."

"Platte's mother knew Joseph Smith?" Eliza questioned in surprise.

"Knew him? Her full name is Eliza Partridge Smith Lyman. She was sealed to the Prophet before he was martyred, as one of his plural wives. That's why I'm not able to speak with her about my dilemma. She simply won't countenance doubt such as I appear to be feeling."

Once again Annie Lyman wiped the tears from her eyes. "Anyway," she said, forcing a smile, "how did your husband gain access to such things? Surely he isn't old enough to have known the Prophet personally."

"He isn't. But in that small cowhide trunk there on the shelf against the wall he has forty or fifty small daybooks, all filled with sayings and sermons and ideas he found or formulated while he worked as secretary to President Brigham Young. You simply can't imagine all the things he's written about."

Now it was Annie's turn to be surprised. "I didn't know Billy was Brigham Young's secretary."

"He was, as was his father before him. Anyway, Billy's been trying to get me to understand the same things you appear to be struggling with—of going before the Lord with the full expectation of receiving counsel from him. Moreover, Annie, I'm sure he must be right. There should be nothing of a personal nature that we can't take before the Lord and, with faith and righteousness, expect revelation about."

"Can you . . . I mean, do you receive such inspiration?"

"I'm . . . well, no, not really." Once again Eliza's expression turned bleak. "I have, though, especially when I was going through that period of repentance I told you about a few weeks ago. But for most of the past year the heavens have seemed as brass to me, and I . . . I don't know what I'm doing wrong. In Billy's last letter he told me it takes time. In fact, he quoted something from Joseph Smith that says we must all grow into the principle of revelation. And maybe that's it. Maybe I just need to grow some more. But Annie, if it takes much longer I'll wither up and die from fear, or little Willy will pass away from starvation, and I . . . I won't have had any idea of how to help either one of us—"

Denver and Rio Grand Railroad Tie Lot, West of Cortez, Colorado

"I don't know about you Mormons, always picking up strays the way you do." Hard Tartar grinned. "Henry W. here is a good man, but where'd you pick up this other young leppy calf?"

Like the smoke from the various adjacent campfires, the question hung, unanswered, in the still night air. Jimmy Heaton, reclining on his saddle, took a drag on the smoke he had rolled only moments before. Occasionally he still spilled more of the tobacco than he got in the paper, and though he detested the taste of the acrid tobacco smoke, at least he had stopped coughing whenever he inhaled, and his older brother had stopped making fun of him—at least about smoking. Of course he was still riding drag on a thousand and one of his other jokes and pranks—

"Hey Jimmy, why don't you answer the man's question? How'd you come to join up with these Mormon folks?"

Jimmy Heaton grinned into the darkness, trying to think of the best way to reply. In the nearby hills a chorus of coyotes were *ki-yiing* into the night, their short barks and howls a song so common he hardly even noticed it anymore. Somewhere nearby an owl hooted, a sound he did note, and at another fire one of the men guffawed at something somebody else was saying.

"Me?" he finally replied, his words slow and drawled out. "The question, by Tophet, had ought to be how these fine upstanding Mormon fellers came to be hooked up with the likes of you hardrock boys."

"That'd be the better question, all right." Wiley Tartar, Hard Tartar's brother, snorted. "I don't know why I didn't think of that afore I made my own fool inquiry."

"And?" Jimmy pressed.

"And what?"

"What're you boys doing here at the D&RG tie lot?"

Hard Tartar nodded wisely. "Well, Henry W., looks like you can tell your folks their baby boy Jimmy at least ain't gone blind. He can see this here is a railroad tie camp, which takes mighty good eyes. Howsomever, you'll also have to tell 'em their boy's brain is sure dead, for he cain't tell that on account of we're all camped here permanent-like, and have been for months, we must be cutting and squaring ties for Otto Mears's gallivanting and never-ending railroad."

"You boys've been doing this all winter?" Jimmy Heaton was astounded. "Why, I had no idea! Hard, I saw you in town not two, three weeks ago. You too, Tom. And now I find out—Well, if that don't beat all! Why aren't you boys still hardrock mining at the Colorado Belle?"

"On account of the fool superintendent closed the mine down last fall."

"Besides which," Tom Click added, "there ain't much difference between swinging a pick and swinging an ax."

"'Cept in the size of the paycheck," Wiley Tartar grumbled. "The mines at least pay a man a decent wage. That Otto Mears and his railroad, on the other hand—"

"That's enough, brother mine," Hard responded quietly. "A man never knows where listening ears might be lurking." The man abruptly grinned. "Or when a leppy calf like Jimmy here might show up to provide us an evening's entertainment."

"Entertaining or not," Jimmy replied in his easy way, "this whole shebang has me buffaloed. Here I finally find me a Mormon who's well versed in the fine art of marrying older women and willing to teach me the same, and it turns out he's already hooked up with Henry W.'s and my onliest ornery neighbors and the dredges of Rico society, to boot."

"You'd have knowed who wasn't around," Wiley Tartar cackled, "if'n you'd stuck your head outside the batwings of Mona's Emporium for more'n half a minute in any given week."

Jimmy Heaton grinned. "Boys, I am amazed. I don't frequent that emporium more'n once a night, and you know it!"

"You don't?"

"He says he don't, don't he."

"Why, I don't hardly believe this here conversation," Tom Click finally scolded. "You fellers know you can't count on young Jimmy here for the straight truth—especially when he's so dadburned addlepated over the lovely Miss Sally."

"Is that the same Miss Sally who's the school marm?" Jim Hall teased.

"Why," Dick Baumgartner replied with relish, "that's more'n likely what she does during the day, all right. At night, though, whilst she's singing, them fancy shoes of hers is wearing out that poor old bar down at Mona's Emporium."

"Dancing?" Hard Tartar questioned, "or trying to get away from her numerous suitors?"

"As ever," Jordan Bean declared, joining in the laughter. "But she don't run too fast, boys, because I got me a good smooch from her when I was home just a week ago Saturday. And everybody knows I ain't as fast on my feet as I used to be."

"Why, she done the same for me," Tim Jenkins declared to the merriment of everyone but young Jimmy Heaton. "Two big, wet kisses that like to have lasted half an hour if they lasted a minute. And on account of my rheumatiz and poor constitution in general I was busting my gut trying to get away from her when she caught me and planted 'em! Why, a feller my age can't stand all that smooching! Bad for the heart and the liver both, or at least that's what my wife says."

"Go ahead, boys," Jimmy declared amiably while the men were laughing all around, "make fun of us two poor, innocent children. Come fall though, after Billy Foreman teaches me what he knows and you get your invites to our wedding, you'd best come serious and sober. Once that reverend says his pronouncements and me and Miss Sally say our I do's, you boys are going to see some smooching the likes of which most of you have only dreamed."

"And the rest of us?" Wiley Tartar pressed.

"The rest of you," Jimmy grinned widely as he flicked away his distasteful cigarette, "ain't had the pluck to even begin such a dream. But come anyway, boys, because me'n Miss Sally'll have a thing or two to teach the whole blamed bunch of you."

"Well," Wiley Tartar sighed elaborately, "you got your work cut out for you, Billy Foreman. You surely do. I know you Mormons are mighty marrying folks, but neither Jimmy nor Miss Sally strike me as the marrying kind—"

"The next thing that's going to strike you, Willy Tartar, happen you don't lay off on me and Miss Sally, is my fist!" Jimmy was still smiling, but most everyone around the fire could see the glint in his eyes, and every one of them knew what it meant.

"Don't worry, Jimmy," Dick Butt said as he took up his bedroll and rose to his feet, completely silencing the noisy group of men. "It's a long way to Bluff and your Pa's cattle, and you and Billy will have plenty of time for palavering about marriage without these noisy jaybirds interrupting things."

"That's right," George Ipson agreed as he arose. "I wisht Dick and I were going along just so's we could listen in. But I'll tell you this, Jimmy. Billy Foreman's got him a mighty fine wife waiting back at the fort, and you just ain't never seen anything like that little towheaded kid that's Billy's own son. If he can help you get a family like he has, then more power to you is all I've got to say."

"Well, I'll be getting one!" Jimmy Heaton declared, glaring at his neighbors. "In spite of these cackling yahoos, it's going to be me'n Miss Sally and a whole passel of young'uns, and every one of you addlepated so-and-sos can take that to the bank!"

Slowly the camp grew still as one after another of the men rolled themselves in their bedrolls and dropped off. Except for the wakeful Dick Baumgartner, who had drawn first watch, Jimmy Heaton was the last to sleep, and he drifted off in the midst of one of his favorite mental visions of the more than lovely Miss Sally, and of what he was certain their future together was going to be.

Bluff Fort

"I simply can't imagine that you brought all those lovely pieces of china and crystal into this horrid country. Whatever possessed you to do that?"

It was late, long after dark, and for most in the fort, the day was drawing to a close. But for some reason Annie had not departed, and so Eliza was simply keeping busy, allowing the younger woman to stay as she wished. Moths were constantly streaming through the open window and gathering to the flame of the lamp, fluttering about and frequently singeing their wings and then perishing in the hot grease. Both women ignored them just as they ignored the occasional yipping of coyotes that echoed back and forth between the high bluffs. Usually coyotes were no more to be feared than moths, and neither they nor anything else in the country caused Eliza as much stress as the two-legged pests that brought such terror to her heart.

Unfortunately, those pests were impossible to ignore—

"Actually," she replied as she carefully rubbed the dust from a delicate gravy boat, "I debated bringing these things with me for some time, but that was before I left Salt Lake City with Billy. I had no trouble making such a decision when I left Cedar City to come to the San Juan."

"But . . . they seem so inappropriate to the hard, simple life that is required here."

"Yes, Annie, they do. But once I got to Cedar I never stopped being thankful for them, and here in this horrid country my gratitude has known no bounds."

"I . . . I don't understand."

"And I don't know if I'm able to explain. They—well, there are times when these things are all that help me keep my head up. When everything else becomes impossibly difficult; when because of the Indians or whatever my life feels absolutely out of control; when I'm missing my husband and my baby's starvation has grown even more obvious, then I can take these things off the shelf and dust them, and somehow I feel a little better."

Annie was absolutely perplexed. "But, why?"

"I don't exactly know why." Eliza's voice had grown soft. "Perhaps they remind me of long-ago scenes that I pine for. Perhaps they represent stability—civilization—which goodness knows we all need on this river. And perhaps it's nothing more than that they give me a way to occupy my mind, my hands."

Eliza smiled sadly. "Of a truth, though? I'm a vain old woman, Annie, and I'm the first to admit it. I take pride in surrounding myself with fine things, for somehow they make me feel better about myself. More than likely I'm acknowledging a great sin, but of all the reasons I've given you, I expect this is the real one. These things somehow stroke my pride, and when nothing else does—when I feel a failure no matter what I put my hand to—then it's comforting to caress the delicate features and exquisite beauty of these pieces, and to remind myself that they are mine."

"Oh. I . . . see."

Obviously, Annie was suddenly uncomfortable, and Eliza supposed it was because of her bluntness. Yet she had told the truth—at least part of it. These things did comfort her, but only during the bleak and lonely times when Billy was away, little Willy was asleep, and all the daily chores were behind her. Otherwise, she thought as she picked up a cream pitcher and began polishing it with her sudden, silent tears, she no longer noticed—or even cared—that the China was on the shelf!

5

Friday, April 1, 1881

Tyende Mesa, Navajo Reservation

The elderly Navajo woman had been sitting on her sheepskins in the traditional place for women when the three *belacani* had ridden over the rise and toward her *hogan.* Though alone in her years she still had respect for the proper ways of the *Diné,* the People. That was why the place of honor where her husband or sons or other men would have been sitting, though easier to get to because it was closer to the door, always remained empty. Instead she passed by it each time she wished to take a seat inside her *hogan* or to go out through the doorway, shuffling the extra few feet around the fire as a simple sign of respect for the old ways that she knew were also the right ways.

The old woman did not spend any time thinking of this, though of a truth she had been thinking more, lately, of other old things she had not thought of in a very long time. For instance, before the three *belacani* had arrived, she had been watching the antics of a packrat who had made her *hogan* his own dwelling. But instead of thinking solely of the packrat, her mind had begun considering Monster Slayer and Sired-by-Water, the twin sons of *Ásdzáá Nádleehi,* Ever Changing Woman, who had gone forth in the first days of this world to slay the monsters that had made living impossible. The old woman knew this to be true, for in her lifetime she had seen many of the remains of these monsters. Near Mount Taylor, she recalled, had lived *Yeíitseh,* the giant who sucked people in. Monster Slayer had struck off his head, and as he died his blood had flowed out in a black stream that had turned to stone and was fully ten miles long. This dried blood was still there, for she had both seen and felt it with her own hands. And off toward the rising sun was the man-eating eagle called Cliff Monster, whose whole body had been turned to stone by Monster Slayer, with sharp feathers pointing upward and wings trailing on the ground. The *belacani,* the old woman knew, called this dead monster Shiprock, but even the little children of the *Diné* knew the truth of what the great rock actually was.

And there had been other monsters, many others, such as Kicking-off-the-Rocks near the great river to the north, which had drowned people, and to the east the Rocks-That-Rushed-Together Monster, which crushed all who ventured near.

With the help of Big Fly, Spider Woman, Bat Woman, and Gopher, the war-god twins, who were the sons of Ever-Changing Woman had slain all of them, leaving alive only the monsters known as Old Age, Sickness, Poverty, and Death, so that mankind might be kept alert and working.

But as the other monsters had died, they had cast off claws and bits of fur or feathers. Trying to make something useful even of these, the twins had turned them into song birds and small animals, saying: "Earth People shall use you in the future." And so it had happened, the old woman had been thinking as she watched the packrat scurrying about the edges of the fire circle. Those small creatures had been very useful. Why, if she were only a little younger or a little faster, this one would have quickly found his way into her mostly empty cooking pot. And if that were so, the hunger that was already starting to gnaw once again at her belly—

It was then that the three *belacani* had entered her *hogan,* and for the old woman, thoughts of eating the tiny packrat were entirely forgotten. Instead she had watched, fascinated, as the three had moved in the proper direction around the fire circle, paused before the traditional seats of honor where men should sit, and at her nod had dropped onto the carefully arranged sheepskins to face her.

She thought, then, of the words of *Natanii nééz,* the tall one who was the son of her sister and who had taken upon himself the *belacani* name of Frank. Many days before, he had brought her fresh mutton and had reminded her that in her lifetime she had carried three names. The first, her infant name, she hardly thought of any more, having long ago set it aside. The second, the name by which she had been known almost all her adult life, Frank also wanted her to set aside. Instead, he had explained, it was once again time for her to be a warrior woman—to call herself *Ahééníbaa,* She Raided in a Circle.

And so the old woman had sat without moving, thinking of herself as *Ahééníbaa* while she watched the three *belacani* as their eyes searched through her *hogan.* That they had come at all had surprised her, for not only was her *hogan* hidden under the rim of Tyende Mesa near the springs at the upper end of *Tseyi-hatsosi,* two days ride from the fort on the big river, but also these were what *Natanii nééz* had told her the *nóódái* or Utes called mormonee—a cowardly people who had no strength to fight. Yet these three, including the one with long white hair and piercing eyes who knew things other men didn't know, had come hard on her heels and had reached her *hogan* only a little time after she herself had arrived.

For long moments they had sat in silence, her eyes and those of at least the one mormonee locked on the nearly dead coals in the fire circle. After an appropriate silence, that one had spoken in her own tongue, his voice so low she had been forced to lean forward just to hear. And he had said little, just enough to let her know that he and the others had observed her recent visit to the mormonee fort on the big river and had come to her *hogan* to gather up a little property that had been lost by the *belacani.*

Sensing that it would be foolish to resist, the old woman had first protested her innocence and then quietly told the man to proceed with a search of her *hogan.* And so now while the one who knew a few things sat without moving, the other two searched, moving sacks, sheepskins, saddles, and some of her own finely woven blankets. And with her almost toothless smile the old woman remained seated upon her sheepskins watching them, thinking of how much joy this one final raid of her life had brought into her heart.

It had been many long seasons since she had thought of herself as the warrior woman *Ahééníbaa*—far too many. In the old days, the good days, she had ridden on many raids; yes, and the warriors of the *Diné* had shown much respect for her. She had ridden against *nóódái,* the Utes; against *nakai,* the Mexicans; and she had even ridden against the *belacani,* the whites. They had been good raids, too, and she had ridden fearlessly and with pride, circling her enemies again and again to show them her power. And thus she had helped in the accumulation of much wealth, not only for herself but also for her people. And that was the good way, the proper way of the *Diné.*

But then the bad times had come, the hard times of Rope Thrower and the destruction of *Diné tah,* the ancient homeland. In all the cycles of the seasons since, there had been little enough to take pride in. Cooking pots had been rarely full. Herds of sheep, goats, and horses remained for the most part small and filled with inferior animals, animals with little value. But the hardest thing of all, *Ahééníbaa* thought sadly, was the fear that yet filled the hearts of the *Diné.* Just as surely as Rope Thrower had killed their peach trees, he had also killed their courage. They had been threatened with more death and another long march if they began their raids against the whites again, and the threats had been believed. Of course, they could still raid the Mexicans and the Utes, and some were doing so—a little. But these peoples seemed as poor as the *Diné,* and so there was little to be gained by such raids. Truly it had become a time of confusion and despair in *Diné tah,* for there had been no *hózhó,* no balance in the universe of the People.

But now her nephew, the one calling himself Frank, was telling everyone that all had changed! *Aoo,* yes! Two cycles of the seasons past, one *haáthali,* a singer who was of her own born-to clan, had performed a prostitution way, a great sing that had cured all of *Diné tah* of the witchcraft brought by Rope Thrower. Shortly thereafter a group of wealthy *belacani* had brought their wagons and their herds to the big river, and there they had settled.

But as her nephew had explained, these *belacani* were not like Rope Thrower and his people. No, these were the mormonee, a cowardly people who sought friendship rather than power, and who did not even enjoy the protection of the *belacani* soldiers. These were a people, therefore, who had come to be raided. These had come so the *Diné* could begin, at last, to recover their lost wealth. These had come so the *Diné* could find again their stolen courage, their stolen heart.

Yes, the old woman thought smugly, Frank had been right. All this was certainly so. And it delighted her to have become the warrior *Ahééníbaa* once again, and to have made a successful raid where she had walked in a circle about the *belacani* fort on the big river. Yes, and to have entered into one or two of their ugly square *hogans*—

"Mother," the *belacani* with the long white hair said softly, interrupting her reverie with his respectful salutation, "we know that you took from their owner the foot coverings for the baby you spent so much time admiring, and we have ridden many miles to get them and return them to that child. With proper courtesy we ask you now to tell us where you have hidden them."

"Have you looked on the other side of my *hogan*?" the old woman asked by way of reply, at the same time indicating the direction with a traditional twitch of her lips. "If I have them, perhaps I placed them over there."

"We have already searched over there, Mother, and you know it. You have no need for such foot coverings, for you are long past the age of bearing children. Tell us what you have done with them, and we will leave you alone."

The old woman cackled joyfully. "I told you in the first place that I did not take them. I have now told you so again. Why is it that you do not believe my words?"

While the one remained seated, the other two moved over to stand beside her, resolute. These two, she knew, had no knowledge of her language or her ways. These she had dismissed instantly, and she gave no thought to them, even now. But the third, he of the long white hair, knew a great deal, and this was starting to trouble her. There were also his eyes, which had a way of looking through a person as though she was made of clear water. This man she feared. But she was also puzzled by him, for though he was an enemy she sensed no animosity in him, no anger or hatred toward her. He knew more than Rope Thrower and his *belacani* soldiers had ever known, much more. Yet he did not hate—

"It is said, Mother, that you were seen leaving the child's cabin with the foot coverings hidden beneath your shawl. Do you deny this?"

Feeling unaccountably nervous, the old woman forced a nearly toothless smile. "Why should I deny such a thing? It is true that I took them from that ugly square *hogan.* But I only did it that all might enjoy the beauty of the foot coverings as I had enjoyed them. That is why I placed them on the end of a log that stuck out from the wall of that *hogan* a little more than the others. It had a flat spot on the top made by an ax, and I placed the foot coverings there so that all who passed by could see their beauty."

"There is such a log on Hy's wall," Kumen Jones said quietly after Haskel had translated her words. "I've seen it, Thales."

"Ben, did either you or Kumen see those booties on that log when we rode out?" Thales's voice was low, so low his two companions also had to strain to hear him. "Because I sure-enough didn't, and happen they'd been there, I believe I would have."

Quietly both men shook their heads.

"Well, boys, I'm convinced this old woman has those booties. Now, as Sister Rachel said, they ain't really all that important. What is important, and this you need to know, is that somehow these Navajo folks must be made to understand that we Mormons mean business, and we won't tolerate such brazen thievery. Happen we don't get that point across at every opportunity, they'll rob us blind. That's their way, boys. It has been for generations, and they're mighty good at it. So, will you back me in my plan?"

"Whatever you want."

"Good." Slowly Thales Haskel rose to his feet and stepped around to where he was directly before the old woman. "When I give the signal, you lift her into the air and stand her up on her feet." Silently Thales sank onto his heels, his gaunt form seeming literally to fold together. Then, his arms clasped around his knees, he stared silently into the dark eyes of the woman.

Old *Ahééníbaa,* She Raided in a Circle, was instantly terrified. Never had she been looked at in such a way. Never! Surely this *belacani* mormonee had a *chinde,* a devil in him. Or maybe he *was* a devil! Yes, that was it, for surely he could see—

"Mother," Thales Haskel said, startling her once again with the

77

quiet of his voice, "will you please rise so that we may look beneath you?"

Forcing her smile back onto her wrinkled old face, the woman cackled again but did not budge. A second time the white man made the same request, and then a third time, and now the old woman knew with certainty that in his eyes was a *chinde*. She did not know exactly what that might mean, for her or for the rest of the *Diné,* but she knew it was so.

More, she knew she could not attempt to deceive this one again, for after three times, a lie becomes part of the person making it, destroying the person's balance, and she did not want such harm to come upon her—especially not with this frightening *belacani* squatting before her, his eyes boring into and through her.

Therefore, when the other two *belacani* abruptly took her by her elbows and gently lifted her to her feet, the old woman did not resist. Neither did she resist when the one with the long hair reached forward and lifted the delicately embroidered white satin foot coverings from where they had lain hidden on the sheepskin beneath her. Instead she cackled delightedly and with amazing sincerity, considering her great fear. And she was still laughing after the three had left her a leg of venison for her nearly empty cooking pot, made the sign of farewell, and departed from her *hogan.*

After all, she reasoned, she was now once again the warrior woman *Ahééníbaa,* She Raided in a Circle. Despite the cycles of her years she had made another raid, a successful one. Yes, and now, she knew, there was hope once again for the heart, the courage of her people!

Unless, her frightened mind warned her, that one with the long white hair and *chinde* eyes happened to be nearby—

Tseyi-hatsosi, Navajo Reservation

"I'll tell you what, Thales. This deal stumps me."

"What deal?" Thales Haskel was smiling, though Kumen Jones had no idea why. "That an old woman would steal baby booties? Or that she'd laugh when we found them?"

"Well, both, I reckon," Kumen Jones responded. It had been an hour since he, Ben Perkins, and Thales Haskel had left the *hogan* of the elderly Navajo woman, and Kumen could not seem to get the incongruity of the experience out of his mind. He knew Ben was troubled as well, though as yet the other man had said nothing. The thing was, neither of them had thought the old woman was the thief. Instead they had suspected a much younger Navajo woman who had also admired the booties, and they had only ridden with Thales to the old woman's *hogan* because the interpreter had insisted on it.

Now they were riding out of the mouth of the wash known as *Tseyi-hatsosi,* and after skirting Boot Mesa they would ride northeastward across Monument Valley and by the next day be back in Bluff. Or they would be, Kumen thought, if they didn't run into any Navajo hostiles, if they didn't somehow stumble onto the trail of the bishop's missing black gelding, and if none of their own horses turned up lame or some other such foolishness.

Of course, should something like that happen, he couldn't imagine anyone he'd rather be with. Kumen had watched the Indian missionary and interpreter intently two years earlier when they had first explored the country, and he had grown convinced, despite the fact that he was somewhat long in the tooth, that no one in the exploring party had more physical strength or pure raw courage than Thales Haskel. Now he was seeing just as clearly the man's apparently unfailing wisdom, as well as his ability to feel correctly, and then follow, the impressions of the Holy Spirit.

"You understand it, Ben?" Thales asked quietly, interrupting Kumen's musings.

"Not at all I don't," the Welshman replied after another moment's thought. "'Tis a puzzle these people be, even more than the Pahutes on the other side of the San Juan. It's doubtful I am that we'll ever understand them."

"Oh, given enough time—and maybe the Second Coming—we'll all understand each other. But you see, Ben, you've hit on the very thing that both you and Kumen are struggling with. The old woman and her folks are Navajo, and the Pahutes are Pahute, and not a one of them thinks like a white man. More important, not hardly a one of them even wants to."

"What do you mean?"

Lifting his hat, Thales wiped his brow and then adjusted the hat back in place. "Navajo ain't the real name of these folks, just like Pahute ain't the real name of those renegades yonder across the river. *Diné* means the People, and the Utes think of themselves the same. In other words, boys, in their minds both tribes think they're the real, original, honest-to-goodness citizens of this earth, and us white-eyes and all others are nothing but interlopers and lesser beings. Fact is, except for a bit of fooforaw such as iron tools, bolted cloth, and lots of livestock, we don't have a thing most of 'em either need or want. What they'd really like, I suspect, is to be left alone to pursue their lives the way they always have—warring and raiding and raising their young'uns to do the same."

"Well, that won't do," Kumen declared. "We can't have them robbing us blind, or killing us at every opportunity, either one."

"No, we can't, Kumen, and that's the rub. We come here without so much as a by-your-leave from any of them, plop ourselves down in the middle of their homeland, and start using up the country for miles around. And then they're the ones who have to change—either that or get out.

"Of course, this ain't exactly a new problem. Both the Utes and the *Diné* started somewhere else themselves and ended up taking over or driving out the old citizens once they'd decided this was their own new Promised Land. More'n likely that's what all these old ruins in this country are about. Fact is, boys, this same drama has been played out time and time again since the world began, including the children of Israel, who kicked the former settlers out of the Promised Land. One night down on the Moenkopi I listened to Jacob Hamblin discourse on this subject for hours, and it was the first time I ever made sense of it all."

"So, is it right? What we're doing, I mean?"

Thales smiled a little sadly. "Depends on who's being asked, I reckon. For myself, I have an absolute knowledge that God is in yonder heavens and that he makes his will known to prophets and apostles, both ancient and modern. That includes Brigham Young, who called and set me apart as a missionary to the Lamanites. That was more'n twenty-five years ago, and so far no one's said anything about me being released."

"That's a long calling." Kumen grinned.

"But not as long as it will be. Boys, I also believe the scriptures are God's word. When I read that his work and glory is to bring to pass the immortality and eternal life of man, the statement rings with truth. When I read that Jesus' name is the only name given through which a man can be saved eternally, and that no man can be saved in ignorance of that name or of the gospel He proclaimed, then I know why I'm here among these people—why we're all here—and I'm at peace with it."

"Of a truth they don't know Jesus," Ben stated quietly.

"Or how to find him, either one. But the biggest question for all of us to ask ourselves, whites and Lamanites alike, is why. Why on earth should any of them wish to stop being who they are and start being who we are? Or why should we wish such a thing upon them?"

"What sort of a fool question is that?" Kumen groused.

"Fool question, Brother Jones?" Thales fixed the red-bearded young man with a piercing glare. "Are you fixing to sit on that scrawny pony of yours and tell me in all seriousness that you think you're better'n the *Diné?*"

"Well, no, I . . . I'm not, at least personally. But the Saints—"

"Kumen, the whole blamed Church full of Saints is nothing but individuals, each one pretty much like you. That's who the Saints are that you were about to credit with being better than other folks! With that in mind, how many individual Mormons do you know who keep *all* the commandments? How many do you know who don't struggle with greed, arrogance, pride, selfishness, worldliness, and every other sin the whole white race seems to have been afflicted with? Are you telling me, Brother Jones, that you want to curse these poor Lamanitish folks with *that?*"

Kumen, his head spinning from trying to keep up with the old Indian missionary's reasoning, shook his head.

"Of course you don't." Now Thales Haskel's voice softened. "In many ways the *Diné,* and even the Pahutes, if the truth were known, are head and shoulders above us white-eyes. What we have that they don't have—and so far as I'm concerned these are the only things— is a knowledge of Jesus Christ and the authority to administer the ordinances necessary to bring us back into Christ's presence. That's what we have to offer these folks, and that's the only reason why any of us is here."

"I agree with that," Ben Perkins said. "Thing is, how do we give them that information, Thales? Or bring them to those ordinances?"

"Not by preachments, that's for certain, or by proselytizing, either one. No, boys, in my opinion the only way these folks can be brought to Christ is by hard work and example, every one of us who have experienced these spiritual blessings showing forth the fruits that a true follower of Christ must show—love, patience, tolerance, long-suffering, gentleness, meekness, and so forth—all the qualities the Lord enumerated to Joseph Smith in section 121 of the Doctrine and Covenants. If each of us will do that, they'll follow us. But every time any of us falls short of that, even a whisper, it sets back the whole process and we become just a bunch of arrogant white-eyes again, trying like the rest of Christianity to convert the Indians."

Again Thales Haskel lifted his hat and wiped his brow, at the same time slicking back his thinning white hair with his fingers. "Now," he finally said with a wry grin, "I ain't made this much chin music since who flung the chunk, and I don't intend doing it again. You boys want any more palavering, you'll have to do it betwixt yourselves. Adios."

And with a light tap of his heels the old Indian missionary and interpreter urged his pony into a bone-rattling, ground-covering trot that made further conversation impossible.

Bluff Fort

Standing in the hot cabin, overheated because of a huge fire that would soon turn to coals for baking bread, Eliza paused to wipe the sweat from her face. Glory, she thought as she licked her dry lips and tried not to think of the foul-tasting water in Platte Lyman's well, this was a hot and miserable country!

Again she wiped her forehead, this time using the back of her rolled-up sleeve instead of the thoroughly soaked hanky she had been dabbing away with for the past hour. Sweat! Back in England and even in Salt Lake City, for pity's sake, refined women referred to it as perspiration. But here on the San Juan, where no refinement was necessary or even possible, Eliza thought grimly, it was sweat! Sticky, salty, smelly sweat!

Bending over her table she began once again to knead the ball of dough she had stirred up for baking in her Dutch oven kettle, pushing it back and forth in the thin layer of flour, back and forth, back and forth, then spinning it halfway around and repeating the process. It was hard, grueling work, made even more difficult by the fact that she could not use her crutch and so had difficulty in keeping her balance. Mercy, her mind groaned, wasn't there anything in this godforsaken country that was easy?

But at least the children were gone for the day, she thought with relief. And Mary had taken little Willy with her to look for a stray cow—which now that the grass was up and strong, was showing a preference for the better graze in the secluded coves or box canyons that irregularly penetrated the bluff north of the fort. Now all she had to do before retiring was finish the bread and set it to baking, finish the stew that would hopefully last her through the weekend, chop firewood for the morrow, milk the cow and feed the chickens, help slop the hogs, feed and clean Willy once he got back, get him ready for bed, stitch up the hole in her apron she had torn earlier, clean herself up for the night, brush out her hair, do a little reading, and finally go to bed. Oh yes, and attend prayers with the community and then have prayers with Willy and herself. The way it felt, she thought as she leaned into the hardening dough, she would be lucky to get to bed at all!

But for a few moments she was as alone as it was possible to be, still waiting for Billy to return from Colorado, still filled with fear that the door behind her would swing open and one of those awful savages would step inside and take her life or worse—

Something, Eliza suddenly realized, was making a funny sort of noise behind the pile of wood she had stacked next to the fireplace the night before. Strange, she thought as she glanced in that direction, her flour-covered hands still grasping the irregular ball of dough. What could possibly—

Abruptly a huge snake slithered out of the woodpile and started across the canvas floor, followed immediately by a second one. In the fraction of a second that Eliza looked at them, she saw only the huge width of their five-foot-long bodies—that and the dark-colored blotches that formed a regular pattern from their flat heads all the way down their writhing backs.

In the next second Eliza was screaming, and when the first of the two snakes began hissing loudly and vibrating its tail as it turned toward her, Eliza abandoned both the bread and her crutch, leaped over the snake in one bound, and ran out the door, still shrieking hysterically.

"Snakes! Rattlesnakes!" she cried as she finally lost her balance and fell against one of the two hollowed-log watering troughs in the commons. "Two! In my cabin—"

Bishop Nielson and Lemuel Redd bolted past Eliza and to the cabin door, where they peered cautiously into the room. Without hesitation Lem then entered, while the bishop turned and came back to help Eliza to her feet.

"R-Rattlesnakes," she stammered as others came hurrying toward her, concern on their faces. "Tell Lem to b-be careful—"

"Bull snakes," Lem shouted as he came out of Eliza's cabin, snakes writhing in each hand. "Hope you don't mind, Eliza. but I used the curved handle of your crutch to catch them."

"They . . . they aren't rattlers?"

"No, ma'am, they aren't." Lem smiled as he loosed one of the snakes and grabbed the tail of the other. "See? No rattles. They'll hiss and thrash around something fierce, and even strike on occasion. But they aren't poisonous, Eliza, and they can't hurt you. Fact is, they do a lot of good against rats, gophers, mice, and so forth. That's why I didn't kill them."

"But . . . what were they doing in . . . in my home?"

"I suspect they crawled under the wall or came up under your tarp and got into the woodpile. The fire you built made them too hot, so out they came, looking for a cooler spot."

"Ya," the bishop said amiably, "dey be harmless. Yust remember, my dear, dat vhen rattlers make de buzzing noise like de locust makes on de hot day, den iss de time to be vorried. Ya?"

Eliza, now trembling from the shock of her experience, nodded.

Then she numbly took her crutch from Jane Walton's outstretched hand.

"Oh, glory," she breathed as Anna Decker put her arm around her and began walking her back toward the cabin, "do I always have to be such a fool?"

Anna smiled sympathetically. "Eliza, every one of us would have done the same, and you know it! Absolutely no one likes snakes, and monsters like the two you found would scare the wits out of anyone. Now—"

"But . . . but what is wrong with me?" Eliza was still in shock and was finding it difficult to express herself. "I . . . I could have seen that they weren't rattlesnakes, but I was so . . . afraid. I could have stopped Pobuy, too, when he stuck his gun into your little daughter's stomach the other day—"

Spinning in front of Eliza, Anna gripped both her arms. "You listen to me, Eliza Foreman! You could not have stopped that boy! Brother Haskel told me so! Had you tried anything other than what you did, Lena and you might both have been killed! Yes, and so might some of the other children. So please stop thinking that way. And believe me, you did the right thing with those snakes, too. Get out of their way and fast! That's what James is always telling me. Get out of their way, and let somebody else take care of them!"

"But . . . but—"

"No more buts, Eliza. Stop blaming yourself for everything, and remember that we're all in this wilderness together. Now—" Entering the cabin, Anna saw the mound of dough still on the table. Abruptly her face turned into a bright smile. "Eliza, my dear, how long has it been since you've had stove-baked bread?"

"What? I don't—"

Scooping up the dough into Eliza's mixing bowl, Anna once again grabbed the taller woman by the arm. "My stove is already hot, Eliza. Let's go put this in pans and put it in the oven. By the time it's baked, I imagine you'll be ready to come home again!"

And Eliza, feeling more and more foolish even as she yearned for her missing husband, allowed herself to be led away from the terrifying loneliness of her home—

Halgaitch Wash, Navajo Reservation

"You know, Thales, you never did answer our questions about that old woman and Rachel Perkins's baby booties."

The three men were camped for the night in a sharp bend in Halgaitch Wash, where water had washed out a cove large enough for them and their horses, and deep enough that a small fire could not be seen from more than a few feet away. While the horses munched on the new green grass that filled the bottom of the wash, the three men huddled close over the fire, not only for warmth but also because Ben Perkins and Kumen Jones were anxious to hear every low-voiced word Thales Haskel uttered.

Nearby a coyote yipped once and then again, and a moment later another answered from off to the east. Overhead the stars burned brightly, hanging like lanterns against an apparently endless curtain of darkness. Though the day had been hot, the air had already grown chill, and Kumen was just thinking of pulling his bedroll over himself when Thales Haskel finally replied.

"Why do you boys think she took 'em?"

"The booties?" Kumen questioned. "I don't know, Thales, unless she thought they were pretty. Women seem to set store by that sort of thing."

"Ben?"

"I'd agree with Kumen, though to Rachel the beauty of the booties is as much because they were sewn for her mother by her grandmother as because of how and with what they were sewn. She's told me that."

Thales smiled. "Well, boys, there you have it. Beauty means different things to different folks, and I reckon that's especially true of the *Diné*. Did you happen to notice the flowers that old woman had planted around her *hogan?*"

Ben and Kumen glanced at each other wonderingly. "There weren't any flowers," Kumen finally responded. "There wasn't anything but rock and brush and a little new grass."

"How about around your home, Kumen?"

Kumen grinned. "Well, Mary's planted flags and a couple of

wildflowers she found that are already blooming. And she's always on the lookout for something new."

"Why does she do that?"

"I reckon because she thinks they're pretty, and she wants our home to be the same."

"To her and most other white folks, that makes sense." Thales stretched out with his head on his saddle and his fingers laced together across his chest, staring upward. "Boys, us white-eyes see things of beauty and want to gather them all in, to own them and possess them and even to hoard them, as if all that beauty we've gathered can rub off on us and we can also become beautiful. And in a small way it works, too, for looking upon flowers and other things of beauty usually eases the soul and helps us be better people.

"But the Navajo, and I reckon most other Indian folks, don't think like that. No sir, from the day a child of the *Diné* draws its first breath and is strapped to the cradleboard, it's taught that beauty is the natural order of things. Beauty means happiness, pure and simple, and happiness is felt most completely when the natural order of things is undisturbed. The Navajo call this *hózhó,* which means balance in the universe—everything in its natural place."

"So a Navajo woman wouldn't see a patch of flowers as being beautiful?"

Thales chuckled. "Of course she would. But she would no more think of cutting them to put in a pot, or of uprooting and moving them and so disturbing their natural order, than you'd think of smoking one of these cigarettes I use when I'm palavering with the Indians. To do such a thing would be to upset the natural order of things and so destroy that person's *hózhó,* her balance.

"Now that don't mean that Navajos don't dig up plants or kill animals or things of that sort, because they do. But in the process they also reverence those things, and they only disturb them when there's a true need. To the Navajo there is beauty in everything just as it is, and that beauty becomes theirs only when they're at one with it. That's one of the ways I think they're head and shoulders above us white-eyes."

"That being the case," Ben asked thoughtfully, "why do they raid and plunder, sometimes killing innocent folks and taking what was never theirs and sometimes can't ever be used by them—things like Rachel's booties?"

"Once again, Ben, it's all a part of *hózhó,* balance. Besides finding beauty in the world, a Navajo with *hózhó* must have beauty within himself. To have this beauty he must be physically strong, able to make decisions that are acceptable to others, industrious, dependable, tractable, skillful, and good-humored, and he must be able to live among his people without friction. Such a person is well-balanced. If he has these qualities, he may be expected to gain wealth, which will help to make him respected.

"For most of the *Diné*—and this has been so since shortly after the Spaniards first came into this country—wealth is counted according to the number of horses a man has, or the number of sheep. Cattle also count toward wealth, but so far they don't mean as much to the *Diné* as they do to us whites. Of course, livestock is accumulated in one of two ways—breeding and raiding, both of which are perfectly acceptable to the Navajo way of thinking. And by doing these things successfully, the *Diné* prove to themselves and each other that they are in balance with the universe.

"The thing is, four years after Kit Carson drove them all off to *Bosque Redondo,* the *Diné* signed a treaty saying they would conduct no more raids against the Americans. And as far as I know, they haven't—at least not any big ones.

"But that 1868 treaty left these folks in a world of hurt. Carson had killed most of their livestock, chopped down their peach trees, and burned their corn. After four years of starvation and disease at The Grove, they were marched back here absolutely destitute, given a few sheep, and told to go out and make do. That's been twelve or thirteen years now, and while some of them seem to be doing all right, most are still hurting.

"Now, the old ways die hard, boys. And though their head men keep telling them to remember the treaty and do no more raiding, there are plenty of warriors ready to seize every little opportunity that comes down the pike just so they can feel a little balance again. Trouble is, of a sudden we're one of those opportunities, sitting smack dab on the edge of their reservation.

"As an added bonus we're a people of peace who can be easily

taken advantage of. And not only are we a long way from any soldiers, but the *Diné* are smart enough to know that us Mormons
haven't always been on the best of terms with other Americans. That
means we're a people without protection, at least of the sort they can
understand, and so we're like a rich, ripe plum ready to be picked.

"As more and more of 'em try to pick us, so to speak, the word is
spreading, and unless we can put a stop to it, these folks and their
raiding will strip us clean."

"So that's what that old woman was doing?" Kumen asked in
wonder. "Making a raid?"

"As ever. And in her mind she was successful, too. We might
have got the booties back, but she wasn't hurt or punished, and now
she knows that it can be done with bigger things. That's why she was
laughing." Thales paused for a moment, thinking. "That," he finally
concluded, "and maybe to cover the fear she felt when I showed her
that I knew all along where she'd hidden the booties."

"Yeah, we noticed that, too. How did you know?"

"Inspiration, I reckon. Ever since we left Bluff I'd been praying
to know where Rachel's baby booties were and, more important,
how I should handle the situation when we found them. While our
local band of renegade Utes seem about as pagan as folks can get, I
give it as my opinion that the *Diné* are sort of like the Sadducees of
the New Testament. They don't believe in individual life after death,
but they're still very religious, and they believe in most everything
else imaginable. For instance, they believe in sorcery, witchcraft, animals becoming human or vice versa, and so forth. We might think
such things foolish, but a Navajo's life is controlled by such beliefs,
and to protect himself and to keep that all-important balance, he wor-
ships all sorts of gods and practices one ritual after another in most
everything he does.

"But that ain't all. For the *Diné* to have balance or inner beauty,
everything has to be understood in terms of the bigger picture. If it
isn't understood, there is fear. When I showed that old woman that
she wasn't fooling me, and that I knew things that couldn't be known
by any natural means, it frightened her. I saw that fear when it
flooded her eyes, and it was still there when she was laughing to try
and hide it. No doubt by now she's figured it out, though."

"Meaning?"

"Meaning she's probably concluded that I'm either a witch or a devil, which explains my power in terms of her world and also causes her to avoid me in the future. My hope, boys—and this is the real reason why we've come all this way after those booties—is that her fear will be enough keep her away from any more raids and also to stop her from spreading the word about us ripe plums up yonder on the San Juan. If that doesn't happen—and soon—we won't last long enough to bring any of them to Christ."

And with that, the old missionary and interpreter rolled over, pulled his blanket over his shoulders, and was almost instantly asleep.

6

Sunday, April 3, 1881

Bluff Fort

"Folks don't look too happy this morning, do they."

It was a statement, not a question, and Eliza had to admit that Mary was right. The mood under the bowery was somber at best, and she knew exactly how they all felt.

"You're always accusing me of being sunny side up," Mary continued, speaking quietly as her eyes scanned the faces of the others who were gathering around them, "and I suppose mostly I am. But not now, Eliza. Not anymore. Besides that, I'm bone-tired from driving that team and scraper day and night since Thursday in a completely wasted effort, and nothing else is going right for us in this awful country! Kumen and Thales couldn't find Bishop Nielson's best horse while they were on the reservation getting those stupid baby booties, the railroad paid Kumen in scrip instead of cash money and some of the stores in Durango aren't honoring it, and now that our fields are covered with that sticky blue clay that the sun is already baking brick-hard, we'll get no crops again this year! I'm telling you, I think we should go back to Cedar and dismiss this mission as a bad dream!"

"I wish Billy was home and we could go back," Eliza said as she stroked her son's fine hair as he lay with his head on her lap. "I just don't feel like I'm the right sort of person for a mission like this!"

"Eliza, you simply must stop tearing yourself down!"

"I'm just trying to face reality. That's why I believe I'd be better off leaving. Only I . . . I don't think little Willy could stand the trip—"

"Is he worse?" Mary asked, her voice filled with instant concern.

Her eyes suddenly brimming with tears, Eliza nodded. "He . . . he's definitely weaker. This morning he could hardly toddle along beside me. And look, Mary. He's already sound asleep, and that's after sleeping nearly twelve hours last night. I . . . I've worn my knees out praying for an answer, but nothing ever changes. I . . . Oh, glory, Mary, if only I knew what to do."

"My dear Eliza—"And Mary, unable to think of anything else to say, reached out and pulled her friend's face down onto her own tired and aching shoulders.

———o—o—o———

"Brothers and sisters, now that our worship service is over, Bishop Nielson has asked me to speak with you for a few moments about our situation." Drawing a deep breath, Kumen Jones did his best to keep his eyes moving so that he didn't have to look too deeply into the faces of the discouraged congregation. Not that he blamed them, he thought bleakly. No matter which way any of them tried to turn, there didn't seem to be much about the mission that was encouraging—

"I'm thankful for the ordinance of the sacrament of the Lord's supper, for through it we can renew our covenants and be reminded of who we are and why we're here. I believe we should all keep that in mind.

"I reckon you all know that the river has pretty well wiped out our efforts again, not just with the ditch but in destroying our fields. That blue clay is about an inch thick and hardening up something fierce, and while we can plow it without a lot of trouble, we'll definitely lose most of our seed when we do. And with our headgate and maybe fifty yards of ditch gone somewhere into the new channel of the river, we're going to need another survey to see where to build a new headgate and the head of another ditch. Finally, since what's left of the old ditch is so filled with silt, we've got to start digging it out again, too."

"What's the point, Kumen? That fool river's licked us, and you know it!"

"We all know it!" someone else shouted. "This'll be our second year in a row without crops, and nobody can live on weed greens and no money forever. I say we abandon this place and give it back to the sandfleas and the Indians!"

Holding up his hand, Kumen waited until the congregation had quieted. "You're right, of course," he admitted candidly. "Nobody can live like that forever—not unless God wills it and gives us the strength to do so."

"Which he isn't," Henry Holyoak growled from the rear of the congregation. "I for one am tired of this nonsense. My family deserves better than a dugout in Peak City or anyplace else along this fool river, and I intend to take them to where we can make a decent living."

"I'd settle for any sort of a living at all," someone quipped in response. Laughter followed, and Eliza could tell that Kumen was struggling with knowing what he might say next—most likely because he had told Mary the night before that he agreed perfectly with the sentiments being expressed. It had been as hard on the men being away from their families all winter as it had on the women being left alone, Eliza knew, and all who had come back looked drawn, tattered, and exhausted. And they were coming back to a second summer of sandstorms, heat, and unrelenting physical labor that would result, at least from all appearances so far, in nothing more than failed crops, wasted effort, and another lonely winter spent away from their homes and loved ones. It was no wonder so many were struggling with a will to stay.

"Did you and Hy and Haskel find those stolen horses?" a woman asked.

"We did not." Kumen's admission was blunt. "Fact is, we aren't even positive they were stolen. They may have just jumped the rope and drifted with the storm."

"With none of the others following? Not likely, Kumen, and you know it. This morning my two best horses were missing, and I know doggone well it's them miserable Navajos that have taken 'em."

"Either them or some wandering, flea-brained outlaw!"

"And it was the Pahutes that killed and roasted my three milk cows! I found where they done it, including what was left of the heads and tails. They took everything but a few charred bones, and now my family is a daily charity case for whoever else has a little extra milk."

"And you know doggone well what that kid Posey about did to little Lena Decker the other day—"

Again Kumen raised his hand, doing his best to quell the outburst of anger and indignation. "We all have grievances," he acknowledged, "and no one's denying it. No one will ever know my feelings when I returned from the reservation last evening to find my sweetheart dirty, sweaty, and bone-tired from following a team and scraper for three days and nights. Of a truth this is a terribly hard land filled with even harder inhabitants, and we've run head-on into just about every one of them.

"We're also discovering how difficult it's going to be to farm this country, let alone make it blossom as a rose. There's no doubt that some of us will wear out our lives just making the effort, and maybe never really succeeding. But I ask you, is that a reason to leave? Is it? Were we called to the San Juan to become gentleman farmers and to relax and grow old in our prosperity, or were we called to this country on a mission of peace, our goal the gentling down of the harsher elements of earth and humanity no matter the cost to ourselves? You tell me, brothers and sisters. To what were each of you called?"

Kumen paused and allowed his eyes to bore into those of every member of the congregation who would look at him. "I've thought about this a great deal," he finally continued, "and I give it as my opinion that the road we built through the Hole-in-the-Rock is the roughest, most difficult wagon road ever built in North America, if not the entire world. But why was it so? Couldn't the Lord have warned us to go another way, an easier way? Of course he could have. But he didn't, and I think he didn't because he wanted to prepare us, to toughen us and strengthen us and stretch to the limit our ability to endure hardship, adversity, and affliction. Why, you might ask? Because the Lord knew full well what we would encounter when we got to this place. He knew how hard it was going to be, and so he wanted a people sufficiently humbled and strengthened and trained in the overcoming of adversity through united effort that they could endure it.

"Well, the Lord trained us and got us here, and now the enduring part is up to us. The brethren in Salt Lake City have promised time and again that we will eventually succeed. They haven't said when or how, but we have their promise, and that is good enough for me. I intend to stay no matter the personal cost, and I'll trust the Lord to provide for the needs of my family when all my efforts fail. Just as he led us through six months of grueling winter work and starvation on that awful road without death, disease, or even serious accident, so he will lead us through however many years it will take to bring peace to this harsh and unfriendly land he has called us to serve and to save.

"I know this to be true, brothers and sisters, and I bear witness of it in Christ's holy name. Now, by the raise of hands, how many of you will cease from your murmuring and complaining and pitch to on the morrow, starting again to build a ditch and tame our unruly river?"

And slowly, ever so slowly, hands started lifting skyward.

Coyote Wash, Colorado

"Oh, nooooo—"

For a moment Henry W. and Jimmy Heaton were too surprised to react. Instead they watched in wonder as Billy flew from the back of the bucking mule, sailed through the air with arms and legs flailing, and finally crashed into earth and brush a dozen feet off the trail. Only then did Henry W. pull his pistol and shoot the offending rattlesnake, while Jimmy loosed his rope and caught the still-bucking mule.

"Did you shoot the snake or the mule?" Billy asked from where he sat in the dust, gingerly rubbing his shoulder.

"The snake."

Billy shook his head. "Too bad. The mule deserved it more. Wonder isn't supposed to buck like that, and the Prophet Joseph told us we would never lessen the enmity between man and beast until we started treating creatures like rattlesnakes with kindness."

"I ain't never heard nothing like that afore," Henry W. said as he thumbed a new cartridge into his pistol, still wondering about this frail-looking Mormon with the strange ideas. "How long you say you been riding?"

"I didn't say," Billy responded as he began groping around for his spectacles. "But obviously it hasn't been long enough—"

"Looks like a young robin feeling after his first worm," Jimmy Heaton grinned as he led the mule back. "I declare, Billy, you're as much a wonder as this here mule, which didn't hardly buck enough to unseat a little kid, let alone a growed man. Whatcha looking for?"

"My spectacles. Can't see a lick without 'em."

"Reckon we ought to help him, Henry W.?" Jimmy was still grinning.

"I don't know. To my way of thinking, the way he's hunkered down and groping, he's after something far more important than them specs."

"Such as?"

"Why, maybe more gold plates or some such treasure. Maybe that's how that Smith feller found the ones he found, too. Lost his specs and came up with gold."

"If you young ladies are through tittering and giggling," Billy said as Jimmy started laughing, "I could use some help. If you have the time, that is. Oh, and Henry W., when Joseph Smith found the gold plates, there was indeed a set of spectacles with them—two ancient stones set in a silver bow and called by the ancients Urim and Thummim."

Too surprised to react with further teasing, Henry W. and Jimmy got off their mounts and dropped to their knees, and in a matter of moments they found Billy's spectacles.

"That true, what you said about them ancient spectacles?" Jimmy asked as Billy wiped his glasses, placed them on his nose and over his ears, and then rose to his feet.

"It is. And it's just as true that no matter how I try, I can't keep my seat on a bucking horse."

"Maybe you haven't had enough practice."

"I've had all I want and then some." Billy shook his head in disgust. "Boys, I've given this rugged frontier the past year and a half of my life, and I'm some better at it than when I started. But about once or twice a day I'm brought up short in my pride by gentle reminders such as this, and I remember that I'm not much more than a clerk and a dreamer with callouses on his hands."

"Of a truth you haven't ridden much?"

Billy smiled. "Jimmy, I never even owned a horse until two years ago, and then I bought a sway-backed old fleabag mare with one good eye. I haven't ridden her but twice since I bought her on account of she's so old and brittle. Dick Butt taught me to ride on one of his horses, or at least he tried. I learned how to mount on the left side, sit in a saddle, and pull the reins one way or the other. Beyond that—well, you just saw my amazing skills."

"But Dick Butt said you were a real hand with livestock of all sorts." Henry W. Heaton looked perplexed. "Hard Tartar and a couple of the others agreed with him."

"Not riding them, I'm not!"

"Then what—?"

Billy smiled a little sadly. "What they were talking about, Henry W., is that I sort of have an eye for a good animal. I can spot an outlaw horse or one with a lot of bottom, or I can pick out the culls in a herd of cattle or sheep without much trouble. Then, too, I can talk to most critters. I mean, the sound of my voice seems to gentle them down so they can be worked with. Usually. But sometimes it doesn't work, and it's never worked when it comes to staying on a bucking horse. That's why Dick always lends me his mule Wonder. In a year and a half I haven't ever seen him buck. Dick knows that, feels sorry for me, and gives him to me whenever I can't polish my britches on the seat of a wagon."

"Well, I'll be dogged!" Henry W. Heaton was amazed. "Billy, you're the first man I ever met who admitted he couldn't ride a horse. I've known others who couldn't ride, mind you; but they wouldn't admit it for sour apples."

"If that's a compliment, Henry W.," Billy said as he rubbed Wonder's neck and did his best to calm the animal before remounting, "I accept."

"Let's get going, then," Jimmy urged impatiently as his horse pranced in a tight circle. "I'll even ride close and keep your mule from bucking, Billy, if'n you'll just tell us more about them ancient silver spectacles—"

Bluff Fort

It was late, and for the moment Eliza was simply sitting in the darkened cabin, soaking in the blissful silence. Willy had not had a good afternoon or evening, and he had cried almost constantly. For a time Eliza had even wept with him, grieving not only for Willy's pain but also for her own inability to help him get past it.

Annie Lyman, bless her heart, had offered to hold the child while Eliza saw to the milking and the rest of the chores, and that hour had been a blessed respite for her. Thank goodness no one had mentioned those horrid snakes. Joseph Barton had come and put rocks wherever it looked like they might have gained entrance, and so Eliza was feeling a little more relaxed in her home. Even Willy had seemed to do a little better. But as the evening had worn on, his crying and struggling had increased again, and now it was after eleven and he had only just barely fallen into a fitful sleep. But at least he was sleeping, Eliza thought with a sigh. Most likely he would sleep through the night, too, which meant that she would also get some much-needed rest.

With another sigh she struck a match and lit the end of a twisted rag that sat in a small bowl of grease on the table. Called a bitch lantern or light, it was what most of the settlers were using now that they had run out of coal oil for their lanterns. And it did provide enough light to read by, if one could endure the stench of burning animal fat that always filled the room.

Kumen's words had struck Eliza forcibly that morning, and when she had joined the others in making the covenant to stop murmuring, she had also made a mental promise to renew her daily scripture study and prayers—things that seemed so easy to ignore when her discouragement and despair grew deep enough.

Now, though, as she prayed for the Lord to lead her to the verses of scripture he wanted her to study, she felt firm in her resolution to do better. After all, during the journey from Cedar City she had been able to feel the Holy Spirit and obtain guidance from the Lord.

Though that seemed to have stopped, Billy would have told her that the problem—if there was one—was hers and not the Lord's. The solution, therefore, would also have to be hers. Now, if only—

Opening her copy of the Book of Mormon randomly, Eliza prayerfully began reading by the flickering light the first verse her eyes landed upon: "And a portion of that Spirit dwelleth in me, which giveth me knowledge, and also power according to my faith and desires which are in God."

Surprised that the verse seemed so clearly to be speaking to her, Eliza read it again and then turned to the front of the chapter to discover that she was reading the thirty-fifth verse of Alma, chapter eighteen. Reading from the beginning of the chapter she discovered that the speaker was Ammon, one of the four sons of King Mosiah. He was speaking to the Lamanite King Lamoni shortly after he had defended the king's flocks at the waters of Sebus, and he was describing the source of the power that had enabled him to do all he had done. And in the midst of that explanation, Eliza now saw, was his remark concerning the Holy Spirit giving knowledge and power.

Convinced that the Lord had directed her to that particular verse, Eliza read it again, doing her best to analyze it just as she had seen Billy do on numerous occasions.

"Very well, woman," she murmured to herself as she pored over the verse again and again, "I think the Lord wants you to learn that all who have the gift of the Holy Ghost and who are at least somewhat worthy of his presence can receive knowledge and therefore power. Knowledge equals power. Of course.

"But it's also apparent that, according to this statement of Ammon's, receiving knowledge and power isn't automatic just because one prays. That's why Ammon used the phrase 'according to my faith and desires.' Knowledge and power are given only to those who show faith by desiring to do the work God has called them to."

Slowly Eliza lowered her book and leaned back, her mind deep in thought. Faith and desire. Faith and desire! Oh, glory, she thought with a heavy sigh, would she never manage to get things right? Would she always find herself in need of repentance?

"Right now, Eliza Foreman," she admitted, speaking quietly once again, "that's exactly what you are struggling with. You can't help Willy or yourself because you don't have enough faith to get knowledge or power, either one! Why not? Desire, woman! You don't have the desire to be obedient, or the faith! As Mary would put it, you flat-out don't want to stay here and remain a part of this peace mission. One way or another, you want out. And that's in spite of the fact that you know perfectly well that God has called you to come to this place and stay!"

Her mind reeling with the scope as well as the content of what she had just learned, Eliza closed the book and snuffed out the flame burning the end of the twisted rag. "Dear Heavenly Father," she breathed tearfully as the burning logs in the fireplace settled upon each other, sending a shower of sparks up the chimney, "I . . . I'm sorry for my lack of faith. I truly am! I don't mean to waver so much from what is right. Only, I'm so powerful lonely for Billy, I'm sick to death of never having enough of the right things for Willy to eat, and . . . and I can't possibly bear watching that dear little soul die!

"Oh, dear Father, please help me want to stay in this awful San Juan country. Grant me the power and faith to somehow stop feeling so afraid of . . . of, well, of everything! And . . . help me especially to have knowledge sufficient to know what to do to save the life of Billy's and my precious little boy—"

7

---○─○─○---

Monday, April 4, 1881

Mouth of Recapture Creek

"So, that's the trail to the LC? Twenty-five miles up this creek and we'll run plumb into it?"

It was a beautiful morning, with clear sky and pleasant temperature that boded to become hot by afternoon. But Billy Foreman didn't mind that, not at all. He was less than twenty miles from home, twenty miles from his Eliza and little Willy, and by nightfall he knew he would be with them again.

"Well, that's what I've been told." Billy smiled pleasantly at the two Heaton brothers. "Of course I haven't actually been there, but I've been told that's the trail, and that the LC headquarters are in plain sight on a bench up above the creek. You certain you boys don't want to come on into Bluff first, though, and meet my Eliza and little Willy?"

"I'd like to, Billy. I truly would." Jimmy Heaton nodded subtly toward where his older brother was seated by the fire mending a tear in his shirt. "But Pa told us to hurry, so I reckon that's what we ought to do."

Billy nodded. "That's right as rain, Jimmy. Once a man learns the principle of obedience, he'll never go far wrong."

"Amen," Henry W. Heaton declared without looking up.

"For folks your age, Jimmy," Billy continued, "it's learning obedience to their parents, which now that I look back on it seems nothing more than simple training in obedience to God."

Jimmy Heaton's expression turned serious. "You think a lot about God, don't you. Are all Mormons like that?"

"More or less, I suppose. After all, our faith is a religion, and all true religion comes from God."

"Makes sense. So, you think there are also false religions?"

"What makes you ask that?"

Jimmy Heaton grinned, enjoying himself immensely. "Well, you said true religion. Doesn't that mean there must also be false ones?"

"Or religions that are less true," Billy agreed. "You see, according to the New Testament, Christ established his church when he was alive. And since he was perfect, it follows that his church would also have been perfect—not the members, mind you, but the structure, the organization. For instance, anciently he called twelve men to be apostles. When Judas Iscariot committed suicide after betraying Jesus, the other eleven met together and chose another man to take the betrayer's place. So, twelve apostles must have been important to Christ's church."

"So if a church doesn't have twelve apostles in it today," Jimmy breathed, his mind racing—

"Then at least to that degree it would be less true than Christ's ancient church," Billy concluded.

"And of course the Mormons have twelve apostles," Henry W. Heaton sneered from across the nearly dead fire.

"We do, Henry W."

"Well, I reckon any church can make apostles."

Billy nodded. "They could, I suppose. Do you know of any who have?"

"I . . . ah . . . well, not offhand, I don't."

"Neither do I," Billy said as he rose to his feet and stretched, pretending not to notice Jimmy's satisfied grin. "And I've looked, Henry W. But that's only one thing. I've been studying the gospel nearly all of my life, and there are all sorts of things besides apostles that a feller should find in Christ's true church."

"And you've found them in the Mormon Church?" Jimmy asked eagerly.

"I have. And now you should understand why we prefer calling it The Church of Jesus Christ of Latter-day Saints. If it's Jesus' true church, then surely it ought to be called by his name."

"By Tophet, that does make sense!"

"And I suppose you're going to stand there and tell me all you Mormons are honest-to-goodness saints?" Henry W. Heaton was obviously skeptical.

Billy smiled patiently. "Not according to the definition most Christians give the word. As a matter of fact, I've never known a Latter-day Saint who wasn't decidedly human, me probably most of all. I have all sorts of weaknesses and sins I'm trying to overcome. And it seems like I barely get on top of one when two more show up to plague me. But anciently—and here it is again—the Bible tells us that members in Jesus' church were referred to as Saints. Since that was in former days, and we are in the latter days, we naturally refer to ourselves as—"

"Latter-day Saints," Jimmy concluded. "See, Henry W.? Just like Billy said yesterday, once you learn the straight of it, the whole kit and caboodle of religion all sort of fits together."

Henry W. Heaton shook his head in disgust. "Jimmy, you're young, and you ain't seen enough of life to go jumping to them kinds of conclusions."

"You may be right about your brother, Henry W.," Billy declared softly. "But remember, age isn't particularly important to the Lord. Samuel and David in the Old Testament were both young when God called them, and in our day Joseph Smith was only fourteen. On the other hand I'm several years older than them or you, and I've slowly and very carefully come to the same conclusions young Jimmy seems to be jumping to. So would you, Henry W., happen your mind was open enough to give such ideas a chance."

"Maybe," the young man groused as he pulled his shirt over his head and rose to his feet, "but I doubt it. Come on, Jimmy, daylight's a-burning and we've got to get Pa's cattle."

"All right, Henry W., I'm coming." Jimmy turned to face his new friend. "Billy, thanks for the company and for showing us the way to the LC. Henry W. and me are mighty obliged."

Billy took the young man's proffered hand. "My pleasure,

Jimmy. Remember, you do what your Pa tells you, and you'll be just fine."

"That, I admit, is good advice." Henry W. Heaton grinned crookedly. "And like Jimmy says, Billy, we do appreciate your help. No offense about your religion, either. I just don't happen to agree with you, is all."

"No offense taken. Good luck with that herd—"

"Hello the fire!"

"Hello yourselves," Billy called as two mounted men and a pack horse came up and out of the willows fifty yards away. "You're too late for breakfast, though. Between the three of us there isn't so much as a crumb left to offer you boys."

And boys they were, Billy saw as the two rode closer. Neither of them was much older than Jimmy Heaton, though the one in front had a sparse growth of facial hair. They were also alone, at least so far as Billy could tell, and they were dirty enough to have been on the road for some time.

"Is this the way to the Mormon settlement at Bluff?"

"It is." Billy stepped forward to shake hands. "I'm Billy Foreman, and I'm from Bluff. These boys are Henry W. and Jimmy Heaton, from Rico, Colorado."

The two nodded politely. "We're the Wilson brothers. I'm Alfred, and the feller eating my dust back there is Isadore—Ise, most folks call him. So, you're Church members?"

Billy smiled. "I am. Came through the Hole-in-the-Rock a year ago. You boys from the LC?"

"No, but we was there yesterday. Cook fed us mighty well, too. Pa wanted us to see about buying a few cows, so we went there to see Bill Ball, the foreman. We hear he's offering better prices by a mile than either Spud Hudson or old man Peters."

"That's what our pa said, too," Jimmy Heaton declared while he watched Isadore Wilson stop his horse, loop the lead to the pack horse around his saddle horn, and climb down to stretch. "Word is that Spud's trying to sell out and doesn't want to deplete his herd."

"No fooling." Alfred Wilson grinned. "He wouldn't tell us that, but I can say for certain that neither Peters nor Hudson would even talk to us about selling a few cows."

"Did Bill Ball make a deal with you?"

Alfred Wilson was about to reply when his younger brother spoke up. "Not yet he ain't. He wasn't even there. The Cookie told us Ball and his hands were out trying to get a herd together for some folks from Colorado. That'd be you fellers, I reckon?"

"I reckon."

"Well, don't get in too big a hurry to get there, then." Isadore Wilson took a swig from his canteen, swished it around in his mouth a couple of times, and then spat it out. "That cook told us Bill Ball wouldn't be back with his gather before this next weekend. So we figure to head on into Bluff, meet the folks there, lend them a hand for a day or two if they need us, and then head back to the LC just in time to pick up the fifty head Pa says he wants."

"Where are you from?" Billy asked.

"Moab, in Grand Valley away to the north of here. Used to be called Elk Mountain Mission. Pa's in the bishopric there. A few weeks ago a Brother Holyoak came by looking at land, said he was from Bluff, and told us about you folks. Ever since then, Ise and me have been wanting to see the place he kept describing as the cross-roads of hell. Is he right?"

Billy grinned. "You could say that. We settled on the only ford on the San Juan for twenty or thirty miles in each direction, and Navajos, Pahutes, and outlaws use it every bit as much as we do. It's a busy place."

"That's what that Holyoak feller said. Thing is, there ain't no real road from Moab to here, not the way we came anyway. So Ise and me have had hard going the past two weeks and feel plumb lucky just to be here."

"I heard there was a road down Spanish and Lisbon Valleys," Henry W. Heaton commented. "You know, the same way Father Escalante went through when he was blazing out the old Spanish Trail."

Isadore Wilson nodded. "There is, and we took it for a ways. But there's precious little water on that road, and besides, we needed to meet with Hudson and Peters about Pa's cows. So at the end of Spanish Valley where the road turns southeast to Big Indian and

Lisbon Valley, we turned southwest instead and cut up across a bunch of mesas."

"Yeah," Isadore grinned, "and discovered us some of them natural bridges while we was about it."

"Arches, Ise. Natural arches."

"Bridges, arches, whatever. One of 'em was a real purty one, too. So Alf and me, we drug a dead log up under it, stood it up in a hole we dug, and carved our names and the date on it. We named it Wilson natural bridge."

"Arch."

"Doggone it, Alf, what does it matter?"

Alfred looked disgusted. "A bridge you can ride over, Ise. It's pretty much level. An arch goes up and then down again, and nobody can ride over it, at least not easily. That was an arch we discovered, and that's what I carved on that log."

Isadore still didn't lose his enthusiasm. "All right, Alf, whatever you say. Anyhow, the next folks past that natural arch'll know it was Alfred and Isadore Wilson what discovered it, and someday folks everywhere'll know it and we'll be famous. Shucks, maybe it'll even be on a map, which would make me right proud. And someday I'll take my kids and grandkids out there and show it to 'em, and they'll be proud, too. Just think of it: Wilson Natural Arch!"

"It has a fine sound to it," Billy agreed while the two Heaton brothers only smiled.

"Anyhow," Alfred continued, a little embarrassed by his younger brother's enthusiasm, "we crossed over Dry Valley and climbed up Peters' Hill to his place, and when he wouldn't sell us nothing but a few old scrubs, we went from there to Hudson's Double Cabins under the Blue Mountains. Hudson wasn't as cantankerous as Peters, but the results were the same; he didn't have any cows for sale. So from there we skirted the east side of the Blues, heading south, and dropped on down Recapture to the LC. That was hard going but not near so bad as it's been from there to here."

"Any Indian trouble?"

"Never saw a one." Isadore Wilson said. "Saw sign of two or three big bands headed east, but that was all."

"You were lucky," Henry W. Heaton declared soberly. "Those

were more'n likely Ute trails you crossed, headed for what they call the Shining Mountains, in Colorado. Every spring they gather from every which way to hold a big powwow and horserace up in those mountains, and every spring the young bucks and chiefs spread back out to raise cain and kill a few unsuspecting whites. A year or two back it was the Indian Agent Nathan Meeker and practically the whole command under that idiot Major Thornburg who got killed. Last year it was some ranchers in the mountains east of us, and no telling who it might be this year. I know Pa told us to keep a sharp eye for 'em while we were bringing back his cattle."

Alfred Wilson nodded. "Our Pa told us the Saints in Moab would pray us back to Moab in safety, and I reckon so far they've done their job. Tell the truth, boys, I'm not worried."

"Our Indians over in this country are called Pahutes," Billy added quietly. "They don't seem as dangerous as the Utes you're describing."

Henry W. Heaton was deadly serious. "They're the same people, Billy. Some use one name and some the other, but they're exactly the same. And you can count on it when we tell you they're dangerous!"

Isadore Wilson grinned slyly. "Well, we may not have seen any wild Indians, but we did spend a night with some honest-to-gosh rustlers—the McCarty brothers from over in Coyote, under the south end of the LaSals. They had a herd of cows with mighty fresh brands on every critter, so Alf and me, we kept looking the other direction the whole time we was with 'em."

Jimmy Heaton nodded. "Safer that way."

"No foolin'!" Alfred continued, taking up the tale. "Ise and me know the McCarty boys, at least Tom and Bill, as them and some of their *compañeros* stop from time to time at our ranch over in Castle Valley. I haven't ever met the older brother, George, who went with the pa, Doc McCarty, to settle in Oregon. But Tom and Bill are fine fellers, too, happen we're playing cards or telling yarns. I reckon we knew they'd been in a couple of scrapes with the law, but until that night we never did figure 'em for rustlers."

"Their wives are fine folks, too," Isadore added fervently. "Especially Teenie, sister to Willard Christiansen from over in Ephraim, the feller who's now calling himself Matt Warner. He wants to be an outlaw, and I reckon he's well on his way. But that Teenie is a fine woman, and I do think highly of her. Wouldn't surprise me to learn she doesn't know what her husband or the rest of them are up to. Wouldn't surprise me a bit!"

"That's only because she's a fine-looking little filly," Alfred grinned knowingly, "and she does have a fetching smile. I do think my little brother's sweet on her."

"Am not! I ain't only talked to her once or twice, and you know it!"

"Apparently that's all it takes, Ise."

"Quit it, Alf, or I'll whup you within an inch, so help me!"

Alfred Wilson grinned and then turned away from his fuming younger brother. "Brother Foreman, if you're going into Bluff and don't mind the company, we'll ride along with you."

"You're mighty welcome," Billy exclaimed. Then he turned to Henry W. and Jimmy Heaton. "Boys, since it won't do you any good to get to the LC before the weekend, my offer stands. You're welcome to come on to Bluff with us and meet my family. Our home may be a little primitive, but we'll treat you to the best we have."

"I sure do reckon I'd like that." Jimmy Heaton was looking at his brother.

"Ahh, all right," Henry W. muttered as he slammed his hat on his head. "Just one thing, Billy—and it goes the same for you Wilsons, too—no trying to convert us into Mormons, either me or Jimmy. We're only there to meet your folks and see the country. Understand?"

Billy smiled patiently. "Of course, Henry W. Besides, no man's ever converted against his will." And still smiling, Billy headed out to saddle his mule.

Bluff Fort

"Eliza!" Annie Lyman's voice was quiet but urgent as she pushed open Eliza's door. "There're two Navajo women on burros here in the fort, and I'd say they're headed this way!"

Her heart suddenly in her throat, Eliza turned from the children she was watching, four of whom were at the moment crying, to the window. They were there, she saw, in the common area, riding toward her cabin. *They were riding toward her—*

"Who else is coming, Annie?" she asked, feeling as if she were about to faint. In spite of her resolutions of the night before, and in spite of her prayers, Eliza felt paralyzed with fear. These women were her enemies—deadly enemies who would stop at nothing to steal or maim—

"Annie," she nearly shrieked, *"who else is coming?"*

"I . . . I was the closest, Eliza, and I got sent. I . . . I'm sure others will be along directly. But don't worry, dear. We're all being protected by the Lord. You know that."

Frantically Eliza picked up little Willy, who was crying loudest of all, and then in terror she backed up against the log wall, ignoring the calming words of her friend—

———o—o—o———

The Navajo woman Hádapa was nervous. Even though she was the wife of the great warrior Natanii nééz, who had taken upon himself the *belacani* name of Frank, she was still nervous. This was her first raid since before Rope Thrower had rounded up her parents and brother and taken them and many others on the long walk. There her brother had slowly died, and her parents had grown old before their time, passing away during the trek back to the reservation. But now she who had been less than the dust was the wife of a great warrior, a truly great warrior, and Hádapa wanted nothing to come in the way of her *hózhó,* the balance with the universe she was finally feeling.

The thing was, she knew a paper had been signed between the leaders of her people and the *belacani,* swearing that the Navajo would conduct no more raids upon the white people. Hádapa knew this for she had seen the paper, and she knew, too, that Rope Thrower would have no difficulty rounding up the *Diné* a second time and perhaps killing them all. And that was why her heart was shrinking within her breast even as she rode forward beside her friend T'anap'a. Truly she had no wish to die or to see death come to her great and marvelous husband.

For one thing it was a great honor to be the wife of Natanii nééz, for with his size, strength, and wisdom he was truly a man among men. For another, despite the seasons of their marriage, Hádapa had been unable to give her great man a son—no, nor even a daughter, which would have been almost as good. Instead she had remained barren and so had seen Natanii nééz spend less and less time in her *hogan.* But now a sing had been performed in behalf of Natanii nééz, a Blessing Way, and she was certain she would soon feel life within her deadened womb. Yes, soon she would present to the great Natanii nééz the son he so desperately craved, and then her *hózhó* would be truly complete. For this reason more than any other, the woman Hádapa feared this raiding.

"Do you see that one?"

Ahead of the two friends a white woman peered out from the doorway of one of the strange square *hogans* of these *belacani,* the only living person they had seen within the structure they called a fort.

"I see her," Hádapa responded quietly, "but I see no others. Where are all the *belacani* who should be filling these ugly dwellings?"

The woman T'anap'a smiled. "Surely the powers of the *yei* are with us," she responded. "Just as your husband foretold, there will be no difficulty in raiding these *belacani* mormonee."

From that same doorway where the woman had peered came the sound of many children crying. With a start the woman Hádapa realized how very much they sounded like the children of the *Diné,* and almost by instinct she nudged her burro in the direction of that open doorway.

"My friend," the woman T'anap'a queried hesitantly, "why do we ride to the one dwelling where we know there are enemies?"

"I . . . do not know." In spite of her fear, Hádapa kept her little burro moving forward. "Perhaps because only in that dwelling will our raiding be of great worth."

Hádapa noted her friend's look of pleased surprise, wondered at the powerful urge toward the single dwelling that seemed to have overcome her, and then pulled her burro to a halt in front of the cabin. Then she dismounted, and with a chant of courage filling her mind, she started for the open door.

———◇—◇—◇———

"What did they say, Eliza? What happened?"

Stunned by the suddenness of it, and still feeling faint because of the rapid pounding of her heart, Eliza could hardly respond. "I . . . I don't know, Annie. I don't think either of them said a word."

Annie was standing in the doorway, looking out at the departing burros. "This makes no sense, Eliza! The two of them walk in here, one stops in the doorway, and the other walks straight to you and Willy. Did she take anything from you?"

Slowly Eliza shook her head. "Nothing. She seemed to hesitate when she first came inside, as if her eyes were adjusting to the gloom. Then she came straight to Willy. To tell the truth, Annie, I don't think that woman even looked at me. Her eyes were for Willy only, and she touched him on the arm, but only lightly. Then she pulled back his blanket and . . . and looked at his body, I suppose. I know she didn't touch anything else. She just stood there for what seemed a long time, looking at him. That was when he stopped crying."

"I saw that, but I couldn't see what she was doing to him."

"She wasn't doing anything, Annie. She was just looking—that and crying. At least tears were coming from her eyes, which I assume is crying for those people the same as it is for us."

Annie looked back into the room. "It might not be, you know. Eliza, what if that woman is planning something? You know, like maybe to kidnap Willy?"

"What?" Instantly the terror within Eliza's breast was mounting again.

"Well," Annie continued, not noticing, "she might be planning such a thing. Like Thales Haskel says, those folks are born to raid, and I've heard all sorts of stories about how women and children have been two of their prime targets. Surely you know that. Besides, why else would she have left so abruptly? She and that other woman are probably planning it right now, devising some cruel scheme to come back after dark tonight, or maybe tomorrow, to steal little Willy from you!"

"I don't know," Eliza mused, trying desperately not to submit to

111

her fears. "Her . . . her face didn't show that, Annie, at least not that I could see. Instead I saw sorrow, pain, maybe even pity—"

"That's it!" Annie declared as she closed the door, barred it, and turned back into the room. "That woman's lost a child of her own, and she intends to take Willy to fill the void. Oh, mercy, Eliza, you've got to watch that child or you'll surely lose him. Of course, I'll stay with you to help, my dear, but it would be so much better if Billy were here!"

Eliza, once again in the viselike grip of terror because of Annie's words, could only nod in agreement.

———◇—◇—◇———

"Well, hello, Billy. Welcome home. Looks like you dragged along some strays."

Grinning widely at his friend Lemuel Redd, who had come riding up the trail toward them, Billy climbed down from the back of the mule and stretched. Turning then, he introduced the man to his four riding companions.

"Howdy, boys. Billy been taking good care of you?"

"As ever," Isadore Wilson replied. "You're the tax assessor, ain't you."

Surprised, Lem Redd looked at the young man more closely. "How'd you know that? Did Billy tell you?"

"Nope. Spud Hudson mentioned you, and so did the cook at the LC. Seems you're famous, Brother Redd."

"Or infamous," Billy teased. "Where you headed, Lem?"

The taller man shook his head. "Billy, we've got troubles like you wouldn't believe. The past few days the San Juan's been flooding badly, and we've lost the headgate and fifty, sixty yards of ditch."

Billy was stunned. "We've noticed it running high, Lem, but I didn't give it much thought. What about the rest of the ditch? Or the crops? Were they already in the ground?"

"Unfortunately, and the fields are covered with blue clay, which along with normal silt has also filled the ditch for practically the whole five miles."

"So," Billy breathed, "we're starting over again. Again!"

"A man sort of loses count, doesn't he. Anyway, we need all the help we can get. The rest of the brethren are yonder at the Jump, trying to figure out what to do about a new and more permanent headgate. Not five minutes ago I left them to their cogitations and started for Montezuma Creek to see if I could pick up a little extra help. Were they hit bad, did you notice?"

Billy shook his head. "There aren't many folks left there, Lem. But I spoke with a new feller name of Hyde, and he didn't say a word about any flooding."

"That'd be William Hyde. His daughter Feenie's our new school marm. And he said nothing about any flooding?"

"No, he didn't."

Lem Redd smiled tiredly. "Well, then, maybe we have a little hope from that quarter. Thing is, Billy, we just don't have enough manpower to do everything that's got to be done. I don't—"

"Mr. Redd?" Jimmy Heaton had dismounted, taken off his wide-brimmed hat, and been slicking back his wavy hair with his hand, trying to get it to dry. "My brother Henry W. and me, we ain't got nothing to do for two, maybe three days. If Henry W.'s willing, we'd both be right pleased to lend a hand."

"So would Ise and me," Alfred Wilson declared quickly. "Fact is, we mostly came all this way to see if maybe we could do just that." Pausing, he grinned at Isadore and Henry W., who nodded his willingness. "If four of us can help for a few days, you've sure got us."

"We could use you, all right." Turning his horse around, Lem Redd looked back. "Mount up, fellers, and I'll ride back to the Jump with you—or leastwise what used to be called the Jump. Most likely they'll hand you shovels and put you right to work. And Billy, I reckon I'd better fill you in a little on the situation with Eliza and little Willy—"

8

Bluff Fort

As the huge shadow of Billy's scratching pen moved across the log wall and up onto the stained factory muslin above her, Eliza did her best to focus her mind. But the grease lamp on the table continued to cast shadows in the early morning darkness, Billy continued penning his letter to Elder Brigham Young Jr.—young Brig, he called him—and so Eliza remained mesmerized by the shadows as she stared upward.

It was so interesting, she was thinking, how comfortable this sorry little cabin seemed when Billy was home, and how bleak it appeared when he was away. Who would have ever thought she would become so dependent upon him? Who could ever have imagined how empty and useless she felt when he was not nearby? And now with the added burden and blessing of their precious little Willy—

"Finished," Billy said as he tapped his pen against the ink bottle to cleanse the tip. "Two and a half weeks to finish one little letter. Who'd have thought life would ever be this busy?"

"Or that we'd be fighting so much opposition," Eliza added quietly.

Turning around to face the bed, Billy smiled. "I'm sorry, honbun. I thought you were still asleep."

Eliza smiled. "Well, it is coming on morning, and I wanted to tell you once again how sorry I am for not writing you about Willy. I know I should have told you, but I was trying to spare you."

Looking away, Billy did not immediately respond. "I feel bad that you didn't allow me to exercise my faith," he finally said. "Maybe that would have made the difference with Willy, and he would be well by now."

Knowing that Billy's comment was the closest thing to a rebuke that he had ever given her, Eliza was deeply affected. "I was definitely wrong," she acknowledged humbly, "and once again, I'm more sorry than I can say."

Abruptly Billy smiled brightly. "Well, don't worry about it, honbun. First chance we get, the bishop and I will give him a blessing, and that should take care of whatever the problem is."

"I'm so glad that's finally going to happen. Mary's been after me for weeks to have her father do it, but I felt so strongly that you needed to be here. Now, thank the Lord, you are—"

Smiling down at his wife, Billy pulled off his long nightshirt and then struggled into his britches and clean shirt. Then he checked his son to make sure he was properly covered. Blowing out the twisted wick, he pulled back the curtain over the window and gazed out into the early dawn.

"Mighty good to be home," he said softly. Then, moving to the bed, he leaned down and kissed Eliza on the forehead. "That ornery so-and-so Dick Butt wouldn't even let me kiss him good morning!"

"Billy—" Eliza giggled.

"Well, he wouldn't. Worse, even the soft, sandy floor of our cave wasn't as comfy as this bed."

"Is that where you stayed? In a cave?"

"A good part of the time. With some old ruins, a few ghosts, a little spring, and on one night at least, a powerful lot of rain coming down only a few feet away."

"Was it recent?"

"A week and a half ago. It came down by the bucketful. If some of those snooty, high-society folks from back east had been out walking in it with their noses in the air, they'd have drowned for sure."

"Billy! What's got into you?"

"Dick Butt, I reckon." Billy grinned mischievously. "But I'm serious; it was some rain."

"I'll bet that was the rain that raised the river," Eliza said. "Oh, Billy, I'm so afraid we won't have any crops again!"

"Now, Eliza, we'll raise some food this year. And even if we don't, the Lord will take care of us. He did last year, didn't he?"

"Yes, but I can't stand for you to be gone, especially not for another whole winter! There are too many things going on—awful things—and I just don't think I can face them alone!"

"Why hon-bun, what awful things are you talking about?"

"I'm talking about the people we've settled in the midst of."

Eliza was upset, and Billy could see it. "Those cowboys or outlaws or whatever they are have the meanest eyes I've ever seen in my life! And the way they look at our sisters, especially the young, pretty ones—"

"Like you?"

"Billy, be serious! You know when you see them riding real slow or leaning against a wall somewhere smoking their smelly cigarettes and eyeing things over that they're planning things, awful things. And the Indians aren't much better. Practically every day somebody discovers something else the Navajos have stolen, and poor Brother Haskel is hardly ever out of his saddle, taking Kumen and Lem or two or three of the others with him, tracking them down. Just yesterday two women came into this very cabin! They didn't take anything that I'm aware of, but one of them walked right up and touched Willy, like she was thinking of stealing him or something."

"A Navajo woman?"

"Yes! I'm telling you, Billy, I was terrified! I'm not a woman who faints, but I thought sure I was going to pass out I was so afraid."

"Did she do anything else?"

"Well, she lifted Willy's blanket and looked at his legs, but she said nothing, not even in Navajo. It was eerie, and I had the most terrible feeling about it!

"Add that awful woman to the evil Pahutes, and—well, I'm frightened to death of those two Pahute boys! Do you know they never show up when you're here, but when I'm alone with little Willy and sometimes the other children they barge in and demand that I feed them. And all the time I can see them staring at me or

Willy, or looking around for something or other they can steal. Billy, they frighten me something awful! Especially the one called Posey. I've never seen such hatred and scorn in a person's eyes. Why, last week he tried to kill little Lena Decker right here on this bed! He jammed that ugly old rifle of his right into her stomach when I didn't have any bread to give him. And he would have killed her, too, if it hadn't been that Thales Haskel just happened by and put a stop to it. Billy," and now Eliza's breath caught again, "what if Posey decides to come back when you or Thales aren't around, to kill or kidnap little Willy—"

"Is this what you weren't willing to tell me last night?"

Eliza sighed deeply. "Most of it, I suppose. But there's more. The past two or three weeks Mary has been feeling more and more oppressed, as though something terrible was happening or was about to happen that would put us in extreme danger."

"Us?"

"Yes, us. Her, Kumen, you, me, Willy, and every other member of the mission who is still here. She doesn't know for certain any details, but practically every day now something else happens that is bad for us—the weather, the river, the ditch, the outlaws, the Navajos, the Pahutes—all of which go to show that she's right! We're on the verge of being destroyed, and no matter how hard we try, it doesn't seem to change!"

Slowly Billy sat back on the bed and took his wife's hand. "Lem told me yesterday that except for a young fellow named Henry, who apparently has something he wants to discuss with Thales Haskel, the Pahutes are gone. Most likely—and this is according to both Brother Haskel and Henry W.—they've headed for the mountains and we won't see any of them for the rest of the summer. So, that's at least one thing we can stop worrying about."

"It doesn't matter if they're gone or not. They're somewhere nearby, and it terrifies me even to think about what they must be doing. Besides, you know very well they'll be coming back sooner or later. And then—and then—Oh, lawsy, Billy! It just feels like all the forces of hell are combined against us, every day they're getting stronger and more powerful, and I don't know if I can stand it much longer. I don't blame folks for pulling out. I want to leave, too! I want to take you and little Willy and never stop running! I want to go back to Cedar or Salt Lake or . . . or—Well, I don't know where I want to go. I've prayed and pleaded and begged the Lord for forgiveness for my bad feelings, and for the strength to change. But it just doesn't happen, not any more than the fact that he doesn't help little Willy. So every day I feel a little worse about things. Every day I see Willy dying a little more. And every day I feel more strongly that I just don't want to be here in this pathetic fort on this awful river in the midst of all these horrid people!"

With that, Eliza burst into tears, and Billy was left with the prospects of trying to comfort her—trying when all along he'd been having the same feelings—at least about wanting to leave. For Mary Jones was right, and Billy knew it. They *were* under siege; every last man, woman, and child of the mission, with threats so deadly that they were every one in mortal danger. All winter long he had been terrified for Eliza and little Willy, and of a truth he was no longer so certain of who was going to win.

"There . . . there's something else," Eliza whispered as her tears gradually diminished, "something else I didn't write and tell you about. Billy darling, I . . . I'm going to have another baby sometime in the fall, and I'm scared to death about raising it in this awful, god-forsaken country—"

———o—o—o———

To the east the morning sun was just showing above the hills, brightly illuminating the looming sandstone bluffs under which the Mormons and others who had come through the Hole-in-the-Rock the year before were building their community. Already most of the folks were up and about, taking care of livestock and in general starting to get ready for the day.

Bluff City, they had named the tiny settlement, which so far consisted of a few corrals, some brush sheds, and a series of tiny, rough-hewn log cabins built in four rows facing each other across the wide square that Jimmy Heaton was presently negotiating. On the north side of the square, in the midst of the cabins, was the new log meetinghouse, which also served as the school. In each of the four corners was an opening that would one day be gated—when they had the time and the logs, Jimmy assumed—and inside each gate, far from the community well that was near the center of the fort, were the community commodes or outhouses. They were not a great distance from any of the cabins, but they were definitely not all that convenient. Of course, Jimmy thought wryly, that's what thunder mugs were for—

When all the gaps were finally fenced in and the four gates completed, the structure would be a real fort. Still, Jimmy thought as he gazed around, it didn't look as though the fort would provide much protection from those who truly wanted to get in.

"Morning, little brother," Henry W. Heaton said as he emerged from the cabin next to the one where Jimmy had spent the night. He was stroking the ears of a large dog that had followed him. "These Mormon folks treat you all right?"

"As ever!" Jimmy grinned. "Who's your friend?"

"Mutt, they call him. Seems like a good enough dog. Who'd you stay with?"

"The Jones family—Kumen and Mary. Good food, a comfy quilt on the floor, some interesting conversation, and that was about it. Oh, I asked Kumen about his name, and he said it came from their Book of Mormon."

"Did he try and get you to read it?" Henry W. was instantly tense.

Jimmy laughed at his brother's reaction. "Naw, didn't even mention it again, big brother, so stop worrying. The rest of the night we talked about the Navajos and their endless raids. Kumen and Mary are both picking up a little of their language and hope before long to make a little medicine with 'em and maybe stop the stealing. Who did you stay with?"

"The bishop and his wife. I found out she's his second wife; the first one is back in what they call the settlements. Another thing; he may be Mormon and he may be crippled, but he's a tough old codger, I'll give him that. We did a couple of arm wrestles after supper, and I didn't have a prayer. I'd hate to go up against him in serious fighting."

"That stove-up old man beat the great Henry W. Heaton?"

"As ever!"

"Well, don't that beat all." Jimmy was truly amazed. "Kumen's his son-in-law. He told me the old man walked all the way here through six months of mud and snow and every other possible condition, and that's in spite of his gimped-up feet, which was froze before you and me was even born."

"I believe it. He's one tough hombre!"

"Kumen says Billy's wife Eliza got crippled in the same blizzards as the bishop, and she made the same winter trek to this place as he did. And she was expecting their baby at the time! From what I heard, it must have been quite a journey for all of 'em."

"I reckon." Henry W. looked around. "You seen the Wilson brothers?"

"Not since last night. We going to help with their ditch?"

Henry W. grinned. "Despite that me and shovels don't normally mix, I don't see a good way out of it. And the good Lord knows they do need the help. I was hoping to meet Billy's wife and son first, though. I'm almighty curious about 'em—"

"Top of the morning, boys!" Isadore and then Alfred Wilson stepped out of a cabin across the way, followed by Lemuel Redd, who turned immediately toward the corrals. "You ready to go dig ditches?"

"Not yet, Ise," Jimmy responded with a wave. "We was figuring on meeting Billy's family first—"

"Then turn around and meet them," Billy said as he swung open the door of the cabin directly behind where Jimmy was standing. "Morning, fellers! I hope the Saints here treated you well."

"Mighty well," Jimmy said as he and his brother waited for the Wilsons to cross the compound and join them.

"Good." Billy stepped outside, which seemed almost like a signal for everybody else to begin pouring out of the other cabins on their way to wherever they were going. And to the amazement of the four brothers, who by now understood at least a little of the dire straits the Saints were enduring, there was no sign of the gloom and despair they had expected. Instead the people acted happy, even jovial in their greetings to each other and the four young men. And as livestock was cared for, teams harnessed, and other preparations begun for the workday ahead, the two young Heatons found themselves amazed at the unity they were seeing—the apparent commonality and sincere friendship of every man, woman, and child within the unfinished fort.

"Is this the way Mormons always are?" Jimmy asked Isadore Wilson, who was now standing beside him. "I mean, all friendly and happy-like?"

Isadore smiled. "Purty much, I reckon. Pa says joy is one of the fruits of the gospel of Christ, and if a feller ain't joyful, then he ain't keeping the commandments. It's true enough of me, I know that!"

"So does everybody else in the country know it," Alfred agreed teasingly. "Whenever Ise starts getting mean and ornery, Ma says it's time for a sit-down talk."

"Yeah," Isadore replied with a wry grin, "and I end up having to repent of something or other purt near every time, too. Ma sure can tell."

Wonderingly Jimmy gazed at the two Wilson brothers. Even in their bantering and teasing of each other there was something different, unusual, even fine—

"Well," Billy interrupted, once again catching Jimmy's attention, "Jimmy and Henry Heaton, Alfred and Isadore Wilson, may I introduce you to my wife, Eliza Foreman, and our son, Willy. Fellers, this is the family I've been bragging about the past many days."

And Jimmy Heaton, who was suddenly staring into the haunted, hollow eyes of the reed-thin Eliza Foreman and her equally gaunt son, could find no words to mask his surprise.

———◇–◇–◇———

Her entire body trembling with fear, the Navajo woman Hádapa—the wife of the great warrior Natanii nééz—urged her little burro across the amazingly crowded compound. She had been traveling since long before daylight, even crossing the big river in darkness. But she had not expected to find such crowds here in the *belacani* fort. No, she had expected it to be almost empty, just as she had found it the day before—

Doing her best to ignore the furtive glances of the *belacani* mormonee, Hádapa instead looked into her mind and saw once again the wasted form of the little white boy, an image that had refused to leave, even in her sleep. For in that little child she had seen, to her great surprise, her own younger brother—the child who had slowly died of hunger so many years before.

How his death had agonized her and her mother, who had kept the child alive only as long as their one remaining goat had remained alive to give her nourishing milk. But with the goat's death had also perished the source of food necessary for her younger brother—the only source of strength her imprisoned parents could find. And so the boy had gradually starved to death, looking so much like the white child during the process that it had terrified Hádapa when she had seen him.

That was why she had left the ugly square cabin so quickly. It was why she had abandoned the raid and said nothing to her friend T'anap'a during the entire journey back to the new *hogan* her husband had built not too far south of the big river.

Despite T'anap'a's protests, Hádapa knew she could not raid such a people, such a woman and child. They were to be sorrowed over, not raided. They should have a sing held in their behalf, a Blessing Way, and many should come to the feasting so that *hózhó* might be restored to their unhappy lives.

Of course, Hádapa knew such a sing would never be held, particularly when her husband, the great Natanii nééz, was so intent upon seeing the mormonee as enemies and raiding them until they were driven from the big river. But as she had lain alone in the darkness of her *hogan* the night before, she had come to know that she must never again attempt to raid these strange people. Instead she must try to help them—particularly the tall, thin woman and the starving boy she had been clutching so fearfully in her arms.

And truly Hádapa had known how the *belacani* woman had felt. For big in her mind was the memory of herself, still a child, clutching her tiny brother to her breast in fear as Rope Thrower had burst through the closed doorway of her parents' *hogan,* threatening death to all who were within. Yes, and his threat had been carried out, though not so immediately as they had at first feared—

Doing her best to wipe the terrible memory from behind her eyes, Hádapa reined her burro toward the appropriate cabin. Then she laid her hand gently on the tanned goatskin udder she herself had prepared two seasons before, the udder from a butchered goat which that very morning she had filled with fresh, nourishing goat's milk. It was the very thing the starving white child needed, she knew, just as it had been the very thing her own dying brother had needed. Now she had only to somehow communicate that fact to the *belacani* child's mother—

———◦—◦—◦———

"Billy, Mrs. Foreman, ma'am, this little feller's . . . well, he . . . he's . . . well doggone it if he ain't being starved plumb to death!" Jimmy Heaton took a deep breath. "I know, on account of Pa and me stumbled on a family of nesters in Disappointment Valley a year ago whose kids all looked the same as Willy here. We brung 'em food two, maybe three times, but it was way too late for the little ones. Two of 'em died afore the rest pulled out, and all we ever found was the crosses and the little graves. Ain't he eating good, ma'am, or what?"

"He eats just fine," Eliza replied softly as she gazed at the child in her arms. "Thing is, it doesn't seem to be doing him any good. Mary Jones and I have tried the milk of every cow in Bluff. We've boiled beef and greens and given him the broth, and we've done the same with wheat and barley. Nothing works. Day after day he gets thinner and more weak, and . . . and—"

"Ma'am," Jimmy said with alarm when Eliza started to weep, "I didn't mean to upset you. Honest I didn't! I was just concerned for the boy here, and feeling fearful that you and Billy might lose him—"

"He isn't going to die," Billy declared emphatically as he took the child from his mother's arms. "Are you, Willy. Fact is, boys, Eliza told me last night she's prayed to the Lord about Willy and been given peace, and I had the same experience after I got home. I feel certain he isn't appointed unto death, and so either tonight or tomorrow night we'll meet with the bishop, and he and I will give the child a priesthood blessing. If it's the Lord's will that Willy recover—and both of us feel that it is—then he will, no doubt about it."

"What . . . what's a blessing?" Jimmy asked, feeling confused.

"It's a prayer, but a mighty particular one." Isadore Wilson was speaking. "Worthy men in the Church hold the priesthood or authority of God. When they give a person a blessing, they speak in God's name, and what happens afterward is the same as if God himself had spoken it.

"Alf and me have had blessings our own selves," Isadore continued, "and both of us have seen some mighty peculiar miracles. If the Lord commands Billy to heal him tonight, then one way or another, that child will be healed."

Jimmy Heaton shook his head. "If that don't beat all," he mumbled almost to himself. "If that just don't beat all—"

"Anyway, fellers," Billy declared, instantly lightening the mood, "this here is my beautiful Eliza, and this is our humble home!"

"Pleased, ma'am," Jimmy said, belatedly removing his hat and elbowing his older brother to do the same. "Billy ain't stopped talking about you since the day we met, though if I do say so, he ain't half done you justice!"

"Why, thank you," Eliza responded, instantly flustered. "You are . . . uh . . . "

"Jimmy, ma'am; Jimmy Heaton. This is my brother Henry W., and we hail from Rico, over in Colorado. These two fellers are the Wilson brothers, from Moab, up in Grand Valley. This is Alfred, the oldest, and this real puny one is Isadore. They're Mormons, ma'am, but Henry W. and me, we ain't. Other than that, we're all four nothing but cowpokes, wanting to buy cattle from Bill Ball of the LC. But since he ain't there yet, and since we didn't have nothing constructive to do, why, Billy brung us here and offered to give us the honor of meeting you and little Willy. And Mrs. Foreman, ma'am, a distinct honor it is, too!"

"Well, my goodness," Eliza exclaimed, looking from Jimmy to the others and then back again, "the honor is mine, Jimmy, I assure you. While Billy is liberal in his views toward all men, I have learned that he doesn't take well to those whose hearts are not good. Since he brought the four of you here, then it can only be because he's seen a great deal of good in each of you. Welcome to our home!"

Jimmy Heaton beamed as he took Eliza's hand and bowed. Henry W. and the Wilson brothers looked at each other in amazement before returning their gaze to the loquacious youth, and they were still staring when the spell was broken by a soft knock on the door.

"Yes?" Billy asked as he turned and swung open the plank door. And then he simply stared at the Navajo woman who stood trembling before him, a bulging, hair-covered goat's udder clutched in her arms.

9

Wednesday, April 6, 1881

Bluff Fort

The young Pahute who was calling himself Henry crouched under the overspreading edge of a large clump of sagebrush. The frequent winds had piled the sand beneath his moccasins into wave-like ridges, though of a truth he paid little attention to such things. Instead his entire focus was riveted on the tall, thin form of a man who was seated in an old chair leaning back against the wall of a log *wickiup*—what the whites were calling a cabin—that had been built separately from all the others of their large encampment.

The seated one was *nan-i-peds,* an old man with hair that was long and white. He was also very still, his only movement the occasional lifting of his hand to remove one cigarette from the corner of his mouth and replace it with another. His head never turned, his eyes never strayed from the distant bluff. Yet Henry had the distinct impression that he was the one being watched rather than the other way around. After all, this man had *myshoot-te quoop,* he had powerful medicine. It had been he who had brought the mormonee people to this place. He had been one of those who had so thoroughly shamed old Peagament two summers past that not only his people but even his young wives had turned from the old chief. And it had been he who had spoken the words that had snuffed the life from the evil Navajo called Peokon. *Oo-ah,* yes, this one with the pale blue eyes and the tall, straight frame was a man to be feared.

For long minutes Henry remained where he was, considering

what might happen should he reveal himself. Yet if he did not, how could he ask this one who was called Thales Haskel why the mormonee had come to this place, and what they intended to do now that they were here. These questions were terribly important to the young Pahute, not only because he feared this one who had brought them but also because his nights for many moons had been filled with strange dreams about them—dreams that were causing him terrible discomfort.

Henry remembered vividly the day when some chiefs of the Pahutes had returned from their own visit with this *nan-i-peds* who was now seated before him. They had found him inside his wooden *wickiup,* his moccasined feet toward the flame in his open fireplace, drowsily puffing a cigarette. He had paid them no heed when they had looked into his open door but merely grunted when they asked if he understood them. Even as they had quietly encircled him he had not looked up but had continued to study the fire through his cigarette smoke.

"Where do you come from?" one of the chiefs had finally asked.

Haskel's answer had been an indolent pointing of his chin toward the west.

"How long are you going to stay?" was the next question, which the thin old man had answered by spreading the fingers of both his hands and moving them up and down, indicating an indefinite period of time.

Regarding him with awe, the Pahute chiefs had backed out of the cabin and departed. They had heard scarcely a word, but around their fires Haskel was now spoken of with reverence and not a little fear, for he was surely one of the most remarkable men any of them had ever encountered. Truly he was one who knew things, great things, that perhaps one day he would reveal.

Many times Henry had heard this telling, and now it was in his heart to also meet this great man, to ask him some questions of his own, and to see if he could get some peace about his nighttime dreams. This was why he had not gone to the Shining Mountains with his father and the others to the racing of the ponies. This was why he had wanted to stay near these strange whites who were unlike any others he had known, to speak with this man he so feared, and to learn the great secrets he must surely know.

Like a shadow Henry finally rose to his feet and moved forward, slowly approaching the silent white man. His heart was hammering with fear, although when nothing unusual happened, he was not altogether surprised.

Reaching the side of the cabin Henry stood patiently, as was the way of the People, waiting for an acknowledgement that he could proceed. When Thales Haskel did not look at him, did not even blink his eyes or do anything but breathe out the smoke from his cigarette, Henry wondered. Truly the chiefs were right. This man was as one of the People. Truly he was *to-wats,* a true man.

Minutes passed, many of them, Henry standing silently while his mind worked itself to a fever pitch with worry and wonderment. What did this man know? What had been in his mind when he had brought the mormonee to this place on the big river? How deeply into the souls of the warriors of the People could he see?

"*Impo ashanty?*" Henry finally breathed when he could stand the silence no longer. "What do you want in this place?"

Again the moments stretched out in silence, Thales Haskel saying nothing, not even acknowledging Henry's presence. Now the young man was filled with even more wonderment, with even more fear. Only the greatest headmen, only the most powerful chiefs, had the power to remain silent under such circumstances. It was almost more than the young Pahute could endure.

"*Impo ashanty?*" he breathed again, knowing within himself that if no answer came from the white medicine man after this inquiry, he, Henry, would be finished. He would turn and go away, never again having the courage to seek the great things that were most surely hidden within this pale *to-wats'* heart.

But still the white man said nothing, staring along the bridge of his nose and off into the distance as though Henry were not even there.

Sorrowing now, for he knew that his desires had been in vain, knew also that the wisdom of Thales Haskel was too great for such a one as himself to hear, Henry started to turn away.

"*Shin-op,*" Thales Haskel said then, his voice so low that Henry had to turn back and strain to hear it, "*Shin-op,* the Great God, sent his three servants to talk to the mormonee."

Realizing that the white man was speaking in Henry's own tongue, the young Pahute was still not surprised. No, nor would he be surprised by anything this white man might do, for truly he was a man of *myshoot-te quoop,* powerful medicine. Meanwhile he was remembering vividly the three men who had come the previous fall, staying only a few days and then leaving in their buckboard up the big river. It was they who must be the servants of *Shin-op!* It was they—

"*Shin-op,*" Thales Haskel continued, his voice so low it was still almost silent, "wants the mormonee to stay here and be the friends of the People. The mormonee have many things to say to the warriors of the People about *Shin-op* and his way of life. The mormonee are *Shin-op's* friends. *Shin-op* tells us that if the warriors of the People continue stealing horses and cattle from the mormonee, they will die."

Hardly daring to breathe, Henry listened intently as the man's voice continued—as his eyes bored into the very depths of Henry's soul.

"Maybe the warriors of the People will get sick and die," Thales Haskel declared, speaking or grunting the words with all the guttural inflection Henry knew so well. "Maybe the warriors will kill each other. Maybe *Shin-op* will send the lightning to kill them. Maybe he will reach out with his unseen hand and touch them, and they will wither up like the grass under the summer sun. If the warriors of the People continue to steal our horses or kill our cattle, they will die!"

With visions of the Navajo Peokon's withered frame filling his mind, Henry knew that his audience with the feared Thales Haskel was over. Yet, he thought as he backed silently away from the still-seated man, not even noticing that the ever-present cigarette, now that it was no longer needed, had been snuffed out, he had learned much. He had learned that the mormonee were friends. He had learned that the way of his father and the others, the way of making raids upon these people at every opportunity, was wrong. Despite that the mormonee were white and in many ways acted foolish, as did all the whites whom Henry had known, the mormonee were nevertheless the people of *Shin-op* the great Spirit, and so they must be befriended. To do otherwise would be foolish. To do otherwise, he thought with a shudder as he turned and fled into the tall brush, would surely bring *e-i*, death, upon them all!

———◦—◦—◦———

Jimmy Heaton had never felt such emotions, not in his entire life. He and the others had just listened as Billy, Bishop Nielson, and a long-haired old man named Thales Haskel had given a blessing to little Willy. It had been a fine blessing, too, though it wasn't the words that had affected Jimmy so deeply. At least he didn't think it was the words. Instead it had been something else, some powerful but indescribable feeling, he supposed, that had made him feel like he was about to smother, or burn up, maybe. Yet it hadn't been so much unpleasant as overwhelming, and Jimmy Heaton was suddenly anxious to find out what was going on.

For two days he and the others had labored with the citizens of Bluff, working on cleaning out the ditch while others replowed the fields and prepared them for another planting. It had been hard, hot work, and the day before they hadn't returned to the fort until long after dark. But today they had returned a little early, not just because Willy needed a blessing but also because no one was certain how to go about building a new headgate for their ditch—a headgate that wouldn't just wash away with the next flood.

A short prayer meeting had been held under the bowery, and it was then that someone had come up with the idea of placing cribs out into the river as a means of controlling the current. Billy had become involved then, explaining how the cribs could be built, and though Jimmy hadn't understood much of what had followed, it was not possible to miss the excitement among the people as they had voted unanimously to begin construction.

Jimmy had marveled at such unity, and he was marveling even more now as a tearful Eliza held her son while she thanked the bishop and Thales Haskel for their assistance. It had been a remarkable two days for Jimmy, his brother, and even the two Mormon youth from Moab, and he knew, as he leaned against the log wall watching the proceedings, that he had much to consider in the days ahead. There was truly something about these people—

———o—o—o———

"Sister Eliza, ma'am," Thales Haskel said as he licked the white liquid from his finger, "though it's starting to clabber up, this ain't nothing but goat's milk. You say it's the second time the same woman's brung it to you?"

"That's right." It was Billy who answered. "She came yesterday morning and again this morning—early both times."

"Was the milk in one of these tanned udder bags yesterday?"

Billy nodded. "Eliza threw it out first thing, though—I reckon on account of she was afraid of it. But this morning I hung onto it—curiosity, I suppose. The poor woman was so scared she was shaking in her moccasins both times, and I wanted to find out what it was she was giving us."

"What'd she say?"

"A few Navajo words, Brother Haskel. That's about all I can tell you. But she tilted her head back and stuck her thumb toward her mouth like she was sucking it, so I figured this was food of some sort."

"That's right, for the baby, since he's the one she figures is still suckling." Thales thought for a moment. "Billy, did she say something like *dichin bá neilé?* Or *tl ízítsaii?* Or *tl ízíkági?* Or maybe *bíká hil naayá?*"

"Well, some of it sounds familiar. Maybe all of it does. I can't exactly tell."

Thales Haskel nodded. "Most likely what she was saying was that your child was sick with hunger, and that she had made a journey to her *hogan* and back to bring the child a goatskin filled with milk from a nanny goat. For some reason it looks like she's taken a liking to your son, and it wouldn't surprise me none if you found her on your stoop every morning from now until he gets better."

Eliza was stunned. "Are you actually suggesting that I feed that . . . that Indian woman's goat's milk to my Willy?"

"Why, yes, ma'am, I reckon I am."

"I won't do it!" Eliza actually stamped her foot she was so

adamant, which caused Billy to jump and all four of the young cowboys standing against the wall to begin fighting back smiles. "I can't stand those people, Pahute or Navajo either one, and you can bet your last silver dollar I won't be trusting Willy's life to a . . . a squaw!"

"Vell, Sister Foreman," Bishop Nielson declared slowly, "there be yust vone ting I tink you should consider—vone ting beyond de fact dat you haff been called by de Lord to bring peace und love to dese peoples. Und dat vone ting is dat de Lord may very vell be using dis Navajo voman to bring about de healing your husband has yust promised your son—de healing I know you haff also been praying for."

Eliza was aghast. "He . . . he wouldn't do that! After the terrible things the Indians have done to me, the Lord would never require such a thing at my hand!"

"Ya, my dear Eliza, he vould." Bishop Nielson smiled tenderly. "Especially he vould iff he could see dat in dis vay your heart vould be softened tovard some off his lost children."

"But . . . but I can't stand them—"

"They ain't all bad like that young feller called Posey, ma'am." Thales Haskel turned his chair so he could better face the still-standing Eliza. "Fact is, I met earlier today with a young Pahute name of Henry, and I can tell you the Lord has been working with him for some time, giving him dreams and preparing him to help his people receive the gospel. Henry doesn't understand all that, but when it happens he'll understand. Meanwhile he has a good heart and wants to be helpful. So does old Chief Peagament and his wife, Peeats.

"As far as the Navajos go, there's good and bad there, too. Natanii nééz, or Frank, as he is calling himself, is a bad one, and I wouldn't trust him as far as I could throw him. On the other hand, corpulent old Pee-jon-kaley is a fine man, always smiling and always ready with a new joke to tell me. Notice the children when he comes into the fort, ma'am. They flock to him, and children can usually tell about folks' hearts that way. Pishleki is another old fellow the children love because he is so happy, and he'll always pitch in to help when he sees a need."

Thales Haskel scratched his chin thoughtfully. "Eliza, ma'am, you need to remember that Indians are just folks—ordinary people like the rest of us, and most of 'em are struggling to get through life just the same as you and me. Why, the other night during that storm when Charlie Walton was playing his fiddle, an old Navajo fellow and his grown daughter were staying with Maggie and me. After she'd listened to Charlie's music for a few minutes, that poor Navajo girl slumped down in her chair and sobbed like a brokenhearted child. The old man stood behind her with a mighty tender look on his face, and when I asked him what was wrong, he told me she'd recently lost a little boy, and she could hear him calling out to her in the music. Wouldn't surprise me none to learn the woman that's bringing you the goat's milk has been through something similar."

Slowly Eliza sank into a chair, her sleeping baby held tightly against her breast. "But . . . but I'm so afraid—"

"Hon-hun," Billy said as he reached out and took his wife's hand, "you have a ton of faith, more than nearly anyone else I've ever known. That's what brought you across the ocean and the plains, and it's what brought you here. Now's the time to use it again."

"Ya, Sister Foreman, dat be right." The tall old Danish bishop pulled himself to his feet and hobbled to Eliza's side, where he placed his big hand tenderly upon her shoulder. "Yust remember dat de Lord has promised you dat de child vill live. All off us, including dese fine young men, heard dat promise vith their own ears, und so did you. If de goat's milk helps or not, you haff de peace of knowing dat it can't possibly hurt your little Villy. De Lord simply von't let it happen! Do you understand?"

Wiping at her now tear-filled eyes, Eliza slowly nodded.

"Goot!" The bishop smiled tenderly. "Und I feel to promise you, dear sister, by de authority off my calling as de bishop, dat de goat's milk vill help your child, und dat de voman vill become to both of you a dear friend indeed!"

———◇—◇—◇———

"Pa, they've done it again!" Joseph Nielson was so upset he hadn't knocked or even closed the door to his father's cabin behind him. "Those durn Navajos have stolen three more horses!"

"Hello, Yoseph." Bishop Nielson took his hand from Eliza's shoulder and faced his son. "Vill you please close de door?"

Feeling foolish that he had interrupted what had obviously been a private gathering, the young man turned to do so. "Billy, Eliza, Brother Haskel—well, every one of you. I . . . uh . . . I didn't realize you and Pa were meeting—"

"Well," Thales Haskel replied with a sly grin, instantly putting the young man at ease, "my Maggie says there's getting to be less and less of me to see anyway." Thales then stood and extended his hand. "Nice to see you again, Joe. What makes you think it was the Navajo took your horses?"

"Well," the youth replied, now ignoring everyone else in the small room, "for one thing there weren't any tracks—not ponies, not moccasins, nothing! Pahutes never go anywhere without their ponies, and every time they've been hanging around, I've been able to cut their sign. Tell the truth, Brother Haskel, except for Henry's foot-prints I ain't seen fresh Pahute sign in going on a week, nor Pahutes either, for that matter. Besides, the tracks of those three horses make a beeline straight for the river and then come out the other side and keep going south. They weren't wandering or looking for graze, I can tell you that!"

Thales looked thoughtful. "Sounds like you've got 'em pegged, all right. Most Navajo are mighty good at raiding horses, and the rest are even better. Speaking of the devil, I've got me a hunch this is the work of my old friend Natanii nééz."

"Natanii nééz?"

"That's right," Thales nodded. "Translates out to the Tall One, or something like that. He also calls himself Frank, and he's a real piece of work—fancies himself a gambler as well as a horse thief, and like I just told Eliza and Billy, he can't be trusted for nothing."

For a moment it was silent in the small cabin, and young Joseph took the opportunity of backing up against the wall with the other young men. He didn't know where his stepmother had gone, but he suspected that this little meeting was official Church business, and so the woman had probably taken the smaller children and gone visiting. Joseph knew it was customary of her to do that since his father had been called as bishop, and he respected her for it. He also respected his father, for despite the fact that Jens Nielson was severely crippled, he had become a dynamic spiritual leader among the Saints of Bluff Fort as well as Montezuma Fort. Now, as the fire crackled in the fireplace, Joseph watched spellbound as the old man stood silently, deep in his own thoughts.

"Vell, Tales," Bishop Nielson finally responded, "iss it possible dat it vas de Pahute Henry who took dese horses?"

"No, Bishop, it ain't. I already told you about his visit today, so I'm certain Henry wouldn't do it. That boy has a good spirit about him, you mark my words on that. He believed what I told him, most likely because the Holy Ghost bore witness of it to him, and so I'm certain we've got us another friend among the Pahutes. And Joe's right about the rest of 'em, too. The three main bands left Sand Island near a week ago, and their tracks went straight enough that I figure they was on a real journey."

"You think they've pulled out for good?" Joseph asked hopefully.

"Not hardly. We're making living too good for 'em to pull a stunt like that. But I am feeling antsy about 'em. Mary Jones told me yesterday she has a bad feeling about what they might be up to, and I reckon I agree. They're up to something no good, and any day now we'll get word of what it is. More'n likely it'll be to our hurt, too."

"They could be headed for that big Ute powwow in the mountains of Colorado," Jimmy Heaton volunteered helpfully. "They gather there about once a year, I know that."

"And raise quite a stink when they do," Henry W. Heaton added.

"I thought of that," Thales agreed, "and it wouldn't surprise me if you boys're right. Happen you are, it'll be a chancy time to be driving cattle back into that country."

"Yeah," Jimmy grinned, "it will at that. But Alf and Ise Wilson here have decided to join their herd to ours, so at least there'll be four of us if we get attacked."

"Good idea."

"We'll travel together as far as the Dolores River," Isadore declared. "Then Alf and I will take our fifty head and skedaddle on up to Lisbon Valley, on to Big Indian, and then down Spanish Valley to home. Shouldn't take us more'n seven, maybe eight days."

"And it'll take us about half that to get to Rico," Jimmy stated. "In terms of traveling together, it's the best we can do."

Bishop Nielson sighed, took his seat, and moved his stocking-covered feet so the heat from the fire would hit them from a slightly different direction. It was no secret the damage the winter snows of Wyoming had done to his feet twenty-six years before—the same sort of damage that had been done to the feet of Eliza Foreman—and everyone knew of the constant pain the old man was forced to endure. Yet like Eliza he did it without complaint, doing his share of the work and sometimes more, and the people of the settlements along the San Juan loved him for it.

"Vell," he said softly, thoughtfully, "I tink you are right in your decision, boys. Und de Holy Spirit vhispers dat you vill all get home safely. Yust remember not to take any foolish risks, und never, ever tirst after de blood off dose Lamanites!"

"Lamanwhats?" Jimmy asked.

"Lamanites. Means Indians." Isadore was grinning. "It's another word from the Book of Mormon."

"Ahh. Well, give me a little more time—"

"Ven do you boys plan to leaf de fort?"

"Tomorrow," Alfred Wilson responded. "We're all bunking with Billy and Eliza tonight—wall-to-wall beds, I reckon—and come first light we'll head on up to the LC. We figure to get there about the same time Bill Ball arrives with our cattle."

Bishop Nielson smiled kindly. "Vell, go vith God. Und tank you so much for your help dese past two days. Ve are all getting a little vorn, und it vas good dat you came to raise our spirits.

"Und, Tales," the old man continued, now turning from the boys, "I hope you are wrong about dat tall Navajo thief. If you are not, do ve haff any of de udder headmen who might be our friends?"

"Not that I know of, Bishop. Course if old Dah nishuánt is still alive, he'd be a friend."

"Dah nishuánt?"

"Yeah, good old fellow. Fact is, Ira Hatch married his daughter, Sarah Maraboots. We used to call him Spaneshanks, on account of Dah nishuánt sort of sounds like Danish Yank, and that sort of sounds like Spanish Yank, and that sort of sounds like Spaneshanks.

Shows you what the white tongue can do to good, sensible Indian words. Anyhow, I ain't seen him in years. Heard a rumor now and then, mostly about him protecting one sorry soul or another from his ornery son Peokon, but I ain't seen him."

"It vould be nice to know if he iss still alive."

Thales nodded. "I'll keep my eyes and ears open—see what I can learn."

"Tank you. Und before I forget again, tank you also for bringing back de baby booties of Sister Perkins."

"It weren't no problem, Bishop, no more'n any other four-day ride. Sorry we couldn't find your black. If it was stole, it was stole by somebody slick   mighty slick.

"Anyway, me being gone so much is why Maggie says I'm getting so scrawny, living off jerked beef and beans while her fine home cooking of rough bran and weed greens sits and goes bad and then goes to the pigs. At least they're putting on a little lard." Thales smiled one of his rare smiles. "That old Navajo woman who took the booties, Bishop? I ain't had time to tell you, but she was conducting a raid too, just like Natanii nééz and this newest thief, whoever he is. Looks to me like the word's being spread among the *Diné* that we're easy pickings, and I'm getting mighty concerned about it."

"As am I, Brudder Haskel. As am I." Jens Nielson then turned to his son. "Ver dose draft animals dat ver taken, Yoseph?"

"Yeah, Pa, good horses. Two belonged to Lem Redd, and the other was another one of ours. We'll miss 'em, all right."

"Vell, Tales," Bishop Nielson said as he once again adjusted his twisted feet, "are you up to anudder ride into de Navajo country? Ve must haff dose horses, you see."

Thales nodded briefly. "Reckon I am, Bishop. That's what I'm here for. I'll get your horses back, and maybe I can throw the fear of God into a few more of the *Diné* while I'm about it. Fact is, I reckon I'll have Maggie cut my hair tonight—good and short. Then first thing in the morning I'll be on the trail of our newest thief."

"Goot. Be sure und choose a couple of brudders to go vith you, yust like last time. Und be careful, Tales. You're more important dan de horses."

The Indian interpreter rose easily to his feet. "We'll be careful,

Bishop; don't worry. And in spite of what I told you about befriending that Navajo woman, Eliza ma'am, you folks here at the fort need to do the same. And you young cowboys, too. Be careful! Like I said, I've got me a bad feeling about those missing Pahutes, and it wouldn't surprise me if whatever deviltry they're up to doesn't all come down around us one of these first days. You hear me?"

Soberly the old man nodded. "Ya, Tales, ve hear you. Und knowing how miserable de devil vants us all to be, it vouldn't surprise me too much, eidder."

10

Friday, April 8, 1881

Bluff Fort

"Billy, are you awake?"

"Uh-huh." Quietly Billy rolled onto his back. "I've been lying here listening to little Willy's breathing, wondering how quickly the Lord is going to heal him."

Though the window shown faintly because of what little light was coming from the low-hanging sliver of moon, the inside of the cabin was dark as pitch. There weren't even any coals left glowing in the fireplace, at least none that Billy could see. Actually, though, he liked it this way, when no matter if he closed his eyes or not, the things around him were not a distraction. This was Billy's favorite time to pray, and he had been doing so with his eyes wide open, mentally talking to the Lord about his beloved companion and their emaciated little son—

"Yesterday, when I thought I was all prepared to accept her, the Navajo woman didn't come."

"I know." Billy sighed deeply. "It makes me wonder if maybe we were all wrong about her and the goat's milk. Thing is, hon-bun, I've been praying this morning, and I keep getting the same impressions." In the darkness Billy sighed again. "Wouldn't it be nice to have a clear understanding of all the impressions and answers we get to our prayers?"

"Wouldn't it, though!"

"I've even asked the Lord that very question—why I keep muddling up and misinterpreting the information he gives me."

"And?" Eliza asked.

Billy adjusted the feather pillow beneath his head. "And I just keep having the feeling that if I knew everything and had a perfect understanding of everything, then mortality wouldn't be a test and a growing experience for me, and there'd be no point in my being here. However, I also feel that the more pure I can make myself, the more clear and comprehensible the Lord's directions will become."

Now Eliza sighed into the darkness. "That's hard, isn't it, especially when we all seem so filled with weaknesses. Last week I finally humbled myself enough to start pleading with the Lord for a way to deal with my fear of the Indians and everything else in this country, and so Sunday after meetings God led me to a verse of scripture that told me not only why I was so fearful but also what to do about it. I just wept because I was so thrilled and grateful to the Lord for his answer, and I promised him I would implement his instructions and follow them from then on."

"That's wonderful!" Billy declared as he squeezed his wife's hand.

"Not very," Eliza admitted sadly. "On Monday morning those two Navajo women showed up at my door, and in less time than it takes to tell about it, I was right back where I'd been before all my great promises to the Lord! I'm not exaggerating, Billy. In less than a heartbeat I was as terrified, angry, and bitter as I've ever been! My call from the Lord was forgotten, and all I wanted was to get out of this awful country—the sooner the better. You know how I felt because we talked about it."

Billy chuckled quietly. "I know, all right."

"Why am I so weak? How can I make the Lord a promise, a sincere promise that I mean with all my heart to keep, and then in a flash turn against it and do just the opposite?"

"Because you're human, Eliza."

"But . . . that's no excuse!"

"I don't mean it as an excuse; I mean it as a reason. Remember when King Benjamin says in the Book of Mormon that the natural man is an enemy to God? Well, that's what he's talking about—our natural or human tendencies. We want to be one way, but we continue to discover tendencies within ourselves that tell us we are the other. That's the natural man showing up.

"Now I don't know that I'm exactly right, but it seems to me that the natural man—which the apostle Paul tells us we must put off before we can truly belong to Christ—is composed of three parts. First are the weaknesses that we inherit from our parents, grandparents, and so on—the curses of the fathers the scriptures call some of these; second is the circumstances in which we're raised; and third are our own poor decisions, which bring the consequences we end up suffering. I believe these three elements comprise our natural man, for together they create the worldly tendencies that keep us from the presence of the Lord."

"But . . . everybody inherits different things, experiences different situations, and makes different decisions. I don't—"

"You're right," Billy interrupted, "because every person's 'natural man' is unique to himself or herself—you might say tailor-made to provide the perfect challenges and thus to generate the perfect humility and thus growth through Christ. The Savior explained this to Moroni when he said, 'If men come unto me I will show unto them their weakness. I give unto men weakness that they may be humble; and my grace is sufficient for all men that humble themselves before me; for if they humble themselves before me, and have faith in me, then will I make weak things become strong unto them.'"

Eliza sighed heavily. "This is too deep for me, Billy, and too discouraging. I don't even want—"

Reaching over, Billy gently laid a finger over his wife's lips. "Don't say any more, hon-bun. Just listen, and think. You're now perfectly aware of this great weakness called fear. Right?"

Silently Eliza nodded.

"And the knowledge of that weakness makes you feel how?"

"Discouraged."

Billy smiled. "Okay, but what's another word for that? Are you arrogant or haughty because you think so highly of yourself? Are you filled with pride because of your great valor in the face of adversity and opposition?"

"Not hardly!" Eliza responded with a harsh chuckle.

"No, of course not. As a matter of fact you are humble—very humble—which is exactly why the Lord told Moroni he had given you that particular weakness in the first place. And now that you are humble enough, you are willing to begin supplicating for the Lord's grace, and then to begin learning how to do exactly what he tells you. Once that is all in place, and you've stopped letting down and making mistakes in it, then this weakness will become a great strength to you."

"Do you . . . really think that might happen?"

Billy smiled. "Of course I do—for myself in my weaknesses as well as for you in yours. That's how each of us must put off the natural man—one effort at a time to overcome one weakness at a time."

"But . . . that could take the rest of our lives!"

"It could." Billy chuckled. "Maybe it's even supposed to. But no matter. There's still no better time than right now to start working on it. If we don't, then I'm afraid not one of us, little Willy included, will survive our mission to this country, let alone obtain the blessings the Lord has ordained it to provide for us!"

For a moment Eliza was silent, thinking. "How do you do this?" she finally asked as she turned toward her husband. "How do you always seem to know the right words to help me keep going?"

Billy chuckled. "I don't, and it isn't really you I'm preaching to. I just keep being forced to give myself little sermons for my own well-being, and you bear the burden of listening in. But I do want to do things right, Eliza! More than anything in the world I long to be worthy of having you and Willy and our new little child as my eternal family!"

Lying back, Billy again stared up into the darkness. "You know, I still can't believe I'm a father, and that we have an actual, real-life son. When I'm away sometimes, it gets to feeling like this is all a dream—Willy, you, and everything. But then when I get home and Willy's crawling on my chest and you're yonder by the fire fixing vittles or mending socks or whatever—well, life becomes real again, and I spend half my waking hours thanking the good Lord for you and Willy and even this wonderful, drafty cabin, and the other half feeling sure I don't deserve everything and it will soon be taken away. I'm telling you, Eliza, I can hardly understand how much beauty and joy you have brought to my life, how amazing it feels to be recognized and loved by little Willy, and how much I've grown to love the folks of this settlement. So I lie here in bed listening to Willy breathe, knowing he's going to be healed and wondering why in the world a sorry little clerk like me has been so wonderfully touched by the loving hand of God."

Wiping the sudden tears from her eyes, Eliza curled up against her husband. "I feel the same, darling. I truly do. At night, especially when I'm alone and you aren't here, I find myself listening to Willy's breathing and feeling absolutely certain that his next breath will be his last. Then he'll pause in his breathing the way he does sometimes. I'll know I'm right, and I seem to freeze up with the worst terror a person can imagine. Oh, Billy, I honestly don't know what I'd ever do if little Willy were to . . . to be taken from us. I've never felt this way—have never even imagined I could feel like this. Do you know I actually find myself trying to breathe for him?"

Billy chuckled quietly. "You too, huh. Well, hon-bun, if you figure out how to do it, be sure and let me know."

Eliza sighed. "Billy darling, I love you so much that sometimes it actually hurts. I'm literally in awe of the way I feel about you— the way I suffer when you're gone and the way my heart pounds when I first catch sight of you coming home again. And yet—and I hope this doesn't hurt your feelings—what I feel for little Willy seems so much greater, more intense, that I can't comprehend it. I . . . I think that's why I'm so afraid."

"Of course it is, and it makes perfect sense!" Billy tightened his arm around his wife's shoulders and pulled her closer. "You're Willy's mother, and from what I've been given to understand, there's no bond in mortality so powerful as the love of a righteous mother for her children. I'm just thankful that you feel that way. I can't even imagine it when the Lord says in the last days the love of some mothers will wax cold toward their own children, and they'll kill them for their own convenience. I'm so grateful that you aren't that sort of mother, and I feel at peace knowing Willy is receiving the best care he possibly could."

"Only it . . . it isn't enough," Eliza breathed, suddenly beginning to weep. "No matter what I try to do—"

"Hush," Billy said as he again placed his finger on Eliza's lips. "You've done all you could, hon-bun, and soon we'll know what else we need to do so the child can get well."

Swiping at her eyes, Eliza snuggled even closer to her husband. And when, moments later, a rooster crowed and something else set all the dogs in the fort barking furiously in response, she managed to ignore them altogether.

Tseya Neechee, Navajo Reservation

"Indians up ahead, Thales. Three of 'em. Navajos, by their looks."

"I see 'em," Thales Haskel replied quietly from behind his two companions. "They've seen us, too. Keep up a steady pace, boys, and no matter what happens, don't act surprised or nervous."

"What if we are? Nervous, I mean."

"Then smile, and if that don't do it, hum a little song. And do it softly, like it's something you'd do naturally, all the time. But don't try whistling, boys, not if your mouths have gone dry with fear. That's a dead giveaway in any man's tongue."

For most of that day, which had started at Thales Haskel's usual time of rising—just after 3:00 A.M.—he and his two companions had followed the trail of the stolen horses southwestward, crossing Monument Valley west of the Mittens and Merrick Butte but just to the east of Mitchell Butte, and so passing between, where the bodies of prospectors James Merrick and Ernest Mitchell had been found only a little more than a year before. Passing Gray Whiskers Rock they had turned southward across Mystery Valley, and it was where the valley narrowed into the finger-like branches of *Tseya Neechee* that Thales had lost sign of the tracks.

Casting about, the old interpreter had felt certain that the thieves had climbed one of the draws southeastward, up onto the sprawling highland that would one day be called Wetherill Mesa. Following a ghost of a trail one of the others had spotted, the three had started up one of the draws, moving slowly. About halfway up they had rounded a point of rock, and it was then that they had seen the three Navajos sitting their horses on the trail ahead.

144

"You think these are the thieves?" Thales was asked as they rode slowly forward.

"I doubt it," he responded quietly. "No tracks. But they may know something. Won't much hurt to ask."

The man grinned with wry humor. "Then you'd better do it, Thales. I'm so gut-shrunk with nerves I'd probably just squeak."

Smiling at the honesty of his companion, the old Indian missionary and interpreter removed his hat and hung it on his saddlehorn, exposing his newly shorn head to the hot sun. Then he gradually kneed his horse past the others and into the lead, making it look like it was simply the landscape of the trail and the eagerness of his horse that had put him in front of the others.

Tseya Neechee, Navajo Reservation

It was the young Navajo Bitseel who first noticed the three *bela-cani* approaching up the trail. He had been listening silently as his father Tsabekiss and his father's older cousin, a man who was called Bizaadii, idly discussed the *beesh ligai,* the white iron or silver that Tsabekiss and the elderly Hoskaninni had recently been led to find. Of course old Bizaadii, whose name meant "one who spoke with many words," was anxious to know the source of the silver so he could make ornaments for trade the way Hoskaninni was now doing. But by the same token, Hoskaninni, whose name meant "the angry one," would tell his too-talkative cousin nothing of the sort. So old Bizaadii had asked Tsabekiss to come for a visit so he might pry the information from him. But Tsabekiss was wise to such things, Bitseel knew, and had revealed nothing.

To Bitseel the conversation had grown tiresome, and so he had been sitting at ease upon his pony's back while his eyes saw nothing and his mind thought of the card games he would soon be playing with his uncle, Natanii nééz.

Several times a year he and his tall uncle sat at cards for two or three days at a time, and with each occasion Bitseel could feel his skills increasing. Of course, this was the intention of Natanii nééz, who was known far and wide as a great gambler, a man who could make the white man's cards do things that others could not even begin to comprehend. Through the seasons he had been teaching Bitseel those same skills, until now the young Navajo was truly beginning to master the art of the cards.

Natanii nééz was also a great raider, Bitseel knew, and had amassed great wealth through his ability to take horses, livestock, and even women and children from those who were less than prepared to defend themselves. In fact, only once in all his memory could Bitseel recall a raid led by Natanii nééz that had not turned out well for everyone involved. That raid had occurred between one and two years before, when the tall one had led a raid against the mormonee *belacani* who dwelt far to the north of the Kaibab, the mountain lying down.

Though the raid itself had been successful, afterward Taddytin and Zon Kelli had disappeared with all the horses, only to show up later with much gold but no animals, and with nothing they were willing to share with the others. Even worse, returning from that raid, old Hoskaninni had been afflicted in the leg with a *chinde,* a devil, that even an Enemy Way sing had not driven out—

The only good thing that had come from it all, Bitseel now thought, was that his father and old Hoskaninni had been led to find the *beesh ligai,* the white iron that the old man was now learning to beat into ornaments the Mexicans called silver conchos.

And perhaps that wasn't as good as it seemed, for not only were one after another of the *belacani* wandering through the country seeking the white iron and killing themselves and even occasional Navajos in the process, but even many of the *Diné,* mostly relatives, were eager to learn the location of the mine. Of course neither man would reveal it, for that was not their way. Of a truth, Tsabekiss had not even told his own son the way of going. All Bitseel knew was that the silver was somewhere down off Navajo Mountain toward the big river, in a place that was easily overlooked.

Of course, those two *belacani* who had been killed the year before by the *Nóódái,* the Utes, had most certainly found it—

"My father," Bitseel said abruptly as his pony raised its head and began to nicker, "there are three *belacani* down the trail. They *baa nisháah,* they approach us."

Turning his head and seeing the three for the first time, Tsabekiss grew silent as he studied them.

"*Bééhooziih?*" Bizaadii questioned. "Have you come to know these men?"

"*Háí'nsha,*" Tsabekiss replied quietly as the white men rode nearer. "I do not know who they are. But I see no guns in their hands, and so I think perhaps they are the mormonee from across the big river."

"These?" Bizaadii questioned with a sneer. "Natanii nééz has spoken some few things to mc about these mormonee. He tells me they are *gáagii,* crows. He tells me they are cowards, fit for nothing but to be raided by the *Diné.*"

Tsabekiss thought for a moment while the three rode closer. "It is said by others," he finally muttered, "that among these people are those with great power; and some who speak well the tongue of the *Diné.* One of these is called by the name *bináá dootízhi,* blue eyes. It is said that his white hair hangs long and is never in a bun. Some think perhaps he is *yenaldolooshi,* a skinwalker."

Bizaadii laughed outright. "And you believe these things, my cousin?"

Tsabekiss did not smile. "I believe the old ones who gave us these traditions saw some terrible things they could explain in no other way. Who am I to say whether or not they were right?"

Bizaadii blinked, for once not knowing what to say. But then he smiled again and was almost instantly filled with his own assurance. "Come, my cousin," he said with great merriment, "let us see if one of these three wears his hair as you have described. If he does, then perhaps it is time for us to grow worried."

Tseya Neechee, Navajo Reservation

"Do you see?"

Bizaadii, the Navajo of many words, had questioned the three white men and had now turned to face Bitseel and his father. "These *belacani* are indeed mormonee, but not one of them speaks the tongue of the People. And as you also see, none of these three have the long white hair of the one called *bináá dootízhi.*"

147

"What is it that they want in this country?" Tsabekiss questioned, not understanding at all the broken English that had been spoken. "And how does it happen that you speak their tongue?"

"I learned a little of it at the Grove—enough of it to understand at least this old *belacani's* foolish words. They seek horses some of the People have raided from their fort. I told them I had not seen any, and I told them I would ask you and your son if you had seen any. But what is in my mind, cousin, is that the horses these mormonee ride are very fine animals. Yes, and they have fine saddles upon their backs. Since neither of us took the horses they have lost, perhaps it is proper that we should take from them the horses they ride now."

"And how would you do that, my cousin?"

Bizaadii indicated the direction toward the top of the hill with a twitch of his lips. "We will ride with them to where the earth goes flat again. I will talk with them in their tongue and be very friendly, as if we are relatives. They will be expecting nothing, for they will think we are all good friends. Then when we top out I will kill this one, you can kill that one, and Bitseel can kill the third one. Then these fine animals will be ours."

Startled by the audacity of the plan, the youthful Bitseel glanced nervously at the young, bearded man he was to kill, then at the second man, who was also quite young. Finally he looked at the older, balding man who had done all the speaking. But there was no suspicion in any of their eyes, no flinching of muscle or any other sign that they had understood what was being planned. More important, his father had been right; not one of the mormonee was armed.

For an instant, then, Bitseel wondered if his father would agree to this great thing that had been planned by Bizaadii. But then he remembered that the talkative one was the eldest of them all and would thus be deferred to. Besides, this was his country, and a man of the People had great say in what was done in his own country. Thus Bitseel knew that his father would agree.

Moments later they were moving up the trail, traveling together while the talkative one smiled often, waved his hands about, and said many innocent things in the tongue of the *belacani*. Bitseel wondered that a man of the People could learn so much about the strange tongue of these foolish whites, and he also found himself wondering which of the fine animals they rode would belong to him. Each appeared to be a strong horse, but if it fell his lot to be given the horse of the man he was to kill, then he would have the least fine of the three animals. Bitseel also wondered at that, thinking perhaps there might be another way—

They were now near where the ground leveled off, and the youthful warrior found himself tensing, trying to make himself ready for what he was about to do. This was a new thing for him, very new, for in his life he had slain only one other, an old Pahute who had hardly been able to put up a struggle. Now he was about to slay a *belacani*, a white man whom some of the People had agreed to fight and raid no longer. Were he and his father also bound by that treaty? he wondered. Even if they had never gone near *Bosque Redondo?* Of course, these particular *belacani* were only mormonee, cowardly like crows and unfit even to live—

Without warning the old *belacani* who was wearing no hat indicated with hand signs that the chattering Bizaadii was to be still. Too startled to say anything further, Bizaadii obeyed. And then this old man, who supposedly knew nothing of the tongue of the *Diné,* spoke, and his words were in the soft, fluid language of the People.

"You," he said quietly as he fixed Bizaadii with his pale blue eyes, "are a brave man; a very brave man. You are going to kill me, he is going to kill him, and he is going to kill him." And Bitseel was startled to see the *belacani* indicate each of them with a perfectly formed twitch of his lips, exactly as if he were a man of the People. "Then you are going to have our horses," the old one concluded. "Brave men."

Of a truth, Bitseel was as surprised by the change in Bizaadii as he was by the powerful words of the old and balding *belacani.* The talkative one's mouth fell open, his eyes widened in terror, and he yanked his horse about once and then again as he sought in his mind for an explanation. Finding none, he finally steadied himself and then lifted his hands and made the sign of apology.

"Ho, b-brother," he stammered, for truly he had been shamed, though more by himself than by the *belacani,* "I . . . I did not know that your ears were hearing my foolish words. It is in me to say that

. . . that those words should not have been spoken. Your life is safe with me; the lives of these two others are also safe. Yes, and if it is your desire, I will ride with you in search of those lost horses. Such a thing would please me greatly."

From beside Bitseel his father grunted his approval. This that the talkative one had planned had not been a good thing, a wise thing, and the young man could see that Tsabekiss wanted his cousin to understand that he knew it.

And young Bitseel was also breathing more easily, for he had little desire to shed the blood of any man. Instead he had been given the gift of knowing the white man cards, and it was in that way that he intended to do his raiding. Besides, he could see without difficulty that these mormonee were indeed men of great power, men who feared not to ride unarmed into *Diné tah,* the land of the People. Who was he to go against such men and perhaps disrupt the *hózhó,* the balance in his life?

Who, indeed?

Bluff Fort

"I wonder how the boys are doing?"

Billy, who had just finished straining what little milk their cow had given them, looked up. "It's interesting, but I was thinking about those four youngsters myself. Right now I'd guess Bill Ball has delivered to them their herd and they've already started back down Recapture with them. I know all four are early risers."

"Wasn't it something the way Jimmy seemed to naturally gravitate toward the truths of the gospel?" Eliza was busy changing and dressing little Willy, who was having a difficult time waking up. "I wonder why there was such a difference between him and his brother."

"I don't know, but I reckon that's what the prophet Jeremiah meant when he wrote that the Lord would take one of a city and two of a family and bring them to Zion. Not everybody will listen when the Lord calls. The Wilson brothers were a great help, though. I can't tell you how many times I heard Jimmy asking questions, especially of Isadore. That youngster has a real ability to explain things."

Eliza nodded. "The Wilsons are good boys. But there was something about Alfred that I felt a little uncomfortable with—"

"I wondered if you noticed it." Billy's voice was subdued.

"You know what it was?"

"Yeah—the natural man he's getting ready to discover within himself. The way I see it, although they have the gospel, both brothers want to keep at least one foot back in Babylon—the world. They like hanging around with the rougher element of society, they like gambling with face cards, they like—Well, at this point, at least, neither of them is totally converted to the Lord. But they're also very young, and I feel certain that their experiences with the Heatons and the rest of us will one day prove beneficial."

Eliza nodded thoughtfully. "Either that or their downfall." Abruptly she brightened. "It's interesting, though, how quickly the four of them worked their way into my heart. I grew to love those boys, Billy. I truly did. They were always so happy, so willing to work—even at the most grueling of chores. And the way Jimmy took to little Willy—"

"He did, didn't he." Billy smiled. "Did he ever tell you about his Miss Sally?"

Eliza giggled. "Only about thirty times. He's dead set on marrying her this coming fall. And Henry W.'s dead set against it."

"I know. It'll be interesting to see how it all works out. I—"

Billy was interrupted by a soft tapping on the door, and instantly Eliza's face froze with fear. "Do you want me to answer it?" he asked quietly.

For a moment Eliza was silent, her eyes on the empty goatskin bags she had cleaned two days before. But then, with a look of fierce determination, she shook her head. "I want to do it," she breathed as she picked up her son. "Willy and I want to greet her—and see if we can get her to come in." Eliza took a deep breath and then reached for her crutch. "If everybody's right, maybe she . . . she will show me how to feed her milk to our son—"

Then, with her heart in her throat, Eliza limped toward the door.

PART TWO

THE CURSE

11

○─○─○

Tuesday, April 19, 1881

Bluff Fort

"Are you minding the children again today?" It was just turning light, and Billy was pulling on his worn boots so he could do his morning chores before going to work on the ditch. He had already checked the woodpile for snakes and would soon go to the well for a bucket of fresh water for his and Eliza's morning oblations.

"I am." Eliza, still barefoot only because of her husband's assurance that the cabin was safe, was stirring up the coals in the fireplace. "The bishop must be keeping me from hard work, because this is the fifth week in a row I've minded them."

Billy smiled, thinking of how Eliza was being watched over and protected now folks knew she was pregnant again. "He just knows a good thing when he sees it. Any troubles now that you're allowing that Navajo woman into our home?"

Eliza looked up, her expression suddenly hard. "Not exactly. But I'll tell you something interesting, Billy. I absolutely cannot turn my back to her, and I can't leave her alone with the children—even for a moment or so. Oh, she seems peaceful enough, and if pressed I couldn't think of a single reason why I feel the way I do. But if she happens to get behind me while I'm working about the room, or if during the day I must respond to a call of nature, I get the most terrified feeling! Chills go up and down my back, and—well, you know what I'm saying!"

"Do you suppose you're being warned by the Lord?"

155

"Humph! What else could it be?" Leaning down, Eliza began blowing on the hot coals, trying to coax the fire back to life.

"Are you left alone with her much? I mean, I could speak with the bishop—"

Arising now that a small tongue of flame was licking up the side of the log she'd placed in the fireplace, Eliza shook her head. "There's no need for that. The other women regularly check on me, so I feel safe enough. And I must admit, she does have a way with the children. They do seem to respond to her."

"Willy, too?"

"Especially Willy. I don't particularly like that, but on the other hand I don't know what to do about it. After all, she is bringing that goat's milk every morning—"

Billy was now standing at the door, the bucket in his hand. "Is it doing any good?" he asked softly.

"I . . . I can't tell." Eliza was in a chair but leaning over now, awkwardly straining at the buttons on her high-topped shoes with a buttonhook. "The child does seem a little stronger, but for all I know, that's because of your blessing. I . . . I'm willing to put up with that woman a little longer, I suppose, just to give the goat's milk a chance. But I don't trust her, Billy! You can bet I don't!"

"Do you know her name?"

"Not hardly! For all I know, she doesn't even have one. I believe Mary's tried to learn a little about her, but I don't think she's picked up much. And I don't want to know anything!"

Smiling his sympathy and understanding, Billy took his hat off the peg by the door. "Well, at least the other sisters are seeing to it that you aren't left alone with her. While I'm away, though, I reckon you should be extra careful—"

Eliza's face turned white. "You . . . you're leaving again?"

"Tomorrow, first thing." Billy pulled on his shapeless old hat. "Dick Butt, George Ipson, and I have been asked to go cut a couple of wagonloads of logs for the cribs they're building up at the Jump. We plan on getting an early start."

"Billy, can't they send someone else—"

"Hans Bayless and his crew are already out cutting, Eliza. Besides, the three of us are mighty good at cutting and trimming

cedar logs, so we're the best choice Bishop Nielson has. I'll be gone
a week at the most, and everybody in the fort will be keeping an eye
on you and Willy for me. So don't be worried."

"I'm not worried!" Eliza stormed, suddenly upset. "I'm not even
afraid! Oh, Billy darling, I . . . I'm just so gosh-awful tired of your
being gone!"

And Billy, stunned by his wife's anger and even more by her
coarse language, could do nothing but put down his bucket and take
her into his tender embrace.

The Jump

"Kumen, you look troubled."

Nodding at Billy's assessment, Kumen Jones stopped digging
and leaned on his shovel. He, Billy, and several others had spent the
past several days driving logs into the bed of the river to shore up
the bank, then filling in rocks and gravel behind them. When they
were finished, the structure, which they were once again calling the
Jump, would be the new headgate, where the water from the river
would be directed into their five-mile-long ditch. That is, it would
be if the river was high enough, they all joked without humor. Or if it
wasn't flooding. Or if the headgate hadn't washed out again. Or if
the ditch were ever dug out all the way to the Bluff fields. Or if they
could ever figure out how to keep the water from washing out the
sides of the sandy ditch once they got it started. Or if, finally, cows
could fly and every Pahute and Navajo in the country became anxious to sue for peace and accept the gospel of Christ. In short, the
ditch, which was essential to their success as a farming community,
had thus far proven absolutely unworkable, and few had much hope
for its future.

Yet Bishop Nielson's constant reminder that faith without
works was dead kept the majority of Bluff's exhausted citizens at
work on the ditch, the Jump, or in the fields from daylight to dark
six days a week, with time off only for chores or other essential
assignments. And all of them hoped, as they labored on the so-far-
thankless task, that their works and faith would help the Lord see

the desperate straits they were in and temper the wild San Juan for their sakes.

"Troubled?" Kumen asked as he stared off toward the sandstone bluffs that lined the south side of the river, preventing any entrance onto the Navajo Reservation except south of Sand Island. During the winter, both Kumen and Lemuel Redd had been called by Bishop Nielson to work as often as possible with Thales Haskel, learning the Navajo language and doing everything they could to become acquainted with the *Diné* and their ways. But more than half a year had now passed since his calling, and most days Kumen felt that he'd made far too little progress and that his and Mary's efforts with the Navajo were wasted.

"Well, Billy," he finally concluded, "I reckon *troubled* is a good word for what I'm feeling."

"The ditch?"

Kumen grinned. "This grim monster'd be enough to trouble anybody. I'm so tired of digging and redigging it that I want to scream! But no, I reckon this time it's something else."

Billy looked at his friend closely. "Anything I can do to help?"

Kumen, still leaning on his shovel, was looking off toward the south as before, although Billy could tell he was thinking rather than seeing.

"Kumen?"

Without turning, the man shook his head. "Nobody can help," he responded quietly. "I just keep having the feeling that something's going on with one of our Navajo neighbors that hadn't ought to be—something downriver but not all the way to the fort. I think—Billy, which way did Bishop Nielson go?"

"Last I noticed, he was headed back toward the fort."

"Thanks." Kumen scrambled from the ditch. "If I don't find him, you tell him I'll be back as soon as I can."

"Kumen," Hyrum Perkins called as Kumen started to walk away, "I didn't call break, you know! Bishop Nielson put me in charge today, and we've got a pile of work to do!"

"Hy," Billy urged, "let the man go. He'll be back directly—"

"It's okay, Billy." Kumen had turned around and returned. "Sorry, Hy. I forgot the bishop put you in as manager today. Thing is, yesterday my best horse turned up missing, and for the past few minutes I've been having the feeling that it's being taken across the river by a Navajo. Since one of my callings is with the *Diné*, I'd like time off to go deal with that fellow—right now!"

Hyrum Perkins gazed at Kumen, saw that he was serious, and immediately gave his blessing to the endeavor. "If you need help," he called as Kumen once again strode away, "just give a holler."

San Juan River

Still shivering from the cold water, Kumen stood in the willows that lined the south bank of the river and dressed. He had stripped to the buff to cross, but though the water had been chin deep in places, not once had he been forced to swim. Instead he had walked where no ford had ever been discovered, holding his clothes above his head, and so he was quickly ready to begin his search.

Of course, he had no real idea where to look, or even what he would find. For a fact, Kumen was feeling sort of strange, for if anything had ever seemed like a wild goose chase, this certainly did. Yet the feeling within him remained so strong—

Emerging from the willows, he climbed the sandy bank and started toward the towering bluffs, walking slowly and looking for he knew not what. Yet his impression was to move forward, keeping his eyes open and his soul receptive.

Stepping from beneath the spring-green canopy of a huge cottonwood, Kumen was surprised to see a man on a horse—*his missing horse*—about half a mile away. The man was obviously a Navajo, and he was just as obviously headed for the only hairline of a trail through the sandstone cliffs that existed east of Sand Island. Few but Navajos knew of this dangerous trail, but Thales Haskel had pointed it out to both Kumen and Lem Redd some time before, and now Kumen thought he knew why.

Moving steadily, he walked straight to where the trail started upward into the cliffs, and as if by some sort of divine plan he arrived there only minutes before the Navajo, who apparently had not yet seen him. Kumen had seen him before, however, and knew immediately that he was facing the one who called himself Frank but in the Navajo tongue was called Natanii nééz, the tall one.

"I see that you've stolen my horse," Kumen stated bluntly in Navajo, his voice low and quiet just as Thales had taught him. And what surprised him, as he spoke, was that for the first time he somehow knew all the right words—knew them and understood them.

Dumbfounded that this white man would be standing there, accusing him in his own tongue of stealing the very horse he was sitting on, Natanii nééz could do little but admit the truth. But, of course, he could put his own spin upon it, which he was quick to do.

"Yes," he said, at the same time making the sign of acknowledgement, "I have taken this horse from across the big river. My own horse has strayed away, and so *ba ígeeh,* I borrowed this one to go look for it. It will be returned to the big pasture across the river as soon as I find my own mount."

"No," Kumen replied evenly, "that is not what has happened, and you know that the truth is not in you. Natanii nééz, you will not steal my horse. You will get off it now and return it to me."

His mind spinning with this man's knowledge of his true identity, the tall Navajo hurriedly dismounted and handed the reins to the white man. "You know my name," he muttered as he averted his eyes from the much shorter white man, thus hoping to retain at least a little of his power. "I would know how you are called."

"I am called *Daghaa chíí,*" Kumen replied with one of his rare smiles.

"Red Whiskers? Yes, and your woman is called Tam askiiji, the toothless one. I have heard a little concerning you."

Kumen, thinking of Mary's loosely fitting store-bought teeth, which she had worn since even before their marriage, made the sign that it was so. "If you have heard of us, then remember us," he said as he swung onto his horse. "And remember this brand. If this animal or any other animal with this brand turns up missing, I will search you out again. Do you hear my words, Natanii nééz?"

The tall Navajo, still not meeting Kumen's gaze, made the sign of hearing. And then without another word he turned and scrambled afoot up the steep, hidden trail.

Nokaito Bench, Navajo Reservation

Tsabekiss looked across the backs of the vast herd of sheep he was following and *bi 'diilá,* felt worried. Above him two *jeeshóó,* two buzzards, wheeled in wide circles. Tsabekiss knew they were there, yet he kept his eyes from them so they might not become intent upon him. He would rather they simply go away and look for death in other places.

It was late afternoon, and the bleating of the hungry, thirsty sheep, as well as the calling of the new lambs for their mothers and the ewes for their lambs was so continuous in his ears that he no longer even heard. His son Bitseel, however, who was troubled enough by the noise to call it *há hodoonih,* a nuisance, had begun putting small mounds of wool in his ears to stop it. Others with this herd were doing the same. And of a truth, Tsabekiss was forced to admit that the noise was great. But then, what could one expect from more than five thousand sheep and goats that had gone more than a day without water and had stripped the mesa of everything that was edible?

Tsabekiss, who was of the Streams Come Together Clan and born for the Standing Rock People, thought again of his cousin Ganado Mucho, the one to whom all of these sheep belonged. Older than Tsabekiss, that one had always seemed wealthy. Even after the terrible days at *Bosque Redondo* his few sheep had multiplied rapidly, and his wonderful horses—

Turning his mind away from such things, for it was not good that a man should envy another, Tsabekiss thought again of his cousin. Upon the return of the *Diné* from The Grove, the *belacani* government had appointed the great orator Barboncito as head chief of the People. Manuelito had been appointed subchief for the eastern side of the mountains, and Ganado Mucho had been appointed subchief for the western side.

Of course, Ganado Mucho had also been reduced to poverty by Rope Thrower, but each time the People had come together to receive their government allotments, the old man had stood in their midst and urged them not to eat their sheep, warning them that if they did they would always be poor. Now, looking at the vast sea of sheep spread out before him and moving slowly northward toward the big river, Tsabekiss could see that Ganado Mucho had certainly heeded his own words.

And Tsabekiss had tried to do the same. Only there had been on the mountain above his *hogan* the evil *nóódái*—filthy, lazy Pahutes who had stolen from him so many animals—sheep and horses alike—that Tsabekiss had never been able to get ahead. Reduced to starvation, he and his family had been forced, from time to time, to eat their sheep and to trade their horses, so that now he continued to exist almost in poverty while his cousin and many others had grown wealthy.

And that was why he was where he was, caring for the sheep of his cousin rather than his own. Of course, a man would help out a relative no matter the circumstances, and Tsabekiss was happy he and his son could do what little they could for Ganado Mucho. Only it had been such a dry season, and the herd of sheep was so large that helping his cousin was proving more difficult than Tsabekiss had imagined. Now they had been directed to move the sheep toward the grass-covered hills on the north side of the big river, and that was what made Tsabekiss so *ntsinishtláád,* so apprehensive.

For a moment he halted his pony, looking northward. The grass there was good—he knew that. And the sheep could easily satisfy their thirst at the river for many weeks to come. But the first of his worries was that the land across the big river was the true home of the hated *nóódái,* and one could never tell where they were or what evil they next intended.

Tsabekiss thought then of the sing he and his family had held more than a year before, the Enemy Way ceremony where his son Bitseel had been the scalp shooter. Held to drive the evil *nóódái* away from their land forever, Tsabekiss was certain the ceremony was proving effective. He was losing fewer animals, and there were long periods of time when he could find no sign whatever of the hated Pahutes. But by taking his wealthy cousin's sheep onto their lands, he reasoned, the ceremony might lose its power, and the *nóódái* might rise up in greater anger than ever. If not a thing to be feared, it was certainly a thing to be considered.

But there was also that other, larger issue—

"My father, a man of the *Diné* comes toward us."

Blinking in surprise that his son had ridden so near without his knowledge, Tsabekiss looked in the direction Bitseel was indicating. "Natanii nééz," he said, wondering as he spoke that the tall one, who was also his cousin, was afoot.

"His countenance is not good," Bitseel said a moment later as the man started through the herd of sheep.

Tsabekiss noted the same thing and wondered at it. The tall Navajo was the favorite uncle of his son, and for many years he had been teaching Bitseel the way of gambling with cards, as well as the proper way of raiding. Bitseel honored and respected him in all things, and for him to even see the anger on the face of Natanii nééz, let alone to speak of it, meant there was truly a lack of balance in his cousin's life.

"Ho, cousin!" the tall one called as he impatiently pushed the sheep out of his way. "I have great need of a horse."

"Yes, we see that you are afoot."

"I can return the horse within one day—at the most, two. When I return I will have another horse with it. Thus the one who is inconvenienced will be paid well for his trouble."

"Uncle, my horse is your horse!" Instantly Bitseel was off his animal and holding his reins toward his tall relative. "But there is no need for another horse when you return it."

At that Natanii nééz smiled—thinly. "For you, my nephew, the second horse will be a prize mount of the mormonee. That is my word."

Instantly warning bells rang in the mind of Tsabekiss, and he had no difficulty seeing the same alarm in the eyes of his son. "Is that who raided your mount from you? The mormonee?"

With great irritation the tall Navajo made the sign that it was so.

"And did he use our tongue as if he were a man of the People?" Tsabekiss pressed.

Again Natanii nééz made the sign of agreement.

"Yes," Tsabekiss said as the great herd of sheep continued to surge around him, "some days ago we also ran into that one. He hears our words, he speaks them as well as us, and it is said that he also speaks words of great power."

"I know nothing of that!" the tall one growled. "I know only that this *Daghaa chíí* will lose his horse again before this night has ended—"

"Red Whiskers?" Tsabekiss asked in surprise.

"Yes, that is how he is called; he told me so himself. The whiskers on his face are red!"

"He . . . is an old man?"

Natanii nééz was growing more irritated by the moment. "No, he is young. Very young. Now, I must be riding—"

"But the man we encountered," Tsabekiss was saying, exactly as if he hadn't heard his cousin at all, "was not young. He was old, and he wore no whiskers. More, his white hair on top of his head had been shorn as if he were a sheep—as if he had no dignity!"

"What is that to me?" Natanii nééz asked irritably.

"He was mormonee, this Red Whiskers?"

"Yes, that is so."

Now Tsabekiss looked stricken. "Then . . . there is more than one," he said, speaking only to himself. "Either that, or—"

"Bah!" Natanii nééz growled as he yanked the reins of Bitseel's fine horse from his hands, "I have no time for this! The mormonee mocked me, and it will not happen again! I ride!"

In silence the two watched the tall one ride away. Then without a word Tsabekiss held out his hand, and Bitseel pulled himself up onto the horse behind his father.

"That one is a great raider," Bitseel ventured, his thoughts following his rapidly disappearing uncle.

"It is so."

"He is unmatched with the white man's cards."

"That is also true."

For long moments Tsabekiss and his son stared silently into the distance, the sea of long-haired sheep unheeded. Both knew that for more than one full cycle of the seasons Natanii nééz had been telling his relatives, all who would listen, that the *belacani* mormonee had come into the country to be raided, and that their wealth was destined to be the wealth of the *Diné*.

What was not so well known among the tall one's relatives, both Tsabekiss and his son now understood, was that some among those mormonee were men with great power, men who would surely lose their patience with the raiding before much longer. Why, the *Diné* had only to recall the fate of Peokon, who had withered and died like a stalk of grass after a long, hot summer. It was being said by some that his death—as well as the deaths of his woman and children and all his livestock—had been the work of a mormonee witch or even *yenaldolooshi,* a skinwalker who could change forms from man to animal and perhaps even from one sort of man to another.

"My father," Bitseel said as Tsabekiss reined his horse around and nudged it toward the far edge of the vast herd of sheep, "is it in your mind that the old mormonee without hair might be the same as this young, red-whiskered one?"

"Those are indeed my thoughts."

Bitseel's mind was racing. "*Yenaldolooshi,*" he breathed. "I . . . did not believe these creatures were real."

"And I did not know they were among the *belacani* mormonee, my son."

"Ahhh." Now Bitseel was looking into the distance without seeing. "Do you think there might be more than just one mormonee with this power?"

Tsabekiss didn't answer, but his mind was following the same, twisted path as that of his son. Was it possible that every one of those strange and seemingly peaceful people was so terrifyingly powerful? And if it turned out that all had such power, would it not be better to keep the sheep on the south side of the river and thus avoid them altogether?

To Tsabekiss the answer was obvious. And that was why, as he and Bitseel helped drive his cousin's slow-moving sheep northward toward the big river, he was growing more and more apprehensive.

12

Wednesday, April 20, 1881

San Juan River

For Natanii nééz the perilous trail up through the sandstone cliffs was of little consequence. He had used it for raiding more times, almost, than he could count, in daylight as well as in darkness, and so he gave it little thought as the horse of Bitseel carried him upward.

To the east the dawn-star glowed brightly above the blackness of the bluffs, indicating that dawn was still a little more than an hour away, and the tall Navajo nodded his head with satisfaction. It had been a good raid, he thought smugly, very good. He had crossed the river just at darkness, ridden to the mormonee fort, entered by stealth into the corral inside the fort after all the mormonee had slept, and without difficulty located the horse belonging to the mormonee *Daghaa chíí*—Red Whiskers. Of course, there had also been other animals in the corral, but Natanii nééz had left them alone, preferring instead to raid just this one horse. By so doing he could save the other horses for other raids and at the same time notify *Daghaa chíí* that his threats were of no consequence. In this manner he would show the foolish mormonee firmly that he, Natanii nééz, could not be stopped or frightened away and that his raids would continue.

Now he was back on the south side of the river with the raided horse in tow, nearly at the top of the hairline trail, and he was already thinking of how proud his nephew would be, not only to have his own horse returned but also to receive the horse of the foolish mormonee as a gift. Yes! It would be a fine gift, with—

Suddenly a stone rolled beneath the outside rear hoof of the borrowed mount being ridden by Natanii nééz. With a squeal the terrified horse bunched its muscles and then lunged. More stones rolled or gave way, and before the tall Navajo raider could do little more than register alarm, he was airborne, falling outward and down into the darkness while the terrified horse still squealed and struggled between his legs.

For what seemed a long time Natanii nééz fell, and then with a terrible sound that tore a scream from his own lips, both he and the horse of Bitseel slammed into a mound of detritus, bounced, and then rolled downward. The snapping sound of bones breaking now joined the screams. The odor of blood and raw flesh assailed the Navajo's nostrils, and just before his mind went dark the tall one saw the form of another animal—the one he had raided from the mormonee called *Daghaa chíí*—as it leaped over him and disappeared into the darkness, galloping hard but unhurt toward the mormonee fort on the big river!

Dolores Valley, Colorado

Though it was hardly past the crack of dawn, Jimmy Heaton had already eaten a good breakfast and was in the saddle, helping the Wilson brothers cut their fifty cattle out of his father's herd. They had traveled a good way together, the four of them, down Recapture from the LC headquarters, where they had picked up their own five hundred head, along the San Juan to Mitchell's Trading Post at McElmo Bend and then northeastward along McElmo Creek, skirting the north side of Sleeping Ute Mountain and finally going into pasture just outside the small community of Dolores, Colorado. It had been a good drive, too. The cattle had already been trained to the trail, there was plenty of water, they had seen no Indians, and since they had followed what folks were starting to call the Mormon road, most nights they had had good company.

As he swung his rope and cut a three-year-old steer with the Wilsons' ear crops out of the herd, Jimmy grinned at that. Henry W. might not like Mormons, but try as he might, he sure hadn't been able to get very far away from them. And he was finally admitting to

Jimmy that they seemed like regular folks—decent, honest, and hardworking. That had been true of the folks at the Bluff fort, it had been true of the Mormons who had stopped at their fire, and it was especially true of Alfred and Isadore Wilson, whom Jimmy had grown quite close to. By day they had trailed the herd in a general northeasterly direction, the Wilsons as willing to ride drag as he or Henry W., and by night the four had played cards, sung together, told stories, and listened to their generally Mormon visitors discuss their fascinating religion.

Jimmy never tired of such discussions, and Isadore seemed as willing to listen as him. For some reason, though, Alfred didn't appear to be as interested, or involved. And of course Henry W. said nothing but rolled into his bedroll or stared at the ground while religion was being discussed.

Except for two nights previous, Jimmy thought with another grin. That night a Mormon fellow by the name of Platte Lyman had stopped with them, and instead of them fixing the meal he had done so—some of the best Dutch oven cooking Jimmy had ever eaten. Brother Lyman and the two men with him, one of whom was his brother Jody, were on their way back to the fort with supplies they had purchased in Durango. Jimmy knew how the folks in Bluff needed those supplies, and it was amazing how excited he felt when he saw what they would be receiving.

Anyway, Platte had begun talking that night, telling the story of how Joseph Smith had translated the Book of Mormon from golden plates. The man had such a way with words, and was so animated in his speech, that Alfred and even Henry W. had listened as intently as he and Isadore. Platte had also described the visit of Jesus Christ to America after his resurrection and had shared two or three old Indian legends about a pale god that Jimmy knew were proof positive that the Book of Mormon was telling the truth. Of course, Henry W. had argued with the man about those legends and even the Mormon belief, but his arguments had weakened against Platte Lyman's reason and logic, and he had finally grown quiet.

Still, Jimmy thought smugly, the conversation had sobered his older brother, and the next day he hadn't made one wisecrack about Jimmy learning some of the Mormon songs Isadore was teaching him, or reading little bits out of the Book of Mormon the Wilson brothers' father had sent along for his sons to study. In fact, he hadn't even made any wisecracks about Miss Sally, though of a truth Jimmy himself hadn't mentioned her so often of late. He didn't know why, either, unless it was that his mind was so busy trying to remember everything Billy and Isadore and now Platte Lyman had been telling him. It was almost as if—

"Jimmy! Yo, Jimmy!"

Turning in his saddle, Jimmy smiled in response to the hat-waving Isadore, who had obviously been trying to get his attention for some time.

"Alf and I both count fifty, Jimmy. We've got 'em all!"

"Already?" Jimmy asked as he reined around and nudged his new horse out of the herd.

"Doesn't take you and that new cutting hoss long to cut out fifty head. I'd say Bill Ball did you a favor when he traded horses with you."

Jimmy nodded his agreement. His new gelding was a fine animal, one of those rare horses that seem born with cow-sense, that know exactly what to do when working with cattle. Even better, the horse had bottom and could go all day without appearing tired. Of course, Bill Ball had told him those things when he had made the trade, but most men weren't so honest, and so Jimmy had been pleasantly surprised.

"You fellers think you can handle five hundred head alone?"

"Listen, Ise," Jimmy growled, "me'n Henry W. have been punching cows since afore we was even weaned. The fellers we all ought to be worried about are named Wilson."

Isadore laughed. "That's no joke! Jimmy, you want to borrow that book from us? Alf and me'd be happy to lend it to you, or even give it to you if you want. Pa gives 'em away himself from time to time. Fact is, he even gave one to Matt Warner, the outlaw who's been hanging out with the McCartys. Told him it was to remind him he was baptized and confirmed as Willard Christiansen, and that he ought to remember who he was."

"Did it do any good?"

Isadore shook his head. "Not so far. Matt was with that stolen herd a few weeks ago. I reckon the Book of Mormon doesn't do much good unless a feller's willing to read it and pray about it."

Jimmy grimaced. "I ain't much on praying, Ise. Ain't hardly done it since I was knee-high to a short grasshopper."

"Then now's a good time to start, Jimmy." Isadore smiled brightly. "The Lord's still there, you know, and would probably like to hear from you."

"But . . . I don't know all them fancy thees and thous Billy and Platte Lyman and the others use."

"I ain't learned 'em proper myself," Isadore admitted. "Way I figure it, if the Lord's my friend then I can talk to him plain old regular—least I can until I've learned a better way. I don't always kneel down, either. Fact is, some of my best prayers have been said sitting in my saddle instead of on my knees, and the prayingest prayer I ever prayed was once when an old nag threw me and I was caught by one spur in her stirrup and was bouncing along through the rocks and the brush and the cactus thinking certain I was being kilt. But the Lord sure-enough heard me, because I'd no sooner'n said amen when my foot popped loose and I was fine."

Jimmy laughed as he imagined the scene in his mind. "I bet it was the shortest prayer you ever prayed, too."

Isadore chuckled. "Yep, it was. You keep the book, Jimmy, do what I've told you with it, and we'll call 'er square. Then one day when you're ready you can come to Moab, and Pa can baptize you in the river there."

"I don't know about getting dunked," Jimmy replied, abruptly serious. "I would like to come visit, though. Ma calls me a fiddle-footed young whippersnapper, and I reckon she's right."

"Great! Then come. We'd love to have you stay."

"Then watch out," Jimmy smiled again, "on account of it might be sooner than you think. Like Billy said that first night we was together, it takes two to have a good religious discussion, and maybe that's what I need. Do you suppose Billy's little boy's getting better?"

"Of course. That's what he was promised in that blessing."

"Yeah," Jimmy smiled, "I think that, too. Reckon I'll write him and Eliza when I get back to Rico—see how they all are. You can bet

I'm fixing to tell Miss Sally about you Mormon folks, too. I'll bet she doesn't know a lick more than I did."

The two young men grew silent, and a moment later they were joined by their older brothers.

"You boys know which way to go?"

Alfred nodded. "I reckon so, Henry W. Follow the Dolores left on up to Disappointment Valley. West from there we'll come to Three Step Hill and Lisbon Valley, and I reckon we can find our way home from there."

Henry W. grinned. "It's a ways, Alf, but you'll have good water most of the time, and fifty head ain't enough to give folks grief happen you cross their land."

"I hope not!" Isadore declared. "You're heading east from here?"

"Well, more northeast than east. We'll catch the river where she swings up into the mountains, and that'll lead us straight on to Rico and home. I reckon we'll beat you fellers by a week."

"I reckon." Alfred smiled. "Well, boys, it's been grand. Ise and me have appreciated the company."

"Likewise," Henry W. stated solemnly. "So adios, and we'll see you again when we do."

Quietly the brothers shook hands all around, and then they pulled apart, all of them feeling a reluctance to say good-bye for the last time. "So long," Jimmy finally called as he and Henry W. pushed their horses back to their own herd. His hat was off, and now he was waving it in the air. "Thanks, Ise, for that gift! It'll be used plenty, you can bet!"

Isadore, now waving his own hat in the air, found himself blinking back sudden, unaccountable tears. "Give Miss Sally a big old smooch for me!" he shouted as joyfully as he was able. "And remember, Jimmy, we'll be a'waiting for you in Moab—"

Bluff Fort

A slight breeze was blowing through the open door and window of Eliza's cabin, moving the air a little and giving at least an illusion of coolness to the stifling afternoon. Wiping her face and then blowing upward to cool her skin a bit more, Eliza tucked a long strand of hair above her ear and back into her bun, blinked her eyes against the sweat that trickled through her eyebrows, and then finished ironing the last of Billy's shirts. Thank goodness, she was thinking, that she had taken off those cursed high-buttoned shoes a little earlier. At least her feet and legs were cool, and on a day such as this she felt thankful for any sort of comfort.

Sighing with relief that she could now let the fire die out, she placed the still-hot iron on the mantel above the open fireplace where it would cool out of the reach of the toddlers, noting almost unconsciously the woodpile that was now obviously devoid of those terrible bullsnakes. Then she turned to look at the half-dozen children who were either asleep or playing quietly with the Navajo woman on the bed.

For a moment she felt irritation, not because the Navajo woman was actually helping a little but because once again she had chosen to remain with Eliza once her goat's milk had been delivered. Glory be! Didn't she have a home of her own? Eliza wondered. Or responsibilities, for pity's sake? Couldn't she sense that she wasn't wanted? Or that her presence wasn't disconcerting only to Eliza, who could never for a moment turn her back completely to her, but also to the other sisters of the fort, who regularly had to drop their own work to come check on Eliza and the little ones? It was all terribly bothersome, and for Eliza at least, extremely stressful. She did not like this woman, did not trust her, and for every moment that she remained in the cabin, either standing silently against the wall or sitting on the edge of the bed doing something or other with the little ones, Eliza's heart was growing harder toward her.

Yes, she faithfully brought the goat's milk early every morning. And yes, that same goat's milk seemed to be having a propitious effect on little Willy, giving him more strength and energy than he had shown in months. But that didn't stop her from being Navajo, Eliza reminded herself. It didn't stop her from being a born raider— a threat not just to Eliza and the children but also to the safety and survival of the entire mission.

Why, the woman never smiled! Day after day her expression remained passive, as though she were wearing a mask and simply waiting to reveal the evil of her true sentiments. Stranger yet, despite

Eliza's occasional chatter, the woman had never attempted to repeat one word of English. Of course, Eliza hadn't tried any Navajo, either. But that was different, for the sounds of the Navajo words were so strange, so foreign, that it would be impossible for Eliza to repeat them accurately. And finally, day after day, the woman's long clothing and ornate jewelry appeared to be the same; her hair was always done in the double bun apparently favored by the Navajos of both sexes; and though Eliza had never seen any evidence of it, there was no way on earth that the woman could be anything but dirty! Why, she had to be, living in a mud hut of the sort Kumen had described as the homes of all the Navajo, and having no washing facilities anywhere nearby that he had ever been able to see.

In short, Eliza could find nothing good about the woman whatsoever, and having her there in the cabin was becoming a trial that was greater, almost, than Eliza felt she could bear!

"Here, Willy," she urged as she set her crutch aside and leaned over, "come see Mamma and give the nice lady a rest."

The boy, a happy smile on his face, glanced at his mother but then returned to the small sticks the Navajo woman was teaching him to play with.

"Willy, come to your mother!"

For a moment the child wavered. But then, seeing Eliza's outstretched arms, he scooted his feet off the bed and dropped to the canvas floor.

Bending even lower to receive her son into her arms, Eliza suddenly saw movement beneath the bed. As the huge, mottle-colored form of a snake coiled itself in the shadow directly behind where little Willy would be walking, Eliza's heart felt as though it were about to stop. Another bullsnake! This could not be happening to her again! It couldn't! Not when—

Willy had now started forward, and the snake was hissing just as the other one had. Abruptly Eliza took hold of herself. Lem Redd had said the bite of a bullsnake was harmless, but she was not about to let the horrid creature hurt her son! Better her, she thought as she lunged forward and scooped Willy off the floor and into her arms. Better the stupid snake bite her own bare foot—

Suddenly Eliza was knocked violently backward by the Navajo

woman, who had leaped to her feet to make the push. Still clutching little Willy, Eliza stumbled backward toward the table, trying desperately to keep her balance and not drop her son. Yet her eyes somehow remained on the small Navajo woman, and she knew the expected attack from this dark-eyed enemy had finally come.

Only—

"*Tłíish bichóhí!*" the woman breathed as she looked downward, not paying any attention to Eliza at all. "*Tłíish bichóhí!*"

In that same instant the huge snake struck from beneath the bed, burying its fangs in the side of one of the ankle-high, wrap-around moccasins worn by the Navajo woman. Eliza saw this, saw her execute a quick spin so that the snake's body was swung from beneath the bed, saw the five inches of rattles at the end of the snake's tail that were still buzzing, and then wonder of all wonders, she saw the woman reach quickly down and grab hold of the massive reptile directly behind its wide, flat head.

Seconds later, even as Eliza was still catching her balance against the table and trying to support her clinging son, the Navajo woman had lifted the snake and was holding its head out before her, the creature's mouth wide and venom still dripping from its long, white fangs.

"*Tłíish bichóhí,*" she said again as the snake writhed and twisted, a full third of its long, wide body still on the floor. "*Jóge'énee'dáá.*"

"She says it's a rattlesnake." Mary Jones said quietly from the doorway, where she had appeared without notice or fanfare. "She wants you to see for yourself that it is so."

"I . . . I see—" Eliza's eyes were wide, and she was nodding furiously. She would have been backing even farther away if the table hadn't blocked her way.

Apparently satisfied, the Navajo woman turned and, still holding the snake's head before her, moved out the door and past the woman who was beginning to understand her tongue.

"Is . . . is she killing it?" Eliza breathed fearfully.

"Actually, no," Mary replied as she watched the woman's departure with interest. "She's walking toward the gate, so I think she intends to set it loose. That was a big snake, Eliza! Come and see how much of it is dragging in the dirt! I'll bet it's five, maybe six feet long!"

"I . . . saw already—"

Finally Mary stepped into the room. "Where was it? Under the bed?"

Numbly Eliza nodded.

"What did she do? Pin it down with your crutch, like Lem did with those bullsnakes?"

"It . . . it . . . Oh, Mary!" Eliza's voice was unnaturally shrill and high, yet she couldn't control it. And neither could she control her still-pounding heart. "It was about to strike at Willy, and I . . . I thought it was another bullsnake. Better me than him, I thought, so I stepped in front of it and lifted Willy. But then she pushed me out of the way, and it struck her on her ankle! I . . . I don't know if the fangs went through her moccasin—"

Without another word Mary grabbed a knife, turned, and ran out the door and after the woman. And Eliza, suddenly shaking, sank weakly into the nearest chair. That woman, her mind was now shouting at her, had saved her life! That Navajo woman, whom she had esteemed as her enemy, had placed herself in grave danger to save her life—

Casa del Echo Mesa

Natanii nééz had no idea what day it was or how long he had lain unconscious at the bottom of the detritus slope. All he knew was that when his mind had come back he had been in terrible pain, and in the hours since, that had not changed.

He was thinking, as he stumbled forward through the rocks and brush of Casa del Echo Mesa, that he had no real idea of what had happened. He could remember making the successful raid on the mormonee fort, and he could remember starting up the hidden trail with the stolen horse. After that—nothing! Yet the fine animal that had belonged to his nephew Bitseel was dead—broken and twisted in a terrible manner where it lay in the rocks. That could only have happened if it had fallen from the trail; yes, and fallen with him on its back.

But even that assumption made the tall Navajo wonder. For if he had truly been on the horse, how had he managed to survive the fate that had befallen the animal? As far as he knew, he had no broken bones; no, nor had he sustained even a single injury that was serious. Oh, he was indeed a mass of bruises, and there were a couple of places where his skin had been scraped raw. But other than that he was intact, and in fact the longer he walked, the better he began to feel. It was almost as if he could not be killed—could not even be seriously hurt!

Straightening a little, Natanii nééz managed a thin smile. Not far ahead was the valley and spring where he kept his herd of fine horses. He would go there, clean himself up at the spring, and then choose two of the better animals and ride a third to the *hogan* of his cousin Tsabekiss. It was a pity that the horse belonging to Bitseel had died, and it was a greater pity that the other horse he had raided from the mormonee called Red Whiskers had somehow escaped. But in a few days he would simply make another raid for that animal, and meanwhile the youth Bitseel would be more than happy to have two horses instead of one.

Yes, and perhaps he would be willing to engage in a little gambling with the white man's cards. After all, Natanii nééz thought as his smile grew even wider, there was nothing like a little gambling to take a man's mind off his troubles—

Bluff Fort

"Well, brethren." Kumen Jones looked around at the men Bishop Nielson had assembled in emergency session and then assigned him to address. "For your information, we found no more rattlesnakes in the fort, Eliza Foreman seems to be doing well enough despite her scare, and the Navajo woman has already departed for her home."

"I heard she was bitten."

"Mary says she was, though probably her moccasin saved her at least a little. Maggie says there is a little swelling, but she thinks Mary got the biggest share of the venom out, and the woman should be fine."

"Quite a thing, a Navajo saving Eliza's life like that."

Kumen nodded. "Yes it is. Goes to show, brethren, that not all our Lamanite neighbors are enemies. That's important to keep in mind, especially since this latest invasion may be the most serious threat we've had to deal with thus far. Five thousand Navajo sheep are now foraging between here and Comb Ridge, stripping the earth of virtually every sprig of green and leaving nothing for our livestock this coming winter."

"Five thousand? I didn't know there were that many sheep on the whole reservation!"

"Well, there are," Samuel Rowley declared emphatically. "Five thousand, give or take a few, in this single herd. Lem and I saw 'em crossing the river last night just afore dark, and this morning the herders were spreading them out across the hills."

"I counted 'em, too," Lemuel Redd asserted. "The count's right. There are also eight herders, including old Tsabekiss and his son Bitseel, though from what little I could understand, none of them claims ownership of the sheep."

"Do you have any idea whose they are?"

Lem shook his head emphatically.

"Is it just me, brethren," Charlie Walton asked, "or do the rest of you also have the notion that old Scratch is truly pouring the coals to our fire?"

"It isn't just you, Charlie. Everybody's noticing it, the women included. Fact is, since the warm weather set in, I can hardly think of another thing that could go wrong with this sorry settlement of ours."

"Or be stolen."

"Or attacked."

"Or bit."

"Or dried up and blown away."

"Day after day after everlasting day! It never lets up!"

"That's a purdee fact!" Lem Redd concluded. "So, if any of you boys happen to think of something that *hasn't* gone wrong, besides that the Pahutes seem to have left for the summer, for the love of Hannah McRay don't mention it. I don't want the devil getting any more ideas than he already has."

There was a general chuckle around the room, not out of humor so much as out of commiseration for each other's continuing difficulties. There were also a couple of jabs as to the possible identity of one Hannah McRay, which Lemuel Redd parried without difficulty.

"Well, brethren," Kumen said when the room had grown quiet again, "let's get back to the sheep. If they don't get back across the river, and soon, we'll be left with no winter pasture for our stock. And without winter pasture, well, you all know we'll be in a world of trouble. Any ideas?"

"I suppose if we rode together we could drive the sheep back across the river." David Stevens looked around. "I mean, the Navajo reservation doesn't extend to this side of the river, does it?"

"It does not," Kumen stated emphatically.

"What about the herders?" Charlie Walton asked quietly. "If we drive the sheep back, will we end up in a battle with them?"

"Ya, goot question, Charlie. Ve are missionaries, brudders, und haffing battles vith de Indians iss no vay to do missionary vork. Besides, ve must remember dat Sister Foreman's life vas saved today by a Navajo voman!"

"The bishop's right!" Kumen looked around. "Any ideas that might be a tad more peaceful?"

"What about if we send a delegation to the Indian agent, asking for help?"

"Anybody know who it is? You, Thales?"

"Fellow by the name of Eastman," Thales Haskel replied from his seat near the door. "He's headquartered at Fort Wingate, though he might also be at Manuelito, on the new railroad."

"That's a long ride. Might we get help from anyone else?"

Thales was thoughtful. "Well, *Naakai Saani,* or Old Mexican, Lorenzo Hubbell, runs a trading post that's some closer. He exercises a little influence over the *Diné.* Then there's Thomas Keam down at Keam's Canyon. He was a temporary agent five or six years ago and runs a trading post now. I reckon he knows the ropes as well as Hubbell, but a lot of the Navajo don't trust him much on account of he's always out poking around for white iron and other treasures that they think ought to belong to them. I agree."

"White iron?"

"Yeah, *beesh ligai*—silver. Anyhow, Eastman and the two trading posts are all a good three day's ride from here, and that's if everything goes right."

"That's six days, going and coming. Considering that you only recently returned from the reservation, would you be willing to undertake another such expedition, Brother Haskel?"

"I'm willing if that's what you brethren think is best. I'm here to support your mission, you know."

Kumen looked at the older man. "Do you have any other suggestions, Thales?"

"Not hardly. Fact is, it might be good to get the U.S. government involved—let them know their poor Navajo wards of the state up on this end of the reservation are pretty much ignoring their famous treaty. Oh, by-the-by, I reckon you'll discover that all them sheep belong to one of their big headmen, a fellow by the name of Ganado Mucho or Many Cattle. His herds have become massive, and word is that he's frantic to find more graze for 'em."

Kumen nodded. "I understand his problem. How many men do you need, Thales?"

"A couple. Maybe you and Lem, since the both of you missed the last little journey. I'll be across the river and on my way before first light, though, so tell whoever you ask to get ready tonight, afore they even think of bed."

Kumen nodded his understanding. "Keep your eyes peeled for that Natanii nééz, Thales. That little scrape with him yesterday convinced me he's up to no good. I'm still wondering if my horse being loose outside the corral this morning had anything to do with him."

"It might have, all right, though I can't imagine him turning it loose a'purpose. Someone brought me word last night that the tall fellow's got more than a hundred head of horses stashed somewhere in a secret little valley, more than half of 'em being ours. Worse, though, is the fact that he's been going around to all his relatives, telling them that us Mormons are the easiest raiding he's ever had."

"Somebody coming through the reservation learned all that?" Kumen could not keep the astonishment from his voice.

"No," Thales said quietly as he stood to leave. "Somebody who lives there—one of the Tall One's cousins. Navajo folks call him Bizaadii, which means 'one who uses many words.' It fits."

"Wait a minute. Isn't he the old fellow you said was going to kill you just last week?"

Thales smiled shyly. "Seems he's had a change of heart. He needed it, that's sure. He also told me about the sheep belonging to Ganado Mucho, if you want to know. Claims he's a relative, too. And by-the-by, Kumen, you tell Mary she did a fine thing for that Navajo sister today, cutting and patching up that snakebite the way she done. If we ever survive and bring this peace mission to a successful conclusion, it'll be done through that self-same milk of human kindness."

13

Friday, April 22, 1881

The Jump

"Top of the morning, boys!"

"Well, if it ain't old Platte DeAlton Lyman himself." Hanson Bayless squatted back on his heels, grinning. "Fellers, our fearless but missing leader has returned."

Quickly the other men stopped their work and gathered together. "How're things in Colorado?" Samuel Mackelprang asked.

"If you mean, 'Is there still work on the railroad?' And 'Are they still paying cash money?' Sam, the answers are yes and sometimes. If you want to know is it worthwhile going out there to do it, I'd have to say not anymore—not now that you boys look to have tamed this fool river."

"Humph," Lemuel Redd grunted. "We'll see how tame she is once the water starts to rising. If it ever does, that is."

"It'll hold, Lem," Joshua Stevens declared positively while others nodded their agreement. "Nothing can move these cribs."

"We'd better hope so," Platte declared as he surveyed the work the men had been doing. "This last flood seems to have torn things apart worse than the big one a year ago. Now if we get another flood in June—"

"If we do and these cribs don't hold," Charlie Walton said, "then I reckon we'll have to admit we've been licked."

"A man isn't licked until he says he is," Platte stated

emphatically as he reached down, picked up a small rock, and tossed it into one of the cribs.

"Ya, und dat be de trute," Bishop Jens Nielson chimed in. "Vith a little sticky-to-ity und de Lord's help, Charlie, ve can do everting ve haff been called to do."

Some of the men merely smiled at the bishop's eternal optimism and his use of his favorite phrase, but a few actually muttered about it—a little. However, no one said anything out loud, at least not to the old Danishman's face.

"So, how many cribs have you brethren built?" Platte was now walking out across the small cribs, which had been placed end to end as they had been extended into the river.

"About thirty so far. We figure it'll take about a hundred and ten to do it up right." Lemuel Redd had fallen into step beside Platte. "As you can see, none of them are very big, about the size of a small cabin. But we think Billy's design is a good one—"

"Billy Foreman?"

"That's right. He came up with the idea of using upright logs for the outside corners and then driving the bottom ends into the mud once the wall logs are notched and fit into the corners. That way they don't float apart, and the rock fill pushing out only makes things tighter. He says the Kirtland Temple was built inside exterior upright supports, and that's where he got his idea."

"Interesting. As I remember, he's right. What's to keep the logs from lifting up off the rocks once the water rises?"

"Each crib has two cross-logs low down, so the rocks are piled on top of them. If anything lifts off, it'll be because the whole shooting match has been torn to pieces. Now we just have to pray that the river doesn't get that mean."

"Amen to that. I haven't seen Billy this morning. Is he around?"

Lemuel Redd shook his head. "Not for the past few days. He's off in the Butler with Dick Butt and George Ipson, cutting cedar logs for the rest of these cribs."

"That's too bad. I had a message for him from a young feller name of Jimmy Heaton."

"You met the Heatons? Were they with the Wilson brothers?"

Platte grinned. "All four were together, along with about five hundred or so head of cattle. They said Billy had brought them to Bluff, but I didn't realize they had met all of you."

"They did, and they spent two full days working on this fool ditch, which was a great help to us. They're all good boys, but that Jimmy—well, he's a delight. In a way he reminds me of a young Billy, the way he sort of shines all the time. I'm mighty glad to hear they're all safe."

"Jimmy told me that Eliza had kept Billy in the dark about little Willy's poor health."

"That's about right." Lem explained Eliza's decision to keep Billy uninformed so he wouldn't worry.

"Doggone women," Platte replied when Lem had finished. "I never will figure them out. Happen I start to feeling poorly, first thing I want to do is tell my wives. Only decent way a man can get any sympathy. And I can't hardly imagine not being told my own son is feeling poorly and maybe even dying. That'd rile me up something fierce."

Lem grinned. "It would me, too. But Billy? Mary Jones told me he didn't even get upset. That's what I meant about that kid Jimmy Heaton. He seemed as hard to rile as Billy, and he was forever smiling. Wish my disposition was a little more like that."

"Well, it takes all kinds to make a world, Lem. Even us, thank goodness. So, what else is going on here?"

"David Stevens is in charge of gathering rocks, and he and the other young bucks have been hauling up a storm. We can hardly keep ahead of them."

"More than a hundred cribs, huh?" Platte looked at the rocky jetty the men were building into the river. It didn't run across the current as he had imagined but rather left the bank, curved, and was running upstream almost parallel to it. When the rest of the cribs were built and in place, the jetty would return to the bank far upstream, leaving a huge settling pond from which clearer water would flow into their newly dug ditch. In high water the cribs would act as a dike, turning the floods away, and in low water the upper cribs could be knocked out and moved into and maybe even all the way across the current, thus damming the river and turning even the low water into the ditch.

"As far as I'm concerned," Platte said with approval, "this ought to do it. Who's ramrodding this crew?"

Lemuel Redd grinned. "I'm the county tax assessor, Platte, and today these boys are all working off their tax assessments. I reckon that makes me the boss today."

"Good." Platte grinned. "You can put me and my brothers to work this afternoon. How are our friendly neighborhood ranchers doing with their assessments?"

"Mostly they're current. Spud Hudson did a lot of groaning and moaning about our blankety-blank white man's civilization that was worse than the Pahutes, robbing a man legally so's he couldn't do anything about it. Still, he paid in full with a hundred head of beef. Rumor is, though, he's been trying to sell his spread ever since.

"Both Mr. Peters and Bill Ball, who was representing Mrs. Lacy and the LC spread, paid with cash money. That's what we used to buy some of the supplies we've been freighting out of Colorado."

"Speaking of which," Platte said as they walked together back to the riverbank, "we brought in two wagonloads of flour, some molasses, six weiner pigs, and a whole slew of odds and ends— things I thought we might need."

"Figuring on setting up a cooperative store?"

Platte nodded. "I've been thinking on it. Maybe I'll bring it up next council meeting. I haven't seen any of the Pahutes around. They off in the hills again?"

"I reckon, other than the boy called Henry."

"Henry? I don't recollect him."

"You know. Old Baldy's son. Seems he had a little powwow with Thales Haskel the other day. Thales said they made some good medicine together, and he figures Henry wants to be our friend. If he does, he's about the only one. Much as I don't like the stealing most of them seem so prone to, I believe I'd rather have them in my sight than out of it."

"So would I. Fact is, I wrote the Brethren in Salt Lake City the other day telling them it felt like we were being crucified between two thieves, Pahute and Navajo, and if the stealing continued our people would be sucked dry by it and be forced to leave."

"It'll be interesting to see how they respond."

Platte nodded. "It will. Thales Haskel told me Elder Snow had given him authority to pronounce gloom and destruction upon all the Indians of either tribe who won't respond to the commandments of God. From what I hear, the Navajo hoodlum Peokon was wiped out by the hand of God, and maybe a few more will have to suffer the same fate before they'll learn. I hope it happens soon, because we may be facing a regular invasion."

"What do you mean?"

"There's been talk over in Mancos that the white folks in Colorado are figuring to drive the southern Utes off their reservation—send them into this country."

Lemuel Redd shook his head. "That'd be all we'd need."

"Oh, we could probably deal with it, should it ever happen. Not all the Utes are like our friendly local renegades. What worries me is how even the peaceful ones will react when they get word of what the white folks are figuring on doing to them. Was it me, I'd not take such a notion too kindly."

"Good point. Reckon we'd best keep our ears open and our eyes peeled."

"I think so." Platte scratched his chin through his beard. "Any trouble lately from the Navajos or white desperados?"

"With the desperados, probably." Lem Redd frowned. "With the Navajos, it's a virtual certainty. Kumen caught that tall fellow who calls himself Frank with one of his horses the other day, and last night Thales told us the man has personally stolen more than fifty of our animals. Apparently across the river he's a big cheese of some sort, and he's influencing all he can to join him in his raids.

"Worse, though, is that five thousand head of Navajo sheep were driven across the river a few days ago and are now stripping the hills out west of us. Come fall when our own animals need that graze, it'll create some serious problems."

Soberly Platte nodded his agreement. "Anything being done about it?"

"We had a meeting on Wednesday, and it was decided to send Thales and a couple of others onto the reservation to search out the Indian agent and ask for help. I reckon we'll know in a week or so how he responds."

"I reckon so."

"On the other hand, that Navajo woman who's bringing goat's milk for little Willy Foreman hasn't missed a day. Two days ago she stepped in front of a rattler in Eliza's cabin and took the bite rather than let Eliza get bit."

"Is she okay?"

"Seems to be. Mary Jones cut the wound and sucked out the poison, and Maggie Haskel wrapped it good. She was back yesterday with more goat's milk, and again this morning. I'd say we have at least one friend south of the river, anyway."

"I'd have to agree." Platte fitted his hat back onto his head. "Well, Lem, Jody and I will be back once we get the wagons unloaded, to see if maybe we can work off a little of that terrible assessment you've levied against us. Maybe Walter'll join us, too." And with another smile, as though there had been humor in everything he'd learned, Platte Lyman turned and walked away.

Jackrabbit Canyon

Natanii nééz grunted with surprise and pleasure. For a day and a night he had been playing card games with his nephew, Bitseel, and for a day and a night the tall one had been victorious. Of course, such a thing was to be expected, for he was much older than the young man and much wiser in the ways of these white man's cards. Thus it had been for several cycles of the seasons, the uncle and the nephew getting together several times a year and playing cards for two days at a time, and the uncle always winning.

And he had come to the *hogan* of Tsabekiss this time, the tall Navajo thought grimly, for expressly that purpose! Winning was good for a man, particularly if his life had grown hard for one reason or another, or if some other little thing had not gone quite as planned. Because his body still ached from his terrible fall, and because his mind still burned with humiliation brought about by the red-bearded mormonee, he had needed a new chance at winning. And so he had, through all the hours of the afternoon and night before, hand after hand and game after game, until Natanii nééz had felt the power of his *hózhó* returning.

However, when Natanii nééz played cards with his nephew Bitseel, things were not quite the same as when he played cards with anyone else. Though they gambled for cartridges, silver coins, and anything else that came to hand, the tall Navajo was never endeavoring to win, and never did he keep his winnings. In fact, for many seasons he had been endeavoring to teach the young man the way of face cards just as he had taught him the way of raiding the *belacani* mormonee and stealing their horses, imparting of his vast knowledge so that Bitseel might profit just the way he had always done.

It wasn't that Natanii nééz was teaching Bitseel card tricks, for that was not so. Bitseel already knew his way with a deck of cards, and his fingers were even more nimble than the tall Navajo's. He could cut and shuffle and cut again with greater speed and ease than anyone else Natanii nééz had ever known, placing or removing single cards from the deck with such dexterity that even the tall Navajo had trouble seeing what the young man was doing. Of greater importance, though, was Bitseel's memory. Though undetectable, his counting was swift and accurate, and he never seemed to forget where a card was or to whom it had been dealt. More important, he could recall the rank of the discards, and in two hands he could build up a bottom stock that no one even suspected was there and available. Because of this he was becoming very skilled in the fine art of gambling with the white man's cards, and he would soon be able to take his place across the blanket from anyone.

But this most recent skill—the art of losing intentionally and then looking for all the world like the losses were devastating—that was an art that took gambling to its highest form. It was also what Natanii nééz had been focusing on for the past two years, training his nephew in the subtle but all-important art of deception. And it was the manifestation of this great skill that had so pleased him.

They had been playing for several hours, building up a large pot in the center of the blanket, and as usual Natanii nééz had been winning. Or so he had thought. He had even been feeling sorry for Bitseel, wondering what he might do that would give the young man a few more victories. And Bitseel had indeed appeared troubled, though he was doing his obvious best to keep his face impassive.

Then Bitseel had dealt the tall Navajo his best hand of the day, though from the young man's expression his own hand must have hardly even been average. Yet he had drawn two cards that seemed to improve his spirits, while Natanii nééz had drawn one that had given him an almost perfect hand. Deciding to see just how far he could push his nephew, the tall Navajo had then put all his winnings into the pot. For an instant Bitseel had looked pained. But then with a slight smile he had covered the bet with his two best horses—two that had been taken from the foolish people in the fort across the big river. Then he had called.

Hoping the young man wouldn't be too devastated, Natanii nééz had spread his cards on the blanket and waited for Bitseel to toss his cards and concede defeat. Instead the young man had spread his own cards, showing a perfect hand instead of Frank's almost perfect one, and easily winning the pot. And it was only then that the tall Navajo had realized that Bitseel had been setting him up from the start, doing to him the very things he had been taught to do, and doing them so well that Natanii nééz, the master, had been fooled.

"*Ho!*" he exclaimed with pride as he watched Bitseel draw the pot across the blanket toward himself, "*táá 'n deeshnal,* my nephew, you are able to do it!"

"It was a good game," Bitseel smiled modestly. "Fortunately, my uncle, you did not notice the little things I was doing that caused you to lose."

Rising to his feet and stretching, Natanii nééz stepped around the cooking fire in the center of the *atch í'deezáhi,* the forked stick *hogan* of his cousin Tsabekiss, and seated himself beside the older man. Reaching out, he accepted food from Tsabekiss's wife, and for a few moments he ate in contented silence. It had been some time since he had been to his own *hogan,* and suddenly he was feeling a need to return, to be with his own woman, Hádapa. But he had been so *baa naanish biilhé,* so busy, conducting raids against the weak people the Pahutes called mormonee, teaching Bitseel and a few other young men of his "born to" and "born for" clans the fine art of gambling, and caring for his own rapidly growing herd of fine horses, that of late he had given little time to her.

Of course, he thought grimly, the barren fool was never there when he returned anyway. Instead she was with her sheep and her goats—or riding here and there on her old burro. Weeks before, he had given her orders to begin raiding again, taking what she could from the mormonee across the big river. In that way, he had told the woman, her power might return so that she might bear him a son.

Of course, he himself had not believed that and so had been merely taunting her with the thought, the idea. After all, any woman who had been unable to give the great Natanii nééz a son—or for that matter any children at all—deserved nothing more than contempt.

Still, there were times when a man needed a woman, and so he would see her immediately after he had paid a visit to the *hogan* of his cousin Jim Joe and his two young sons, who had not yet been told of the fine opportunities for raiding that the Mormons were presenting. Yes, he would return to his *hogan* after that, and he and Hádapa would make another great effort to bless the world with a son—

Bluff Fort

"Thank you for all your help, Lula." Eliza smiled from her rocker, where she was feeding little Willy what was left of the Navajo woman's daily delivery of goat's milk. "That's a wonderful fan you made in your demonstration, as fine a work as anything I ever did."

Lula Redd beamed. "Eliza, that ain't . . . I mean, isn't so, and you know it. But thank you. Little Evy Lyman's sure picking this weaving up quick, don't you think?"

"I do. She and—"

"Did I hear someone mention my daughter?"

"Pla . . . I mean, President Lyman!" Eliza exclaimed as she hastily pulled herself to her feet, "I didn't see you standing at the door."

Removing his hat, Platte Lyman stepped inside. "I've only just got here, Eliza. More weaving classes?"

"Yes. Lula's been helping me with the class and clean-up afterward, and we were just saying how well little Evy is doing. But Maggie Mackelprang is also catching on. Alice Louise Rowley,

Caroline Nielson, and Katie Perkins are doing well, and of course Leona Walton is a master weaver just like Lula."

Platte smiled down at Lula Redd. "Well, you women are doing a fine work—both of you. With summer coming on, I suspect we'll need all the fans we can get our hands on.

"It's coming on dark, Lula. Would you mind if I walked you home?"

"Lawsy, Brother Lyman, it's only a few cabins over!"

"True enough. But when I saw you through the open door, I remembered that I needed to see your father." Platte turned with Lula toward the door, then stopped. "Oh, Eliza," he said with some embarrassment, "I spent a night recently with the Wilson boys and the Heatons. They asked that I give you and Billy their love, and to tell you that they're getting along first rate. They . . . well, they were also anxious about your son."

Eliza smiled happily. "He's doing much better, President Lyman. A Navajo woman from across the river has been bringing him goat's milk every morning for the past couple of weeks. Willy thinks it's just the ticket for whatever it is that's been ailing him, and I'm starting to feel the same."

"Good. I'm pleased to hear it." Slowly Platte stroked his beard. "Navajo woman, huh? You and she do much talking?"

"Not hardly. Oh, she talks and I talk, but I don't think either of us has any idea what the other is saying. At least I don't. She . . . uh . . . she saved my life day before yesterday."

"I heard about that. A rattlesnake, wasn't it?"

Eliza nodded. "A huge one! Hádapa was bit, but—"

"Hádapa?"

"Apparently that's her name. Mary found it out yesterday." Eliza smiled brightly. "It has a pretty sound, don't you think?"

"I do."

"Anyway, she has some fearful discoloration on her leg, but this morning she wasn't even limping." Looking sheepish, Eliza continued. "I . . . I had a hard time with her at first, President Lyman. I've not been a very good missionary, I suppose. But I'm starting to believe that she truly loves Willy, and of a truth she's a real help with the other children I've been tending."

"Interesting. It's good to know we have one or two friends across the river. Well, Lula, I reckon we'd best be on our way—" Abruptly Platte stopped. "Eliza, when will Billy be home from the Butler Wash country?"

"I hope by Sunday."

Again Platte smiled. "I hope so too. Seems like you've had some hard times when Billy's been called to leave you alone, and I don't imagine expecting another baby makes it any better. Annie Maude says that, anyway."

"I expect she's right." Eliza was startled that she had been a subject of conversation between her stake president and his wife.

"Besides," Platte declared awkwardly, "there can't be much joy in being alone."

"There isn't. Annie and I have commiserated on that very subject from time to time."

A shadow briefly crossing his face, Platte Lyman dropped his gaze and nodded his understanding. Surely, Eliza thought with surprise, there was sorrow in this man's heart, as well—

14

Sunday, April 24, 1881

Moab Settlement

Isadore Wilson awakened abruptly, bathed in a cold sweat. He was frightened, for he had awakened in the middle of a terribly unsettling dream.

Pulling back his bedding, he swung his feet to the floor of the loft where he and Alfred slept, at least when they were home. For a moment he remained still, listening to his brother's soft snoring, getting his balance, and trying to think. Then he stood and moved quietly to the window.

Off to the southeast, beyond the stock corrals and the line of cottonwoods that marked the course of Mill Creek, the looming bulk of the LaSal Mountains thrust upward into the dawn. Ruggedly steep, the LaSals were a sanctuary for all things wild—man as well as animal. Yet the lower mesas to the north and west of Grandview Mountain, Mount Waas, and Haystack Mountain—the foothills, actually—provided wonderful pasturage for the settlement's livestock, and within the past two years Isadore's father and the others had assigned themselves specific allotments or acreages where they could run their cattle and horses. The Wilson range, as his family called it, extended from upper Castle Valley southward and included the upper drainages of both Placer and Castle Creeks, Pinhook Draw, Harpole and Adobe Mesas, and as much of the steep slopes of Grandview Mountain as they wished to use. It was a fine range, a wonderful range, and Isadore was never so happy as when he was riding it with the family dog, Spot, trotting along at his side.

Now, though, as he looked at the mountains where he was spending so much time, Isadore was not thinking of the range at all. Instead he was thinking of his unsettling dream, trying to remember it, and wondering what in the world it might mean. For he was sure it had a meaning. It had to have one. After all, this was the third time he had dreamed it since his return with the LC cattle more than a week before.

Thing was, Isadore could never remember exactly what the dream was about. He knew he was with Alf up on the range, and he knew there were others around—possibly the McCarty brothers and maybe somebody else. They weren't exactly there with him and Alf, he didn't think, and yet they were. It was very confusing.

Then the dream changed—not so much the location as the people. He and Alf were still on the range, but the McCartys or whoever they were, were gone—replaced somehow by hideous, fierce beings who were coming after him and his brother with terrible anger.

And that was all.

Three times now he had dreamed it, and three times he had awakened at the height of danger—cold, clammy, and frightened to death of he knew not what.

Staring out the small window, Isadore wondered if he should tell someone about it. Probably, he concluded, but who? Not Alfred, he thought grimly. His brother would only laugh and then make fun of him the next time the McCartys happened to drop by. Then there were his folks, good people who would try to understand. But Isadore felt funny about telling them, for by all rights he was now full grown, and telling his parents about his nightmares seemed more the action of a child.

It would be nice, he thought with a wry smile, if he could go back to Bluff and talk with Billy and Eliza Foreman or Kumen Jones or maybe even crippled old Bishop Nielson. All of them thought of him as an adult and would surely treat him that way. Or even, he thought, it would be good to talk to Jimmy Heaton! Jimmy would listen to him, all right, and would never make fun. Maybe he wasn't Mormon, but he was a fine fellow and a good thinker, and something between him and Isadore had really clicked. Almost instantly they had been good friends, and Isadore felt certain their paths would cross again.

Too bad it couldn't be today, he thought as he turned back into the room to dress for chores. Wouldn't it be something if Jimmy came riding into Moab just in time to attend Sunday meetings with Isadore and his family. Now that, he thought, would make it a memorable Sabbath day—

Bluff Fort

It was dark in the cabin, little Willy was asleep, and Eliza sat in her rocker, thinking deeply. The busy sounds of evening had nearly come to an end, and Eliza knew that most in the fort would soon be retiring for the night. Occasionally a cow still lowed, a barking dog would set off the others until every dog in the fort would be carrying on over hopefully nothing, and now and then someone's soft laughter would seep through the log walls.

It was this time of day when she missed Billy the most, Eliza thought as a deep sadness seemed to grip her soul. She missed talking to him, laughing with him, listening to him do his best to answer all the fool questions that seemed to plague her. But most of all she missed *him*—the feeling of him being near, his wonderful spirit, and yes, even the security of his presence. Billy was such a peaceable man, and yet he seemed to be afraid of nothing and troubled by little more. In his mind things were always on the verge of getting better, God was never out of his place in the heavens, and there was nothing but joy to be found in this desolate San Juan country they had been called to settle. In other words, Billy was a faithful optimist, and oh how Eliza envied him that gift—

Suddenly she felt a slight movement within her womb, the first she had felt with this child, and instantly she froze. Seconds later the movement was repeated, and now Eliza knew that another life had been placed in her hands—God was sending another child to join Billy, herself, and little Willy.

"Dear God," she breathed as tears of joy started from her eyes, "thank you for once again allowing me to experience this miracle—"

Outside, the dogs went through another round of barking, Eliza thought for an instant of the possibility of an Indian attack, and then she realized that somehow she was not afraid. Instead, her mind—her whole soul, in fact—was filled with rejoicing over this little child who would soon be cuddled in her anxious arms.

"Dear Father in heaven," she breathed in further prayer as she blew out the rag wick and climbed onto her bed to avoid the possibility of snakes, "thank you for this child. From both Billy and me, thank you so very much. I know it doesn't really matter what the child is, but I would dearly love a little daughter—"

Once her prayers were completed, Eliza crawled under the quilt, closed her eyes, and lay silent, her soul awash with the joy of once again preparing to give birth. "Oh, my darling Dilly," she finally pleaded softly as new tears began trickling down her cheeks, "won't you please hurry home to me? I need you, especially at times like this. Oh, glory! I am so terribly tired of being alone!"

The Shining Mountains, Colorado

The Pahute known as Old Chee sat contentedly only a foot or so from the fire, his head down and his hands busy. He did not mind the warmth, and for all he cared, the dozen moths that fluttered about his face might as well not even have existed. He simply concentrated on the task at hand, an obsidian flake that was rapidly taking shape as an expertly crafted arrowhead.

Off in the darkness he could hear children screeching as they chased each other in their war games, and he grunted with the pleasure of knowing they were getting better at stalking and surprising. So it had been with his own two sons until one or two seasons past, when they had somehow turned from boys into men. Or at least, he thought with another grunt, they thought of themselves as men. And in some ways, he admitted candidly, they were. Posey was fierce in battle and filled with a lust for spilling blood such as Old Chee had never seen. He was also quick and impulsive and made many mistakes. Scotty, the larger but younger of his sons, while not fierce in battle, was more quiet and steady, always seeking for the hidden meaning in things. He was a listener, not a talker like his older brother, but he was willing to follow the older Posey anywhere.

From behind him *o-num-buds* the badger scurried past not a dozen feet away, his clawed feet leaving a peculiar track on the sand. Chee paid no attention, not even stopping his careful work to kill the badger for the dinner pot. At the moment there was plenty, and he was not at war with the creature.

The point in his hand now finished, Chee laid it aside and selected another flake from the block of black obsidian his youngest wife carried always with her. She was a fine wife, Chee thought as he adjusted the flake in the leather pad that curled between the palm and fingers of his left hand. Her temperament was good, she had lots of energy, she was pleasing to look upon, and she was very obedient. Truly he had been fortunate to win her in that game of *ducki* so many seasons before.

Holding the flake between his fingers and palm, the leather protecting him from the sharp shards that he knew were coming, Chee pressed the narrow, whitened tip of a deer antler against the outer edge. Instantly a small shard chipped away from the underside of the flake. Working quickly, he pressed the antler tip time after time against the flake, so that in just a few moments one side of the flake began to take on the sharpened, serrated edge of an arrowhead.

Turning the flake over, he repeated the process on the other side until the general form of an arrowhead had taken shape. Then he flipped the point and began the more exacting work of shaping its other side to match the side he had already chipped. Within a quarter of an hour he was finished, and carefully he held it up for inspection.

"*Pan-now-nup,*" he muttered with satisfaction. "A fine arrow point." Perhaps, he thought, Mike would trade him this point and a few others for one of the two hats he had stolen from the white men who caught with a lasso the long horns of their cattle. Of course, Mike no longer had much use for the bow and arrows that Old Chee preferred. Instead he carried always a big gun—a rifle he had also stolen from the white man. He had stolen other big guns in seasons past, and one of them was now the constant companion of his son Posey, who had become a fine shot and was always anxious to prove himself before others. It was—

"*One-e,*" Mike suddenly said from behind him, startling Chee badly and at the same time reaffirming the knowledge that the warrior who led him was in all ways superior to him. "I do not understand what is troubling that one you call Posey."

Forgetting all about his desire for a white man's hat, Old Chee placed his points and blank flakes in the small bag with his leather pad and antler tip. Then he turned to face the warrior who was leader of Old Chee's band of renegade Utes.

"What has my son done?" he asked quietly.

Carefully Mike lowered himself to the earth, choosing a spot where the smoke from the fire was not blowing. "He no longer finds joy in the ways of a young warrior," he finally responded.

Surprised, Chee did not know how to respond. For more than a week now, Mike's band of *pah* or water Utes had joined in celebration with many others of their people—Utes who dwelt in many parts of the Shining Mountains and beyond. There had been war dances, horse races, much *ducki* or card playing, and much discussing of the best way to live in the midst of the white men who were rapidly filling the country.

Many were for peace, taking the lead of the warrior Ouray and accepting reservation land as their permanent home. But others, such as himself, Mike, and old Norgwinup and his four sons, were for war. To them the whites were enemies who must be put under the grass or driven from the Shining Mountains, and until that was accomplished they would retire to no reservation but would instead continue to hide themselves in the secret places near the San Juan River that were now their home.

Old Chee knew these things, and he also knew that Posey was an ardent supporter of the way of war. Fierce in every competition, he spoke constantly of his desire to shed the blood of the whites, particularly those mormonee in the new fort on the big river. Old Chee did not know where this hatred had come from, but it pleased him greatly, and he did nothing to discourage it.

"I do not see where he has no joy," Chee finally responded. "Did he not win many of the races, and this despite the fact that he was among the youngest of the warriors? And was not his shooting of the *aukage,* the old rifle you gave him, more true than the shooting of almost everyone else? And is he not growing more than skilled in *ducki?*"

"Those things are true enough," Mike admitted. "Posey will indeed make a fine warrior."

"And did those victories not give him joy?"

"They did," Mike again admitted. "But only for a few moments. And this is the thing that is troubling to me. Moments ago I passed by your son, and he was sitting in silence on that big rock yonder, staring off toward the camp of old Norgwinup and his warrior sons. Your other son was also there, but he was busy with his hands, just as you are busy. Not so with Posey. He merely stares, and there is no movement about him—no joy.

"I have seen him thus many times these past few days, and it troubles me. He does not join in the celebration dances around the fires at night; he does not join in the war games with the other young men during the day. Instead he remains on that rock, his face troubled."

Chee made the sign that he understood. "It is the girl," he declared, "the *nan-zitch* called Too-rah. She is the youngest daughter of the old man Norgwinup. Posey thinks much of her, but her older brothers cause him to fear, and so he does nothing but watch."

"Posey fears the sons of old Norgwinup?" Mike asked in surprise.

Sadly Old Chee made the sign that it was so. "They are fierce warriors," he said by way of defending his son. "Especially Poke, who for good reason is called the grizzly. He watches Too-rah as if he were a hawk and she a mouse, and he allows her to draw near none of the young men of the People. It is said that he intends to sell her for a great sum of money, and because she is comely and very skilled about the fire, it may well be true."

Big-mouth Mike was still trying to understand. "Last night there was a bear dance," he grunted, referring to the getting-acquainted ceremony that was the only time during the year when the People countenanced promiscuity. "If he has such great thoughts for the girl, why did he not get her under the robe last night?"

"It was told me by my son Scotty that she did not attend the dance. Poke would not allow it."

"And why does not Posey fight this Poke and take the girl for himself?"

"He is still very young," Chee admitted sadly, "and in this one thing only his heart is small with fear. He has not spoken to me of this, but I see it in his eyes, and I sorrow over it."

"As well you should." Mike was silent for some moments, deep in thought. Finally he pushed himself off the earth and rose to his feet. "It is said by some that a few whites have many horses in a place near the reservation. If this is so, then I will call together a big raid, and I will see to it that both Poke and Posey are among the warriors I will take with me. Not only will this show Ouray and those who follow his foolish way of peace that raiding is still the best way for our people, but Poke will no doubt see Posey's fearlessness in battle, and perhaps his heart will be softened toward him. *Oo-ah,* yes, and then perhaps we will see again the joy that once filled the countenance of your warrior son."

And without another word, he of the big mouth strode off into the darkness.

15

Bluff Fields

"Don't look now, Eliza, but that looks a lot like your husband coming up the road yonder."

Pulling herself up by her crutch and adjusting her bonnet to better shade her eyes against the afternoon sun, Eliza looked to where Jane Walton was pointing. Billy had been gone nearly a week, and the days and nights were getting terribly long for the lonely woman. Now, as she spied the six wagonloads of logs being pulled tandem behind the three assortments of teams, her heart began to beat more urgently.

At Eliza's request, Mary Jones had joined the Navajo woman Hádapa in watching the babies and small children, leaving Eliza free for at least one day to join with the other women in doing a little physical labor—replanting the community's fields. The hard clay had been plowed and harrowed in with the sand, furrows had been dug at approximately thirty-inch intervals, and now the precious seed corn was being hand-planted—for the second time that season—to make certain none was wasted. Then all that would be needed was to bring the water through their heretofore impossible ditch—

"It iss dem!" Kirsten Nielson exclaimed from the other side of Eliza, where she had also risen to her feet. "Gootness, but dis vill excite my Yulie. De poor soul's been pining for Dick Butt until I tought she vould vaste avay."

"Those two need to get married," Jane Walton stated without much sympathy.

"Und dey vill, Yulie tinks dis fall ven ve can make de trip back to St. George. But until den, may de Lord haff mercy on us all, und give us de patience to endure her lonely sorrows."

"Well, thank the Lord they won't have to go back through that awful Hole-in-the-Rock country!"

"That's right." Anna Decker continued to work while she talked, punching holes in the lumpy ground in preparation for the seed. "Colonel Critchlow did say Charlie Hall and his sons have moved to a better crossing."

"It's this side of the Hole, isn't it?" Eliza asked, remembering the railroad man named Critchlow who had come through Bluff from Colorado the winter before, looking for a route to take the Denver and Rio Grande through to St. George. Of course, no such route could be made through that terrible country, as Critchlow had finally discovered. But for a time there had been hope for less isolation.

"Miles and miles this side," Eliza Redd said as she joined the group watching the slow approach of the wagons. "And tons faster and easier. Lem told me Platte found the new crossing when he was out looking for livestock, and when he went back to the settlements to get his family, he told Charlie Hall what he'd found. Lem says that right away Charlie went exploring, and by late last fall the Hole-in-the-Rock crossing was already abandoned."

"Ya," Kirsten grumbled, "und to tink he's called it Hall's Crossing instead off Platte's Crossing or even Lyman's Crossing, for gootness sake. To me it's disgusting!"

"Oh, I don't think Brother Hall named it after himself," young Parthenia Hyde said softly from where she was still on her knees with a handful of corn kernels, following Anna Decker. "Folks have just started calling it that on account of he's the one owns the ferry and runs it. That's how we came out this past winter, if you recollect, and folks back in the settlements were already calling it Hall's Crossing or Hall's Ferry."

Parthenia, or Feenie, as she was called, got no argument, which made Eliza smile. To Eliza's way of thinking, Feenie was a real sweetheart, a fine young woman who had and would yet make a true contribution to the San Juan mission. She had been teaching school most of the past winter in the log meetinghouse, and she had done such an outstanding job of helping the children learn ciphering and numbers that now hardly any of the parents would even think of arguing with her about anything. After all, she was the teacher!

While Feenie had stayed in Bluff to teach, her folks had continued on to Montezuma Creek, where they felt their chances for a successful farm were better. And they were probably right, Eliza thought as she considered the dry, weed-infested land they were calling the Bluff fields, where as yet nothing of any substance had been raised for the hungry settlement.

Of course, this was still fairly early in the new season, and if the brethren could get the cribs in place in the river and the ditch rebuilt before the scorching sun burned everything up, then perhaps this second planting would have a fighting chance. But if they didn't—

"Speaking of heading out for St. George and the temple, Feenie," Harriet Ann Barton said, interrupting Eliza's thoughts, "things between you and my brother-in-law seem to be looking mighty promising."

Having the good graces to blush, Feenie smiled and nodded. "They do, don't they," she responded coyly as she busied herself with her planting.

"Well, Amasa Barton's a fine young man," Jane Walton declared with a laugh. "It's too bad Harriet Ann's Joseph dragged him off to Colorado to work on the railroad all winter. Had he been here, Feenie, your romance might have moved along a little faster."

"And we'd have had a whole lot less schooling done, too," Eliza Redd quipped, bringing forth a chuckle of good humor from them all.

"By the way, Eliza," Anna Decker asked, "how did you talk Mary into staying with the children today? She tells me she's frightened to death with not knowing how to care for them."

"It's a shame that she hasn't been able to have children of her own," Harriet Ann Barton declared before Eliza could respond.

"Und it isn't as iff dey haffn't been trying," Kirsten added tenderly. "Mary iss a fine young voman, und I yust don't understand vy de Lord is trying her und Kumen so fiercely."

"It troubles her a great deal," Eliza agreed, "for she yearns deeply to hold and love a child of her own. That's part of why she agreed to trade places with me today. It gives her a short time, at least, to fulfill her mothering instincts. Besides that, she wanted to work on her Navajo with Hádapa, who is already starting to pick up a little English."

"You set store by that Navajo woman, don't you."

"Wouldn't you, if she'd risked her life to save yours?"

"Maybe, if she did it a'purpose. But she's still Navajo!"

Eliza smiled at the rather accusatory comment. "And I'm still a Latter-day Saint. Billy once told me that when an elephant walks through town, all the dogs bark. But once the noise is over, the elephant is still an elephant, and the dogs are still dogs."

"What's that supposed to mean?"

"It means that if Hádapa is being deceptive or is planning on hurting Willy or me, in the long run it won't matter. Despite all that she or anyone else can do, I'll still be me, Willy will still be my son, and we'll be just fine. And meanwhile, if those awful things are true, she will only diminish herself by her efforts.

"Of a truth, though," and now Eliza smiled again, "I don't believe Hádapa has anything more in mind than to bless and help Willy and me. Of course, I admit that I was dragged to that viewpoint kicking and screaming, for I had as much mistrust as anyone here, and probably more. But I know that Hádapa is singlehandedly saving Willy's life with her daily delivery of goat's milk, and there is no way on this earth I'll ever be able to thank her sufficiently."

"Have you learned much about her?" Anna Decker was definitely curious.

"Hardly anything, Anna. Oh, we talk back and forth now and then, but I understand no Navajo and she understands English only a little better. Yet we're starting to communicate, and I've learned to love and trust that woman completely."

"Quite a turnaround for you, isn't it?" This was the woman who had been so accusatory of Eliza. "Frankly, I'm amazed."

"Ya," Kirsten Nielson quickly agreed, placing her arm around Eliza and drawing her close, "it iss amazing but not surprising. Venever God changes a person's heart, it iss alvays amazing and surprising to dose who are not expecting it or who haff not prayed for it to happen. Because I know how much Eliza hass prayed for dat change to come, I am not surprised at all dat it did."

Carefully the bishop's wife looked around the group. "Vone day, sisters, ve vill all learn to love dose people yust as Eliza hass done vith Hádapa. Ya, ve vill learn dat it iss a gift dat comes only through prayer, for such love iss called charity or de pure love of Christ. Und ven ve obtain from God dat pure love for de Navajo, den iss de day ven dey vill learn to love us in return, und de enmity between our peoples vill cease forever."

In silence the women considered Kirsten Nielson's remarks, and at that moment Billy, who was driving the lead two wagons, saw Eliza. Standing on the dashboard he waved his hat, eagerly she returned the wave, and without so much as a by-your-leave from any of the others, Eliza started across the fields toward her husband.

Navajo Reservation

"What do we do next, Thales?"

Riding beside his traveling companions Amasa Barton and Benjamin Perkins, Thales Haskel wondered how to respond. They had ridden all the way to Fort Wingate and beyond, and he felt more than troubled. They had met the government agent at the fort, and the agent had even ridden with them back across the mountains to meet with Ganado Mucho, the owner of the five thousand head of sheep that were now decimating the entire range west of Bluff—the range the settlers had planned on using for their winter graze.

One of the original Peace Talkers after the People had been taken to *Bosque Redondo,* Ganado Mucho had nevertheless been more than resistant to the suggestion that he remove his sheep from the hills to the north of the big river. He wanted to have peace with the *belacani,* of course. Those words had been big in his mouth. But even peace should not be purchased at so great a price. Besides, the *Diné* were not raiding the mormonee, which was what the peace treaty had addressed. They were only herding their sheep, doing their poor best to eke out a living in the desolate country the *belacani* government had declared to be theirs.

Of course, Thales had argued that the reservation was bordered by the big river, and that land to the north of it belonged to the settlers. But Ganado Mucho was disdainful of such claims, and in the end the agent had done nothing but shrug his shoulders.

"I'm sorry, Mr. Haskel," he had said as they had ridden away from the smug Navajo headman, "but my hands are tied. I can threaten him a little more, but he knows my threats will be hollow. Technically he hasn't broken the treaty we made with the Navajo at Fort Sumner, and so the government won't allow me to withhold his allotment—the only sort of power I hold over him."

"He's raiding," Thales had argued. "Off the reservation, too. He's raiding our grass and destroying our means of sustaining ourselves in that country."

The agent had agreed, but only in terms of the argument being technically correct. In practical terms, he could do nothing about it. And so now—

"Tell the truth, boys," Thales finally answered, "I have no idea what we'll do for graze. But the Lord does, and I reckon in the end he'll take care of us. He always has before, I know that."

Bluff Fields

"Howdy again, hon-bun." Billy Foreman smiled with delight as he looked up from the bottom of the wide ditch he had been working on since shortly after his return. Then, still gazing at his wife and one-year-old son, he pushed the blade of his shovel into the sandy soil, adjusted it, and leaned with his arms folded across the end of the handle. "And howdy to you, too, Willy, my boy. Did your ma bring you all the way out here just to see your papa?"

"Papa," the child replied as he clung to Eliza's skirts and pointed with one little finger at Billy. "Papa, papa."

"Would you listen to that," Billy chuckled proudly. "Hardly more'n a year old, and he's talking plain as day. And look how handsome he is, too. Mercy sakes, hon-bun! He keeps this up much longer, and he'll be most as handsome as his mother is purty."

"Hush your mouth, Billy Foreman! You don't know but what folks up and down this ditch are listening to every word you say."

His smile only growing wider the more she tried to look stern, Billy gazed up at his precious Eliza. To him she was so beautiful it never stopped being a source of wonder. And the fact that she had actually married a fellow like himself, with no brawn and hardly any more brains, was something he would ponder the rest of his life and never come close to understanding. But more, she had courageously carried his unborn son through the terrible ordeal of their winter trek from Cedar City, had given birth to him from her bed in a wagonbox, and had already taught him to walk and now to talk—at least a little.

And now she was doing the same courageous work again, carrying what both of them hoped would be a daughter to join with Willy in making their family complete. Truly Eliza was a woman of miraculous and wondrous strength, a woman whose courage knew no bounds, a woman whose faith was a thing to be studied. Why, it was as if—

"Billy, why on earth are you gawking at us like that? You'd think you hadn't seen us in a coon's age."

"Seems that long," Billy grinned in reply. Lifting his wide, floppy hat, he wiped the sweat from his forehead with the back of his sleeve, then settled the hat back in place where it covered his slightly balding head and badly sunburned neck.

"For April, she sure seems mighty warm. It's no wonder you sisters knocked off a mite early today."

Eliza shook her head. "They didn't—I did. Maggie Haskel told me to go home and lie down. So I picked up little Willy from Mary—"

"Lie down?" Billy was up and out of the ditch in an instant, his teasing entirely forgotten. "You feeling poorly, hon-bun? Is it the baby? What's the matter that Maggie should be sending you home?"

Leaning on her crutch, Eliza shook her head. "I . . . I don't know, Billy. After I'd helped plant for a spell, Maggie put me to driving the team pulling the water wagon, not hardly working at all. We'd just come from the river with the water barrels full, and when I pulled the team to a stop and stepped on the brake handle, I got all light-headed and like to have fallen off the wagon seat, I was that dizzy. A little later it happened again, and that's when Maggie saw me. Fact is, she caught me, or I would have fallen that time."

"Eliza," Billy said, suddenly taking charge, "you need to sit down, pronto. Yonder under the shade of that brush looks to be a fine spot."

"Billy, I don't—"

But Billy had already lifted little Willy, and seconds later Eliza was being led to the scant shade Billy had indicated.

"There are probably ticks and rattlesnakes under here," Eliza grumbled as she carefully lowered herself to the earth and then tightened her bonnet against any invasion that might be launched down her neck. "And scorpions and spiders and fire ants—"

"Yeah, and two or three wild Pahutes, too." Billy grinned as he squatted beside his wife, with little Willy—for the time being, at least—sitting contentedly in his lap. "All right, Eliza, truth time. How long have these dizzy spells been going on? And what else are you feeling that you haven't yet told me about?"

"Now you sound like that busybody Maggie Haskel."

"Happen you don't answer my questions, hon-bun, I'll sound worse than ten busybodies like Margaret Haskel and ten more cranky old biddies like Sariah Jane Oliphant back to Cedar City, all lumped together."

Abruptly Eliza giggled. "You're shameless, Billy. You truly are, speaking ill of good women like that." Then she sighed as she fingered the folds of her apron. "Truthfully, darling, I've felt just fine until this afternoon. No sick headaches, and nothing else except maybe the beginnings of a little headcold! And who ever heard of such a thing as that making a person dizzy?"

For a moment or two Billy sat in silence, studying his wife. Little Willy, tired of cuddling, wriggled away and was soon picking up rocks and trying to throw them into the empty ditch. Willy hadn't yet developed his ability to throw, but Eliza had sewn him a bean-bag for his first birthday, and Billy had tossed it at him half a hundred times or more each evening that he'd been home, encouraging him to pick it up and throw it back. And he was starting to catch on—a little.

"Willy, you stay away from that ditch! You hear?"

Ignoring his mother, the child continued his efforts to fill the

ditch and undo all that Billy and many others had labored so diligently to accomplish.

"Chip off his mother's block," Billy said with a tender grin.
"That'll learn you for being so hard-headed and stubborn, Eliza
Foreman."

"Humph! Pregnant or not, I won't sit idly by feeling useless and
awful, Billy—not when every other woman in the fort is off planting or hauling water!"

"I never said you should sit idly by, Eliza, and you know it. I
merely suggested that you stop trading folks and doing work that's
so gosh-awful hard on that beautiful but fragile body of yours."

"And why should work be any less hard on me than it is on any
of those other poor sisters? You should see them, Billy, either on
their knees planting or else lifting bucket after bucket of water out
of that miserable river and passing them up the line until they're
dumped into barrels to be hauled to the fields. And those buckets of
water aren't light, either. I tried lifting one this morning, and I
know."

"You shouldn't even be trying such a fool thing! Mercy sakes,
Eliza, you're more'n twice the age of most of these sisters, you're
carrying your second baby in as many years, and you've already
been through more than most of them will ever have to endure their
whole lives. I'm just thankful Maggie Haskel was there to put you
to work driving the water wagon. That was inspired."

"She's a good woman," Eliza admitted quietly. "And considering that she's never had any real training, she's a wonderful doctor.
Our settlement is lucky to have her. And Mary, too! You should have
seen her the other day when she found out that Hádapa had been bitten by that huge rattlesnake—"

"What's this? I haven't heard anything about a rattlesnake striking anyone. And who in blue thunder is Hádapa?"

"I . . . I haven't had a chance to tell you." Eliza looked away
from her husband, not wanting him to see what was in her eyes. "It
was under our bed . . ."

"Well, I'll be snickered!" Billy said after Eliza had told him the
whole story. "Who'd have ever thought a Navajo would do such a
thing for one of us? That woman has my eternal gratitude, I'll tell

you that! I aim to show it to her, too. And you say her name is Hádapa?"

"Uh-huh, although I'm certain my pronunciation is wrong. Mary talked to her a little and told me. Apparently her *hogan* is only a short distance south of the river, a mile or so, Mary thinks, and she has many sheep and goats but no children. I know nothing about her husband, or even if she has one. But it seems her younger brother starved to death several years ago when they were in Kit Carson's prison camp, and that's what drew her to Willy. She recognized his symptoms and wanted to help."

"So, is the goat's milk helping?"

Eliza nodded. "I'm sure of it. Aren't you?"

For a moment Billy watched his son at play. "Well, he does seem to be getting stronger and more active, all right."

"And he's sleeping less, too. I absolutely believe the child is getting better. Of course, the process is slow, but Willy does like goat's milk, and Hádapa has no trouble getting him to take it. In fact, some days he suckles it right out of those udders she brings it in. She sings to him, too, though for the life of me I can't find the tune or rhythm to her songs. But Willy seems to like them, and I suppose that's what's important."

"It is! For a fact, Eliza, I believe the veil of mortality is slow to develop, and tiny children have no difficulty whatever sensing people's spirits, good or evil. For you and I, now, it's a bit more difficult."

"If not practically impossible," Eliza stated sadly. "Had that snake not appeared, I don't suppose I'd have ever seen Hádapa's inner beauty or felt the love she's developed for Willy. It almost makes me want to thank the Lord for sending that fool snake, but I won't on account of I don't want any more of them to visit my home—ever!"

Billy chuckled. "I don't blame you. I'm just glad you finally have a little peace about our Lamanite neighbors."

Instantly Eliza grew serious. "I'm trying to reach that peace, Billy, and maybe I am—toward one or two of the Navajos. But as for the rest of them, why, they're awful thieves. Except for Hádapa, even the women are guilty of it. And as for every single Pahute on the face of this earth, I have no peace at all! I don't know where those savages are or what they're up to, but I know they're going to do us hurt. I can see it especially in the eyes of the one called Posey. And Bishop Nielson told us last Sunday that so much livestock is being stolen by both tribes that he doesn't know if we'll have enough draft animals left to work our fields."

Billy nodded soberly. "Yeah, he told us that today, too. I know Brother Haskel is kept on the run just chasing down the thieves. And Joe Nielson and the other boys with the herd are having a terrible time trying to keep the animals from being stolen. But the Lord wants us here, Eliza, so I know he'll help us manage it somehow. Maybe he'll bring more women like Hádapa to our aid or give us ways to aid them. Serving others is the best way to develop love."

"Maybe so." Eliza called out to Willy, who had wandered a few yards down the ditch and was looking to go farther. Beyond him loomed the two rock spires the Saints were calling the Navajo Twins, while beneath them, on the valley floor itself, a smaller, tilted formation called Sunbonnet Rock could hardly be seen. To Eliza the latter formation looked terribly precarious, and she didn't want her son getting anywhere near it. To her satisfaction, however, the child turned immediately around and began his toddling return.

"How's this awful ditch coming along, Billy? Are we soon going to have water in it?"

"I hope so!" Billy shook his head disgustedly. "All we have to avoid is another flood."

"Mary says this last one was worse than the floods a year ago."

Billy nodded. "In terms of damage, it was. But some of the problems with this ditch have been our fault, or at least mine when I fouled up the original survey. Everybody knows water won't run uphill, and that's exactly what we were trying to get it to do. I reckon I was just in too big of a hurry. Anyway, the survey is correct this time. I know, because I've checked it again and again. Only, what with work on the cribs and replowing all the fields, we haven't had enough men to get the ditch finished, and I'm not sure we're going to."

"What . . . will we do?"

Billy sighed. "I don't know, hon-bun. Everyone's working themselves into the ground, though, so whatever happens, it won't be from lack of effort."

Eliza nodded her understanding. "The sisters were commenting on how fast the river is dropping."

"They're right. The fool thing is dropping way too fast, which is part of the reason we're building those cribs. I just hope we can get them finished in time and that the ditch will hold water once we do."

"My only prayer," Eliza said wistfully, "is that I will give you a daughter, and that our crops will be sufficient this summer that you can spend next winter here instead of off in Colorado working on that railroad."

Billy smiled as he took his beloved wife's hand and helped her to her feet. "My prayer's the same as yours. Now, what say we take ourselves back to the fort and see what we can scrape together for supper?"

16

Tuesday, April 26, 1881

Chinle Creek, Navajo Reservation

The *atchí'deezá'hi,* or forked-stick *hogan,* was almost invisible the way it sat huddled against the talus slope near the spring that was east of what would one day be known as Moses Rock. It was an old *hogan,* many years old, and there had been times when it had stood empty for several seasons. But now it was inhabited by a young Navajo who was calling himself Jim Joe, his one wife, and his three small children. And yes, it was also inhabited by a very old man whom the others called *hachaii,* or uncle, and who was in reality the great-uncle of Jim Joe's wife.

Natanii nééz, the tall Navajo who was calling himself Frank, had come to visit the people of this old *hogan,* but he did not know the old man. Neither did he know that the old man's name was Dah nish uáant, and that his ears and his mind were still as keen as they had been during the long-ago days of his youth. But because he sat in silence in the place of honor directly to the west of the *hogan's* entrance, and because his head was bowed and his nearly dead eyes were always upon the earth before him, the tall Navajo had dismissed the old man and focused his attention instead on Jim Joe and his two sons.

These people were relatives, of course, cousins of Natanii nééz, because Jim Joe's woman was of the same "born for" clan as his father. It was because of this that Natanii nééz had made his way to their *hogan.* Now he had been with them the better part of the day, visiting idly, helping to gather into the corral near the springs a nice herd of horses, and sharing out of the cooking pot prepared by Jim Joe's wife a satisfying mutton stew.

And though it was already past the season of cold, which is also the season for telling stories, nevertheless in the afternoon Jim Joe rehearsed a short version of the long-ago time, before Monster Slayer came, when the *Yei* and the Horned Monster had eaten the old ones—the people called *Anasazi* by the *Diné*. Jim Joe wanted his children to understand that the ghosts of those old ones stayed around, and that it was not a good idea to spend much time in their abandoned cliff houses.

In his turn Natanii nééz had told a humorous story of a man who had slain a frog—a rainbringer—and of the terrible crippling that had come upon him. Then he had told them of the *belacani* mormonee who had come to the crossing on the big river, of their womanlike ways, and of the ease with which he had been conducting his raids upon them. It had been a good telling, too, and during it Natanii nééz had chanted two new songs, both of his own composition, that proclaimed the balance, the way of beauty, he had gained through his raids.

It was not difficult for Natanii nééz to tell that Jim Joe and his sons, as well as his wife and daughter, were affected by his powerful words, and so he had gone on a little longer, proclaiming with quiet pride even more of his great accomplishments, with raiding as well as with cards, and of the easy accumulation of his newfound wealth.

Of course, the tall Navajo knew that boasters were scorned by the People. And he understood as well that wealth, while obviously desired and eagerly sought after, could just as easily become a liability. For instance, if a man acquired wealth too quickly—which usually meant faster than those around him—he might be accused of chicanery, or worse, of practicing sorcery. And this was especially so if the man happened to be stingy with his wealth, and if he also happened to be skilled at chanting—a thing Natanii nééz was definitely discovering a gift for.

But these were his people, his clan, the tall one told himself as his voice flowed softly and easily as the big river. They would never think such things. Besides which, hadn't he brought for them a gift of one of the *belacani* horses he had raided from the mormonee? True, it wasn't one of his better animals, but still—

"This old man, too, would make a telling," the old one stated suddenly from his place of honor, surprising Natanii nééz with the firmness of his voice. "It is a telling of the true old ones, the *Anasazi.*" The old one did not look up, and he spoke in the old way, referring to himself as if he were another person so that his humility might be known. Instantly the *hogan* was quiet, and Natanii nééz knew he was about to hear some things he might never hear again.

"But first," the old man continued, "in our old days many wished to know why the *hogan* faces east. For these beloved children, this will be briefly explained. Long ago, at the emergence place of this fifth world, Talking God performed a 'No Sleep' ceremony. At that sing the people could not find anyone to do the bathing of patients. Talking God gathered sand from where the ground was black, blue, red, and white, and he made a picture in a round shape with the colored sand. This became the ceremonial basket, which had the finishing outlet toward the east. It was very beautiful, and it showed the design of a true *hogan*.

"Later, again at Huerfano Mountain, which is the true emergence place, the first Blessing Way was held at a place called Mating of the Corn. Again the question of who would do the bathing was brought up, as well as how it should be done. Talking God was sent to the *hogan* that was exactly at the place of emergence to get what he had hidden in the far side of the *hogan*. He ran and brought it back. It was then copied, and the design was kept. Today the ceremonial basket, with that same design, is used for ceremonial baths. It was granted to the People for use in the Blessing Way sings. Its outlet faces the east, and thus the doorway of the *hogan* faces the east. This reminds us that all good things in our lives enter with the dawn from the east."

The old man paused, and Natanii nééz had almost concluded that he was finished when he spoke again. "It is good for the People to offer their thanks at dawn by sprinkling cornmeal toward the east to thank Talking God and Calling God and the other People of the Dawn for the night's rest, and to greet another pleasant day. The men offer white cornmeal in the morning and in the evening. The women offer yellow cornmeal each time. At noon corn pollen is offered to the sun because the sun prefers pollen. These offerings are made for good health and prosperity, and they help the People have *hózhó* in their lives. These things should not be forgotten."

Natanii nééz shifted uneasily on his seat of sheepskins. He could not remember the last time he had made such offerings, certainly not that morning when the others had quietly done so, or at noontime, either, and he had the distinct impression that the old man was speaking directly to him. It was almost as if—

"Now this old man will tell a real story, briefly," the old one declared, once again interrupting the tall one's thoughts. "He would tell the whole account, but that would take until long after tomorrow, and this is not the season for such long tales.

"The location was Chaco Canyon. There was a man named One-Who-Wins-You. He was like a wizard with all gambling games. He won everything from his opponents. It was not known what he did to have such remarkable luck. Maybe it was made possible by mere instinct. He was born as a twin, but no one has told us exactly who he really was. This man who speaks to you thinks he may have been born a *belacani* of some kind. The people from whom he won had practically become his slaves. They all worked hard. They carried limestone on their backs from a rock quarry to Chaco Canyon, where the rocks were chipped into blocks to make stone houses with many rooms. These are still there today. One-Who-Wins-You lived above the canyon, and below his home was where the slaves built the houses.

"Someone dreamed that the wizard would be a loser not too far in the future. He had a brother who was his identical twin. The only way to tell them apart was that his brother was an honest man. He lived at Bird Knoll. The people all said, 'Let his own twin be his next opponent. That will change his luck, you will see.' It is said that twins are extraordinary beings. In this telling you will hear where his brother personally encountered him.

"In those days the Holy People communicated closer with each other and knew what was happening. This also happened during the time when all people, no matter who they were, mixed and intermarried indiscriminately. It is told that these mixed tribes inhabited

215

Chaco Canyon, a place used as a retreat. From the activities that occurred there, new tribes were added and other races were born.

"As has been said, One-Who-Wins-You might have been *bela-cani,* or at least one who was different. It was told that a real brother could win from his own brother only after having betrayed him. That was what happened when the gambling wizard's brother came to his home. The visiting brother was advised by the people not to greet his wizard brother as 'My dear brother.' Neither was he to take his hand. The only greeting was to be 'My opponent.' After a song, the gambler would say, 'Let's play a game and see who wins.' The wizard knew he always won, so they started with the shinny game. One game after another the gambler lost. The last was the tree-breaking game. Soon, the only possessions One-Who-Wins-You had left were his wife and children. 'We will bet our wives and our children,' he said.

"The two trees were at the far end of the race track. They got set, and the race was on. About halfway, One-Who-Wins-You shot a witch missile at his brother's feet, but he missed. That was how he had won all the races from his opponents before. However, his brother caught the missile and tossed it back to the wizard's feet. By that time, the honest twin was ahead. Before he got to the trees, Horned Toad was running beside him. Horned Toad told the twin that of the two trees ahead, one was a cane reed tree and the other was a hard oak tree. Horned Toad pointed out the oak. Usually the one who broke the tree lost. The twin was struggling with the oak when One-Who-Wins-You got to his tree and broke it without a struggle. We all know the hard oak cannot be broken, so we know that the gambling wizard lost everything he had, even his wife, children, and home.

"His honest twin brother had redeemed all the people, with their belongings, as well as their children and wives. Everyone was happy. One-Who-Wins-You was downhearted. He told his brother to take good care of his family, and he began to speak to the people, but they ignored him. 'Send him away,' they shouted. 'Put him on a strong, swift Black Arrow and shoot him up yonder.'

"Long ago the Holy People used holy arrows. The gambling wizard was placed on such an arrow. Before he left, he yelled, 'Even if you send me up there I will return. I will see you, and I will be above you. Wait and see.' One-Who-Wins-You also said to the people, 'In the future there will be round objects which the people will play games with, to gamble and to win. They will be a reminder of me.' Today there are many round objects to play with, things the *belacani* call balls, which remind us of the gambling wizard who became a loser. These balls were brought to our children by the *belacani* when we were imprisoned by Rope Thrower at The Grove. The gambling wizard also said that the lightning flash would be his power, and the wind, and the rolling rainbow arc. He added, 'When I return you will see in your homes by the power of lightning, and everything that is round will roll beneath you with the wind.' Today when we see the *belacani* wagons carrying people inside them and going fast, we can see that part of this is so.

"These are the reasons why this old man thinks One-Who-Wins-You must have been a *belacani*. Soon, this old one thinks, the *belacani* will also show us how to capture the lightning to put in our *hogans* for a light, and we will somehow travel with the wind on the rolling rainbow arc. These things should be enough to let us know that the gambling wizard has still not gone away, and that he is still looking for more slaves. That is all this old man will tell you about the gambling wizard."

In the silence that followed, Natanii nééz stared into the flames of the small cooking fire that yet flickered in the center of the *hogan*. As shadows danced on the rounded walls, he found himself wondering if the old man had been speaking directly to him, warning him. Of course he was a great gambler, but what of that? Why would such a thing bother this old man? Perhaps the old fool was suspicious of his methods. But how could he have known that Natanii nééz had ways of making certain that he usually won? No, more than likely the foolish old man's tale was a warning to the others to stay away from the *belacani*—his way of trying to force the others to continue in the old ways and so remain in poverty. And they could most certainly do as they wished, the tall one thought smugly. That would only leave more wealth for him—

"Natanii nééz," the old man declared suddenly, once again startling the tall Navajo with his strong voice, "it is said that along with your raids upon the mormonee you have taken upon yourself the *belacani* name of Frank."

In wonder the tall Navajo admitted that it was so.

"Long ago this old man was acquainted with a few *belacani* mormonee. These were good men who had the interest of the *Diné* at heart, and they were trying to do a little good among the People by speaking to them of holy things. They were not like the *belacani* soldiers. But then two brave warriors of the People came among a few of them and shed the blood of a young mormonee who was not expecting such treatment at their hands. First they shot him with his own gun, and then they lifted his shirt and drove many arrows into his back. Leaving him where he fell in the rocks to die alone, they rode away laughing. It is said," and now the old man's voice grew quiet, "that one of these men who killed without good reason had taken upon himself the *belacani* name of Frank."

His heart hammering with fear, Natanii nééz could not force his eyes toward the face of the old man who sat beside him. Instead he stared only at the fire circle, wondering. How could the old fool know such things? How could—

"The Holy Ones were not pleased by such bad behavior," the old man continued, his voice grown so low that Natanii nééz had to strain to hear him. "Especially they were not pleased to see a boy killed with such cruelty. And so the Holy Ones waited a little, and then they sent Rope Thrower and the *belacani* soldiers to take away the wealth and perhaps even the lives of the *Diné*. Soon it was done, and the People were taken far away to the place of suffering. When they had suffered enough, the Holy Ones allowed them to return to *Diné tah* to see if they had learned anything—to see how they would behave. The Holy Ones even sent more *belacani* mormonee among them—people still filled with goodness and a desire to speak of holy things. This was so the Holy Ones could see if the *Diné* had learned their lesson.

"One of those two warriors, a man with a heart of flint, had avoided going to the place of suffering and so had learned nothing. When the Holy Ones saw that this was so, they sorrowed, and then they gave holy words to the *belacani* mormonee, words that had the power to end that warrior's life. Soon it was done, and that warrior was no more. Neither was anything left alive that had been called his, including his wife and children. As it was with the gambling wizard called One-Who-Wins-You, so it was with him.

"Now it remains to be seen what will happen to the other warrior, the one who now and then still calls himself Frank. Will holy words also be spoken against him? Will they be spoken against all who follow him against the *belacani* mormonee? No one knows this thing, but it is thought by some that the Holy Ones have come close again to watch this warrior's behavior to see if it is still bad. If that is so, then perhaps they have already seen enough and have made their decision. For this day, this old man has spoken."

His mind reeling with what he had just heard, the tall Navajo sat on the sheepskins in the *hogan* of the one called Jim Joe, still not daring to look at the old man who was seated beside him. But he was having difficulty breathing, and for some reason the muscles beneath his right eye were jumping as if they were being poked with a sharp stick.

How, he was asking himself again and again, could this old man have known such things? How could he have known of the long-ago killing by him and Peokon? And how could he have known of the terrible curse spoken so recently against Peokon by the *belacani* mormonee called Thales Haskel—the curse that had brought to an end not only Peokon's life but also the lives of all he had once possessed? And finally, how could he have known that Natanii nééz's secret intention, as he went among his relatives, was to gather a following who would take everything from the *belacani* mormonee who dwelt in the unfinished fort on the big river? Such questions screamed in the tall one's mind. They tormented him, for there were no answers to any of them, no answers at all.

At length, unable to remain seated an instant longer, he rose to his feet, mumbled something of gratitude to Jim Joe, and then stumbled from the *hogan,* vowing never again to return. In the brightness of the late afternoon, he took many deep breaths to steady himself. Then finally he slid up onto his horse and rode away, not once looking back.

And so he did not see the tears that flowed from the nearly blind eyes of the old man who had risen to follow him from the *hogan,* tears of sorrow not only that Natanii nééz's heart had remained hard but also that the old one had not been able to soften the flintlike heart of Peokon, the dead warrior who had been his only son.

Chinle Creek, Navajo Reservation

"Natanii nééz!"

Reining in his mount and spinning in surprise, the tall Navajo stared into the shade of the large juniper, trying to determine the identity of the man who sat his pony there, the warrior who had called his name.

"I see you, brother," he said bravely as he made the sign of greeting, "but I do not recognize you. How are you called?"

"I am called by many names," the man replied as he held his pony still in the shade of the tree. "Most of them mean nothing to me."

The man had to be of the *Diné*, Natanii nééz knew, for he spoke like one. Yet there was something about him that did not seem quite as it should—

"It is said among the People that you are becoming a wealthy man—that you own many fine horses."

Suddenly pleased, Natanii nééz sat a little straighter on his fine new mount. This was better, he thought, much better than the treatment he had received in the *hogan* of the one called Jim Joe. Finally his great skill and wisdom were being recognized. Finally there were men among the *Diné* who were seeking him out—

"It is said that you make frequent raids upon the *belacani* mormonee who dwell near the big river. It is said that many of your horses were once their horses, and that *líshcháázh,* you take unfair advantage of their *hóózhó*—the balance they bring into their lives with their kindness and goodness."

Stunned, Natanii nééz could do nothing more than stare. This could not be happening to him, not twice in one day—

"It is also said that long ago you did the same to an innocent boy, helping another to *yish'a naastseed,* to kill him when he was not prepared. Yet there was no need to kill, for the boy had nothing of value to the People, and he was not an enemy about to strike a blow against you. Yet, Natanii nééz, you willingly assisted in his death."

"How . . . how are you called?" Natanii nééz asked as he fought to maintain composure. "It is my right to know—"

"Now the one who rode with you is *ánishdin,* Natanii nééz. He is dead! And you are running hard in Peokon's footsteps!"

"*Bináá dootízhi,*" Natanii nééz breathed in fear as he involuntarily backed his pony away. "You are the one known as Blue Eyes."

"That is one of the names I am called," the man replied as he urged his horse from the shade, pacing Natanii nééz's backing mount.

"You . . . blew a bone into the one called Peokon," Natanii nééz breathed, his eyes wide. "You are *yenaldolooshi.*"

"I am no skinwalker, Natanii nééz, and I blew no bone into that evil one. You know that, for you were there, and you watched all I did. My *belacani* name is Haskel, and like all the mormonee you think of as weak and foolish, I have power from the one true God that is greater than many hundred *yenaldolooshi*—power that is much greater than the power of Talking God and Monster Slayer and all the other gods of the *Diné.*"

"But . . . I saw you . . . blow a bone into—"

Thales Haskel urged his horse close beside the mount of the tall one, his eyes blazing. "No, Natanii nééz, you did not see me blow a bone, for you know I have no need of such things. Such deeds are for entertainment tales around winter fires. Indeed, Natanii nééz, my power is in the words of my mouth, for the great God Jehovah, the God of Israel, has given it to me and to many others of the mormonee.

"You heard me speak those words to the evil one called Peokon. With the words of the one true God that the mormonee have been given, I *binisdzin,* I put a curse upon him, and now he is no more. Neither is his wife, or his children, or his horses, or his sheep and his goats—no, not even his fine spring of water remains alive. All this is done by the power of the words of the Lord God Jehovah."

Natanii nééz could hardly breathe he was so terrified. Yet he could not make a fleeing, for that would do no good at all. The God of this mormonee had such great power that he could no doubt reach out and pluck him back again—

"Natanii nééz, you have also become evil. It is always in your heart now to *líshcháázh,* to take unfair advantage of others. Because you killed that unarmed boy, and because these many seasons later you continue to hate and destroy both your people and the mormonee people who have come to this place to help you and to be your friends, the Lord God of Israel curses you." Abruptly Thales Haskel stretched out his hand. "In his holy name I curse you, Natanii nééz, and I say, be it unto you according to His will."

———◦—◦—◦———

"Think he'll die, Thales?"

Once again with Amasa Barton and Benjamin Perkins, his traveling companions of the past several days, Thales Haskel rode steadily forward. This had now become a good journey, a very good journey, for quite by accident—or quite by the Lord's design, which was often the same thing—he had found Natanii nééz and delivered the Lord's warning.

Riding past Chinle Creek Wash, he had spotted the thief flailing at his pony, riding hard toward them. Instructing his companions to wait behind some large boulders that had fallen in ancient times, Thales had ridden into the dark shade of a huge old juniper, and there he had waited.

"To tell the truth," he finally answered, "I have no idea. But like I said before, the Lord does, and I reckon he'll do what Natanii nééz most deserves. That," and Thales Haskel's eyes flashed again as he said it, "and make a powerful example out of him for the rest of these benighted Israelites who call themselves the People."

And with that, the old missionary and interpreter pushed his pony into a hard and determined lope homeward.

PART THREE

ON THE FIRING LINE

17

Saturday, April 30, 1881

Bluff Fort

Breathing deeply of the fresh morning air, Eliza hitched her skirts, swung her crutch, and maneuvered expertly around a stack of twisted cottonwood logs. In the distance she could hear children laughing on their way to school—boys teasing girls, no doubt—and she smiled at the thought of it. Would her unborn baby be a girl? she wondered. And would little Willy turn out to be her protector or her tormentor?

Expertly the tall, thin woman negotiated the narrow pathway that led between a pig wallow and the walls of Ben and Mary Ann Perkins's cabin, her son following immediately behind her. "That's it, Willy," she encouraged as the child toddled forward, gripping her skirt with one chubby, clenched fist. "That's Mommy's big boy. Don't step in that dirty old wallow. The pigs have been in there already, and you don't want to look like they do!"

It was astounding, Eliza thought, that moisture could stay in that wallow but would not for ten minutes stay in the bed of their pathetic and still uncompleted ditch. It was almost as if what some of the folks were saying, was right—the ditch was cursed.

To the east the morning sun was already above the hills, brightly illuminating the looming sandstone bluffs under which she and the others who had come through the Hole-in-the-Rock the year before were building their community. So far it wasn't much to look at, Eliza thought wistfully—one large corral and three smaller ones, some brush sheds, and a series of small, rough-hewn log cabins built in four rows facing each other across the wide square she was presently negotiating.

"Morning, Eliza. Morning, Willy."

Looking up, Eliza smiled. "Morning, Nellie. How are you this bright and cheerful day?"

"First rate, thank you." Nellie Grayson Lyman smiled. "Look at you, Willy! You look healthy as a small colt!"

In response the child ducked his head and gazed up at her shyly before sliding out of sight behind his mother's skirts.

"He looks absolutely marvelous, Eliza. That goat's milk is doing him a world of good."

"It is, Nellie. There's no doubt in my mind that Hádapa has saved the boy's life. I just wish there were something I could do to repay her kindness."

"Well," Nellie smiled, "maybe something will come up. Congratulations, by the way! I think it's wonderful you're expecting another child."

"Thank you." Self-consciously Eliza looked down at her stomach. "I'm not due until fall, but already I feel as big as a barn."

Nellie Lyman snickered. "Well, you aren't big at all, and you're so thin I doubt you ever will be. Are you feeling all right?"

"I've felt wonderful—not even a touch of morning sickness."

"What a blessing!"

At that moment a team and wagon clattered past on its way to the Jump, Joseph Barton driving. "Morning, sisters," he said as he touched his hat. "You too, Willy boy! Top of the morning!"

Politely both women curtsied. "Have you been out to the Jump already?" Nellie asked as Joseph's wagon, loaded with logs, disappeared into its own dust. "Am I right that your assignment this week is breakfast for the brethren?"

Eliza smiled. "It is, but that's too far for me to walk, especially with Willy. But Elizabeth Stevens has been taking it out for me, bless her heart. She left nearly an hour ago. Willy and I just came from swinging under the old surveyor's cottonwood. He finds it nearly as soothing as I do."

"It's a great swing, isn't it! I've been glad since last summer that the boys hung it. And that old cottonwood tree, it must be hundreds of years old."

"Just think what it must have seen," Eliza mused. Then she smiled radiantly. "I'll bet you're enjoying having Jody . . . I mean, Joseph, home again."

Nellie smiled. "Eliza, you can call him Jody if you're of a mind to. Every soul in this fort but his mother and me does the same. And yes, it is so good to have him back with us. Him, Platte, Walter, George Lewis, and Sam Rowley—they all came in together. And mercy sakes, Eliza, they're all thin as rails."

"Maybe it's that Colorado water they've been drinking."

"More than likely it's Colorado starvation, the same as the Bluff City starvation we've all been enduring here at home. We're getting starved out, Eliza. Joseph says that betwixt here and Montezuma Fort we're down to thirty-six men, and that's counting the boys who are big enough to do a man's work. I heard yesterday that Henry and Sarah Ann Holyoak abandoned the new settlement at Peak City and headed out, figuring to settle at the old Elk Mountain Mission up in Grand Valley."

"Elk Mountain Mission?" Eliza was puzzled. "Sarah Ann told me they were going to Moab—where Alfred and Isadore Wilson live."

Nellie smiled. "You're right; it is called Moab now. According to what my husband told me, twenty, maybe thirty years ago a mission was established there at the base of what folks today call the LaSals but which were known at that time as the Elk Mountains. Platte says the mission only lasted until the Utes killed some of the missionaries and drove the rest out. But folks are back there again— the Wilsons, Walt Moore and his family, Joseph Burkholder, and Platte says twelve or fifteen other families whose names he doesn't know. From what I hear, they have a right nice little settlement, which will now be augmented by the Holyoaks."

Eliza nodded, her expression somber. "It certainly will, though we'll miss them terribly. I'm thankful Sarah Ann brought little Mary Luella over to tell me good-bye."

"Sarah Ann is thoughtful that way. Besides which, Eliza, you've surely had a way with those girls. But mercy sakes, if folks keep leaving we won't even have need for this fool fort."

"I've been wondering since they left what they're doing about their call."

Nellie's expression was serious. "You mean the call by the Brethren to settle here as peace missionaries? Who knows, Eliza? To some folks it wasn't considered a call at all—just an opportunity that didn't work out. Probably that's how the Duntons, Robbs, Fieldings, Goddards, Hutchings, and goodness only knows who else felt about it. Before the three Pace families left, Pauline told me she felt like God wouldn't hold anybody to such a call if it meant starving to death."

"I received a letter from Maggie Sevy a couple of months ago," Eliza said as she leaned against the rough-hewn logs of the cabin to ease the strain on her feet. "You know she and Bishop Sevy left here for Colorado last fall, but now they're figuring on heading back to Panguitch and settling in as though they'd never left. Maggie says they felt inspired to leave here, and now she wonders if it wasn't so the rest of us would have a little more to live on."

"That's an interesting thought. I wonder if she's right."

"Maggie's a wonderful woman," Eliza declared, "so I'd hate to call into question her inspiration. Or Bishop Sevy's either, for that matter. But Billy says the actual call wasn't to Bluff City or Montezuma Fort either one, but to the San Juan country in general. That covers a lot of territory, including a good portion of southern Colorado where Silas Smith has settled his family."

Nellie Lyman sighed deeply. "Billy's right, of course. But when I start to thinking that life is too thin for good health here in the fort and that maybe we should move on, too, Joseph and Platte and even old Bishop Nielson all remind me that while the original call wasn't that specific, the instructions we received last fall from Elders Snow and Young were very clear. We are to stay and build up a settlement right here on this horrid little river bottom. Of course, if the ditch fails again this summer and we lose *these* crops, Platte says he'll seriously petition the Brethren in Salt Lake for all of us to be released. It just doesn't seem logical that the Lord would want all of us to continue living on sand and alkali water, weed greens, dried berries, a little flour hauled in from Colorado, and now and again a few fish or a stringy beef."

"The ditch won't fail again," Eliza declared as she pushed herself from the wall to go after her son, who was now venturing back toward the wallow. "Billy says he's sure these cribs they're building will tame that old river right down."

"Well," Nellie said as she too moved away, "I'll believe it when I see it. That river is a monster—there's no two ways about it! Nice visiting, Eliza. You and Willy have a good morning now, you hear?"

Alderson/Thurman Ranch at Ute Springs, Southwestern Colorado

Despite the early season, it was hot, hot and muggy. Dark clouds billowed and roiled in the late afternoon sky, steam misted even the near distances, and Dick May, looking up from the back of his horse, found himself worrying, of a sudden, about lightning. He was riding in the open, and if those distant rumbles of thunder got any closer, he could be in trouble.

Not that he'd ever seen lightning strike a man, he admitted to himself as he deftly undid the bandanna from around his neck. But he'd heard stories, more than one of them, and every one of those who'd lived swore he'd had himself a bad feeling just before being struck. Just like he was having now, Dick thought nervously as he pulled his eyes from the sky to gaze across the vast, grass-covered park.

With quick movements he wiped the sweat from his face with the bandanna, which he then reknotted around his neck. Lifting his hat he tousled his wet hair and slicked it back, hoping to redirect the sweat that had been trickling into his eyes.

"A feller'd think the shade from those gol-durned clouds would cool things off a bit," he groused to no one in particular as he clamped his hat back into place. "Not make it hotter. The way these poor hosses is foaming up, a feller'd think it was an afternoon in August and we was down by Sonora."

Standing in his stirrups, Dick looked across the backs of the sea of horses he and his partner Byron Smith were cutting their thirty selections from. Fifteen hundred head. It was a huge number of horses that John Thurman and Josh Alderson had gathered the year before out in Oregon and Nevada. Not only that, but some of them were outstanding animals, including the twenty-nine he and Smith had cut out and were paying cash money for—to the tune of $50 a head.

For a moment Dick thought of the money belt wrapped around his body. In it was $1,500 in greenbacks, with one exception the most actual cash money he had ever seen in one place. Truth be known, he would be relieved by more than somewhat to complete the purchase of the horses and hand John Thurman the money. To Dick's way of thinking, it was too much cash for any one man ever to be responsible for—too much cash to tempt others with!

Suddenly nervous, Dick let his eyes search the park and then the trees that rimmed it. Was that what he was feeling? A sixth sense that others were nearby, waiting for an opportunity to rob him? Of course, nobody knew Thurman had brought him and Smith to the ranch, nobody but that ragtag knot of Ute braves they had run across a few days before. They knew, all right. But they hadn't seemed in the least dangerous, not to him or either of his companions. Of course, that Indian agent Nathan Meeker that the Utes had killed the year before up on the White River, he hadn't thought his killers were dangerous either. But then, Meeker'd also been dumber than a fencepost—

Abruptly Dick May chuckled. "Seems to me," he muttered quietly, "I'm acting jittery as a kid who just locked the school marm in the outhouse. Especially since this entire spread of Thurman's is on the edge of the southern Ute reservation. If them Injuns is around, well, they do have a right.

"There," he muttered as his eyes caught sight of the high, arching neck and head of a beautiful steeldust stallion. "I reckon that'll be number thirty—unless Smith's found something better."

Moments later, his rope around the steeldust's neck, Dick May was moving toward the cabin and corrals at Ute Springs where he and Smith were holding their purchases. Now he had nothing to do but lazy around until the others returned—most likely in the morning, he thought with a grin. It was a hard life, but somebody had to do it.

Smelling the water at the springs, both his mount and the steel-dust quickened their pace. Dick May was already anticipating his late afternoon siesta at the cabin, and he had forgotten altogether his worry about lightning or Indians either one. It was a fine time to be alive, he was thinking, and with their thirty head of prime horseflesh—well, luck had finally dealt him and Smith a winning hand.

18

◦─◦─◦

Sunday, May 1, 1881

Alderson/Thurman Ranch at Ute Springs, Southwestern Colorado

"*Wagh!*"

In awe the young warrior Posey yanked his pony to a stop. Beside him Scotty did the same, as did all the other warriors who were riding with Mike to make a big raid. They stared out from the piñon and juniper trees and across the vast, grassy park, their eyes big with surprise and anticipation.

"*Soos,*" Scotty began counting carefully, "*so-use, wiuni, piuni, watso-wi-uni—*"

"Do not be foolish, Beogah." Posey was scornful. "One might as well attempt to count *poot-se,* the stars, as to try and count so many horses as there are before us."

In an instant the larger youth's jaw was set with defiance. "*Ni-yaani,*" he snarled. "My name is Scotty, just as your name is now Posey instead of Sowagerie. And I will number these horses just as I choose to number them!"

Amazed that his brother would think of numbering a herd of horses so vast they could not all be seen even with many long looks, Posey forgot him and turned his attention back to the horses. There were hundreds of the animals in the park before them, many hundreds—far more than Posey had ever seen. Thus Mike had been right. Here was wealth unimaginable! Here was power so vast that even such notable warriors as Canalla, who had slain the fool Nathan Meeker, would be forced to pay attention.

232

Glancing quickly to the right and then to the left, Posey noted the nearly forty warriors who now rode with Mike. Of course, his father, Chee, was there. So, too, were Survipe, Wolf Tail, and Tavagutts, who had been with them from before Posey could remember. But now others had joined the band: fierce warriors such as Tobuck-ne-ab, who was now calling himself Mancos Jim; Poke, the older brother of the comely but troubling young girl called Too-rah; and several who had been with Canalla at the *puck-ki,* the killing of the fool Meeker, or with Nicaagat at the killing of the white soldier Thornburgh.

These were brave warriors, Posey knew; fierce men who scorned the whites and refused to go with the Uncompahgres under Ouray to the Uintah reservation, or to stay with the Muuches, the Capotes, and the Weeminuches on the new southern Ute reservation.

Of course, Posey and the others were on that reservation even as they sat staring at the vast herd of horses, but it was not because they had chosen to join these southern Utes. No, Mike and his followers had come only to make a big raid on these animals and then to drive them in a hurry into the wild country off to *pe-tan-er tavi-awk-er,* the southwest, on either side of the San Juan. There they would not only have this vast wealth of horses they were now observing, but there also they would set up an ambush that would be talked about for many generations to come—an ambush in which a great number of whites would be put under the grass—an ambush so well executed that all the warriors of the People would see the power of the Utes of the San Juan country and decide to follow after them.

In that country they could live free and unmolested, they could partake at will of the wealth of both the Navajo and the newly arrived mormonee, and they could be known as Pahute because they had the courage to challenge the whites and live where they chose, along the waters of the big river—

"Ungh!" Mike grunted from atop his pony several yards away. "Were my words not true, brother?"

Tobuck-ne-ab or Mancos Jim, who had been educated by the whites and spoke their language fluently, also grunted. "They were true," he acknowledged, his dark eyes flashing with anticipation. "With this many *kuvah-u,* horses, my brother, we should have little trouble killing many mericats and showing even the weakling Ouray that the land of the big river is the best land for the People. Yes, and showing him, too, that the way of the whites will never be as good as the way of the People."

"All this *at-am-bar,* this fine talk, is good for nothing more than what a bunch of women would be doing," the surly Poke snarled from nearby.

"Are you saying that those of us who speak are women?" Mike countered, his voice low and dangerous.

Seeing not just the change in Mike's demeanor but also the worry that blossomed on the faces of Posey and some of the others who sat their ponies close by, Poke was suddenly cautious.

"My meaning," he replied, at the same time making the sign of humility or acquiescence to Mike, "is that we are not women but warriors of the People. While we sit here jabbering like foolish birds, brothers, *ang-iv-its ung nax-wosik-ai ung,* the gnats are bothering us, the horses are still not ours, and the white fools who have them sit undisturbed in that log *wickiup* yonder."

Balefully Mike glared at the warrior, who though fierce was not much older than Posey. "Yes," he growled, "and one very big fool jabbers like a magpie because he has not opened his eyes to see what we are doing in these trees. Wagh! Even the young warrior Posey can tell you this thing. Is it not so, my son?"

Amazed and proud that the great Mike had singled him out from the others and called him his son, Posey made the sign that it was indeed so.

"And what does this *tow-ats-en,* this child, know?" the angry Poke snarled.

"I know from the tracks in the earth that one sun back the three whites rode in different directions," Posey answered with confidence. "When they are found, it will be a simple matter to *puck-ki,* to put them all under the grass. Yes, and that will be especially so of the one yonder who waits in the log *wickiup.* Even a young warrior such as I could kill him there."

Slowly the downturned corners of Mike's cavernous mouth lifted in a rare smile. "Ungh," he grunted with satisfaction, "it is so, even as Posey has declared. Soon, my brother, your eyes will see that we people of the big river do not make idle boasts. Soon you will see that we few have taken to ourselves greater wealth, greater power, than all the others of the Shining Mountains."

"Perhaps," Poke snarled, still unappeased. "But perhaps you will see that I, too, have great power, and that I will let no chattering *tow-ats-en* stand before me in battle!" Balefully then he glared at the slight youth who appeared so smug.

"*Aru-pax-ai ung-tu-rásun-av,*" Scotty breathed scornfully as the angry warrior yanked his pony away. "The wolf is talking, brother. Hear it."

"I hear," Posey snickered in reply, "but he sounds like *sikuts* the squirrel to me." And grinning wickedly he turned again to watch the distant log cabin.

Ute Springs, Monument Creek

Dick May knew, the instant he saw the Indians through the open door of the cabin, that he was in trouble. He was alone, his two associates still having not returned, and there were at least fifteen painted warriors sitting on their horses before the only door, silently waiting. None of them looked happy, and to Dick's way of thinking there were some downright hostile faces glaring at him through the narrow opening.

"How," he said as he stepped into the early morning light, wishing he had taken time to learn a little of the Ute tongue. "Ute ponies all-the-same heap hungry. Many grain this place, heap many grain. Feed Ute horses, heap good."

No one answered; no one even moved. Despite the fact that he was holding a twelve-gauge goose gun with both barrels primed with black powder and double-aught slugs and both hammers drawn and cocked, Dick May licked his lips and wished he'd relieved himself a little earlier. Things did not feel right to him, they did not feel right at all. Blast! Where was John Thurman when he was needed, or that sorry complainer Byron Smith? For that matter, where were the Indian agents on the new reservation who were supposed to keep these Utes under control?

Abruptly Dick May thought of the cowboys he and Smith had

run into a couple of days before at the head of Yellowjacket Canyon. There had been Erastus Thomas, Henry Goodman, the Quick brothers, and a few others. But it had been Goodman who had warned him and Smith about the Utes, explaining that the cowboys had run onto a bunch a day or two earlier who were angry about something and looked to be spoiling for a fight.

"Was it me," Henry Goodman had advised, "I'd not go near that reservation, boys, not at least for a week or so."

With an empty feeling in the pit of his stomach, Dick May recalled his scornful laughter; that and his threat, as he had waved his goose gun in the air, to blow the red sons to kingdom come. Now though, despite that both barrels of that same weapon were trained on the bare belly of one of the more threatening of the Utes, he felt naked and alone, hardly capable even of spitting, his mouth had gone so dry—

"Want horses?" he croaked through parched lips. "Heap many horses, all-the-same Utes have 'em, one each. No, two! There, take the ones we've got in that corral yonder. Heap fine ponies, the very best!"

Abruptly one of the Utes, an ugly man with a huge mouth, smiled and nodded. Dick May felt instant hope, though if he had been more observant he would have seen that the smile never entered the man's eyes.

"Food heap good," the warrior declared in the guttural English Dick May had been trying to use. "Maybeso white man fixum food, giveum Utes!"

"Why," the frightened man replied with sincerity, "I'd do it in a minute, only there ain't a thing to eat in this blasted cabin but oats—horsefeed. I already looked when I got here last night."

"Heap hungry," the warrior persisted, his eyes flicking to the ring of warriors who sat silently around him.

"Well," Dick May declared hopelessly, thinking ruefully of the last of the coffee he had already consumed and wishing it was still in the pot so he could offer it, "I may not have any food, but I have . . . I have greenbacks, heap many greenbacks!"

Frantically he thrust one hand inside his shirt, yanked at the bulging money belt, and in an instant was holding before the staring Utes a handful of twenty-dollar bills.

"Greenbacks!" he shouted, his voice high and shrill. "See? Heap many greenbacks! Utes takeum one, takeum all. Takeum horses, too! Takeum all, but p-please just leave me alone—"

The spring morning was already warming, and to Dick May it felt for all the world like it was already summer. He could feel sweat coursing down his back, down his sides, and for an instant he worried that the sweat that had suddenly appeared on his brow might somehow impair his vision.

Breathing deeply to steady his nerves, he glanced off toward the grassy meadows where John Thurman and Byron Smith had vanished, and where Thurman's hundreds of horses were now grazing peacefully. The buzzing of a bee came from somewhere nearby, and off behind the cabin a crow screeched raucously. A breeze moved through the clumps of aspen, and for some reason their rapidly trembling new leaves served to remind him why he and the other locals called the trees quakies. But despite these signs of peace and normalcy, there was no sign of his friends, no indication that either of them would ride up and help him out of this trouble he could feel building.

Oh, lordy! he moaned inwardly. Why had those sorry fools ever thought they could build a ranch so near the Utes? Right on their new reservation, as a matter of fact. It was a fool thing to do, one Dick was sure they would soon live to regret.

Still, it was a lovely place for a ranch—good water, plenty of timber, lush meadow grass. Even better, he thought, than his own spread down in the Big Bend country, which he shared with his two brothers and Byron Smith. Too bad this place had to be wasted on the Indians. Too bad—

"*Wagh!*"

Warned by the tone of the Ute's voice, Dick May's mind focused on the Indians again, and he was surprised to see a huge rifle in the man's hand, a rifle that was pointed directly at him.

"Now, see here—" he protested as he started to shift his shotgun, belatedly noticing that the other Ute warriors had spread out and had their rifles and other weapons aimed in his general direction.

"Heap be still!" the ugly Ute ordered, his countenance finally betraying his true feelings. "White man heap fool!"

"What? Listen to me—"

"Say take ponies and go. Say take greenbacks and go. Heap good idea. We do. Heap good idea we killum white man first. We do."

Deliberately the Ute warrior extended the heavy rifle. Dick May's eyes grew wide with the realization of what was about to happen; then they narrowed with his fierce determination to give as much as he was going to get. But before he could do more than begin to depress the double triggers of his shotgun, the Ute fired.

Dick May grunted with surprise as something heavy slammed into him. His finger spasmed then, and fire belched from both barrels of his favorite goose gun. As the smoke from both weapons dissipated he looked down with surprise to see a gaping red hole in his abdomen. Strangely he felt no pain, just a sudden numbness, which made him wonder if somehow the bullet had merely grazed him. Yes, he thought as he looked back up to see a Ute warrior writhing on the ground beneath his horse, he himself wasn't badly injured at all. In fact—

With a strange feeling of exhilaration Dick dropped his goose gun and pulled his pistol from his belt. He had never done it better, more smoothly, and as he raised it and began firing he was aware that more bullets were splattering into the log doorframe beside him— that, and horses and men were suddenly down in the yard, the horses squealing and kicking in pain.

Quickly he stepped back into the room, wondering as he did so that the pistol was becoming so heavy. He could hardly hold it level, could hardly raise his left hand to palm the hammer.

Blinking his eyes to clear them he realized, abruptly, that the cabin floor was rushing up at him, and Dick May couldn't get his hands up quickly enough to catch himself. The jolt that followed was terrific, and with agonizing effort he turned his face to clear the oats on the floor from his nose and mouth. Only somehow that did no good, for now his breath wouldn't come, and frantically he let go of his pistol and with both hands pushed himself off the rough planks, struggling to breathe.

A final explosion and a smashing blow to his body were the last mortal memories Dick May ever had—those and a diminishing wonderment that he had somehow been shot and killed. Then he seemed to be moving away from everyone and everything, gathering speed—

———o—o—o———

With a grunt of satisfaction Mike slipped down from his pony, entered the cabin, and used his foot to roll the man over. Only after he had determined that the man was dead did he look up to see what his warriors were doing. Gunfire echoed in the distance, either that or thunder, and he felt confident that others of his followers had put a second foolish white man under the grass. Somewhere a third would also go down, and a good portion of the wealth of these whites would then be his.

"Come and gather these greenbacks," he ordered expansively, looking directly at Posey as he spoke. "Some say they are good for playing *ducki* with the whites. Yes, and perhaps they will be of even greater value in the day when we return with our wealth to the Shining Mountains."

Two or three warriors chuckled at Mike's humor and dismounted to do his bidding, and once again the ugly leader looked down at the still form of the erstwhile horse-buyer, whose wide, empty eyes were now staring upward.

Nonchalantly the powerfully built man exited the cabin and walked back to his pony, completely ignoring the two dying horses and the shotgun-blasted Ute brave he had been forced to step over. The horses he felt badly about, and usually he did not like to see warriors of the People fall in battle. But this one had been *katz-te-suah,* he had been a fool to sit in the way of the man's shotgun blast. *Wagh!* It would not have been wise to ride with him; it would not have been wise to take him into the wild land of the big river.

"*Ungh,*" he grunted with satisfaction as he watched Posey stuffing greenbacks into the trousers he had stripped from that dying white man on the far side of the big river more than a year before. "Now the fool Poke will see who are the true men of the People. Now he will see how many braves are ready to ride with the warriors of the big river."

Moments later, when Mike saw that flames were licking up the log walls of the cabin, he shouted his fierce war cry once again. Then without another word he reined around and followed after the vast herd of horses—his destination the slickrock country of the San Juan.

Bluff Fort

"Billy, do you mind if I ask you a question? A gospel question?"

Carefully recording the events of the past week in one of his small daybooks, Billy lifted his pen from the page, looked up, and smiled. "Of course not—not if you don't mind my admitting that I might not know the answer."

It was Sunday evening, not quite dark, and the activity in the fort was winding down for the night. Since it was the first of May, the Saints would normally have held a Mayday celebration, with feasting, dancing, and children winding strips of cloth around a planted Maypole to signify the springtime coming-together of all aspects of their lives in unity and happiness. But because it was Sunday, Bishop Nielson had decided to halt work on the ditch, the cribs, and the fields a little early the next day, and to have the community do their celebrating then.

Eliza shook her head as though she were out of patience with her husband. "You always know the answers, darling. That's why I ask you."

"I'm glad you think that," Billy teased, blowing on the fingernails of his right hand and then rubbing them on his shirt as though he were cleaning something that was already the epitome of perfection. "You think I'm great, and so now at least I have one person on this earth fooled. What's your question?"

"It has to do with Joseph Barton's sermon in meeting today. Or maybe it was Harriet Ann who said it. I disremember. Anyway, they quoted a verse of scripture where the Lord said we had to have faith, hope, and charity."

"That was Joseph, and he was reading the eighth verse of section 12 of the Doctrine and Covenants. The Lord was saying that no one can assist in the work of the restoration unless they are humble and full of love, having faith, hope, and charity." Billy grinned. "Was that it? Your question, I mean?"

"No, silly, I haven't asked it yet. For the past little while I've been looking up other scriptural passages, and I've found several others that also use the phrase *faith, hope, and charity*. My question is, why does the Lord always put those three attributes together?"

For a moment Billy looked at his wife, his smile apparently frozen in place. Then it slowly faded, to be replaced by a look of complete puzzlement. "Truthfully, hon-bun, I have no idea."

"Are you serious?"

"I am," Billy replied as he nodded slowly. "I've never asked that question of myself or anyone else, and I've never heard another soul address it. Oh, I've read or listened to a great many sermons and discourses that quote those various passages, and I'm aware that the Standard Works contain upwards of a dozen such references. And you're right—they are attributes that the Lord wants us to have. But as to why he always lumps those three together? Well, I really don't know."

Eliza was astounded. "If you don't know, darling, then maybe it isn't important."

Billy immediately disagreed. "Of course it is! Think about it for a moment, Eliza. Why have you been pondering those words since Joseph read them? Why have you been hunting out scriptures on the topic this evening? And why did you ask me about it? The logical answer is because the Spirit is impressing upon your mind that this is something you need to study out."

"But . . . I've read the passages of scripture, Billy. I think I know what they're saying. What I don't know is why—"

"You don't know why the Lord always lumps them together," Billy finished for her. "That's right; you don't know, and neither do I. So, ask him."

"What?"

Billy smiled. "Ask the Lord, Eliza. Study it as deeply as you are able, and then go to him in prayer and ask him to explain what you've been studying. He'll respond, and then you can teach me."

"Me?" Eliza giggled. "That'll be the day."

Billy nodded his confidence in his wife. "You're right, it will be.

Tuesday, or maybe Wednesday. By then I'll bet the Lord will have given you a firm grasp of the subject. Oh, by the way, the prophet Mormon once addressed the topic of faith, hope, and charity. His son Moroni was so impressed with his father's words that he added them to his own little book, and today we call that sermon the seventh chapter of Moroni in the Book of Mormon. Every time I've read it, however, I've wondered what Moroni saw in it. Personally, I find it somewhat confusing."

"Thanks a lot, Billy." Eliza was only partially feigning her disgust. "You've been a real help."

Billy grinned at his wife's sarcasm. "You're welcome," he replied sweetly, and with that he re-inked his pen and went back to work in his daybook.

19

◦─◦─◦

Monday, May 2, 1881

Rico, Western Colorado

"Well, if it ain't the youngest Heaton kid, home already from his jaunt through the wilderness. Couldn't find your way to them cows your pa was trying to buy, huh?"

Hard Tartar looked up at the younger but taller Jimmy Heaton as they joined in step and walked along the dusty main street of Rico, a mining town of fifteen hundred men and a few women set in the mountains at the eastern end of Disappointment Valley. It was morning, and a storm that had threatened them the past day or so looked to have blown over. Word had just spread through town of some trouble somewhere, and both Hard Tartar and Jimmy Heaton were responding to the call for help.

"We found 'em, Hard," Jimmy said, "all five hundred head, and drove 'em home with nary a hitch. But I hear tell you tie-cutting galloots from here in the valley got sent home by the railroad without meeting your quotas and ended up getting paid in scrip."

"We got paid in scrip, all right," Hard growled, truly upset, "but not because we didn't meet our quotas. Why, us and them Mormon fellers from Bluff filled half another team's quotas as well as our own. Way I figure it, that dadburned railroad's running short of funds; either that or some scallywag's pulling some mighty dishonest shenanigans. So, you and Henry W. actually did find that ranch you was looking for?"

"For a fact. Billy showed us the way, and he was right. He also took us into Bluff, which is a ramshackle fort that's more wide open than a politician's mouth. Tell the truth, Hard, I don't know why they call it a fort. But I do know them Mormon folks are fine people."

"Do tell?" Hard looked at Jimmy. "Some folks don't believe a word they say. Born-again liars, they call 'em, and worse. Did you actually meet Billy's wife and son, or were they conveniently someplace else?"

Now it was Jimmy's turn to look askance at the older man. "What's the matter with you, Hard? I thought you knew those folks. You spent all winter working with Billy, Dick Butt, and George Ipson."

"I did, at that. They was hard workers, I admit, and most of the time I enjoyed their company. But word gets around in spite of such doings, and Billy's the least likely looking husband a man ever saw. Besides, there are times when a man can't be too careful—"

"This time there's no need!" Jimmy was upset, and it showed. "Those Mormon folks are the real thing, Hard. Fact is, Henry W. and I met both Eliza and little Willy. Stayed with 'em, ate with 'em, worked beside 'em, and even learned some about their religion. Eliza's a fine woman, near tall as me, and sweet as honey. Turns out little Willy's been mighty sick, so Billy, he and the bishop, who's a tall, gimped-up old Danishman who's still strong enough to outdo Henry W. in arm wrestling, gave the boy what they call a blessing. The laying on of hands, they said it was. You can bet he'll be getting better now, too. Those folks have a powerful lot of faith, Hard, and I admire 'em for it."

For a moment the two walked in silence, and Jimmy found himself wondering at the discord that had come between them. He was surprised, for the same feeling came between himself and Henry W. whenever Mormons were brought up, and he didn't understand it. But neither did he want it to continue, at least not this morning. Hard Tartar had been too good a friend.

"Speaking of politicians," he said, pushing his hat back on his head and forcing his grin back into place, "who's old Dawson trying to impress now?"

"That's *Captain* Dawson, you young squirt," Hard Tartar replied sarcastically, glad himself to be off the subject of Mormons. "Either that or Sheriff, at least to the likes of you. And he ain't trying to impress anybody 'cept those he's raising a posse to chase after."

Jimmy was filled with sudden anticipation. "No fooling? We going after horse thieves this time, or more murderers?"

"What do you mean, 'we,' youngster? Posses are for men, not young bucks what're still green behind the ears."

Jimmy's grin continued, for he had learned to have almost infinite patience with the teasing of the calloused men who were his neighbors and teachers. "Hard, Hard, Hard," he said soothingly. "Just on account of that's your name, it don't give you no call to be so hard on innocent young folks like me. Besides, I rode with old Dawson once before, last year, in fact, and I don't recollect you being around that time to wipe my nose."

Hard Tartar smiled in return. "I wasn't, all right, not that you didn't need it. Me'n my brother Wiley was punching a useless hole in the ground for Isaac Stewart up in San Miguel County when old man Phelander was shot, and we plumb didn't hear about it. We did hear, though, that while you maybe started out with the posse, you didn't make it all the way to the finish."

"On account of my fool cayuse going lame on me," Jimmy groused. "But you can bet that won't happen this time. When Henry W. and me bought them five hundred head of cows off the LC, Bill Ball took pity on me and threw in a fine horse and a practically new saddle—"

"They to go along with that new little gal of yours?"

Jimmy's smile grew wider. "That's right. I told you boys about Miss Sally that night in camp, didn't I. Have you seen her yet, Hard? She's a sight! Especially when she dances up on that bar the way she does. Whooee! Did I tell you that come fall she and me are fixing on getting hitched?"

Suspiciously Hard Tartar eyed the tall youngster who was walking beside him. "Hitched? The two of you? Your pa know about this? Or your brother?"

"Henry W. does. Leastwise he knows me'n Sally have been sparking a little. But he's such an old fussbudget that I've about stopped telling him anything at all. But I'll tell Pa about it when things is more definite. You know how he and Ma are, and Sally doing what she does to hold body and soul together. Well, no sense pouring the milk out before the cow's put her hoof in the pail, I always say."

"You ain't had time in this life to always say much of anything." Hard Tartar, despite his crusty approach to life, truly loved Jimmy Heaton. Not only did Jimmy withstand his teasing with amazing grace, but he was also a good hand with a rope and could ride and punch cows with the best. Everybody in the country got along with him, and Hard had never heard of his losing a rough-and-tumble with anybody. For a fact—

"Morning, boys. We headed for Mona's Emporium?"

Hard Tartar glanced at Hiram Melvin and John Galloway, who now joined them in the roadway. "That's the word I said to spread around," he declared. "Sheriff Dawson's there, raising him a posse, and since our crew's only been home a couple of days, I figure we got nothing better to do than ride with him. The other fellers coming?"

"Far as I know, Hard, the whole crew'll be there. Morning, Jimmy. You joining us?"

"I reckon so, Hiram."

"You heard why the posse's getting raised?"

"We ain't even heard when." Jimmy Heaton smiled with his endless humor.

"When is now," John Galloway grumbled, his dark eyes flashing, "and why is on account of them murdering redskin Utes. Way I heard it from George Taylor, Pat and Mike O'Donnel and that Navajo they call Little Captain was camped at Willow Springs and saw smoke, too much of it, coming from Thurman's place at Ute Springs over on Monument Creek. Soon as they could they rode over and found it burned to the ground and Dick May's body badly burned and lying under a pile of oats. All of his money except for a little silver was missing from his belt. Outside was two dead Injun ponies, a sight of blood, and a whole slug of shell casings, and all Thurman's horses are gone, every last one of them."

"That whole blamed herd?"

"That's right. Fourteen hundred head of horses! Anyhow, the O'Donnel boys lit a shuck on back to guard their own place and sent

Little Captain off to find Dick's brother Bill May. Bill's madder'n hops and has been getting up a posse at Mancos and on the Dolores, and Sheriff Dawson and his boy are here recruiting men in Rico."

"Dick May, huh. What about John Thurman? He was a friend of mine."

Hiram Melvin shook his head. "No one knows," he responded. "But he ain't been seen. Another man by the name of Smith ain't been seen either, and Davis Willis, Thurman's partner, is mighty worried. I reckon Josh Alderson's a little worried too, seeing as how all those horses was half his. Thing is, those Utes have been robbing and killing around here for years, and no one's had the nerve to do a blamed thing about it. Seems like it's high time a few of us boys got together and taught 'em a lesson."

"Seems like," Hard Tartar agreed. "Which way did they head with the horses?"

"Northwest, over toward the Blue Mountain country where Spud Hudson has his range. George Taylor thinks the Indians'll hit Hudson and his neighbors next, and it wouldn't surprise me none if they did."

"Anybody know that country?"

"Not very well. But Bill May was told the trail is plain, and with that many horses the Indians won't be moving too fast. So that's it, boys, except that we'll be riding out within the hour, heading first for Thurman's burnt cabin to see if we can find him or Smith. We all in?"

Hard Tartar nodded firmly. "Well, I am, and I reckon my brother Wiley'll go too. He wintered with Dick May once and thought highly of him."

For a moment Jimmy Heaton thought of his new Mormon friends and their philosophy of feeding rather than fighting the Indians. He also thought of Bishop Jens Nielson's counsel to never thirst after their blood. But this was different, the young man instantly reasoned. These were murderers he would be riding after— outlaws that truly did need to be brought to justice. Surely that would make a difference—

"Count me in," Jimmy Heaton declared, his smile abruptly gone. "I'll float my stick with George Taylor's opinion, too. I reckon it's high time we taught them thieving varmints a lesson they won't soon forget."

And without another word the young man turned toward the livery stable and his new horse and saddle. Before he rode out, he was thinking, there should be a minute or so to say good-bye to Miss Sally, at least if she was awake and dressed. And maybe, by golly, to get a smooch or two out of her. And that, Jimmy Heaton thought with another of his wide, pleasant smiles, was worth more than all the posse rides in the whole blamed world!

Bluff Fort

"I'll tell you this much," George Lewis laughed as he swung Parley Butt in a Virginia Reel on the sandy commons of the Bluff fort, "I'd a whole lot rather be celebrating Mayday by dancing with my wife."

Parley laughed. "So would I with mine, George. All we have to do is find 'em and then talk 'em into marrying us."

"Course, at least you ain't expecting a baby any minute like Harriet Gower, there. Or Anna Decker, either one."

"No, George, I ain't. But from the size of that pot belly of your'n, maybe you'd ought to let Maggie Haskel take a look at you."

Several in the group of dancers laughed at that, and the good-natured bantering continued as number after number was sawed out on Charlie Walton's lone fiddle, Lem Redd doing the calling. It was late afternoon, the sun was low over the sandstone bluffs to the west, and the San Juan Saints were doing what most of them enjoyed more than almost anything else—dancing and bantering with each other in good-hearted fun.

In honor of the occasion, Platte Lyman and his brother Joseph had cut and then planted in the commons a cottonwood pole that was more crooked than any of them would have wished, and a few moments before, the children had danced in a circle around it, weaving and wrapping their strips of rag until the pole was covered with colored fabric. Several of the men had then fired their guns in salute, and now the celebration was in full swing.

While as many as cared to danced, Hanson Bayles, Walter Lyman, his sister May, and Mary Ann Perkins tended the roasting of a beef that had been butchered early that morning. Young William

Mackelprang and his friend Sammy Rowley had been given the job of tending the fire, and they had already dragged up more wood than would ever be needed. But in their enthusiasm the boys had gone after more, and no one was going to discourage them.

"That Navajo woman over there with Eliza Foreman makes me nervous," John Gower declared as he watched Hanson Bayless turn the large spit.

"But John, that's Hádapa." May Lyman was startled at the man's attitude, and she was determined to set the matter straight. "She's the one who took that snakebite for Eliza and saved little Willy's life with her goat's milk."

"Makes no matter. She's Navajo, and every one of those people are thieves from the get-go. Besides, this ought to be a celebration for our people. Period."

"I suspect Eliza thinks that's who Hádapa is," Walter replied quietly. "For a fact, John, I agree with her."

"And I agree with Walter," Hanson Bayles stated without looking up. "Billy looks on her as a true friend, and Thales Haskel says we need all those we can get."

"Well, I still say she shouldn't be here. She makes me as nervous as old Peokon did when we first came into this country two years ago, exploring. Or the one called Frank, for that matter. Those two would've killed us in a heartbeat if they'd dared, and even Thales says he believes Frank is at the heart of our livestock losses now."

"All that may be true, but it has nothing to do with Hádapa." May Lyman was insistent. "Look at the happiness on her face, John, and tell me she's plotting evil. Look at her! She's even teaching little Willy how to clap in time with Charlie's fiddle."

Unconvinced, John Gower merely grunted. "Well, with her here, we're likely to be up to our earlobes in Lamanites before the day is over. But like some are saying, I reckon I can love the Lamanites and still hate the Indians."

"Mighty strange attitude for folks called on a mission to bring the gospel of peace to these people," Kumen Jones remonstrated as he walked past. "If Christ loved them, I reckon we can too."

"Yeah," another man grumbled from nearby, "but they couldn't kill Christ, either. He'd been resurrected. Anyway, I agree with John.

I've about had it with this mission. Being around so many of these murderous red sons gives me the willies. And I'll say this while I'm at it. I'm mighty tired of watching my family sacrifice and starve year in and year out, and I'm just as tired of scratching at that fool ditch and knowing full well it ain't never going to hold a lick of water. I think Billy and Eliza Foreman are crazy for letting that woman near their son, and I think the rest of us are just as crazy for letting her help tend the rest of the little ones. And I think all of you who plan on staying and continuing this fool mission are crazy as coots!"

"Crazy as coots," Kumen Jones stated quietly, "or full of faith."

"Did you folks hear what Billy was just saying?" Joshua Stevens asked as he sauntered to the fire with his wife Elizabeth, unwittingly interrupting the other conversation.

"Not a word, Josh. What was it?"

"It was an amazing mathematical trick," Elizabeth declared enthusiastically. "How that man comes up with such things, I'll never know!"

"So, tell us about it."

Joshua laughed. "Are you serious? I couldn't begin to remember that crazy formula. Say, Billy," he then called to where Billy was standing next to Eliza and Hádapa, "these folks want to learn a little higher mathematics. Come on over and tell them about that new formula of yours."

"It's hardly new," Billy declared after he had moved past the dancers and reached the fire. "I learned it when I was a boy and happened to think of it when I heard Francis Webster doing a little calculating the hard way."

"Well," May asked with a smile, "are you going to tell us what it is?"

"If you'd like." Billy was obviously nervous, but he continued anyway. "Any number you want to multiply by five will give you the same result if divided by two, a much quicker operation; but you have to add a zero to the answer when there's no remainder, and when there is a remainder, you discard it and add a five."

"Say that again?"

Slowly Billy repeated himself.

"That's it?"

"That's it, Walter. For instance, if you multiply 464 by 5, the answer is 2,320. Divide 464 by 2, and you have 232; there's no remainder, so you add a 0, which again gives you 2,320. Now, take 357, multiply it by 5, and the answer comes out as 1,785. If you divide 357 by 2, you get 178 and a remainder. Discard the remainder, place a 5 at the end of the figure, and once again you end up with 1,785."

"Amazing," May breathed.

"Not really. It's just a simple formula."

"No, not that part. I'm amazed you can do all that in your head. It'd take me three slates and a whole hunk of chalk, and then I'd probably get it wrong. Have you told Feenie about this?"

Billy smiled. "No, but I'm sure she knows it. After all, she is the schoolteacher."

"That's right," Elizabeth Stevens agreed. "And schoolteachers are supposed to know everything. By the by, where is Feenie?"

"I saw her and Amasa Barton heading out through the gate a little bit ago," May said with a smile. "Maybe that romance of theirs is heating up a little."

"Like the off side of this beef?" Billy teased. "Come on, Hans, either turn it a little faster or turn it over to me."

With a flourish Hanson Bayless bowed and backed away. "She's yours, Billy. Turn her fast, and I'll go see if Eliza'll take a fast turn or two around the commons with me."

Everyone laughed, Hanson Bayless walked away, and Billy was just starting to turn the roasting animal when Charlie's fiddle stopped and Bishop Nielson pulled himself up into the bed of a wagon.

"Ya, brudders," he called out, waving his hat for attention. "Sisters und children—you, too! Gadder around, und ve vill haff us a meeting!"

Without hurry the people sauntered together around the wagon. "Tank you," the old Danishman declared once they had all gathered and grown reasonably quiet. "Yim Decker vill lead us in singing "Come, Come, Ye Saints," after vich my son Yoseph vill offer de prayer. After dat I haff a few tings to say about our mission und de blessings off de Lord dat ve all enyoy in dis vondrous land.

Following my remarks, ve vill see how much damage ve can do to de beef Billy iss turning yonder on de spit."

There were a few quick cheers, and then the whole assembly, Hádapa included, joined in singing the favorite hymn. Truly things seemed to be looking up for the besieged Saints on the San Juan.

20

The Ditch

"Haw!" Samuel Rowley shouted to the two oxen, at the same time goading them to the left with a pole he was carrying. "Haw, you miserable critters. Haw!"

Half a dozen feet away David Stevens was shouting the same directions to his team, also goading them to the left, and beyond him Charlie Walton was doing the same with a third team. Behind the three men and their yokes of oxen dragged a massive forked cottonwood log to which trace chains had been attached, and this dragging log was breaking up the clay and smashing down the willows and greasewood. And behind them all came Dick Butt, his mules dragging the scraper that was opening the first cut of the ditch.

"All right, now, straighten it!" Billy called from where he stood off to the side behind Platte Lyman's transom, spotting the direction the oxen should go. "Good! Hold 'em steady, boys. That's it, that's it. Okay, now to the right a little, just to the side of that rock outcropping directly ahead. Good, good!"

"Gee!" Samuel Rowley shouted in response. "Gee, you four-legged numskulls! Gee! Gee!" And immediately David Stevens and Charlie Walton picked up the same refrain.

It was coming onto a hot day, Billy thought as he lifted his hat and wiped his brow, and the sun was not even two hours into the sky. It was also clear, with no hope of rain, and therefore no hope of wetting the settlers' precious seed—seed that needed a good soaking in order to germinate.

"Beats me how that river can work so fast," George Westwood grumbled as he and several others followed after the scraper with their shovels. "I know our ditch ran through here before that flood, but I'll be dogged if I can see any sign of it now."

"It is amazing," Ben Perkins agreed as he shoveled behind the younger man. "Compared to God's power made manifest through the elements, man's arm is puny indeed."

"Hey, fellers!" Joseph Barton called from behind the two men with shovels, "you're digging a little soon, aren't you? Amasa's coming right along with another scraper, and it's him you ought to be following."

With sighs the men climbed up out of the ditch, where they saw that Joseph Barton was right. Fifty yards back, Amasa was coming along behind another team and scraper, completely negating all the clean-up they had been doing.

"Billy," George called, his voice filled with frustration, "who the devil is ramrodding this outfit today? Didn't the bishop assign somebody?"

"Reckon you boys are looking for me," Jim Decker said as he rode out of a thick stand of greasewood. "What'd I foul up this time?"

"If we're going to get five miles of this ditch dug out," Joseph Barton declared, "we've got to work together. Jim, today that's your job. Everybody wants to work, but it's got to be coordinated so the boys aren't stumbling over each other or undoing what somebody else's just done."

Jim Decker shook his head. "I know it, Joseph, and I'm sorry. Parley was showing me the torn hoof of one of his mules, and . . . well, I just got behind. Boys, remember; we have two scrapers, and there ain't no sense in shoveling anything out until they've both taken a pass at it, and Billy and Kumen have surveyed the bottom for level. If it's still high, then we need to take another pass or two with the scrapers, and I don't want anybody shoveling anything until the scrapers are gone for good."

As first Amasa Barton and then the shoveling crew continued

forward and past him, Billy strained his eyes through the glare, watching for the end of Kumen's marked stick. Digging the ditch was slow going, he thought as he sighted on the distant stick, too slow. The river was starting to drop, the cribs weren't finished, and they still had several miles of ground to put a ditch through before they came near the plowed and planted area of the Bluff fields.

But at least, he thought wearily as he gave Kumen the signal for level, folded his transom, and trudged after the others, they were all being blessed in other ways. The Pahutes were still out of the country, for some reason the Navajo raiding had slacked off, and little Willy was getting stronger by the day. Yes, and Eliza was also doing better, especially now that he had put his foot down and told her to stay with the work of tending the little children. That didn't tax her too heavily, and she could sit down as often as needed.

Besides, he thought as he passed the men and set up his transom in a new location, it gave her a little more time to do the studying he had suggested she do—

———o—o—o———

"I'm telling you, Billy, I have no idea what's going on with Mary. She's more troubled than I've ever seen her, and I don't have any idea how to help."

The sun was now a little past straight overhead, and with tired sighs the men had left their teams yoked or in harness and their shovels planted in the dirt, then moved to the shade of a large cottonwood. The sisters had already placed a couple of buckets of wellwater there, not clear and sparkling but nearly liquid enough, as one of them joked, to sustain life. And so with thankful looks the men used the water to slake their thirst and soak their faces, after which they gathered to the communal meal that had been prepared earlier by the same women.

"What's she troubled about?" Billy asked as he chewed thoughtfully.

Kumen shook his head. "That's just it, Billy. She doesn't know, at least exactly. For weeks she's been consumed with a feeling that something awful is about to happen to all of us. Now she's even having dreams—of a terrible fierce battle of some sort—and every time she dreams it, she wakes up bawling her eyes out."

"Has she had a blessing?"

"Two of 'em. They haven't helped that I can see, and to tell the truth, Billy, I'm stumped. I've even talked to her pa, and he can't figure it any more than the rest of us. I was wondering if maybe she'd said anything to Eliza that might be of help."

For a moment Billy was quiet. "Well, Eliza has mentioned that Mary was feeling troubled—something about all of us being in danger—but I haven't heard anything more specific. In her dreams, is there ever any sort of solution?"

Kumen smiled thinly. "Yeah, sort of. She always wakes up saying we have to be more pure of heart, more united in our work. I don't know about you, Billy, but I can't give it much more. I mean, daylight to dark I'm dead beat, and more and more this season's looking to be as big a bust as last year. Happen it is, short of starving to death, I have no idea what Mary and I are going to do."

"Just go forward, I reckon," Billy stated quietly. "That and pray for a little more purity of heart. If she's right, Kumen, we're all going to need it—"

Hills above Coal Bed Creek, Colorado

"Damnation and double damnation!" Captain William Dawson growled as he gazed at the partially butchered remains of two horses. "I can abide murder and robbery, boys, but when it comes to killing and eating perfectly good horses, my whole stomach turns."

In silence the men of the Rico posse sat their horses around the two carcasses, picturing in their minds what had happened around the various fires in the encampment. To an individual they were as disgusted as their captain, and as furious.

Earlier they had examined the remains of Dick May, as well as the burned cabins at the spring where he had been slain. The J. H. Alderson ranch, of which John Thurman was foreman, was located in the hills above Monument Creek, a small stream that ran mostly southwestward through precipitous gorges until it entered into Utah and Montezuma Creek. That stream, in turn, flowed southward until it emptied into the San Juan.

Jimmy Heaton and Hard Tartar, scouting around on Cedar Point while the others had remained at the burned cabins to bury Dick May, had also found the body of John Thurman—stripped, scalped, and fly-bloated. He, too, had been buried where he had been found.

To a man the Rico posse was now so determined to exact retribution on the Ute warriors that nothing on earth would have turned them back. The Dolores posse, under Bill May, apparently felt the same, and so upwards of sixty men, mostly hardened men of the frontier, were presently riding northwestward in two groups toward Spud Hudson's range below the Blue Mountains of southeastern Utah.

"They was Thurman's and May's horses, all right." Wiley Tartar was normally as quiet as his brother was loquacious, but not now. "Brand's still there on both of 'em."

"They just et the juicy parts," Tim Jenkins added, though from the way the two animals had been butchered, his conclusion was obvious to all the Rico posse. "The way it looks to me, fellers, those brands were left a'purpose for us to see. These Utes is just laughing at us, making it clear exactly what they think."

"Then let's show 'em what we think!" Tom Click growled angrily. "The trail's still plain. If it's all the same to you, Captain Dawson, I say we ride till we can't see it no more on account of the dark."

"My plan exactly," Captain Dawson responded. "Boys, I—"

"Captain?" Dick Baumgartner called as he and Jordan Bean rode up the hill toward the group. "There's another trail down yonder, maybe two, three hundred yards. Looks to be a couple of days older."

"More Indians?"

"As ever!" Jordan Bean declared. "They were dragging travois poles, and they have a fair-sized herd of sheep and goats, so it's a bunch of women and kids—more'n likely the squaws and papooses of this bunch that took the horses."

"We ain't going to kill the women and kids, are we?"

Some of the men guffawed at Jimmy Heaton's concern, but

Captain Dawson held up his hand. "No, Jimmy," he responded, "we ain't. Some would, I reckon, figuring that nits make lice, but I don't hold with that sort of thinking a'tall! No sir, we're after the murderers of Dick May and John Thurman. Them we'll fight to the last man, but never women and children. Any of you boys who think differently, now's the time to leave."

Nobody moved, nobody spoke. "Good!" Captain William Dawson said, his voice ringing with authority. "Then let's ride!"

Nokai Canyon, Navajo Reservation

Natanii nééz could not understand what was happening. He had ridden, with the coming of the dawn, to the fine herd of horses he was in the midst of acquiring and developing. And most assuredly they were fine animals that he had taken from here and there; a strong stallion and many mares, every one fit for breeding fine colts. Yes, and fine geldings, too—every animal already bred for the trail and fit to carry a man long and far. So the tall Navajo was pleased, and justifiably so.

Of course, he was not so pleased with the woman Hádapa, whom he had taken to wife a few years before because of her great beauty. That beauty was now fading, he felt, and she no longer seemed so desirable to him. Worse, though, was that she had been unable to give him a son to ride beside him; no, nor even a daughter to brighten his days. Instead, the woman had proven *doo áshchíí da,* barren, and thus she was unworthy of him.

Still, Hádapa was a hard worker, and Natanii nééz knew this. Especially of late this had proven true, for on the rare occasions when he had returned to spend the night with her, upon awakening with the dawn he had found her already gone to spend the day with her growing flocks of sheep and goats. That was good. It was also good that she never rode away without leaving fresh meat in the pot for him to eat.

On the other hand, Natanii nééz reminded himself, she had failed to give him children, and not once had he seen the spoils of her raids against the mormonee *belacani*—raids he had directed her to make.

No one would blame him, therefore, if he were to take to himself another wife—

Shaking his head to clear his mind of such small worries, the tall one noted with pleasure the beauty of the afternoon. The sun, far along on its journey across the sky, was hot upon a land that had been well watered by the recent rains. In fact, not all of the cloud and thunder people had gone away with the darkness of the night before, for here and there in the sky, long streamers of walking rain once again hung downward, providing even more moisture for the ever-thirsty land.

Natanii nééz enjoyed these things, enjoyed seeing them, feeling them. They were part of the *hózhó,* the balance in his life. And so as a few droplets from a streamer of walking rain wet his upturned face, he rejoiced, not only that there was such beauty in this land of *Dine tah* and among his fine horses but also that there was beauty in the way he had been able to take the best of the horses from the foolish mormonee *belacani* who had settled along the big river to the north.

Small in his thoughts now grew his worry over the woman Hádapa; small in his thoughts had already grown the memory of *Daghaa chíí,* the red-bearded mormonee *belacani* who had shamed him by so easily taking back his horse more than two weeks before. Yes, and though they were more recent, even smaller had grown his memory of the words of the mormonee *belacani* known as Bin'a'a dootl'izh'i, Blue Eyes. Yes, they had been strong words—words of warning—or so it had been claimed. But the words had in truth held no power, for Natanii nééz had seen no change within himself. No, not for eight days and eight nights had he seen any change at all.

And so with the woman Hádapa once again gone to her flocks, he had ridden this day to his herd of horses with one intent, and one only. He would choose the finest mount in his herd of fine horses, and on its back he would ride once again to the fort and take for himself the fine mare that Red Whiskers had stolen back from him. *Aoo,* yes, and he would do it before darkness, and in that manner defy the weak mormonee to do anything about it! Besides, he thought without mirth, in daylight there would be less chance for his mount to slip on that treacherous trail—

Throwing his rope on a powerful bay gelding, which he had also stolen from the people on the big river, Natanii nééz exchanged his bridle and good saddle, mounted the gelding, and reined it around toward the big river.

"Hiyii," he shouted joyfully as he nudged the gelding hard with his heels. And it was in that same instant, as the bay lunged forward, that something terrible struck the tall Navajo hard in the chest. His breath was driven from his lungs, he doubled over above the gelding's neck with pain, and for a moment he thought he had been shot.

But no, there had been no sound, no explosion of gunfire. Besides, as he struggled to examine himself he found no wound, no blood. Yet the pain in his chest was incredible, and no matter how he struggled and gasped, the tall Navajo could not draw in sufficient air.

In agony he fell from the still-running gelding, and when he had dragged himself to his feet he found, to his surprise and horror, that he could no longer stand erect. His back was now bent as if he were an old man, his neck ached simply with the effort of trying to see ahead of himself, and all the while he continued gasping and wheezing, feeling as if he were being suffocated under a heavy blanket.

Weakly he raised his voice, hoping to call back the gelding. But the fleeing animal paid him no attention and was soon out of sight over a low hill. Stumbling about, Natanii nééz then made for the other animals in his fine herd, and in dismay he heard more than saw them galloping off, apparently frightened of this bent and deformed creature who was stumbling toward them.

His mind whirling with more questions that he knew how to ask, the tall Navajo, no longer so tall, turned again and began stumbling in the direction of his own distant *hogan*. And as he stumbled and gasped and wheezed and moaned with pain, trying to see what was ahead of him, bigger and bigger in his memory grew the words of the old mormonee who was becoming known among the *Diné* as Blue Eyes, the terrible words of power that had been spoken only eight days before.

Bluff Fort

"Well, Eliza, that's another day behind us."

Seated in her rocker with Willy in her arms, Eliza pushed a

strand of graying hair behind her ear and nodded. "A long day, too, Annie. The way those children were crying a little earlier, I didn't know if we'd ever get them calmed down. But thank you so much for your help. When two do the tending, it's so much easier."

Annie Lyman smiled warmly. "The pleasure's been mine, Eliza."

For a moment the two were silent, Eliza rocking her son with closed eyes and Annie standing by the door, looking at but not seeing the Regulator clock.

"Eliza," she asked abruptly, "remember when we spoke a few weeks ago of prayer—of getting personal answers?"

"I do." Eliza still didn't open her eyes.

"Well, I've been praying like I've never prayed in my life, and nothing's happening. Absolutely nothing! What am I doing wrong?"

Now Eliza's eyes opened wide. "Glory be, Annie, how should I know that?"

"I . . . I don't know. I was just hoping that you'd come on a solution or something."

Slowly Eliza shook her head. "I don't mean to make light of your struggles, Annie. But if the truth be known, I may be in worse difficulty than you."

Annie raised one eyebrow inquisitively.

"I made the mistake of asking Billy a gospel question the other night, and he claimed he didn't know the answer. Worse, he told me to study and pray about it and get the answer for myself."

"Have you? Received your answer, I mean?"

Eliza chuckled. "Lawsy, no! We were supposed to talk about it last evening, but it was long after dark by the time Billy finished the chores, and I think he was asleep before he even hit the pillow. It wouldn't surprise me if tonight turns out the same. I certainly hope so."

"Are you . . . are you trying to get an answer?"

"I'm trying, all right. I've read Mormon's address on faith, hope, and charity twenty times if I've read it once; I've prayed about the meaning of it more often than that, and I still find it confusing. Truthfully, Annie, short of fasting I don't know what else to do."

"And you can't fast?"

Slowly Eliza shook her head. "Not according to Maggie

Haskel—not at least until the baby's born." She sighed deeply, her concern obvious. "Still, Annie, I'm going to have to do something! I know I'm supposed to understand it. I do!"

21

The Ford at Sand Island

The sun was high in the sky, too high, and Hádapa gripped the ropes more tightly and kicked her burro, urging it to hurry. She was finally at the ford over the big river, and she knew there were only two miles left until she would be at the fort. But that would take time, and she felt terrible that little Willy, whom she had fondly named *Haskéts'ósi,* or Slender Warrior, would for that time be without food. She was also considering her friend *Ásdzáán nééz* or Tall Woman, Slender Warrior's mother, and perhaps even Slender Warrior's father, whom Hádapa laughingly called *nákéeáznilii* because he was always adjusting his spectacles on his nose and thus bringing attention to them. These two would be worrying about her, about why she was late, and Hádapa knew it.

These three people the Navajo woman truly cared for— *baa áháshyá*—and she was certain that they felt the same about her. She also cared for Mary Jones, who was barren just as she was barren, whose heart was also breaking, and who could speak enough of her tongue that they could talk a little of this great sadness. Of course, she also felt fondness for many of the others in the fort, especially the children, and she was always surprised at how willingly she was accepted among them. But it was the three, Slender Warrior, Tall Woman, and the one who wears spectacles, who had found a true place in her heart and over whom she was now grieving.

"'*Aeeskés!*'" she called anxiously as she kicked her burro and yanked again at the two ropes in her hand. "We must travel fast!"

At last across the ford and climbing the sandy banks on the north side of the river, Hádapa continued worrying about this or that and wondering. Within the past few days her cousin Jim Joe and his wife's aging father, Dah nishuánt, had stopped at her fire for a little nourishment. She and Jim Joe had enjoyed a pleasant visit, and she had told him a little of the starving mormonee *belacani* child and her efforts to help him. Dah nishuánt had then spoken a few words about the goodness and power of the words of these mormonee people, and his telling had lodged firmly in Hádapa's mind.

She knew of the goodness, of course, for the mormonee were a people of peaceable ways toward her and all others, which was a thing she greatly favored. But she hadn't known about the power of which the old man spoke. In all her days in the fort on the big river she had seen no sign of this—had heard no words that brought blessing or destruction upon anyone. It was not that she hadn't believed the telling of Dah nishuánt; it was just that he was very old, and Hádapa knew that age sometimes dimmed the mind. Despite this, she had not been able to stop thinking of what he had said, worrying about what sort of power the mormonee *belacani* might hold—

As sudden tears started from her eyes, the Navajo woman kicked her burro again, urging it into a slow trot. She had to hurry, to get to the fort and then back to her *hogan*—

When Natanii nééz, he who was her husband, had come staggering into the *hogan* that morning before the dawning, Hádapa had not known him and had cried out with fear. Not only had his appearance changed, but even his voice was different, causing him to sound older than most old men. Yet within a few moments she had come to realize that this man who was now *nánishhod,* a cripple, was also the tall one who was her husband. Or at least he had been tall when she had last seen him—

Words of power. She thought again of old Dah nishuánt, and of his brief telling of the mormonee. Natanii nééz had also made a telling this morning, or rather he had gasped it out after he had fallen upon his sheepskins. His telling was of killing and raiding, and of a blue-eyed mormonee who had spoken words of power against the tall one because of it. Yes, and this same *belacani* had also spoken his words of power against Peokon, a man whom Hádapa had once feared and even hated. That one was now dead, he and all his household, and Natanii nééz was filled with terror, for he knew that the same fate lay ahead for him and his woman.

More tears flowed from Hádapa's eyes, and again she jerked the ropes and kicked the ribs of the hapless little burro, urging it forward. She did not fear death at the hands of her friends the mormonee, for she was certain those words of power had not been spoken against her. She did not even fear the death of her tall husband, for she knew that if it came, it would be the way things should be. No, that which she feared—and it was the thing that brought tears to her eyes and sorrow to her heart—was that now she was needed always in the *hogan* of her husband.

No longer would she be able to spend her mornings and sometimes even her days with Slender Warrior or Tall Woman or even the one who wears spectacles. No longer could she learn the words of the *belacani* tongue from Mary. Worst of all, no longer would she feel the love she always felt when approaching the unfinished log fort—

Choking back the sobs that were suddenly wracking her body, Hádapa kicked her burro and yanked again on the two ropes—the ropes that led back to her two finest nanny goats. At least, her sorrowing mind told her, if she could no longer come to the aid of Slender Warrior and his family, if she could no longer come to their cabin and bask in the warmth of their love—at least they would not be deprived of the precious milk the child so desperately needed!

Yes, she thought as her tears continued, and perhaps she herself would be fondly remembered—

Piute Springs

"Hell's tinkling hot brass bells!" The curser, Joshua "Spud" Hudson, Blue Mountain rancher and stockman, was staring at the torn-up earth beneath his horse's hooves. "I don't know, Curly. This here's either a new-fangled toll road somebody's building from nowhere to nowhere else, or it's the biggest doggone stock trail I ever saw. You see any cow tracks in this mess?"

Curly Jenkins, a tall, gaunt-looking man who was now Spud Hudson's foreman, rode slowly across the churned ground—at that point more than sixty yards across. "Nary a one," he growled when he had returned. "Them's hosses, Spud; every last one of 'em. But that ain't the bad news."

Spud looked at his hired hand questioningly.

"The bad news, Spud, is that scattered around out there are the tracks of a few unshod ponies—Injun ponies, I make 'em. These may be white man hosses, Spud, all shod and broke to the saddle, but they sure ain't being driven by white men. Worse, the Injuns driving this herd are headed straight for the Double Cabins, and you know what that means."

For a moment Spud sat his horse in silence, thinking. Ahead of them the cattle they had been moving westward toward the higher pastures of the Blue Mountains continued slowly forward, drawn by the smell of the nearby water. Behind them a crow called raucously from the top of a juniper where it had watched the herd trail past, and other than that, all was still.

"Curly," Spud finally replied, for once too dumbfounded to cuss, "you got any idea how many?"

"I didn't take time to work out the tracks," the lanky man replied helplessly. "Maybe a dozen?"

"That's a lot, but it ain't too many. You truly figure they're headed for my hoss herd next?"

"Well, if I was them, Spud, that's where I'd be headed."

Angrily Spud yanked his hat off and threw it to the ground. "Of all the dad-burned, low-down, rotten tricks! I'm telling you, Curly, it don't do a man a lick of good trying to get ahead in this world. What with drought and winter storms and thieving outlaws and Mormon tax collectors and these durn-fool plundering Injuns, it just can't be done! Come the day I sell out and head off to find a more free and decent country, I hope by thunder you'll recollect this miscarriage of justice and understand why."

"I'll remember," Curly replied while Spud swung from his horse, clapped his hat back on his head, kicked a couple of rocks as hard as he could, and then clambered back aboard.

"Spud, maybe that prospector feller what's been staying at the springs got a look at these varmints."

Spud's expression changed instantly. "Well, I'll be dogged, Curly. I never even thought of that old feller. Seems to me he'd be in more danger than my horses, and of a sudden I've got me a bad feeling about him. Forget the cows; we can come back for them later. Let's ride!"

They did, for not quite a mile, and then just over a small rise and not a hundred yards from the springs, they rode right onto the naked, mutilated body of the old man.

"Thunderation," Spud growled as the two gentled their terrified mounts, which had shied violently at the grisly sight and smell, "what we're following ain't no raiding party, not by a long sight. What she is, by jings, is a murdering war party of either Utes or Navajos what's up to the same no good deviltry as I hear tell Geronimo and his Mimbreno braves are executing down in Arizona and old Mexico."

"That ain't good news," Curly declared quietly.

"It's bad as sulfur stink in the moonlight and getting worse right along," Spud said. "These Injuns may have stolen a passel of hosses, Curly, but you mark my words: that ain't what they're after, at least not altogether. Just like Geronimo, the whole kit and caboodle of 'em is out to kill whites, and all this is just bait to draw us along."

"So, what do we do?"

Spud spat to the side. "Do? Well, we're too late by more than somewhat to save my herd, and I'd bet my last gold eagle that by now they'll have Mr. Peters's herd and whatever they can gather from some of the smaller ranchers, too. So one of us buries this sorry old soul, and the other starts riding to round up every white man he can find. Then we take the bait and go after 'em, just like they want!"

"Sounds right to me, Spud."

"Good, on account of if it didn't, I'd fire you! Take your pick, Curly. I ain't assigning either job to anyone."

"I'll bury the old man," the lanky cowpoke said as he swung down and tied his horse to some trampled brush. "Fellers around here know you, Spud, so you'll gather more men than I ever could."

Tipping his hat to show his gratitude, the rancher spun his horse and was off to the west. Doing his best to stay upwind of the old man's body, Curly Jenkins watched his boss disappear. And then, sucking in his breath and pulling his bandanna up over his nose and mouth, he turned to the gruesome task at hand.

Bluff Fort

"You're not coming?" Billy, cleaned up after evening chores, was struggling to tie the bow in his tie. "But hon-bun, it's fast and testimony meeting tonight."

"I know," Eliza replied dully. "I just don't feel like going."

"Of course—it's what happened with Hádapa," Billy concluded as he shrugged into his coat. "That's what has you so upset."

Numbly Eliza nodded. "She handed me her two goats, and we embraced. Then she cried, held little Willy, and cried some more, and I had no idea of what was happening. Then Mary appeared, she and Hádapa talked a little, they both cried, and Hádapa climbed on her burro and rode away."

"So . . . what did Mary learn?"

Eliza shook her head. "Not much, beyond that the goats were for Willy because Hádapa wouldn't be coming back. Something terrible happened to her husband—do you suppose that's what Mary has been fearing? The terrible calamity she has been so certain we were all headed for?"

"I don't know." Billy was silent for a moment, thinking. "Perhaps it is," he finally concluded, "though it doesn't seem like the whole community is suffering the way you are."

"No, I . . . don't suppose they—Oh, Billy, what are we going to do? What am I going to do? Hádapa and I have never spoken so much as a whole sentence to each other, yet I love that woman as if she were my own sister! I can't bear to think that she won't be coming back!"

Tenderly Billy took his wife's hand. "Eliza, it's all going to work out. I promise you, it will. Now, I'll take little Willy to meeting, and you stay home and see if you can get some rest."

Smiling through her tears, Eliza pulled herself to her feet and embraced her husband. "Thank you, darling."

Much later Eliza was on her knees beside her bed, taking advantage of the remarkable quiet while she pleaded with the Lord to grant her a little peace and understanding. That morning she had been reading section 84 of the Doctrine and Covenants, and the first part, especially verses 19 through 21, had put her in mind of her temple endowment, where she had received the sacred ordinances alluded to in the scripture. After Billy's departure she had begun thinking again of the temple, wishing she had taken advantage of the one in St. George, where she could have done work for the dead and then presented herself before the Lord to receive the light and knowledge she so desperately needed.

In her mind she visualized herself as she was the day she first participated in the sacred ceremony in the Endowment House in Salt Lake City and received her own endowment or gift from the Lord. Billy had been there with her, of course, and with remarkable clarity she could remember the very words—the instructions of the brother who had been officiating that day, as well as her own responses in reply—the eternal covenants she had made.

For some time Eliza rehearsed those memories in her mind, going over everything to the best of her memory. It was all a part of her prayer, the peaceable yearnings of her heart. But a little later, as she was pleading for the well-being of Hádapa and her husband, as well as peace for herself and little Willy, Eliza realized that her mind seemed almost to be exploding with thoughts about the very thing she had asked Billy about, the very thing he had told her to study and pray about for herself—faith, hope, and charity.

"Oh, glory," she breathed in wonder as she pulled herself to her feet and struck a match to light the twisted rag of their grease lamp so she could see her open scriptures. "Dear Lord, please help me to get this right—"

"Billy," Eliza said excitedly as her husband led little Willy through the door an hour later, "I think I know what faith, hope, and charity mean, at least when they're used together."

Closing the door, Billy gazed at his wife. "Eliza, what has

happened to you? If I put out the wick and doused the fire, I do believe your countenance would illuminate the room."

"Don't be silly," Eliza beamed. "Still, I think I know what Mormon was talking about—his entire address. It's remarkable! It's—"

"It's got to wait until this child is in bed," Billy teased. "Now, if you'll just help me, we can soon be discussing your new understanding."

———o—o—o———

"Now that, hon-bun, is what I've always found confusing." Willy was now asleep, and together Billy and Eliza had just read all forty-eight verses of the seventh chapter of Moroni. "Moroni says his father is going to speak on faith, hope, and charity," Billy declared, "and then Mormon takes over and rambles around for twenty verses before he even so much as mentions faith. Then he does a little more rambling, briefly mentions hope and charity, and finishes. Orson Pratt told me once that this was one of the three most profound addresses in the scriptures, the other two being the Sermon on the Mount and King Benjamin's discourse. But frankly, Eliza, I've never been able to see it."

Eliza looked at her husband in wonder. "I . . . I must be wrong then, Billy, because it all seems so clear to me. But if you can't see it—"

Reaching out, Billy took Eliza's hand. "Because I'm blind doesn't mean you can't see. Now, tell me what you've learned, because I truly would like to understand."

"Very well. But no making fun!" Seeing the instant seriousness of Billy's expression, Eliza began. "First, I don't think Mormon was rambling. He was addressing his congregation, complimenting them on their righteousness before Christ, and then, beginning in verse 5, explaining what had made their righteousness possible."

Pulling the scriptures closer, Billy scanned the verses. "Hmm," he said quietly, "I'd not seen that before. But I'm still puzzled over why he gave this tiny discourse on the differences between good and evil."

"Why, to make certain those ancient Saints understood their own accountability," Eliza responded. "They had to make choices every day, just as we do, and Mormon wanted to remind them that they had been given the ability to always choose righteously, which of course made them accountable when they didn't. That's why he said that 'a man being a servant of the devil cannot follow Christ; and if he follow Christ he cannot be a servant of the devil.' In other words, we can't have it both ways. We can't walk with one foot in Babylon and the other in Zion. Each is mutually exclusive of the other."

Thoughtfully Billy reexamined the verses, though half his mind was wondering at his wife.

"Then Mormon declares why these people—and everyone else, apparently—will be accountable. He says, 'The Spirit of Christ is given to every man, that he may know good from evil; wherefore, I show unto you the way to judge; for every thing which inviteth to do good, and to persuade to believe in Christ, is sent forth by the power and gift of Christ; wherefore ye may know with a perfect knowledge it is of God.' On the other hand, he continues, 'Whatsoever thing persuadeth men to do evil, and believe not in Christ, and deny him, and serve not God, then ye may know with a perfect knowledge it is of the devil; for after this manner doth the devil work, for he persuadeth no man to do good, no, not one; neither do his angels; neither do they who subject themselves unto him. And now, my brethren, seeing that ye know the light by which ye may judge, which light is the light of Christ, see that ye do not judge wrongfully.'"

"All right, I see that, and I agree with it. But I still don't see the connection with faith—"

"Billy, it's right here in the next verse, where Mormon tells us to search diligently in the light of Christ to know good from evil, and to lay hold upon every good thing and condemn it not. Then, he says, we certainly will be the children of Christ."

"Children of Christ," Billy said thoughtfully. "Now, that's interesting—"

Eliza smiled. "I knew you'd think so! Remember during our trek, when I was going through so much suffering for my sins? You told me I was going through a part of what you called my own spiritual progression? Later, when I'd been born of the Spirit and had received a remission of those sins, you showed me King Benjamin's statement that his own people, who had also had their sins remitted that day, had become the children of Christ, his sons and his daughters.'"

"Mosiah chapter 5 verse 7," Billy breathed. "I also showed you Ether chapter 3 verse 14, where the premortal Christ told the brother of Jared that all who believed on His name would become his sons and his daughters."

"That's right, Billy. Believing on Christ's name, making a covenant to do his will and keep his commandments, or searching diligently to know and choose good over evil—all these seem one and the same to me. They are precise directions leading those who desire righteousness to the point where they can experience the mighty change of heart and be spiritually reborn as children of Christ. When Mormon counsels us to lay hold on every good thing, I believe he is referring in part to those divine instructions."

Billy was astounded. "Eliza, I never would have thought of that—"

"Me neither, until tonight," Eliza said with a smile. "Remember, Billy: spiritual progression—drawing ever closer to God and his Beloved Son. And from what Mormon is saying, I believe such progression requires that spiritual rebirth before any of us can exercise the kind of faith necessary to save our souls in the kingdom of God."

"Where do you get that?"

"Right here, in Moronin chapter 7 verse 21. Mormon says, 'And now I come to that faith, of which I said I would speak; and I will tell you the way whereby ye may lay hold on every good thing.' Do you see, Billy? To lay hold on every good thing is to exercise faith. But what is every good thing? It is Christ and his atonement. Again according to Mormon: 'God knowing all things, being from everlasting to everlasting, behold, he sent angels to minister unto the children of men, to make manifest concerning the coming of Christ; and *in Christ there should come every good thing.*'

"In other words, there is no faith unless it is in the Lord Jesus Christ. Otherwise it is only a belief or an idea and does not have the power to save."

"Remarkable," Billy declared softly.

Eliza tapped the open scriptures. "It is, isn't it. And to make certain we understand that God will deny no one this understanding of Christ so that their faith in him can develop, Mormon then launches into a brief discourse on the ways God uses to inform mankind of his Beloved Son and his redemptive mission."

"Maybe that's why he speaks so strongly about the ministering of angels," Billy said. "You know, that's another bit of knowledge that always seemed out of place in this chapter. Until now, I never saw the connection between angels and faith."

"But it's there, isn't it. Mormon says, 'There were divers ways that [God] did manifest things unto the children of men. . . . Wherefore, by the ministering of angels, and by every word which proceeded forth out of the mouth of God, men began to exercise faith in Christ; and thus by faith, they did lay hold upon every good thing; and . . . become the sons of God.'"

"Yes," Billy continued, sounding more and more excited, "and on down here around verse 30 Mormon again speaks of angels, saying that they are to declare 'the word of Christ unto the chosen vessels of the Lord, that they may bear testimony of him. And by so doing, the Lord God prepareth the way that the residue of men may have faith in Christ, that the Holy Ghost may have place in their hearts.'"

"In other words, Billy, so that all mankind might know in whom to exercise faith. In every way possible, God has declared his Beloved Son to the rest of us. 'For no man can be saved, according to the words of Christ, save they shall have faith in his name.'"

"And this is the only type of faith," Billy continued, "that can lead to hope. So faith and hope are connected, just as you said. Beginning in verse 40, Mormon says, 'How is it that ye can attain unto faith, save ye shall have hope? And what is it that ye shall hope for? Behold I say unto you that ye shall have hope through the atonement of Christ and the power of his resurrection, to be raised unto life eternal, and this because of your faith in him according to the promise. Wherefore, if a man have faith he must needs have hope; for without faith there cannot be any hope.'"

Eliza nodded. "That's right. Our hope can't be in worldly things or even worldly leaders, for ultimately those things will fail. True hope must be centered in Christ—a hope that as his children we will be raised to life eternal."

"Yes, I see that." Billy's expression had again grown thoughtful. "But now I'm troubled by something else. Mormon continues, 'None is acceptable before God, save the meek and lowly in heart; and if a man be meek and lowly in heart, and confesses by the power of the Holy Ghost that Jesus is the Christ, he must needs have charity; for if he have not charity he is nothing; wherefore he must needs have charity.'" Billy gave Eliza a wry grin. "I'm probably going to regret admitting this, but here especially I don't see the connection. What does charity have to do with faith and hope?"

"Are you serious, Billy? You don't see it?"

Billy shook his head. "I don't. Is Mormon saying that people who are filled with faith and hope must start reaching out to the needy, or what?"

"Yes, he most certainly is. But I think it's more than that. Do you remember when you told me once that the scriptures were layered like an onion, with different meanings to the same verses, depending upon our needs and understandings?"

"You feel that you've discovered a deeper meaning?"

Eliza smiled. "A different one, at least—one that I feel the Lord wants me to understand. Here in verse 45 he defines charity by saying, 'Charity suffereth long, and is kind, and envieth not, and is not puffed up, seeketh not her own, is not easily provoked, thinketh no evil, and rejoiceth not in iniquity but rejoiceth in the truth, beareth all things, believeth all things, hopeth all things, endureth all things.'"

"Yes, those are attributes of a charitable person. Paul taught them as well. But I still don't see how that is connected to a faith and hope in Christ—"

"Billy, those qualities are most completely the attributes of Christ."

Stunned, Billy could only look at his wife. "Are . . . you saying that charity is Christ?"

"In a sense, perhaps, but I think Mormon takes his line of reasoning in a slightly different direction. He says, 'If ye have not charity, ye are nothing, for charity never faileth. Wherefore, cleave unto charity, which is the greatest of all.' How could it be the greatest of all, Billy, or 'never faileth,' if it weren't the eternal Christ, or rather the most pure manifestation of him?"

"The most pure manifestation?"

"That's right. His pure, eternal love. Mormon says, 'Charity is the pure love of Christ.' But more than being his love, Billy, I believe it must be his love made manifest in completeness in our own lives. That's why Mormon said, 'Whoso is found possessed of it at the last day, it shall be well with him.'" Eliza smiled as she took Billy's hand. "Remember, darling, spiritual progression, step following step as we progress toward Christ and life eternal. You taught me that."

His mind racing, Billy gazed at the open scriptures. "Very well, if we have the pure love of Christ, then we must have all those Christlike attributes—"

"Billy," Eliza interrupted, "that's true enough. No one can have charity without showing those attributes with greater and greater power. But for now, stop thinking of the results of charity and consider charity itself. And while you're about it, think of a person's spiritual progression. Do you remember quoting for me what Joseph Smith said?"

"I . . . don't think so—"

"Yes, you do, darling. As I recollect, it pertained to making one's calling and election a sure thing."

"That's right!" Leaping to his feet Billy grabbed his small trunk, opened it, and began rummaging through his collection of daybooks. "This is the one," he said a moment later as he took his seat. "Now give me a minute—All right, Eliza, here's Joseph's quote, just as I copied it: 'After a person has faith in Christ, repents of his sins, and is baptized for the remission of his sins and receives the Holy Ghost, (by the laying on of hands), which is the first Comforter, then let him continue to humble himself before God, hungering and thirsting after righteousness, and living by every word of God, and the Lord will soon say unto him, Son, thou shalt be exalted. When the Lord has thoroughly proved him, and finds that the man is determined to serve Him at all hazards, then the man will find his calling and his election made sure.' It goes on, but is that the part you wanted?"

"That's it." Eliza's look was serious. "The next step in spiritual progression, after people have become sons or daughters of Christ by being born of the water and the Spirit, is to continue forward until they can obtain from God the promise of exaltation and eternal lives—to have the Lord make their calling and election sure, just as you quoted Joseph Smith as saying.

"Can you imagine how that would feel, Billy?" Eliza seemed almost enraptured at the thought. "Can you imagine feeling Christ's pure love to that degree? Can you imagine the peace that would come to your soul if God had given you that knowledge?"

Billy chuckled. "Tell the truth, hon-bun, I can't. But it does sound like you've been reading my daybook. Listen to this other statement Brother Joseph made about one's calling and election being made sure—of being sealed in the heavens and having the promise of eternal life: 'Having this promise sealed unto them, it was an anchor to the soul, sure and steadfast. Though the thunders might roll and lightnings flash, and earthquakes bellow, and war gather thick around, yet this hope and knowledge would support the soul in every hour of trial, trouble and tribulation.'"

"Yes," Eliza beamed, "that's exactly what I mean! An anchor to the soul, no matter the difficulties one may encounter. In my opinion, Billy, obtaining such an anchor, such a manifestation of Christ's love, is another meaning of charity or the pure love of Christ."

Thoughtfully Billy drummed his fingers on the table. "Well," he finally declared, "that does make sense. What greater manifestation of Christ's love could he make, than to make an individual such a promise? It would also give greater meaning to Mormon's comment that charity, or the pure love of Christ, 'endureth forever.' Such a promise would surely endure forever and would most certainly anchor the soul."

Eliza nodded. "It also—"

"Wait a minute," Billy interrupted. "I just thought of something else. The scripture says—and I believe this is repeated in 1 John and in Moroni, that 'perfect love casteth out all fear.' I've always interpreted that as a condemnation of fear in general—which I still believe. But when you think of Christ's pure love—or charity—as being perfect love, and then you think of Joseph Smith's statement that the promise of exaltation as granted through Christ's love is as an anchor to the soul during all fearsome times—"

"Then you have another layer or definition of that scripture, too."

Billy nodded. "And another witness that the understanding of this chapter that you were given tonight is likely accurate. Hon-bun, this is exciting!"

"It is." Eliza's tender expression showed her gratitude for Billy's acceptance. "It also explains why Mormon concludes his address by practically thundering, 'Wherefore, my beloved brethren, pray unto the Father with all the energy of heart, that ye may be filled with this love, which he hath bestowed upon all who are true followers of his Son, Jesus Christ; that ye may become the sons of God; that when he shall appear we shall be like him, for we shall see him as he is; that we may have this hope; that we may be purified even as he is pure. Amen.'"

Billy grinned. "He makes it sound mighty important, all right."

"Yes, because he wants us to pray with all the energy of our hearts that this gift of charity—this loving promise from Christ of eternal life—will be ours. And of course the connection—that we exercise faith and hope until Christ gives us charity—is now obvious."

"Only to folks such as you, hon-bun. Until tonight it has never been obvious to me."

Eliza smiled at her husband and then stared off, instantly deep in thought. "There is a negative side," she finally said, her voice quiet. "Earlier tonight, while I was going through Mormon's sermon and reading about hope, I had an awful feeling. I pushed it aside, of course, and tried to forget about it. But then when you read that quotation by Joseph Smith and quoted those verses about perfect love casting out fear—"

"Hon," Billy said as Eliza's face turned bleak, "what is it? What did I read?"

"It was . . . the answer about why we're going through such trials here on the San Juan—maybe even the answer as to why Hádapa has been taken from Willy and me. Do you recollect reading where Joseph said, 'When the Lord has thoroughly proved him, and finds that the man is determined to serve Him at all hazards'? Do you see, Billy? All of us on this mission are learning to exercise faith in Christ so we may have hope in him, and so he is proving us. Through one round of adversity and privation and hazardous endeavor after another, the Lord Jesus is teaching us, proving that we are not to have hope in the world but in him alone!

"But . . . but . . . Oh, Billy, darling, so far I haven't done very well at all. If Mary's right, and our circumstances become even more frightening, more desperate, I . . . well, I don't think I know how to handle it!"

"Of course you do," Billy smiled as he rose to his feet, pinched out the braided wick, and pulled Eliza up to him. "We just get up every morning, pray for help and guidance, and then grit our teeth and do our best to hold on until nightfall. Just exactly like you did today—"

22

————○─○─○————

Friday, May 6, 1881

Recapture Pocket

Despite the fact that his body was numb with fatigue, the warrior Posey rode with his head held high. Not only had he proven himself in battle again and again during this big raid, but he had also been the one to think of adding the horses of the foolish mormonee to the already vast wealth Mike and the other warriors of the People had accumulated. Now they were nearly to the place where that herd was usually kept, and Posey could feel the excitement growing within him.

The sky had barely been showing light when he, Scotty, his father Chee, Mike, and the others had taken a few of their newfound wealth of horses and ridden south from Dodge Springs, leaving Mancos Jim, Poke, and the rest of the warriors to ride west and lead the much-anticipated posse of whites into an ambush. Of course, Posey felt bad about missing that ambush, for no warrior desired to miss a great battle—especially not a warrior such as himself, in whose future lay such great promise.

Of course, there was always the possibility that the posse would take longer than expected to catch up with the raiders. Posey grinned at that thought, for the foolishness of the whites was large in his mind, and he did want to be a part of the battle when they finally came together.

Stretching himself as well as he could while still remaining mounted and riding, Posey tried to ease his aching muscles. For hours he and the others had driven the horses south along Montezuma Creek, slowing only to go up the trail onto what would soon be called Alkali Point. From there they had ridden across McCracken Mesa—where they had crossed the trail of their own women and children who were fleeing westward—and dropped off the rimrock into Recapture Pocket. Now, with *tabby,* the sun, still high enough to give them good light, they had only to cross the creek called Recapture and then move up onto the sand hills of the Bluff Bench. There they would kill the mormonee herders and take the herd, and when the mormonee followed—if any actually had such courage—he and the others would do just as they had done to the three from whom they had stolen the large herd; them and the foolish man at the place of water two days before. *Puck-ki,* they would kill them all, showing not only the warriors who had held back with Ouray and the other Utes but the white mericats as well that the warriors of the river, the Pahutes, had true power and were men to be reckoned with.

Oo-ah, yes, Posey thought as his exhaustion was forgotten and his eyes flashed with excited anticipation. This too would be a great raid, and once again Mike and the others would recognize him as a man of the People. Yes, and perhaps the fearsome grizzly Poke would also recognize him—he and his comely younger sister who was called Too-rah.

Dodge Springs

Spud Hudson glowered at his foreman, Curly Jenkins, though he thoughtfully kept his name out of the conversation. "I thought there was only a dozen of 'em," he snarled. "Where in Hades' hot smoking cinders did the rest of these thieving devils come from?"

His eyes never leaving the ground as he moved around the periphery of the camp, John B. Brown shrugged. "Tell the truth, Spud, I reckon they've been together all along. We've followed 'em thirty miles now, and except for little raiding parties that come and go, nothing's changed. From the fires and tracks, I'd say there's got to be sixty, maybe seventy of 'em all told, every one armed to the teeth, and not a squaw or papoose among 'em!"

"How in the deuce can you tell that?" a cowboy asked in disbelief.

"The way they make water, you nitwit," Spud growled without much malice. Now the leader of a posse of eleven heavily armed ranchers and cowboys who were at that moment examining an empty encampment at Dodge Springs, Spud had a right to be concerned, and he knew it. He'd lost close to seventy-five head of prime horseflesh, twice what all the rest of the men had lost together. Still, to a man they were as anxious to get their livestock back as he was, and every one of them was ready to fight to do it.

"John," he asked, "can you tell who they are and where they're headed?"

John B. Brown straightened from his search and looked at his neighbor. "Well, Spud, the biggest bunch of them is headed west, and the rest are going south toward that new Mormon settlement on the San Juan. They ain't Navajo, because their camp is too messy, so all the signs say they're Pahute."

"That's just a fancy name for renegade Utes, John, and you know it."

The tracker grinned but remained silent, watching and waiting.

Spitting into one of the dead fires, Spud wiped his mouth on his sleeve. "Ute or Pahute, I don't give a tinker's tin cup, and that's a fact! Curly, what do you figure about our horses? Which way did they go?"

Curly Jenkins gazed off to the west where the largest trail led. "This is the bunch that have 'em," he answered laconically as he pointed with one gnarled finger, "or at least most of 'em. The tracks of that old splay-foot mare are right here, and the notched shoe on your blood bay shows up plain." Curly scratched his grizzled chin. "Thing is, boss, besides the hundred or so head they took from all of us, there must be hundreds and hundreds more in this herd."

"More'n a thousand, I'd say. Maybe fourteen, fifteen hundred head."

Curly glanced at the speaker, Dudley Reece, to see if he was funning. But the man looked serious as a stepped-on lizard, so Curly decided to accept his evaluation.

"Fifteen hundred head, of which a hundred is ours. Makes a

feller wonder who in Colorado they stole the other fourteen hundred head from."

"It doesn't make me wonder!" Spud Hudson snarled as he once again spit to the side of his mount. "What it makes me, by thunder, is madder'n a hornet-stung, blue-tick coon hound. These thieving varmints has been gallivanting around the whole blamed country stealing all them hosses—"

"Not to mention killing who knows how many innocent bystanders," Green Robinson interjected, "like that poor prospector feller Curly buried yesterday at Piute Springs."

"No telling how many they murdered off in Colorado before that," a rancher who gave out his name as Mr. Peters added quietly. A taciturn man who had never even told any of them his first name, he was nevertheless disliked by Spud Hudson and some of the others in the posse for no other reason than because he'd gone about his cattle range a year or so before, naming various landmarks after himself. Such arrogance was unheard of. Then he had spread the word about the new names of things, and that had truly raised their ire. Mr. Peters knew full well how the others felt, but it seemed to bother him not at all. Instead he rode with them when he could, against them when he had to, and was as eager as any of the rest to reclaim the horses the Pahutes had taken from his range.

"Mr. Peters is right," Dudley Reece agreed. "We don't know how many innocent folks these Utes have murdered."

"Or how many they might kill in the future. Maybe we should ride on south and warn the Mormons."

Spud glowered at his neighbor. "We'd get there too late, Peters, and you know it. Besides which, them Mormons likely have more men armed and ready than we could scrape together in a month of Sundays. They also have that fort folks keep talking about, so the women and children are already better protected than anything we could do for them. No, by Tophet! What we've got to do, boys, is stick to the business at hand—getting back our horses."

"Which brings up the question of the other posse," Curly ventured. "Where in by howdy are the boys from Colorado that by all rights ought to be chasing down these other fourteen hundred head of hossflesh?"

"Good question, Curly."

"Humph," Spud muttered disgustedly. "Good question or not, there ain't no good answer, because we just don't know."

"Could be," Curly mused, ignoring his boss's sensible conclusion, "they all got killed off before they came to Piute Springs. Or maybe they're too durn scared to follow such a crowd. Or maybe they somehow lost the trail—"

"Maybe, maybe, maybe!" Mr. Peters ejaculated with disgust. "What good are all these maybes? I say we stick to what we know, which is that this bunch that's rode to the west has at least most of our horses and enough warriors to outnumber us five to one."

"You suggesting we tuck tail and run home?" Spud growled fiercely, expertly concealing his own opinion on the subject.

"Not hardly. But I am suggesting we go back and round up more men. Even if another posse never shows up, twenty, twenty-five of us ought to make the fight with these Utes about even, I'd say."

The men chuckled, and Spud glowered at them. "They'll likely be waiting for us, you know. Them hosses and dead folks is likely just bait, and if we go after 'em, we'll be marching right into their trap."

"Maybe so," Green Robinson growled. "But like Mr. Peters said, a third as many of us had ought to be twice as good as all of them put together!"

Slowly Spud nodded his agreement. "Good thinking, Green. I want my horses back, and even without reinforcements I reckon the bunch of us could take 'em. But if these varmints get thumped good while we're at it, which more of us will be able to do a whole lot easier than less of us, then I expect the red sons'll be a little less anxious to steal the next time. Boys, let's head back to the Double Cabins and see who else we can roust out of the woodwork. Curly, you ride to the LC and see if Bill Ball has any men he can spare. We'll meet back here tomorrow at high noon. And bring supplies to last at least a week, the rest of you, because this time we ain't quitting till the job is done!"

And without further comment or consideration the Blue Mountain posse turned around and headed back north.

Bluff Fort

"Billy, come a'running!" Kumen Jones had shoved open the door of Billy and Eliza's cabin without even knocking and was standing with his wife, Mary, both of their faces showing shock. "The Pahutes are back, and they're back with a vengeance! They've shot at Joe Nielson and stolen our entire herd of horses from where he had them on the Sand Hills!"

"The whole herd?" Billy was so surprised that for a moment he remained where he had been on the bed, playing with his son.

Kumen and then Mary stepped into the home. "That's right, and you know what that means. Without those horses, we're done for!"

"Has somebody notified Brother Haskel?"

Kumen shook his head. "Can't. He's still off across the river chasing Navajo horse thieves. That means it's up to us to deal with the Pahute variety. Billy, we've got to go and get those animals back!"

Eliza, who had been kneeling before the fireplace stirring a pot of stew, pulled herself to her feet and then almost collapsed onto the earthen floor. "Oh, Mary," she breathed after she had caught herself on her crutch, "this is it! This is the terrible calamity the Holy Spirit has been warning you of—"

Her eyes wide and her face a ghostly chalk-white, Mary could do nothing more than nod.

Instantly Eliza's heart was racing, her head was spinning, and for a few seconds she thought she was about to faint. That quickly passed, however, and then she was gripped by the cold hand of fear—a stark terror over what her dear Billy would be facing that dried her mouth and took her breath right out of her chest.

"Was Joe hurt?" Billy asked as he finally rose from the bed, his still-laughing son in his arms.

Kumen shook his head. "I don't think so, though they did put a scare into him. Platte says we're going to need everybody, Billy, and we're going to need them now. You and Eliza feel okay about you going?"

"Of course we do." Billy glanced at his wife, then reached over to take her hand. "You do want me to go and help the brethren, don't you, hon-bun?"

Still dizzy, Eliza wondered that she was even standing. Why, the way her legs were shaking was a caution. And she knew she didn't have the ability to speak. If she did, then for certain Billy would hear the terror in her voice—

"Eliza?"

Silently, numbly, she nodded.

"We'll likely be back by tomorrow," Kumen said, doing his best to allay what he could see were Eliza's fears. "I reckon you and Mary ought to get together with the rest of the sisters. Bishop Nielson can't ride with us, so he'll remain here at the fort to watch over everything."

Reaching out, Billy took his coat from the peg near the door. "I don't know what else to take, Kumen. My saddle's down at the tack shed, but I don't even have a horse. That old glass-eyed mare we brought with us from Cedar was with the herd up on the Sand Hills."

"Platte's got extra horses, Billy, and—oh, I plumb forgot; he also called for us to bring our guns."

Surprised, Billy glanced at his friend. "I didn't know Platte held with guns."

"I didn't either." Kumen was shaking his head. "I know I sure don't. Guns lead to killing, and that's the last thing in the world I came to the San Juan for."

His heart now racing, Billy looked at his wife and for the first time saw the terror in her eyes. Tenderly he took her in his arms, little Willy between them, and then led her to a seat on the edge of the bed.

"Here, hon-bun," he said as he handed her their son, "you watch over little Willy until I get back." Then he turned to face his young friend.

"Well," he drawled, forcing his voice to be slow and soft, "this is a pickle, Kumen. It surely is. Seems like we're durned if we do and durned if we don't. One thing I do know: those Pahutes understand the power of guns even when they don't much respect us."

"Or the might and power of God," Kumen admitted sadly. "Still, it goes smack against the grain—"

For a long moment Billy's and Kumen's eyes locked together, each of them trying to determine the best course of action.

"Billy," Eliza whispered as she reached out and took his hand, her own mind suddenly firm, "you really don't have a choice, you know. Neither of you do. Not, at least, if you're still sustaining Elder Snow and the rest of the Brethren, who have set Platte apart by the laying on of hands as president of this stake of Zion."

Silent until now, Mary made her way to the bed and sat next to Eliza, where she reached out and took her hand. "Do . . . do you really think that's right, Eliza?"

"I know it is," Eliza breathed.

Slowly Billy nodded. "That's the straight of it, all right. Thanks, hon-bun." Swiftly he turned toward his friend. "I reckon it's guns we'll be taking, Kumen. I have a fine model 1873 Winchester carbine and a single-action model 1872 Colt's revolver, and to tell the truth I've never fired either one. Fact is, I've only shot a rifle once or twice in my life, and I've never once fired a pistol. Which one do you think I should bring?"

Kumen appeared just as perplexed. "I don't rightly know, Billy. Why don't you take the carbine and lend me your pistol, seeing as how I don't even know if my old Remington 44–77 rifle still fires, let alone shoots straight. I'll tell a man, though, it's hard for me to see how this helps me be a missionary!"

"Kumen," Mary said as Billy pulled his weapons from under the bed near her feet, "I hate this! Missionaries or not, I'm terrified to death to send you and Billy out after those Pahute people. I know some of them have murder in their hearts, for I've seen it in their eyes. Others, however, are good people, and it is them we must think of. It is for their sakes that we must have our livestock! Otherwise we won't be able to survive in this country and be any sort of missionaries at all."

There was silence in the cabin as Eliza and the men absorbed Mary's words. Outside several men on horses galloped past, and from every direction dogs were barking as folks gathered near the gate from which the party would be leaving. In the cabin, though, all was still. Even little Willy was sitting on Eliza's lap without movement, his eyes large as he tried to understand what was happening.

"Besides which," Eliza stated quietly, speaking as much to herself as she was to the men, "it seems to me that now's the time for our faith. If you brethren truly represent the Lord, and if he doesn't want you shooting Indians and you don't either, then no matter that you'll all be carrying guns, and no matter what those Indians might believe or not believe, God will make a way so that none of you will have to shoot."

Slowly Kumen's serious face broke into a grin. "Billy's right, Eliza; you do see the straight of things." Taking the gunbelt from Billy's outstretched hand, he buckled it on and then held the door so that Billy could go out before him.

"Adios," he said as he winked at his wife.

"See you soon, hon-bun," Billy added. And then the two hurried off, not seeing—not wanting to see—the tearful embrace the grieving women gave each other once their husbands were out of sight.

Bluff Fort

"Vell, sisters, und you too, you children, I tink it be time for all of us to exercise dat faith in de Lord dat ve all haff."

Bishop Jens Nielson paused, surveying the group of women and children who had gathered in the log meetinghouse. Unable to ride a horse, he was the only man left in the unfinished fort. Which seemed somehow fitting, he thought, inasmuch as he had been called and set apart by the laying on of hands to preside over these dear Saints he had come to love and admire.

"Let us pray," he urged softly as he looked upon this portion of his flock. "Dear Fadder in Heaven, ve tank de for the privilege off being in dis comfortable place. Ve haff gathered here now because all de men-folk haff gone off and placed demselves in mortal danger, and ve vould pray—"

Bishop Nielson continued, reminding the Lord that there was not a soul in Bluff that had not given up everything—nice homes and well-ordered farms, beloved family members and friends, the graves of departed loved ones, and even peace and safety—to come to this wilderness in response to a call from the prophet of God. Surely, he prayed, the Lord must love them for their willingness to obey, their incredible sacrifices as they sought to do God's will. Surely the Lord would bless them for their desires to be righteous. Surely he would bless the menfolk who had ridden out, without fear of the great danger they were placing themselves in, to take back their horses, which were desperately needed if the mission was to succeed.

On he prayed, pleading for the success of the men, pleading as well for the success of the entire mission. Again he reminded the Lord of the faith and righteousness of the women and children who had gathered with him, and then he pleaded that the Lord honor that righteousness by sending forth legions of angels to stop the traditional way of the Pahutes, the way of shooting and killing. Pausing for a moment and then growing slightly emotional, he pronounced a blessing on all of them, but most especially the brethren—that by their righteousness they would see the hand of the Lord unveiled before this experience was concluded.

In the name of the Lord, Bishop Nielson finished his prayer, and then as the next few hours dragged by, he visited with the sisters and the children, wondering all the while at the great outpouring of the Holy Spirit that had filled his mind and heart, as well as the room in general, during his prayer.

Boiling Springs

"How many you reckon are down there?" The voice, hardly more than a whisper, was Jim Decker's.

"Between twenty-five and thirty fires," Lemuel Redd answered just as quietly. "Probably about that many braves, plus squaws and papooses."

"Well," Platte Lyman added, "we knew the women and kids would be there from the tracks we found back on the trail over from Cottonwood. Boys, there's something funny about this situation— maybe lots of things. First, what are they doing raiding with their women and children along? That isn't normal."

"Maybe they weren't along," Billy replied. "Maybe the braves raided the horses and then met up with their families in Cottonwood where we came on their trail. Thales says that's where some of them camp from time to time."

"Could be," Platte acknowledged. "But that brings up an even bigger question, at least in my mind. These Pahutes have been hanging around us for more than a year. Sure they've stolen horses and cows now and then, but our whole herd at one time? Seems to me somebody's put them up to this, either that or put the idea of it into their minds."

The men were quiet, digesting Platte's idea, and Billy had the feeling that the man was right. It was long past dark now, with no wind and no moon, and in the stillness the drums, the chanting, and the loud exulting of the Pahutes was easily heard. They were also dancing around the largest of the fires, their wildly gyrating bodies presenting a sight such as none of the settlers had ever seen before.

Leaving Bluff in the late afternoon, the missionary posse, which included besides Kumen and Billy, Platte Lyman, Lemuel Redd, Joseph Nielson, James Decker, Amasa Barton, Jess Smith, Hyrum Perkins, George Ipson, and Johnny Gower, had ridden up Cottonwood Wash until, after dark, they had reached the trail that crossed over into the Butler. Examining the trail by matchlight, they had quickly discovered the tracks of numerous dogs, horses, and goats, as well as the scars of dragging tent poles, and so they had known that they were now following an encampment of families, not just braves.

In the darkness the men had continued slowly on to the edge of Butler Wash where it overlooked Boiling Springs, and there below them they had discovered the numerous fires they were now watching.

"Quite a celebration they're having," Johnny Gower observed.

"You'd celebrate, too, happen you'd just got rich."

"Now Amasa, since when did our sorry lot of horseflesh amount to enough to make anybody rich."

"Well," Hyrum Perkins opined as the men chuckled, "riches mean different things to different folks. Besides, from the way the trail's been chewed up, they've got a whole lot more horses down there than ours."

"Where do you suppose they got 'em?"

"Who knows, Jess?" Platte Lyman was thoughtful. "More than

likely, though, that's where they've been the past couple of weeks, wherever 'that' might happen to be."

"The Wilson boys, who'd ridden down from Moab, told me they'd crossed the trails of several Indian groups headed east," Billy said.

"That's right," Lem Redd nodded. "And one of the Heaton brothers—I believe it was Henry W.—told my wife and me about the big powwow the Utes hold over in Colorado each year. Ten to one says these fellers stirred up something over Colorado way and are on their way back."

"You're likely right, Lem." Platte continued to gaze down off the high bluff at the distant fires. "Not that it matters very much. It's our horses we've got to be worried about, and they're the only ones we should try to take."

"Then," Kumen interjected, "we'd best be praying powerful hard that the Lord will help us do what we've come here to do, because the way those braves are carrying on, I'd say they're in a mood to see that none of us survives, let alone takes back our horses."

"Kumen's right, boys," Platte responded thoughtfully. "I've been too rattled this evening to think much of prayer, but if we don't invite the Lord to be a part of this little expedition, then I believe we'll be in serious trouble. Billy, will you do us the honors?"

In the darkness Billy listened as the men removed their hats, and then he quietly implored the heavens not just for protection for themselves but also for the Pahutes, so that none of them, red or white, would do anything that might be regretted in the day of the Lord.

"Thank you, Billy," Platte said when he had concluded. "Now brethren, here's what I think we're going to have to do. At first light we'll ride boldly into their herd and cut out our own animals. We won't say anything unless that becomes necessary, and no matter what they do we won't act rattled or frightened."

"And if they shoot?" Johnny Gower asked quietly.

"Then we shoot back. If they threaten, we threaten. In other words, we'll respond in kind. But remember, brethren, we *must not* fire the first shot. We do, and in that instant we'll lose the blessings of the Lord and likely our lives in the bargain!"

Doing their best to absorb and deal with that information, the men settled in to watching the encampment below them—that, and maybe getting a little sleep.

23

——◦─◦─◦——

Saturday, May 7, 1881

Boiling Springs

"*Quir-i-ka!* Get up, brother! I think something is moving among the horses!"

Posey, in the middle of dreaming of the mighty raids he was leading against the despised mormonee who had filled the country along the big river, rolled over and sat up. It was still mostly dark, but the dawn star had lifted above the eastern horizon, so he knew it was close to morning. Rubbing the sleep from his eyes, he strained to see off down the wash where the horses had been left. Of course, in the deeper darkness of the wash nothing was visible, but as he listened he could hear the restiveness of the animals, their snorting and shuffling as though they were being disturbed.

"*Ick-in-ish,*" he breathed. "I say that you are right, my brother. Do you have your weapons ready?"

Posey's younger brother grunted that it was so. Of course, his bow and arrows were not as fine or powerful as the old muzzle-loading cap-and-ball rifle Mike had given Posey. Still, anything that inflicted pain worked against *yohats,* wolves, or even against *moochich,* the great cat. And, Posey knew, it was more than likely it was either a wolf or a cat that was disturbing the horses. It certainly wouldn't be those cowardly mormonee—

"Are any of the others stirring?" Though Posey's voice was quiet, he was trembling with excitement.

292

"They stir, my brother, but I do not think they have heard. Otherwise, one of them would have shouted an alarm."

"Then *pie-ka,* come. We will see for ourselves what it is that moves among our ponies. *Oo-ah,* yes, and perhaps we will kill it or drive it away and become even greater in the eyes of our people."

Without hesitation Posey crept out into the darkness, and with only a little hesitation Scotty followed after his older and infinitely wiser brother.

———o—o—o———

"See anything yet?"

"Not a whole lot," Amasa Barton replied softly. "There're a lot of horses in this bunch, but so far I can't tell which ones are ours."

It was still too dark to see much, but the light was growing rapidly, and everyone knew it would be only a matter of minutes until they were spotted by the Pahutes. Until then it was imperative that they work rapidly—and quietly.

"Well, I've found two of Johnny Gower's nags," Jim Decker said from a few yards away. "The one with most of its left ear gone is a dead giveaway, and the other, as usual, won't leave its side."

"Hold 'em apart, then," Platte ordered, "and don't make any sudden moves or loud noises. We can't afford to spook anything, horses or Pahutes either one."

"You have your gun out, Hy?"

"Not hardly," Hyrum Perkins replied to Jess Smith's question. "It's too busy I am looking for horses to worry about guns."

"Yeah, me too. Besides, mine has a terrible hair trigger, and I don't want to be the one that starts a shooting war."

"Here's one of Pa's nags," Joe Nielson said from nearby, "and here are two more. Good. He was some worried about them. Now if I can only find old Dobber—"

"Remember, boys, don't take anything unless you know it's one of ours."

"All right, Platte. We won't. Well, what do you know! Here's that little mare of my wife's that turned up missing last fall. No wonder we couldn't find it. Dadgummed Pahutes! I sure should have known—"

"Here are Sign and Wonder," Billy breathed in the rapidly increasing light, cutting the other man off. "Dick and Parley will be relieved, probably as much as I am. And this old glass-eyed mare of mine is hanging right with them. Hello there, old lady. Pahutes been treating you all right? Good. Now why don't you tell me what's become of Lots and Little Bit?"

"Boys," George Ipson warned, "a few of their cooking fires are blazing higher, so at least some of the squaws are awake."

"Yeah," Kumen Jones agreed, "and with the noise these horses are making, they're bound to hear us and give the warning. Tell you what I think, boys. It's only a matter of time—"

———○─○─○———

"Can you see anything yet, my brother?"

"I see that it isn't wolves and it isn't a great cat," Posey responded as he slowly lifted his old rifle to sight along the barrel. "It is in my mind to say that the mericats have followed us and are among the horses."

"Are you certain it is the mericats?" Scotty questioned almost fearfully. "The ones from the Shining Mountains?"

"Almost certainly," Posey breathed as his rifle barrel wavered and then settled on what appeared in the gloom to be a target. "Surely it will not be those *katz-te-suah,* those foolish mormonee. Truly, though, it does not matter. Now stop chattering, for one of them *nan-a,* one of them grows beyond the end of my rifle."

"Are you not fearful of what the others might do if you kill that one?" Scotty breathed as he drew back.

"Posey fears nothing!" the young warrior snarled. And so saying, he squeezed the trigger of his old rifle.

———○─○─○———

"What was that?"

"I didn't hear anything."

Joseph Nielson, his rope around the neck of a horse he had just roped, stared into the gray light. "Well, I did, Hy, and my ears are a sight better than yours. Somebody toward that Pahute camp either just cocked a gun or they pulled the trigger and it misfired."

"You certain, Joe?"

"If he ain't," Lemuel Redd declared laconically from close behind them, "I am! And it wasn't a cock—it was a misfire. Get ready, boys, because we've got company!"

———o–o–o———

Posey was so startled when his old rifle failed to discharge that he almost rose to his feet. He didn't, but without thinking of the need to warn the others back in the encampment, or even of changing percussion caps, he pulled the hammer back and squeezed the trigger once more. And again the old rifle misfired.

"Brother," Scotty hissed in alarm, "we must warn the others."

Numbly Posey made the sign of agreement. This had never happened before. Never! For all the times he had used the rifle, it had always fired. More, he had always hit what he had fired at. But now, with an unsuspecting white man squarely in his sights—

Scotty's shrill war cry burst forth from directly behind him, so startling Posey that once again he nearly rose to his feet as he spun about. But then, feeling foolish, he fumbled a new cap onto the nipple of his rifle, turned angrily back, and once again pointed it in the direction of the white man who had ridden so near—and gasped with surprise when he saw that the white man he had been about to put under the grass was the small mormonee whose tall woman had the many fine glass and iron things spread out on the table in her *wick-iup*. More important, that same small mormonee now had a rifle pointed directly at him, and it was not wavering even a little!

———o–o–o———

"Billy," Platte breathed, "fine job keeping those two covered. Don't take your eyes off either one of them."

His rifle held steady now that he had loosed the reins of the horse he had been riding, Billy nodded silently. Of a truth he had no real idea of what he was doing, and he had absolutely no intention of firing. For a fact his whole body was shaking so badly he was amazed he was still on his feet. But for some reason the new rifle was steady in his hands, its muzzle unwavering, and the two Pahute youth were obviously frightened into submission by it.

Climbing back into his saddle, Platte peered toward the Indian camp. "Here they come, boys," he growled as warrior after warrior darted from their *wickiups* to race down the hill toward the horse herd, their shrill war cries beginning to rend the early morning quiet. "Whatever happens, and no matter how many of them there are, don't flinch. And remember, none of us fires the first shot! If possible, shooting must be avoided. With us out of the way, you know what they'll do to our folks back at the fort."

"There's sure a passel of 'em," Jess Smith breathed as he watched the approaching warriors.

"Quite a tangle, all right," Lemuel Redd agreed. "Looks like we've stirred up the swarm, for certain."

"It is many guns they have, Platte."

"You're right, Hy." Platte drew a deep breath. "The rest of you," he finally ordered, uttering what to all of them were terrible words, "draw your guns and let's show 'em what we have. If one of them does shoot, then don't hold back. We'll need to sell our lives as dearly as possible!"

"Whatsamatta white man heap no savvy Injun pony?"

The big-mouthed Pahute, who had given his name in and around Bluff during the past year as Moencopi Mike, appeared seething with hatred as he leaped onto the back of a horse, kneed it forward, and slammed the muzzle of his rifle hard into the stomach of Amasa Barton.

"I savvy, all right," Amasa responded with a growl of his own, and Moencopi Mike gave a surprised grunt as the muzzle of Barton's rifle was pushed hard into his own abdomen. "And these ponies," the young Mormon concluded, "ain't Indian!"

It was coming onto full daylight now, and Billy, on foot, had stepped to within six or seven feet of Posey and his brother Scotty, his carbine steady. Because of what Eliza had told him, he had not been surprised to discover that Posey and his brother were the ones who had attempted to kill him. Though mystified by the fact that these same young men had sat at his table and spent time in his home, Billy now knew that something had turned them, and that they now considered the Mormons, and perhaps especially himself and his family, to be their enemies. Still, as Posey stared slack-jawed at

Billy's carbine while his own weapon remained at the ready, Billy could not feel exultant. Instead he was sorrowing over all the effort so many of the settlers had made with these two—effort that now appeared to have come to naught.

Nearby Billy could see, without turning his head, that Jess Smith and another Pahute, one Billy did not know, had rifles pressed against each other's heads. And without averting his vision from young Posey and his brother, which he dared not do, Billy could also see a Pahute who was known as old Paddy—just as bad a character as Mike, some were saying—holding his old pistol hard against Lem Redd's stomach.

That pistol, Billy knew, had no trigger. But several times he and others had watched Paddy shooting sticks in the river by striking the hammer with a rock—the same rock he now held ready as he snarled his fury at Lemuel Redd. And Lem, meanwhile, had his own pistol cocked and pressed hard against the forehead of the redoubtable Paddy.

"White man heap scared," Paddy suddenly growled, his voice carrying easily to Billy.

"You even think of swinging that rock, Paddy," Lem replied easily, almost conversationally as he smiled and pressed his pistol even harder, pushing Paddy's head back at an unnatural angle, "and we'll see which one of us is scared the most."

It was amazing to Billy how much clarity of mind he was experiencing, especially since the whole Butler Wash seemed filled with such confusion. Platte was behind him somewhere, yelling that the Mormons wanted only their own horses and were not interested in any of the other animals the Pahutes had gathered in their "big round-up." He could also hear Hy Perkins's booming baritone warning someone that he was not afraid to shoot, and just as clearly he could make out the voices of Johnny Gower and George Ipson.

There was also the babble of Indian voices shouting instructions or making threats that Billy did not much understand. One word, *co-que,* he heard again and again, and that word, he knew, meant "Shoot!" Yet strangely, no one had.

Then there were the war cries, horrid shrieks that continually punctuated the morning air, designed no doubt to distract and unnerve opponents. That such a tactic would normally work Billy had no doubt. But not this time, not with him and his brethren made resolute with desperation!

Though Billy could not turn his head to see, he knew that the Pahutes had them outnumbered at least three to one. He also knew some of the Mormons were surrounded by three or four of the Indians, and he supposed, though he couldn't see, that he might be one of them. It gave a man pause, knowing that any second one of these hotheaded, screeching Indians, if not one of the quieter but equally resolute Mormons, was going to shoot, and that within a second or two after that, one or more bullets would almost certainly pierce his own body. And though some of the Pahutes would also die, including this youth called Posey who was now glaring at him with dark, flashing eyes, many others would not. And they would be the ones, Billy knew, who would attack Eliza and little Willy in the unfinished and defenseless fort.

"Dear God in heaven," he pleaded as men and horses raged around him, "please protect Eliza, Willy, and the others, and please don't allow me to kill this boy—"

"*Too itch tickaboo!*"

The shrill, commanding voice pierced the morning air, somehow bringing to an instant stop the amazing cacophony. As one, all eyes turned upward, and there, on a rock high above the valley floor, stood a lone Pahute youth.

"*Too itch tickaboo!*" he shouted again, this time into a stillness broken only by the snorting and movement of a large number of horses. "These men are mormonee—our friends! Don't hurt them! Give them their horses!"

In wonder Billy watched as, without hesitation, every weapon in the hands of the Pahutes was instantly lowered. Every single weapon! And though doubt and confusion appeared on the faces of many, including Posey and his brother, nevertheless the threat was over in an instant and the danger past. No Pahute weapons were raised again, and so Billy and the others lowered their own weapons and quickly finished gathering the Bluff animals from among the large herd.

Bluff Fort

"I hate to admit this," Mary Jones groused as she bent over her washboard in the hot sun of early afternoon, "but I do believe Pa was inspired! The way my back's aching, I couldn't worry about Kumen if I wanted to."

"Why Mary, your pa's the bishop." Jane Gower was acting shocked, but she winked at her sister, Rachel Perkins, to show it was not so. "He's always inspired."

"Maybe. But if you only knew how I hate washdays—"

Shortly after their arrival in Bluff, Platte Lyman and his brothers had dug a well around which the fort was now being built. Though of easy access and only about fifteen feet deep, the well-water was so hard—so filled with minerals—that the Saints had to draw it and then settle it in tubs for days, at the same time soaking bags of wood ash in it to draw out at least some of the minerals before they could even think of using it. Still it tasted awful, and some continued to joke that it remained too thick to drink, too thin to plow.

Because of their limited workforce and the necessity of everyone working together in order to get anything accomplished, washday in Bluff had become a community affair rather than a private one. The boys who were too small for working on the ditch or in the fields kept the fires going and the water boiling, the girls carried hot water to whoever needed it, and the women reserved for themselves the backbreaking labor of washing and hanging out the laundry.

Normally the day began early, almost before daylight, with fires being ignited under the forty or so metal boilers that had been filled with softened water. Raised a foot or so on rocks that were dragged up for the purpose, the boilers were filled with white fabrics that the women brought out when the water was boiling. This first soaking was to loosen the dirt—"matter which is out of place," Eliza called it—and while a few of the women stirred up the clothing with peeled wash sticks, the remainder turned to preparing a community breakfast.

In the cabins water was also being heated as the children fed wood to the fires and three stoves that now graced the fort, and outdoors the several wooden washtubs were kept at least half full of hot water. The women next took their bars of homemade lye soap and peeled small slivers into the water, which they stirred until it was mostly dissolved. Then, leaning over their rippled washboards, which rested against the bottoms of the tubs, they soaped and scrubbed their presoaked clothes by rubbing them up and down, up and down, into the soapy water and back out again, in and out, in and out, constantly turning and wringing each piece of fabric until most of the dirt was left in the water of the tubs.

The boilers were then filled with clean, cold water, and the whites were soaked and stirred for a second time while the water was brought to another boil. They were then lifted out by means of the sticks and placed in tubs of cold water for rinsing. Then each piece of clothing was wrung by hand as tightly as possible, shaken out, and hung on one of several dozen lines that had been strung here and there throughout the fort for that purpose.

The only difference in the treatment of colored clothing was that it was never boiled, and occasionally salt or alum was added to the water to fix the colors. But whether white or colored, washing clothes was hot, grueling, backbreaking work for everyone involved. Yet it needed desperately to be done, both for cleanliness and to preserve the clothing of the Saints for as long as it would last.

"I do wish we'd started earlier," Eliza Ann Redd stated caustically as she pulled one of the washtubs across the ground. "Inspired or not, I wish the bishop wouldn't have waited until practically noon to call a washday."

"It is hot," Adelia Lyman agreed as she tucked a stray lock of hair back into her bun.

"As a blistered boot, Lem would say." Eliza Ann undid her bonnet and wiped her forehead on her rolled-up sleeve. "Still, I'm in complete agreement with you, Mary. Not only do I hate washdays every bit as much as you, but I'm also equally convinced that your father is inspired. My inclination is to sit in the cabin weeping and wailing after poor Lem and doing neither one of us a lick of good. Fact is, that's exactly what I was doing when Lula brought word of washday to me. But now, even though my back is breaking over this relic of barbarism they call a washboard, the time is passing faster, and I'm getting a little good done besides."

"Relic of barbarism is right!" Adelia Mackelprang grumbled as she pushed a tired shirt up and down the cruel board. "Sammy's got an old copy of the *American Agriculturist* magazine, and there's a picture in it of a Monitor washing machine and improved wringer that I swear I'd give my left leg for!"

"Mother has a Novelty brand wringer back home in Cedar," Mary Ann Perkins declared. "She offered to let me have it when we started for this place, but like a silly fool I told her no."

"Does it work well?"

"Oh, Jane, you've never seen anything like it!" Mary Ann's face looked positively dreamy. "No more twisting and twisting until it feels as though your skin is coming off your hands and your arms are on fire. Instead you just feed the clothes into the wringer while you turn the handle; and presto! Clothes ready to be hung out on the line."

"Lawsy! I can't even imagine such a thing."

"Well, I can't imagine a machine that washes," Rachel Perkins declared, "and I've even seen one. In Salt Lake City."

"How did it work?"

Rachel paused for a moment, remembering. "Well, there was a tub with some paddles in the middle, fastened on a drum. Under the tub were some gears, and they were connected by a metal rod to a handle that stuck up outside the tub like the brake handle on a wagon. With the water, soap, and clothing in the tub, all the woman had to do was push and pull that handle back and forth, turning the drum and paddles and agitating the clothes until they were good and clean. I swan, but it was the most amazing thing—"

Anna Decker looked up from her washboard, tears streaming down her cheeks. "Chatter, chatter, chatter! I . . . I don't know how you sisters can carry on like you do, not when—oh, mercy! Maybe it's that I didn't get to say good-bye to Jim, I don't know. I . . . I have this awful feeling in the pit of my stomach, and I can't seem to make it go away no matter how hard I work."

"I think that must be normal," Nellie Lyman said quietly, thoughts of washers and wringers instantly forgotten. "If my Joseph was after the horses instead of across the river with Thales, I know I'd be feeling the same."

"Billy *is* after the horses," Eliza added, "and I do feel the same. I didn't sleep a wink all night long, and though I'm glad Bishop Nielson called a washday today to keep us all busy, I can't seem to stop the gnawing worry in my own stomach."

"Well, Pa says he felt strongly that all will be well with them."

"I . . . I hope he's right, Mary. But . . . what happens if something goes wrong?"

Mary's look was bleak. "Then it'll be like everything else we've had to face since we were called on this peace mission. We'll just have to grit our teeth and bear it."

"Boiling water coming up!" Lula Redd called as she and Leona Walton staggered from one of the large fires with a large pail of steaming water held between them. "Which one of you sisters needs it most?"

Waving her hand, Eliza forced a smile to her face. "Over here, Lula!"

"We're on our way!"

"Lawsy sakes," Leona exclaimed as she looked into Eliza's tub, "are those Willy's diapers?"

"They are, Leona. Stinky, huh?"

"Stinky and almighty colorful!" And with that observation, the girls turned and ran giggling toward the tubs of well-water, where they would refill the pail and get it back over a fire.

"Look at these poor diapers," Eliza exclaimed after the girls had gone. "Practically every one of them is threadbare, and the only passable ones have 'Pride of Durango' printed across them. No wonder Leona and Lula giggled. They are colorful!"

Jane Gower laughed. "The girls' underwear probably says the same thing."

"Lula's certainly does!" Eliza Ann grinned without humor. "So does half the children's underwear in this fort! One thing's for sure—with that many young people wearing unmentionables made of 'Pride of Durango' flour sacks, nobody needs to wonder where we purchase our flour."

"I don't mind seeing the flour sacks and knowing they're covering the children's backsides," Mary said. "What's difficult for me is seeing how thin and patched everybody's outer garments are getting—Kumen's especially. And that's despite the fact that every one of us is spinning and stitching up homespun at every available opportunity. I swan, but our whole community seems destitute, and if we don't get a harvest sufficient to sell for more than our own barest subsistence, I don't know what we'll do."

"Lem's and my clothes are the same as Kumen's," Eliza Ann admitted, "thin enough in some places to see through."

"And everything my children are wearing," Mary Ann added, "was something else before it wore out and got restitched. I can't tell you how fervently I'm praying for a decent harvest."

"Well," Mary said quietly, "I don't give a fig what our clothes look like, so long as the Lord brings Kumen back home in safety—"

"Pa's back!" Lula Redd suddenly shrieked from near the fires. "Hey, everybody! Look! The men are back, and they got the horses!"

24

Sunday, May 8, 1881

Elk Ridge

"*Ungh!*" Scotty grumbled, "that was a strange thing, a strange thing indeed. I do not think I have ever seen anything like it."

"You do not *shu-mi,* you do not think, at all!"

Posey was angry, more so than Scotty had ever seen, and so wisely he grew still. Besides, the insult was an old one, used often, and the large youth hardly even noticed it anymore. Instead he settled himself on the back of his horse, content to ride beside his brother while he thought long thoughts about what they had experienced.

But Posey could not grow still; neither could he enjoy the journey the way his brother seemed to be doing. His heart had turned bad, and he could not shed the thoughts that troubled him so deeply.

It was now past the middle of the second day since the mormonee from the big river had come to claim their animals, and Mike's band of Pahutes and their herd were moving smartly northward across the heights of Elk Ridge. For more than a day they had traveled the secret trails that would take them over the mountain and down again to where the majority of the People who would not follow Ouray—and who had fled the Shining Mountains at the time of the big raid—were now encamped.

It was spring on the mountain now, a glorious time of lush new growth and melting snow that in seasons past had been Posey's favorite time of year. More, he was riding one of the stolen horses, a magnificent blooded animal that at any other time would have thrilled him no end. Now he hardly noticed such things. Instead he rode hard, he rode angrily, and he treated without mercy any living thing that happened to get in his way—horses or otherwise.

In fact, the day before, once the accursed mormonee had taken their pitifully few horses and ridden back toward the big river, the Pahutes had come upon several head of mormonee cattle. In total frustration he, Scotty, and several of the others had ridden these cattle down, shooting arrows into all of them, killing most and mutilating the others by cutting off their ears, udders, or tails. These, too, would die, but not for a time—not until the mormonee had found them and seen the anger and hatred that yet burned in the hearts of the People.

And Posey knew he was not alone in such feelings. Almost without exception the group of warriors were a sullen bunch, deeply troubled by what had happened with the stolen mormonee horses and completely unable to explain why they had allowed it. Posey knew this and knew exactly how they were feeling. In their group were now almost thirty warriors, men who were well armed and fully able to defend the way of the People, the free way of raiding and submitting to no man, which they had left the Shining Mountains to enjoy. Yet without even firing a shot they had submitted themselves to little more than a handful of men, allowing them to reclaim the horses that had been taken only the day before.

Worse, these few were not merely white men, who could at times be very fierce fighters. No, these were *katz-te-suah* mormonee, foolish men from the big river who always acted more like squaws than they did warriors. Yet he and the others, and even the feared and fearsome Mike, had acted more like squaws than the mormonee—

Angrily Posey quirted his fine-blooded mount, not because it was not moving fast enough but because the youth could find no peace, no answers to his burning questions. Why had they allowed such a thing, he asked himself again and again? And each time he asked it and came up with no answers, young Posey grew more angry.

But there was another question that lingered not far behind the first one, something that troubled him even more. Yet it was so unfathomable that Posey could hardly bring himself to acknowledge it, let alone ponder it in a search for solutions. In the past he had always done exactly as he had wished. He had lied and joked with the others and had always been *kee-en,* filled with laughter. No whim had gone unfulfilled, no wish ungranted. He had done what he wanted, taken what he wanted, and had never felt the least sort of restriction.

Yet when the mormonee had come among their horses and he had thought to *puck-ki,* to kill the small one with the glass before his eyes, his rifle had misfired, not once but twice, a thing it had not done either before or since. Of course, Scotty's mind had hearkened back to the foolish words spoken to Posey by the man Haskel—that he would never be able to kill the mormonee—and Scotty had not hesitated to let Posey know of his thoughts.

Of course, such tellings made Posey even more angry, and the swelling mark of his quirt on Scotty's cheek would remind his younger brother for some time to come that Posey's anger was a thing to be reckoned with.

Worse even than that, at least to Posey, was that the same foolish mormonee who had somehow avoided being killed had then held Posey under his own rifle, and Posey had seen no fear whatsoever in the man's pale eyes. At that moment, however, knowing he was close to *e-i,* to death, the humiliated youth had felt his own eyes practically glaze over with terror.

Perhaps, he thought with continued embarrassment, that was why his rifle muzzle had dropped, becoming so heavy that he had been unable even to lift it. Perhaps his terrible fear was why—

But no, that could not be true of all the warriors! It couldn't be! Too many of them were seasoned veterans and had faced death too many times to be frightened. Yet every one of them had lost the power to shoot their guns or their arrows, and they had lost that power in the precise moment when the unknown one—a man of the people whom none of them had recognized—had climbed upon the rock and shouted for them not to shoot but to accept the mormonee as friends.

In wonderment Posey reconsidered that moment. Beyond the sound of the Pahute's shrill voice there had been nothing done, nothing said. Yet almost instantly every weapon held by the Pahutes had been lowered. The few mormonee had in turn lowered their weapons, and soon all had been *tig-a-boo,* great friends. All the horses and mules had been returned to the whites, even one or two that had been taken the year before and had been with the Pahutes through the entire season of cold. More, there had been a great trading for other things belonging to the mormonee—a coat, two hats, a pistol that was even more broken than the one old Paddy used. And instead of being simply taken, as was the way of a true warrior, Posey and the others had willingly handed over many greenbacks for these articles—twenty-five for one hat, sixty for another. Posey could not even fathom all the numbers they were so great.

It didn't matter to Posey that these same greenbacks had been stolen only days before from the murdered Dick May. To him they were now the property of the People, and he could not imagine using them as trade to the foolish mormonee. Yet he had been as anxious to hand greenbacks to the white fools as anyone else. He had been—

Angrily Posey quirted his hapless mount again. It made no sense! It angered him, but when he tried to *shu-mi,* to think it through, he could come up with nothing! All he knew for certain was that some of the warriors—in fact, many of them—now feared the foolish mormonee. And they were saying, as they made a fleeing northward to join Mancos Jim, Poke, and the others, that they would never again make a raid against the people in the unfinished fort on the big river.

And it was that foolishness more than anything else that had turned to stone the heart of Posey!

Bluff Fort

"Who was it, then? Does anyone know?"

Eliza, rocking her son in an effort to put him down for a nap, was still trying to learn the details of the successful expedition to recover the stolen horses. Suffering from another one of her sick headaches, she had not felt well enough to attend worship services at the meetinghouse. Thus she had missed the accounting the brethren had given there. And the evening before, Billy and all the others had simply been too tired to give anything other than a cursory accounting of their expedition. But since his return from Sunday School, he had been repeating everything he could remember, and Eliza was still trying to extricate from him further details.

"Nobody could see him clearly," Billy responded to her question. "But Lem Redd, he's sure it was that young fellow Henry who has been hanging around Thales Haskel's place of late. I understand he had a personal talk with Brother Haskel last month, and I guess he left pretty well convinced that the Mormons are his friends. He and Lem talked a little, too, and according to Lem, Henry thought Brother Haskel was a 'heap good Injun.' It seems likely he's the one who shouted from that rock."

Eliza sighed. "I wish Brother Haskel would talk to those boys Posey and Scotty. Maybe he could find out why they're so angry."

"He already did," Billy replied. And he was thinking, as he spoke, of the way Posey had looked at him the second time he had tried to shoot, just seconds after Billy had "got the drop on him," as Kumen was now putting it. "I guess you didn't see it, Eliza, but after Posey stuck his rifle in little Lena's stomach, Thales took it from him and threw it into the dirt. Then he told Posey that the gun was no good and that he'd never be able to use it to kill Mormons."

"And that's why he couldn't kill you?"

Billy nodded. "Something certainly stopped him. Twice his rifle misfired, and after that he didn't have a chance. I'm telling you, hon-bun, you've never in your life seen anything like it. The minute—practically the second—that Henry stopped speaking, it was over. Without even looking at each other, but all at the same time, every Pahute brave who had attacked us lowered his gun or bow and arrow, and just like that the danger was past."

"Is this Henry a chief?"

"Not hardly. Fact is, he's only a boy, fourteen, maybe fifteen years old. But I don't think it was Henry that brought it to pass, Eliza, I truly don't. The Spirit of the Lord was what wrought upon those Pahutes, probably through a whole legion of angels. It was too miraculous to be otherwise. Henry called out, no doubt trying to help, and that was when the Lord took over. Otherwise somebody would have fired, and most likely none of us would have come back alive."

"But . . . except for Posey they've never been violent before," Eliza protested.

"They were sure-enough ready to be violent yesterday. Besides which, some of those greenbacks they gave us were stained with blood. Now, those poor Pahutes don't understand money—in fact one tried to pay for Joe Nielson's shirt with plain pieces of paper and couldn't understand why they weren't as valuable as greenbacks— so you know they hadn't earned it. No, ma'am, that money had violence behind it, as did all those horses with various brands on them. I don't know where it all came from, but I allow the day will come when we'll get word of some terrible crime that's been committed, and we'll see that we were being truly protected."

Soberly Eliza nodded.

"And I'll allow something else," Billy declared as he picked up little Willy and perched him on his shoulders. "I'm more convinced than ever that the Lord intends to protect us on our mission here on the San Juan, preserving our lives as long as we're obedient and prayerful."

"I believe that, too," Eliza agreed quietly. "I just wish someone would convince the Pahutes."

Bluff Fort

"Good evening, Eliza."

"Why, hello, Annie. Do come in."

"Thank you, but I'd rather not—not unless this is a good time for you and Billy."

Eliza was surprised. "A good time?"

"Yes, for Billy to tell me what he knows about getting answers to prayer. You were going to ask him about it. Remember?"

"Oh, mercy!" Eliza exclaimed as she opened the door even wider. "Annie, I'm embarrassed, but I'd entirely forgotten. Do come in, though, for I'm certain Billy will be happy to speak with you."

"Speak about what?" Billy asked with a smile as he stood his son on the canvas floor of the cabin. "And how-de-do, Sister Lyman. Take a chair, why don't you."

Annie Lyman sat at the table, and Eliza quickly explained to

Billy the woman's concerns about learning to obtain direction from the Lord.

"These past two days have been especially difficult for me," Annie said quietly. "Some of the sisters felt great peace while you men were gone, but I didn't! I was absolutely terrified for Brother Lyman! And no matter how hard I prayed, I could get nothing from the Lord. Why, Billy? What am I doing wrong?"

Soberly Billy shook his head. "I don't know that I can answer that, Annie. There are so many variables, and then I don't have a speck of priesthood authority over you—Well, I suppose I'm saying that I'm probably not the one to help you."

"Fiddlesticks!" Annie murmured. "I'm sorry if I'm troubling you, but I don't know who else to talk to. Brother Lyman is forever running here or there from one meeting or emergency to another, but a little while ago he suggested that maybe you could help—"

Billy smiled warmly. "Well, that does change things. Would you mind if I asked you a couple of questions?"

"Of course not. Ask me anything you wish."

"First, do you study the scriptures—the word of the Lord? Do you read and ponder them every day?"

Vigorously the woman nodded. "I don't always read a lot, but I do read every day."

"Good. Do you pray?"

Now Annie sighed. "Almost all the time, though occasionally it does get discouraging. Is . . . that why I don't feel anything?"

"Possibly." Billy sat back in his chair. "When you do pray, do you wait for the Lord to respond?"

"I . . . uh . . . What do you mean?"

"I mean, if we do all the talking, then we aren't giving the Lord much of an opportunity to respond."

Annie was shocked. "I've never even thought of such a thing."

"Makes sense, though, doesn't it. Another thing—the Lord told Oliver Cowdery that he would respond to Oliver's prayers by causing his bosom to burn within him if his course was right, or by giving him a stupor of thought if it wasn't. Several things can be learned from that, Annie, but one seems particularly important. When we get a response from the Lord, it will be through the power of the Holy

Ghost, and it will affect our feelings and our thoughts." Billy smiled. "To me, that means we're usually waiting in vain if we are waiting for an angel to appear or for the voice of God to thunder revelation out of the heavens. He just doesn't make himself known to most of us in that way."

"So, what am I to expect—to wait for?"

"A feeling, Annie; a simple, gentle impression. The voice of the Lord's Spirit is called the still, small voice—I believe because it is so tiny, so subtle. So we must learn to listen not so much with our ears as with our whole beings. Think about what you're feeling. Think about the ideas that come into your mind, especially those that come immediately after you've asked the Lord a question or made a request. According to the Prophet Joseph, it is important that we heed such impressions.

"Another thing. My physical body responds the same way every time I feel the power of the Spirit, and the few others I've discussed this with say the same. Our bodies don't always respond alike, but each person seems to respond the same way again and again. Pay attention to that, Annie. If you can determine how the Holy Ghost affects you physically—such as Oliver Cowdery's bosom burning or Father Lehi's bones quaking—then you're most certainly beginning to grow into the principle of revelation. Can you do all that?"

Soberly Annie nodded. "I think so. I'll certainly try. Thank you—both of you—for helping to ease a lonely woman's confusion."

25

Monday, May 9, 1881

Moab Settlement

Isadore Wilson was once again checking the rigging on the pack animals, not so much looking for loose knots as just plain stalling. His older brother Alfred was already mounted on his gray, waiting impatiently. But Isadore didn't much care how impatient his brother grew. For one reason or another, he'd been gone from home a good part of the past month, and he wasn't particularly anxious to leave again.

Besides, there was that durn dream he'd been having of late.

"Pa, will you be out afore next week?" he asked.

"Not until a week from today, Isadore," his father answered. "Bishop Stewart's asked me to take charge of the meetings Thursday and again on Sunday, so I reckon you boys will have to handle things until then." Alfred Gideon Wilson stepped to one of the pack animals and helped Isadore with a couple of knots that might have been loose.

"Remember, boys, jimson weed is getting mighty bad up there on Harpole and some of the other mesas, or so Brother Burkholder says. Al Moore agrees with him. So watch for it, and don't let the herd get in it. Keep 'em bunched pretty close if you have to."

"We'll do 'er, Pa." Alfred was confident, much more so than his younger brother.

"Remember, keep 'em on Castle Creek and the east side of Harpole. Cows start wandering up Pinhook and over Porcupine Rim and there's no telling where they'll end up. Burkholder and the others need the range on Wilson and Bald Mesas, every bit of it, and I told them we'd keep our cows off that country."

"We know, Pa. We'll do it."

For a moment the morning was silent. A couple of mourning doves were cooing on the pole fence down by the stock pond. One of the riding horses, restive, stamped a hoof, and the little terrier the boys called Spot plopped onto her stomach, her tongue hanging out in the heat. It was clear and hot, and there was no good reason the two young men were not already on their way toward Castle Valley. But for some reason Alfred Gideon Wilson did not feel like sending them off. Instead he continued looking at them, first one and then the other, almost as if he was trying to memorize their faces, their features. Isadore could sense this reluctance in his father, and it made him feel lonely—lonely and nervous. Too bad, he thought, that they couldn't take Spot with them this trip. The small terrier would have been a comfort.

"There's been talk of some rough characters hanging around Coyote or La Sal," their father said abruptly, "with the McCarty brothers. Their pa's a good man, but those two boys of his, Tom and Bill—well, you boys see any hombres like that, ride shy of 'em. If it looks like trouble, get on over to Burkholder's spread, fast. Do the same thing if any of those dadburned Utes or Pahutes or whatever they are come nosing around."

Isadore ducked his head with shame. Twice since their amble down-country to Bluff, they'd spent a night with the McCarty brothers, playing cards and having a fine old time. Twice, that is, since the night when they'd caught them with that rustled herd. Isadore was ashamed of that, not because he and Alf had done a whole lot wrong but because he knew how disappointed their father would be if he found out. "Avoid even the appearance of evil," he was always saying, and Isadore knew that he and his older brother were now ignoring that good advice.

"Maybe you ought to let us pack a little iron," Alfred suggested with a wry grin, not feeling ashamed at all.

"Nope," Alfred Gideon responded to his oldest son's request. "No guns, boys, and you know it. I don't hold with killing anybody for any reason. Never have and never will. Those Holyoak folks who just came in from Bluff say the Saints there haven't carried weapons in more than a year, and they're practically surrounded by enemies. If they don't need weapons, neither do we."

Isadore didn't know what Alfred was thinking, but in his mind, clear as day, he was seeing Billy Foreman sitting across the table from Jimmy and Henry W. Heaton, explaining that Mormons had too much respect for God and his creations to heedlessly take the life of anything, man or beast. Of course, both Heatons had worn tied-down pistols and carried saddle carbines, and Henry W. had been largely unaffected by Billy's words. But Jimmy? Well, somehow Isadore could tell what Jimmy was thinking, and he had known Billy's words were sinking in. Thing was, they'd also sunk into him—so deep that a week before he'd not even killed a rattlesnake he'd encountered on the trail. And he could still hear old Bishop Nielson, in his heavy Danish accent, warning them all four to avoid lusting after the blood of the Indians.

"All right, Pa," Alfred was saying. "Just thought I'd ask."

"Is Ma coming out to say adios?"

"I thought so, Isadore. But maybe some of the little ones are acting up. Didn't you say good-bye before you left the house?"

"Yeah, Pa, I did." The youth was downcast, for he had finally decided it was his mother he wanted to tell of his dreams. Thing was, with all the youngsters underfoot all the time, he'd never found the right opportunity. And now—

"I . . . I was just sort of hoping," he stammered lamely, "that she would come out—"

"Come on, Ise," Alfred said gruffly by way of interruption, "daylight's a-burning, and we've got a long ride."

Slowly Isadore's face broke into his shy grin. "I reckon we do," he replied simply, and then he stepped into his saddle.

Thoughtfully Alfred Gideon Wilson pulled his big watch out of his vest pocket. "Practically six-thirty," he said, looking up. "It isn't like either one of you to start so late in the morning." Carefully he studied his sons one more time. "Uh . . . anything wrong?"

"No, Pa. Everything's jake."

"Good. You, Isadore?"

Thinking again of his unsettling dream and his desire to share it with his mother, the young man slowly shook his head. Maybe, he was thinking, when he came home again—

"All right, then. Remember who you are, boys, and the Lord will bless you. And be sure to keep the Sabbath day holy next Sunday! Do a little studying for a change—be good for your souls. See you in a week!"

Kicking their horses, the young men moved off, their two pack animals in tow. For a few moments Alfred Gideon Wilson watched them, wondering. But even after he had left the corrals and gone back into his cabin, he could still see his sons vividly in his mind. And far down the road, though the Wilson cabin and outbuildings were long out of sight, young Isadore was still riding with his face turned back toward home, wishing he'd had a decent chance to have a sit-down talk with his mother.

Bluff Fort

"I'll tell you what I think. This is the wrong season for such business as we're about." Harriet Gower was growing frustrated with her task of chopping up bits of cooked pork, and it was obvious.

"It certainly is," Jane Walton agreed as she labored to mix the chopped meat with salt, pepper, and sage. "Butchering hogs is something folks should do along about November, when the cold can help preserve the meat. Hot time of year like this, it's much more difficult."

"I'd rather be butchering now in the heat," Eliza said from her seat between the other two, "than attending the funeral of some child this monster has killed. Did you hear how it went after little Jesse Decker?"

"I did, and I'm with you, Eliza. It was high time for this hog to be butchered! How do the boudins look?"

"Boudins?"

"Intestines, then." Jane smiled. "Charlie says boudins is an old mountain-man term, but I use it because I believe it sounds a little more delicate. The boudins are only supposed to bleach in that lime mixture for twenty-four hours, you know. Since they've been soaking since last Thursday afternoon before meeting, I'm a little nervous about them."

For a moment the women were silent, recalling the terrible emergency caused by the Pahute thieves who had attempted to steal their horses. It was no wonder, Eliza was thinking, that the intestines and everything else in the fort had come to such a screeching halt. Except for the washing, of course, not a thing had been done by anybody from Friday afternoon onward, and so this morning it had been necessary for several volunteers to finish butchering the large hog. Two of the women had salted and were now smoking hams, hocks, and side meat, and she, Jane, and Harriet had volunteered to finish the sausage.

Someone the Thursday before had removed from the intestines the loose fat and outer membranes, turned them inside out, cleaned them in borax water, and set them to bleaching. Eliza's task was now to rinse them in clear water and then scrape away the inner lining, getting them as thin as she possibly could without tearing or puncturing them. When she was finished, the thin skins would be washed repeatedly in warm water, after which they would be ready for packing with the seasoned meat. Finally they would be placed in a large earthenware crock and melted lard would be poured over them, thus preserving the sausages until they could be eaten and enjoyed.

"Truthfully, Jane, they look fine to me. The skin isn't brittle at all, which the bishop told me to watch for, and I'm having very little difficulty tearing away this inner lining."

Jane Walton nodded. "Good. That's usually the most difficult part."

"Without a proper grinder, I believe chopping has overtaken it," Harriet said. "Who has the children today, Eliza?"

"Mary," Eliza replied with a chuckle. "She says if this is the only way she can have children, she's going to make the most of it."

"I don't blame her a bit! This is a discouraging enough place even with a family." Harriet's voice betrayed her sadness. "I don't know how I'd cope without my babies."

"Billy said John is thinking of leaving?"

Harriet nodded. "He is, and I support him wholeheartedly. If that fool ditch fails one more time, we're packing up and heading back to the settlements. I can't let it break his heart again."

Jane nodded her understanding. "It's interesting, isn't it, how little things trouble us women, while only the big ones, like our ditch or having to spend their winters away from home, trouble a man."

"Little things? What do you mean?"

Jane laughed with embarrassment. "Oh, you know. Little things, like poor table manners, unmended holes in clothes, no curtains at the windows, stale body odors—"

"Snakes under the bed or in the woodpile," Eliza added emphatically.

"That's right. To a man such things are simply part of life. You ever heard one of the brethren scream when he ran into a rattlesnake? Why, they hardly even notice such things, and they certainly don't stay awake nights worrying about them. I think we sisters notice them and worry over them because, while our hands are always busy doing one task or another, our minds are quite often idle. Some days when my only company is the buzzing of the flies and my tasks are the very things I've done every day for the past thirty years, I get to thinking the same things over and over until they nearly drive me crazy. For instance, Charlie never goes off to the Jump or anywhere else that I don't worry he'll be killed by Indians, imagining how it might be again and again until I'm positively ill with worry."

"I . . . do the same with my Johnny. I don't think I'm ever shut of my fear!"

"And I thought I was the only one fighting fear," Eliza admitted. "I've had a terrible time forcing myself to want to stay here on this mission, it has been so bad."

"But . . . you seem so peaceful—"

Eliza chuckled as she began stuffing chopped meat into the finally ready skins. "Until recently, that's been the actress in me. Lately, though, I've been finding a little peace."

"Through your faith, no doubt," Jane said as she sat and began helping stuff the intestines. "That, and your sweet willingness to repent. You'll never know, Eliza, how that touched my soul during our trek out here."

"Thank you," Eliza said quietly. "For me, it was simply embarrassing. And it certainly didn't stop my fears from growing once we got here. That's been a whole new trouble to repent of."

"Well," Jane agreed, "I've always thought that fear is a person's greatest sin, for it shows such a lack of faith. It comes between us and the light of Christ, and it prevents us from doing all sorts of things that might otherwise gladden our hearts and glorify our souls. All of this seems to be expressed in the words of the Bible: 'Perfect love casteth out fear.'"

"Then both my love and my faith are sorrowfully lacking," Harriet declared sadly, almost angrily. "This mission isn't at all what I expected, and I'm almost praying that our ditch will fail again just so Johnny will take me away. I . . . I'm sorry, sisters, but that's the truth! And it's exactly how I feel!"

Lower Lisbon Valley

"Anybody have any idea why Captain Dawson's left off following the trail of the horses?"

Jimmy Heaton, lying on his back looking up at the stars, was hardly even listening. Instead, he'd been thinking of something he had read in Isadore Wilson's copy of the Book of Mormon, wondering about it—

"Hey, Jimmy, why don't you answer the man's question?"

Jimmy Heaton grinned into the darkness. "I reckon it's on account of he wanted to stay close to water," he finally replied, knowing full well that this was a dry camp and that the men of the Colorado posse had precious little liquid left in their canteens.

"Water!" Wiley Tartar snorted. "We was near enough to water back at Piute Springs, afore the captain made that hard turn north and missed it altogether. Tell the truth, boys, my nag's getting mighty thirsty, and I got less than half a canteen myself."

"It ain't the water I'm worried about," Tom Click groused. "We was on the trail of them murdering redskins, and then the captain left it a'purpose to come this way. That worries me."

"Why don't you ask him why he done it, then?" Dick Baumgartner was a serious man, and everything he did or said was serious. He was straightforward and expected everyone else to be the same.

Jim Hall scooted a little closer to the fire. "Could be he's afraid of asking a fool question—"

"What fool question is that?" Captain William Dawson asked as he moved into the light of the fire. He had been gone for some time, and Jimmy found himself wondering how long the man had been standing out in the dark, listening.

"Jimmy's already answered it," Wiley responded almost sullenly.

"I didn't either," Jimmy said with a wide smile. "I ain't hardly said a thing. But all of us would like to know, Captain, why we didn't stick to the trail of them hundreds and hundreds of horses."

"Or why we had to climb up and over Three-Step Hill and suffer through this miserable Lisbon Valley country," Jack Galloway responded in his deep, gravelly voice, picking up Jimmy's line of discussion. "This here's the country where they had that silver strike that went bust a year ago, and it was purty well determined then that there wasn't water enough in this country to keep a stove-up lizard alive—let alone a man."

"You boys arguing with my decision?"

Jimmy laughed outright. "Not hardly, Captain Dawson. We're here, ain't we?"

"You are, and every man-jack one of you volunteered to follow me, no matter."

"That's right, Captain," Hard Tartar responded, "and we will. But that don't mean we don't want to understand why we left off the trail yesterday morning. Good chance we'd have caught them varmints by now!"

Slowly Captain William Dawson, sheriff of San Miguel County and rancher of Disappointment Valley, lowered himself into the sand upwind from the smoke of the fire. "Fair enough," he said as he rolled and lighted a cigarette. "You recollect that grubrider we fed night afore last? Well, me and him had us a little talk afore he rode out yesterday morning, and he told me Spud Hudson and about twenty-five others have gone after the Pahutes."

"We figured they would."

"Yeah, we did. What we didn't figure was that Spud thinks he's about four days behind the Pahutes, and that the whole ragtag bunch of them murdering red devils is now circling north around the backside of the Blue Mountains. Spud thinks they're fixing on heading back to the reservation in Colorado. Leastwise that's what he told that grubrider feller, who wanted no part of joining up with his posse. Likewise the sorry so-and-so didn't feel like volunteering for ours."

"Lilly-livered skunk!" Harg Eskridge spat disgustedly.

"More'n likely. Anyhow, boys, I put two and two together and figured that if Spud was chasing the Injuns from behind, I'd strike north northwest and see if maybe I could head 'em off or intercept 'em—sort of box 'em betwixt us and Spud, and then both of us give 'em a good old dose of what for!"

"Sounds reasonable," Pat McKinney said. "You got any notion of where you're going?"

Captain Dawson nodded. "The grubrider drew me a map, Pat. We'll follow up Lisbon Valley to where it cuts into Big Indian Wash. From there we cross to Coyote Wash and skirt westward between a place called Flat Iron Mesa and the little mesas on the southwest end of the LaSals. That'll lead us into Muleshoe Canyon and to a water hole called Kane Springs, which according to the grubrider is the only place in a hundred miles for the Pahutes to water all them hosses they stole, and for us to catch up to them. Seems the flats above the springs are a regular camp for 'em on their travels, or so this feller told me."

"He's seen 'em there, I suppose?"

"Claims he has." Captain Dawson flicked his hardly-smoked butt into the fire. "Says he had a game of cards there once with a Pahute name of Bridger Jack, a medicine man who was the gamblingest fool Injun the grubrider had ever seen. Game lasted two days and two nights, and when it was over he discovered he'd won precious little but his own outfit, which Bridger Jack had somehow stole during the game, hid back in the brush, and put up for booty."

"Sounds like one of them red sons, all right!"

"It does. Now let's get some shut-eye, boys, just like Bill May's outfit is doing over yonder. Dick, you take first watch and I'll take second. We've got two, maybe three days hard riding ahead of us, and then we've got to fight those fool Indians."

Slowly the camp grew still as one after another of the posse rolled into their bedrolls and dropped off. Except for the watchful Dick Baumgartner, Jimmy Heaton was the last to sleep, and he drifted off pondering again the words of the Book of Mormon—that, and wondering when he was finally going to have a chance to speak of these things to the more than lovely Miss Sally—

Indian Canyon

It was late, but still the council fires in the bottom of Indian Canyon burned brightly. The youth Posey, now considered a warrior by all but the fierce Poke, who for some reason continued to disdain him, had been dancing around the main fire with some of the others, each of them showing the way he would fight the hated mormonee when they finally came after their horses. It was an exultant time, a wild time, and the People who had come directly to the canyon had now joined forces with the great warriors who had slain the foolish ranchers and taken their vast herd of horses.

Resting now, for his *weep-pi,* his dancing, had also been a way for him to express his anger with the way the mormonee had fooled them, Posey was suddenly aware that he was being watched from the shadows. Looking up, he saw his brother Scotty, whose glance meant nothing and whom he now ignored. And then, in the semidarkness behind where Scotty sat, Posey was startled to see the dark, luminous eyes of the *nan-zitch* called Too-rah.

He had not seen her since before the big raid, and even then they had not spoken. Instead he had watched her constantly, part of the time wishing to draw near to her, and part of the time remembering the sting of her mockery the year before. But now there was no mockery in her eyes. Instead, Too-rah seemed to be smiling at him, inviting him to follow her into the darkness.

His heart hammering and his hands suddenly sweaty, Posey could not think what to do. Half his mind wished to follow her, to be near her once again. But the other half was filled with sudden fear, for he had no idea what he would say to her, what kind of talk he would make. Then, too, the feared Poke was standing nearby, and Posey was certain the Grizzly would slay him if he found him with his sister.

Still, the dark eyes of Too-rah were bright in the firelight, and her smile was beckoning—

With a start Posey became aware that someone nearby was speaking to the warriors around the fire, making a telling concerning the mormonee who had encamped along the big river. Posey knew the voice, but until he twisted about to see who was speaking, he could not identify old Peagament. And when he did and then turned quickly back again, the *nan-zitch* had vanished.

Almost Posey arose to go seek her. Almost. But then he also caught the eyes of the feared Grizzly resting upon him, and he did not move at all. Instead, he sat sullenly, hardly listening to the voice of the old fool Peagament, who had so long before been shamed by the mormonee—

"It is a true saying, brothers." Peagament struck the ground with his hand to show his conviction, his sincerity. "I have seen this *to-wats,* this man who is called Haskel. His *myshoot-te-quoop,* his medicine, is very strong. He is mormonee, it is true, and yet he is also as one of the People and speaks our tongue. He speaks the words of *Shin-op,* and they come to pass even as he says."

"It is said that this mormonee shamed you," Posey snarled, suddenly, inexplicably angry. "This is why you fear him! This is why you say his words have power."

Old Peagament looked at the young man who had once saved his life, and for a moment he felt tired. Why was it, he wondered, that the young always had to grow old before wisdom would come to their hearts—

"The young warrior Posey's words are true," he acknowledged quietly. "This *to-wats* did shame me. Nevertheless, I do not fear him, for he is not an enemy to me or to any of the People. Neither are any of the mormonee our enemies."

"I say you fear him!"

"No, for I have gazed into his eyes and found nothing fearsome there. But I do fear his words, for they are the words of *Shin-op.* They are words of great power."

"And what are these words you would have us worry ourselves over?" another warrior asked disdainfully.

Peagament looked firmly into the eyes of the warrior. "*Shin-op* says the mormonee are the friends of the People. The mormonee are to be treated as friends—as brothers. The mormonee have many things to say to the warriors of the People about *Shin-op* and his way. The mormonee are *Shin-op's* friends. If we try to put them under the grass we will be stopped, for *Shin-op* protects them, and we cannot *puck-ki,* we cannot kill them. If we continue to steal from them, we will *puck-kon-gah,* we will grow sick. After that, if we keep stealing, we will die."

"These are the ramblings of an old fool!" Posey snorted.

"Fools can also be young," Peagament replied quietly before he returned his gaze to the others. "This man Haskel did not say how we would die. His words of power were, 'Maybe the warriors of the People will get sick and die. Maybe the warriors will kill each other. Maybe *Shin-op* will send the lightning to kill them. Maybe he will reach out with his unseen hand and touch them, and they will wither like the grass under the summer sun. If the warriors of the People continue to steal mormonee horses or kill mormonee cattle, they will die!'"

"The words of Peagament are true," a second voice said from the outer edge of the circle.

Straining, Posey could see a youth of about his own age who looked somewhat familiar, though he had no idea why. But before Posey could challenge him, the youth spoke again.

"I am called Henry," the young man declared. "I am the son of the warrior who is called Baldy, and I have also visited the one called Haskel. He spoke the same words of power to me, and already I have seen some of his words come to pass. Yes, at the place called Boiling Springs *Shin-op* stretched forth his unseen hand and stopped many warriors from slaying a few mormonee. *Oo-ah,* yes, and *Shin-op* also gave back to the mormonee the horses the warriors of the People had stolen from them only one day before. Ask these warriors who have come from Boiling Springs, brothers, and you will see that my words are true."

And the youthful Posey, too startled by the explanation to say anything else, found himself thinking of the words that the mormonee Haskel had spoken to him.

26

◇─◇─◇

Tuesday, May 10, 1881

The Jump

"I'd say the blamed river's dropped five feet!"

"At least, and all in the past week and a half!"

For a moment or so the men were silent, watching the unpredictable San Juan as it swirled and eddied past the bottoms of their carefully constructed cribs. All spring the temperature had climbed rapidly while the level of the river had fallen even faster. Now the newly sprouted crops, painstakingly watered by the sisters with their carried water, were withering in the unrelenting heat. And the river had dropped so low that water was not going to flow into the ditch even after all the cribs were finished. The problem was so pressing that the Pahute raid and the miraculous recovery of their horses, or even the huge invasion of Navajo sheep that were decimating the range to the west of the fort, were no longer even topics for discussion. Instead it was the unpredictable river, that grim monster with which they had contended unsuccessfully for more than a year.

"Does make a body feel sort of discouraged," James Decker said as he kicked a small rock off into the stream.

"As ever," Platte Lyman agreed. "Ideas, anybody?"

"Somebody said Feenie Hyde's pa is building a water-wheel at Montezuma Fort."

"That's true," Platte replied. "I've seen it."

"Maybe we could do the same here."

"Not and do any good this year," Kumen Jones said. "Feenie told

324

me her pa's been working on his wheel all winter, and it still isn't finished. So one of our own would take too long to build, and then it probably wouldn't lift enough water to get to our fields, let alone irrigate them."

"Eight or ten of them would."

"Yeah, maybe. But it would still take a year or more to build them. And that isn't counting the time necessary to build a road up into the mountains where the Ponderosas grow."

"We need Ponderosa pine?"

"Well, that's the straightest lumber in the country, and those wheels will need to be built with straight lumber. Thing is, we don't have the time to go cut it and haul it back."

"Or the time to dry and mill it, either one."

"Vell, den, a vater veel iss not de ting for our fields, I be tinking." Jens Nielson leaned on his cane, staring at the whispering water. "Und dis awful river does make a body discouraged. But brudders, ve must do someting! Ve haff bin called to dis place by de Lord, und by yimminy, vith a little sticky-to-ity ve vill make de desert to blossom as de rose!"

"That's fine, Bishop." Now Jess Smith kicked a rock into the water. "But sticky-to-ity to do what?"

"We've talked about this before," Billy stated quietly, "so it isn't a new idea. But it looks to me like it's time to extend the cribs across the river and dam it off. Either that or run the ditch on upstream so we can grade it down to water level. Either one is a lot of work, but I believe damming it has the best shot."

"Why's that, Billy?"

"One, the river's dropped so low we'd have to take our ditch ten miles farther just to get a decent drop. Tell the truth, I don't even know if we can build such a grade. But if we decide we can, we're still dealing with a ditch made mostly of sand, which won't hold water any better than our present ditch does. Boys, I don't think the water would ever get this far, let alone to our fields."

"So you think damming this fool river's the best bet?" Parley Butt was sarcastic, though Billy didn't seem to notice.

"I don't know, Parl. We've never done it before." Now Billy

grinned. "But Platte didn't call for ideas that would work; he just called for ideas."

"Well, if it's damming the river we'll be doing," Ben Perkins declared, "I'm for getting started on it right away. Another two, three days of this heat and it's a loss our crops will be."

"Amen," two or three agreed quietly.

"Any other ideas?" Platte asked, looking around at the assembled men.

"I reckon we could do a bucket brigade, like the sisters have been doing."

Platte nodded at his younger brother. "We could, Walter, and I've thought of that myself. Trouble is, we'd have to make a trip back to Escalante or over into Colorado to get enough barrels to make a real difference. By the time we could do that, the crops will mostly be gone. Then too, there aren't enough of us left to bucket up the amount of water we need—"

"Not when this blasted sandy soil sucks water up faster'n a herd of thirsty heifers," Hanson Bayless grumbled. "Billy's sure right about that!"

"That's what I mean. Bucketing only helps a little; it's a temporary solution at best."

"Vell den, I say it iss time for a fast. Ya?"

"I agree, Jens. We need to have a community fast no matter what else we do. Boys, spread the word that come Thursday we'll all be fasting for the Lord to temper the elements of this river so it will become useful for the irrigation of our crops. At our regular Thursday night fast and testimony meeting we'll conclude our fasts with solemn prayer.

"In the meantime, we'd better start building cribs to dam the river. Billy, do we have enough logs?"

"Maybe, if we lay off work on the fort. We for sure don't have enough rocks, though."

Platte nodded. "So we need more crews, do we. Any volunteers for rock haulers? Anyone at—"

"Rider coming, Platte. He ain't one of us."

"That's Bill Ball," Lem Redd growled a moment later. "I recognize his big mule."

"Bill Ball?" Platte asked.

"Uh-huh. He's foreman of the LC, on Recapture up under White Mesa. The Brumleys grumbled some about the taxes I assessed Mrs. Lacy last fall, but not Bill Ball. He made sure they got paid right up. Now, though, he looks about as sociable as an ulcerated back tooth and as determined as the grim reaper. If he has more bad news to add to what we've been dealing with the past week or so, well, I just don't hardly know if I even want to hear it!"

———o—o—o———

"Howdy, boys. Sheriff Decker, good to see you again."

James Decker nodded. "Hello, Bill. You ever track down that Hazelton fellow?"

"Sugar Bob? That miserable, gut shrunk son of a gun! No, I didn't find him. Fact is, he seems to have dropped clean off the edge of the earth—either that or dug a hole somewheres and buried hisself in it. Do the world a favor happen he died there and stayed put, though to tell the truth I don't hardly expect such luck. Somebody did say they'd heard he was down on the Navajo reservation hunting the lost Peshlaki silver mine. I don't know, and as long as he stays away from here, I don't care!

"Mr. Redd, good to see you again, too. Happen, that is, you ain't assessing taxes today."

Lem Redd stepped forward and offered his hand. "Howdy, Bill. Name's Lemuel, but I'm Lem to my friends. And no, I'm not assessing taxes today, or collecting them, either one. Still, that's a mighty purty mule you're riding."

Bill Ball grinned lopsidedly. "Yeah, Lem, she is—for a mule. But useless as a wart on a purty gal's kisser. I wouldn't give a wooden nickel for her. Fact is, I'd probably pay some sorry fool to take her off my hands."

Lem and the others chuckled. "I told you I wasn't assessing taxes today. I just admire a purty animal."

Again Bill grinned his lopsided grin. "In that case, Lem, she's a good'un, all right. Most expensive animal I ever owned. I call her Abigail on account of a gal I knew back in Texas. They do favor each other somewhat—narrow bony face, sad round eyes, and teeth long enough to eat corn on the cob through a bob-wire fence. But despite such numerous similarities, that ain't why I named my mule after her. Tell the truth, that Abigail woman was the hardest worker—man or woman—I ever laid eyes on. My mule Abby's the same. So far as I've ever found, there ain't a quitting or sit-down bone in her body, and she don't know the meaning of tired."

"Mules have a reputation for being stubborn and mean," Josh Stevens commented.

"Some are, I reckon, just like some people I know. But not Abby."

"Is that why you ride her?" Jess Smith asked.

"Partly. But mules are thinner'n horses, so they don't stretch a man's legs so wide. At my age I like that. They're also more sure-footed, which in this country of rocks and cliffs is almighty important. And their gait is smoother, which is good for any sorry ol' son what has to live in the saddle daylight to dark. All-in-all, boys, I'll ride a mule every chance I get and wish I was when I ain't. You boys've sure done a pile of work on them cribs."

"And then some. There's more'n a hundred of them now. Trouble is, the river isn't too cooperative."

Bill Ball shook his head sadly. "Never has bin, not at least since I bin around. You gonna try damming it?"

"Looks like that's our last hope."

"More cribs?"

"That's right, straight on across to the far bank."

"Should do it—if she don't run plumb dry afore you're across. Or flood over with some chance storm. Overnight, or so Spud Hudson says, the San Juan can rise fifteen feet or more and turn into a raging monster. That happens once you've got her dammed, you folks could be in real trouble. I heard you didn't get any crops last year."

"How'd you come to hear that?"

"Oh, some young fellers name of Heaton and Wilson bought a couple of small herds of cows for their folks two, maybe three weeks ago. Fine boys. Said they'd spent a little time with you Mormons, digging on your ditch."

Lem Redd nodded. "They did. And you're right, they're all fine boys. And they were right, too. Bishop Nielson raised a few garden vegetables last season, but other than that—nothing."

Bill Ball nodded. "They also said you'd purty well scattered out through the winter, hunting work for groceries. Happen this fool river don't cooperate and you need to do it again, one or two of you come see me. We can always use another hand. You the head honcho here, Lem?"

Lem Redd grinned. "Only when I'm assessing or collecting taxes, which thankfully ain't too often. Bill, this here's Platte Lyman. He and Silas Smith have been the real leaders of this outfit, though with Silas gone and moved to Colorado, Platte's now the president of our company."

"Howdy, Mr. Lyman." Bill tipped his hat. "Pleased to make your acquaintance."

"Name's Platte, Bill." Platte stepped forward to shake hands. "And I'm pleased to make yours. Fact is, I'm a mule man myself. I spent my whole childhood on the back of a gentle, soft-walking mule that I felt as close to as family. I ride one now, every chance I get. What can we do for you?"

"Not much, I reckon. Just being neighborly. On account of some hot-headed, hoss-thieving Paiutes, the country hereabouts is some agitated. I came on the trail of a fair-sized herd of shod hosses and Injun ponies a day or so ago, headed this general direction. Then Curly Jenkins, a rider for Spud Hudson, came and borrowed a couple of my men to trail after what he figured must be twenty-five, thirty warriors. He said they was stealing all the hossflesh in sight, so I thought I'd drop by and give you folks warning."

"They've been here and gone." Samuel Rowley spat in the dust as he said it.

Bill Ball's eyes narrowed. "They get any of your stock?"

"They did," Platte replied with a nod. "They fired on our herder, drove him off, and then skedaddled with our entire herd."

"That's too durned bad." Bill Ball curled his leg around his saddlehorn and then carefully shook out the makings. "Spud'n Curly have a posse of maybe twenty-five men following 'em right now. I don't have any more riders to spare, but if you want to go join him, I'll be more'n happy to ride with you."

"That's mighty kind, Bill, but there's no real need. We went after them right off and caught up with them at Boiling Springs, up in the Butler."

"Ah, them miserable red so-and-sos," Bill breathed sorrowfully. "Some days I almost think they're worse'n the white sidewinders like Sugar Bob Hazelton that we got perambulating around this country. Did you lose many—I mean, was there much shooting?"

"Not any." Lem Redd lifted his hat and wiped his forehead. "For a moment things looked touchy as a teased snake, all right, but that was all."

"Well, I'm right sorry about your stock," Bill stated solemnly, "but at least none of you got hurt."

"No, we didn't." Platte was now smiling, as were the rest of the men. "Thing is, Bill, we also got our stock back—every last head, including a couple of animals we've been missing since last fall."

"You *what?*" Bill Ball looked stunned. "Platte, you can't be telling me the whole story! Those are *mean* Injuns! Plumb mean! And like I said, that bunch in the Butler had twenty-five, maybe thirty of 'em. Did you have 'em outnumbered, or get the drop on 'em maybe?"

"Since there was only ten of us, I doubt we outnumbered them. And the only one of us to get the drop on any of them was Billy Foreman here. For the rest of us it was sort of a Mexican standoff, two or three of them holding their guns on each of us, and each of us doing our best to cover every one of them. It was an interesting predicament, all right."

"Well, if that don't beat all!" Bill shook his head. "Them particular redskins've bin killing white folks here and yonder ever since they left Colorado. Spud reckons they're spoiling for a big war and trying to lead some of us more foolish white folks into it. He also figures they plan on joining up with others right away and turning into a real war party. He knows 'em mighty well, so I reckon he's probably right. What I want to know is, if you sure-enough went in and got your hosses and every one of you ended up being covered by their big guns, why in thunderation didn't they start that same war with you?"

"About the only reason we can give, Bill, is that the Lord was protecting us. We did a powerful lot of praying, and we didn't go with the intent of punishing or killing anybody. Our policy on this mission has always been to feed the Indians, not fight them, and that didn't change just because they stole our horses. All we wanted was our stock, and after those few seconds when things looked so grim, they dropped their weapons, we dropped ours, and our own stock was all we took back. That, and a few bloodstained greenbacks they used to buy hats and such from a couple of us."

"That'd be some of the money they stole from a feller name of Dick May—after they'd drilled him full of holes and burned a cabin down around him." Bill Ball flicked his cigarette butt into the sand. "So like I said, they're a mean bunch. That's why this little expedition of yours beats the stuffing out of anything I ever heard. Maybe you Mormon folks do have the ear of the good Lord, for it's a sure bet nobody else could have prevented a bloodbath there in the Butler. Feed but not fight, huh?"

"That's right." Platte's voice was quiet. "To our way of thinking, Bill, all life is precious to the Lord. He gave it, and he's the one that ought to take it away. When folks go spoiling after the blood of each other, except in the natural recourse of the law, then the Lord is grieved and can't bless them."

"Vengeance is mine," Bill breathed thoughtfully. "I will repay, saith the Lord."

"Exactly."

There was silence as Bill and everyone else contemplated the words from Paul's epistle to the Romans. Not far away the San Juan eddied and swirled noisily past the cribs, somewhere in the distance a dog barked, and in the fort a woman laughed, her voice carrying easily in the still air.

Suddenly Bill Ball broke into a wide smile. "Tell you what, boys. Since we ain't going to be chasing after no Pahutes, it looks like I got me a free day or two. You want a hand with building that dam yonder, Abby's mighty good at snaking logs from one place to another, and I ain't so bad at hanging onto her back while she's about it. What do you say?"

"We'd appreciate all the help we can get." Platte smiled in return and then started back toward the river. "Boys, let's get cracking, before Mr. Ball discovers what a lazy bunch of so-and-sos we all are!"

Bluff Fort

"The brethren are working mighty late tonight."

Without looking up from her stitching, Eliza nodded. "Perhaps we should have done the chores."

"That wouldn't have pleased Kumen very much. He says I have plenty to do without the chores, and I suppose he's right. Only, I get so lonely in my cabin without him around that I can hardly stand it."

Now Eliza looked up. "You're more than welcome here, Mary, and you know it. Besides which, sometimes I get so tired of cleaning silverware and lamp chimneys and everything else that needs it every few days—well, I'm more than grateful for your help."

Earlier Mary had taken Eliza's silver, which seemed always to be getting tarnished in their hot desert climate, and boiled it in potash lye—the same ingredient, derived from their wood ash, that was used in making soap. Next she had taken a soft rag and polished each piece with a mixture of whiting and vinegar, after which she had carefully placed them all in the wooden box where Eliza was now keeping them.

"I had no idea you had whiting for your silver," Mary said as she worked on her next project—the glass lamp chimneys.

"How do you polish yours?"

"I just put the pieces in a pan, pour sour milk over them, and let them soak overnight. In the morning the pigs get the milk, and I polish the silver with the ashes I save from our burned-out lantern mantels."

"I've heard that works, Mary, but I've never tried it. Neither do I—Oh, the salt for cleaning that soot is in that tin on the shelf."

Nodding, Mary pulled down the tin, pinched a little salt on a dry rag, and commenced rubbing the black from the inside of the long, narrow chimneys. "You started to say something?"

Eliza nodded. "Yes. I don't have any burned-out lantern mantels. How on earth do you save such things?"

"I keep them in a little chewing-tobacco can. Unfortunately, I'm about out."

Eliza chuckled grimly. "I understand. Why, plain old wicks are nearly as rare around these parts as enameled bathtubs, which I miss terribly!"

"I probably would too, if I'd ever used one." Mary smiled a little sadly. "I reckon, living on the frontier the way I always have, there's a powerful lot of things I've never seen or done. But I can make do when I have to. Have you tried making wicks out of strips of felt cut from Billy's old hats?"

"No! I've never even thought of such a thing!"

Mary giggled. "Imagine that. Well, strips of felt make wonderful lamp wicks, and I believe they burn brighter than braided rags in these grease lamps. They work even better if you cut them wide enough to fold over three times and then stitch closed, but that does take a little time."

"*Everything* takes a little time," Eliza declared. "Fact is, Mary, I believe a woman could work in her home twenty-four hours a day, seven days a week, and still never get everything done that just naturally needs doing. Stitching, cleaning, polishing, sweeping, washing, cooking, ironing, buttoning up, unbuttoning—I swan if there aren't days when it seems like all I do from morning to night is button up and then unbutton again, every article of Willy's clothes. This coming winter it'll be even worse, for he'll want to go out and play, and children simply don't play outside very long when it's cold. Last winter I was visiting with Adelia Mackelprang one day, and I swear she buttoned and unbuttoned the jersey leggings of her three little girls—all the way from the ankle to the waist or back again—a dozen separate times. And all the while she kept on chattering as though she didn't mind it at all." Eliza giggled. "I left there more thankful than ever that the Lord had sent me a little boy!"

Mary laughed too. "I think frontier life is simply harder for little girls. Mary Ann Perkins says she won't have her daughters looking like ragamuffins, so every day those girls put on a clean gingham pinafore and clean cambric drawers that were white only once, before the first wearing."

"Unless they're our 'Pride of Durango' brand," Eliza chuckled.

"Yes. And no matter the brand, if those little girls are like I was and spend much time astride the top rail of the corral—the natural and best seat for viewing whatever is going on anywhere in the vicinity—their drawers pick up a sort of greenish grime that absolutely never comes out! And if they happen to sit on a lump of pitch or ride bareback on a sweaty horse—well, you can just guess what that can do to a little girl's bloomers! Mary Ann says that every washday, when her back is throbbing from scrubbing all those little pinafores and bloomers, she thinks of her poor, dear mother, who used to plead for her daughters to hold their skirts up out of the dew when they walked out of an evening."

Eliza nodded. "They get dampened just enough to catch all the dust."

"That's right. And then if you add four or five of those many-ruffled petticoats such as the young girls like to wear—Well, Mary Ann says she sometimes weeps just remembering what she put her mother through."

"I suppose we all have to learn. I remember my own mother telling me she hoped I'd get a daughter just as thoughtless as I was."

"You, too?" Mary laughed and then turned instantly sad. "And now I just wish I could have any child, no matter how bothersome or thoughtless it might turn out to be! Mercy sakes, Eliza, do you think I'll ever have a baby?"

"I'm sure you will." Eliza smiled tenderly. "Maybe you need a blessing for that, as badly as Willy needed one for his health."

"I've thought of that. But . . . well, it just doesn't make sense to me that a woman can't conceive! What other purpose can a woman possibly have?"

"I wrestled with that for a long time, Mary, as you might guess, and when it comes right down to it, I don't know. The Lord created us to be nurturers for a reason, and no matter what else I did or tried to do, before little Willy came along I always felt incomplete."

Mary sighed deeply. "I've talked to Annie about it, and she reaches out in wonderful ways to Delia's children—"

"And Willy."

"Yes, to every child in the fort. I know she gets fulfillment out of that, but even she admits there's still an empty place in her soul—

a sense of failure that she can't do anything about. I know there's certainly a sense of failure in mine."

"Hádapa felt it too."

Mary nodded. "Yes, she did—or does. Isn't it interesting. No matter the culture, a woman's role remains essentially the same. We were created to become co-creators with God, and when for some reason that doesn't happen, each one of us struggles. I suppose it's good that we're all so busy."

"You're saying that when we live so close to the bare bones of reality, there isn't much room left for sentiment?"

"That's just what I'm saying."

"I think you're right. But maybe someday, Mary, the Lord will reveal a way to help women conceive."

"You mean through medicine? Wouldn't that be an amazing discovery!" For a moment Mary was silent, thinking. "But there have been other amazing discoveries!" she declared, suddenly brightening. "For instance, I have good, workable teeth in my mouth in spite of the fact that I lost every one of my own to disease when I was sixteen. My poor grandfather had the same disease, and he never had any teeth at all the last forty years of his life. Think how blessed I am not to go about gumming it! Something else! Back in Cedar I read about an actual, flushing toilet that somebody had invented. Have you ever seen one?"

"Yes, I had access to one, in Salt Lake City. They are truly wonderful inventions!"

Mary sighed. "That's something I'd love to see. Or real honest-to-goodness cleaning paper that wasn't torn straight out of a Montgomery Ward catalog."

"It may be softer, but it's nowhere near as entertaining or enlightening," Eliza giggled as she pulled herself to her feet. "There! What do you think of my new curtains?"

Mary nodded her approval. "They look simply beautiful. I especially like how you worked the lace trim. And I must say, Eliza, that you've been about as creative with a pair of old bloomers as anyone I've ever known! Two bits says that Billy will never even guess what his new curtains used to be."

Eliza laughed with Mary at that certainty, the Regulator clock struck 11:00 P.M., and just then they heard the creaking wagons carrying their exhausted husbands through the northeastern gate of the fort.

27

Wednesday, May 11, 1881

Indian Creek

"They were here, all right!" Curly Jenkins looked around the level, sandy floor of the high-walled canyon. "Way it looks to me, Spud, this has been a more or less permanent camp. It's sheltered and warm, feed's good, creek runs clear and cold—good camp for them and not a bad spot for a white man's ranch either, to my way of thinking. Anyhow, it looks like the warriors we've been following, the big bunch and the little bunch both, came here and joined up with a bunch of others."

"They ain't warriors we're following!" Spud ejaculated angrily. "They're renegades and thieves, Curly, and don't you forget it!"

"Whatever name you want to call 'em," John B. Brown interjected, "Curly's right about one thing—this was one big encampment. And like Curly also says, there's plenty of evidence a good lot of 'em have been here for some time."

"How many you think there were?" Mr. Peters asked.

"Way more'n a hundred, I'd say. And that's before our own renegades—both bands of 'em—joined up. Course, that figure includes old folks, women, and kids, but I'd say we've got a band here now that numbers a hundred seventy five, maybe two hundred people. At least half that number are going to be armed and able-bodied, and maybe more, happen the squaws pitch in."

"Hell's tinkling hot brass bells," Spud Hudson growled fiercely as he stared off up the draw where the trail of the departed Indians and their stolen horses obviously led. "Doesn't nothing ever come easy? It don't make no matter that all twenty-five of us are gritty as hard-boiled eggs rolled in sand, or that ever man-jack one of us is packin' enough hardware to cause kidney sores. Twenty-five agin a hundred or more just ain't favorable odds!"

"Particularly not when you figure where they're headed," Green Robinson added.

"Which is?"

"Most likely back to Colorado by way of the Wind Whistle Trail. That there draw yonder is Hart Draw Canyon, Spud, which winds eastward up into the high mesas north of your range on the Blue Mountains. At the end of it there's a narrow trail that leads to the top. It's called the Wind Whistle Trail on account of—"

"Yeah, I can guess! On account of the wind whistles through there, no doubt."

Obviously Spud was not happy, but Green Robinson did not back down from his sometimes cantankerous neighbor. "That's the truth. But Spud, the Wind Whistle Trail is also the best gol-durned place for an ambush this side of I don't know where. These Injuns may have a hundred armed men, but with hardly more'n half a dozen good shooters, they could pick every one of us off that hairline of a trail without even breaking a sweat."

Spud stared up Hart Draw Canyon as he digested the man's statement, while the men around him sat silently, still willing to give him the lead.

"Curly, how far ahead of us you reckon they are?"

"Still three, maybe four days."

"They've been known to hold an ambush that long, too," John B. Brown added helpfully.

"Well," Spud drawled as he spat into the churned-up sand of the campsite, "I may be anxious to get my hosses back as a Blackfoot buck lifting his first scalp, but I ain't altogether dumb to go along with it. No sir, boys, this ain't the time to go charging up that trail in hot pursuit. What it is, by jings, is the time to be slow-acting as wet gunpowder. We'll keep after 'em, all right, but we'll go slow and we'll go careful. That way, by the time we catch these thieves we'll likely be joined by a posse or two out of Colorado, and maybe even some soldiers from Fort Lewis. Then, by thunder, we'll all jump 'em like a roadrunner on a rattler!"

And with that, Joshua "Spud" Hudson dismounted, took off his horse's saddle and blanket, and set about establishing a very early camp.

The Jump

"I'll say this, Billy—it's a good thing this country's hotter than a blistered burn." Samuel Mackelprang pulled himself from the murky water of the San Juan and dragged himself up and into the crib in which Billy was stacking rock. There he did his best to wring the water from his clothing. "Can you imagine having to do this in the middle of a normal cold spring?"

"Makes you appreciate those boys who had to go swimming through the ice, chasing after Charlie Hall's raft that day back at the Hole," Billy grunted. "You know, when the wind tore it loose?"

Samuel looked up and smiled. "From now on they have my respect, all right. Hot day or not, this water's too cold to enjoy sloshing around in, especially when I'm trying to jockey cottonwood trees into place."

"Aw, those trees are hardly big enough to count," Billy teased.

"Maybe." Samuel was just grousing to hear himself talk, and Billy knew it. In reality the man was extremely even-tempered, and Billy had come to admire the way he handled his brood of young children. "But when I'm standing on that quicksand bottom trying to maneuver them around, they don't feel any too little. Do you think this crib will take two more loads of rock, or three?"

"Three, to do it right." Billy paused and wiped the sweat from his forehead. "Charlie Walton ought to be along with another load any time, though. And speaking of Charlie, did you hear that the U.S. Postal Department has taken away both our post office and his postmaster position?"

"Yeah, I heard." Samuel sounded disgusted. "And that's after he's been riding to Mancos and back once a month all winter long just to get the mail! Durn eastern bureaucrats! I hear they rejected the name of Bluff City, too. Seems there's another city of that name somewhere in the country—I think back by Winter Quarters some-where. So either we'll be plain old Bluff from now on, or we'll have to come up with an entirely new name."

"Well," Billy grinned, "at least Bluff's a short name and easy to write." He paused, and for a moment or two he stared at the murky water below them. "Passing strange, wasn't it, how Bill Ball hap-pened by on the two days we needed him the most?"

Samuel Mackelprang grinned. "It was. That man's as big a work-ing fool as his mule." Samuel had sunk onto a log to rest his legs, and now he stretched them out before him. "What with his help, I've never seen a project fly so fast. After this crib and those two more, we'll be all the way across. And that's in two days, Billy. Two days! Then once we've filled in these spaces between the cribs where the main channel runs, we'll have us a dam."

"I know—if it'll just hold." Again Billy lifted his hat and wiped his forehead with his sleeve. "I don't know if it's me or what, Sam, but I don't recollect ever feeling so hot."

"Maybe you'd better take a turn in the river."

"Maybe so." Billy looked eastward into the unrelenting glare of the sun on the water. "Makes a feller wonder if the snows have melted in whatever mountains feed our river, or if this heat's going to do it."

Samuel looked at his friend, sudden interest in his eyes. "Now that's an interesting thought. You think maybe the snows haven't melted yet?"

Slowly Billy shook his head. "I don't know. But this river scares me, Sam. Listening to some of Bill Ball's stories about flash floods has got me feeling spooked."

Samuel grinned. "You're not the only one. I think he was trying to do that a'purpose."

Billy nodded. "He might have been. Thing is, I've got a funny feeling about this dam, and I can't seem to shake it."

"Your feeling start with Bill Ball's stories?"

"Before—out in the Butler when we were cutting timber."

"Interesting. Question now is, are you just spooked, or is the Lord giving you a premonition? Do you happen to know which it is?"

"Not hardly." Billy shook his head. "Fact is, I don't even want to know—especially if I'm right and the dam for some reason is going to fail."

"Yeah, that's the trouble with premonitions, all right. Knowing the future—even a little bit of it—can be a terrible burden. For a fact, Billy, if the Lord revealed to me that this dam was going to break or not work, and if I could see that our crops were going to fail again, I'd load Adelia and our children back in our wagons and head out of here. Tomorrow!"

"I know how you feel. Thoughts of forcing Eliza and little Willy to face another winter without adequate food—"

Bluff Fort

"Drudders und sisters, ve haff great reason to rejoice. Ya, safe for yust a little bit, de dam across de river iss finished, und by tomorrow night de vater should be rising."

Jens Nielson paused and looked around the irregularly shaped room where he had convened the unusual Wednesday night meeting. Though the log meetinghouse wasn't overly large, it was sufficient to hold the diminished congregation of the rapidly dwindling community. Of course, there were one or two who simply found more important things to do than attend such meetings. But the vast majority of the Saints were faithful to their meetings as well as their beliefs, and they were absolutely convinced that because of their faithfulness the Lord's blessings were upon them.

"De Lord hass allowed Brudder Haskel to recover much off our stock und plunder from de Navajos," he continued, "und ve haff also been protected by de hand off de Lord from de Pahutes, a few off whom haff murder in der hearts besides larceny in der souls. But ven ve are prayerful und keep de commandments, brudders und sisters, den in all tings de Lord vill bless us und protect us. Ya, yust as he hass blessed us to be brought to dis goodly land."

Billy, seated on the split-log bench next to his beloved Eliza with the finally dozing Willy in his arms, found himself pondering Bishop Nielson's words. Was Bluff, or the San Juan country in general, a goodly land? In spite of the difficulties they had encountered in subduing it, was it?

Absolutely, Billy thought, though so far it hadn't been very productive as far as crops were concerned. In fact, late that afternoon as work on the dam had been winding down, Platte had stated emphatically that if their crops did fail for a second year, as the newly appointed stake president he would officially request of the Brethren in Salt Lake that the entire mission be released from their assignment and allowed to move on.

With all his heart Billy hoped that wouldn't happen. Crops or no, he was happier on the San Juan than he had ever been before. He felt more needed, more useful. Willy was already starting to learn some of the manly things Billy had never been given the chance to learn, and Eliza seemed finally at peace, both with herself and with her situation. So in spite of the poor showing the crops were making, the San Juan was indeed a goodly land for Billy and his family, and he was more than thankful to be there.

Kane Springs, Muleshoe Canyon

"Captain Dawson," Jimmy Heaton whispered in amazement, "look at what's happening to the moon."

It had been full dark with no moon showing when Captain William Dawson had quietly led his posse of Rico volunteers up Muleshoe Canyon to water at Kane Springs. Though individual Indians might have been anywhere, the glow of numerous fires on the flats below Black Ridge, which loomed above them to the south and east, betrayed the main encampment. Hence the posse had exercised great care, and so far as Captain Dawson could tell, the Utes were completely unaware of their presence.

Now the moon was high and the fires up above were burning low, and as all but two of the posse crouched in the oak brush below the Indian camp awaiting further orders, the captain was feeling more than good. Not only had he and his men crept up unawares on a huge body of Pahutes, but he had also called it right the previous Monday when they had left the wide trail of the horses and set off toward Lisbon Valley. Now they had headed the Indians for sure, and they would successfully end this big raid with first light.

Only, he wondered, where were the other posses? Where were

Bill May and his boys from Mancos, and where in the world was Spud Hudson and his Blue Mountain posse? Despite his careful observations, Captain Dawson had seen no sign of them anywhere—no glow of fires, no snort or whinny of horses—nothing! He and the boys from Rico were alone, and to his way of thinking, that was a mighty big band of Indians camped above him. Too big, unless he could figure some sort of edge—

"You see it, Captain?"

Looking upward, Captain Dawson sucked in his breath. "Well, I'll be," he breathed. "That's an eclipse coming on, Jimmy; an eclipse of the moon."

"Does that mean it's going to go full dark?" Hard Tartar whispered

"It does if the eclipse is full." His mind racing, Captain Dawson tried to think through his suddenly forming plan. It could work, he knew that. And so far as he could figure, even if it didn't work perfectly it couldn't hurt them, even a little.

"John Galloway," he whispered loudly, using the man's formal name instead of Jack, which is what everybody else called him, "where're you at?"

"Right here," the man whispered from not more than a dozen feet away. "What do you want, Captain?"

"Do you still *habla* the Ute lingo?"

"I reckon I can get by." Even whispering, John Galloway's voice remained deep, like coarse gravel.

"Good. Here's what I want you to do. Give a holler or two in their direction, loud enough to get their attention. Then tell 'em the Great Spirit—"

"They call him *Shin-op*."

"Okay, good. Tell 'em *Shin-op* is angry with the Utes, that he's eating up the moon on account of they've killed some white folks and stolen a bunch of their horses. Tell 'em *Shin-op* will swallow the moon for a few minutes to show his anger, and then he'll cough it back up again so the Utes can see to surrender themselves and their horses to the white men who have them surrounded. Can you tell 'em all that?"

"I can tell 'em," John Galloway replied easily. "But what

happens if they cut and run instead of surrendering? Or worse, what happens if they just open fire on us?"

"Then we'll fire right back," Captain Dawson replied easily. "If they run, at first light we'll attack whoever's left, and then we'll go after the rest of 'em. But don't worry so much, John. Between that eclipse yonder and your calling out of the dark in their own tongue, they'll be one startled bunch of redskins. Fact is, superstitious as they are, I'll bet good money they won't neither run nor fight. Instead they'll palaver back and forth with each other the rest of the night, and come morning they'll surrender.

"Now get to hollering, will you, afore that wondrous eclipse is done and over."

The Flats above Kane Springs

Though Posey's heart was pounding with fear, he would never have admitted it, even to himself. Still, he could not keep his eyes from the star-filled heavens, where of a truth *Shin-op* was eating up *mat-oits,* the moon. It was an awesome thing to see, a great and wondrous thing, and there was hardly any sound among the People as they stared upward. Truly he had never thought *Shin-op* might have such a mouth, or that he might have such power. But now with his own *poo-ye,* his eyes, he was seeing the moon being eaten up, and how could he possibly deny it?

Neither could he deny the voice of the white man that had come out of the darkness where no white man had been only a little earlier, waking both him and his brother, telling them of *Shin-op's* anger and urging them to surrender.

Posey didn't know if his people should surrender or not, but in his heart he did not have a good feeling about things. In fact, in his opinion the entire previous two weeks—the time since the big raid on the white man's ranch in Colorado had commenced—had been riddled with failure. That worried him. But what worried him more was his certainty that more failures were coming—failures that he could do nothing about.

Oo-ah, yes, the warriors of the People had taken many fine horses, first from the three whites they had put under the grass and then from the whites who were now coming after them into what all had hoped would be a fine trap. And yes, they had put a fourth white under the grass at that place of water. But to Posey's way of thinking, those were the only good things to come of this big raid. All else that had happened was *katz-at,* it was bad.

"*Ungh!*" Posey grunted softly in disgust as his mind went again to the raid of the mormonee upon the Pahute camp at Boiling Springs. No mormonee should have left that place alive! No, not even after that fool, whoever he had been, had shouted from the cliffs that the mormonee were friends of the People and not to harm them. No, he should have been ignored and his words allowed to mean nothing! With so many warriors armed and ready and only a few yards from the few despised and poorly armed mormonee, all of them should have been put under the grass.

Why, Posey himself had been ready to kill the nearest of them. He would have, too, but for the fact that his old rifle had misfired! Then one by one all the others of the warriors had slowly lowered their weapons. Posey had also lowered his, and that had been a second strange thing, for in his mind there had been no intent to do so. No, he had actually begun to pull the trigger a third time, and when for some reason the trigger had stuck he had looked down to discover that his rifle had not been pointed at the small mormonee at all but had been pointed instead at *tee-weep,* the earth.

Posey still wondered at that, for it had been a strange thing indeed. And though he would not speak of it with Scotty, he was still remembering the strange words of the one called Haskel, words that had been echoed by the old fool Peeagament and the young man who was calling himself Henry. Could it be that Haskel's words were true, he wondered? Could it be that *Shin-op* had stopped him from killing that mormonee?

Of course, he thought disgustedly, who could possibly know such a thing—

Posey thought that the next bad thing had come at the large encampment in Indian Creek, for when they had all joined together, the warriors had also taken upon themselves more squaws and papooses, many more. And they also had a large herd of goats, which could not be made to travel fast.

Of course, the comely *nan-zitch* called Too-rah, Poke the Grizzly's sister, had been there with her mother and father, an ugly older sister, and two more of her crazy brothers. And though just seeing her had warmed Posey's heart, he had not dared speak with her by day or even sneak near her *wickiup* in the moonlight. With Poke watching her like *quan-a-tich* the eagle, he would have been *katz-te-suah* to even consider such a thing. And Posey was no fool!

The trouble was, Posey was now convinced that others of his people were fools indeed. Having become a huge body of men, women, children, and animals, the Pahutes had traveled slowly up Hart Draw Canyon via the treacherous Wind Whistle Trail. Certain that they were being followed by at least one posse, Mike, Wash, Mancos Jim, and some of the other warriors had proposed setting an ambush where the Wind Whistle Trail came onto the Hatch Point country. The trouble was, after three days of waiting, no white men had appeared, and so the band had continued slowly *qui-am-er tavi-maus-er,* northeastward, off of Hatch Point and down into Muleshoe Canyon, encamping that very afternoon on the flats above Kane Springs.

Now, to Posey's way of thinking, circumstances had turned from bad to awful. As he watched the amazing hunger of *Shin-op* finishing the moon, he could already hear the voice of old Peeagament urging the warriors to do as the white man had ordered—surrender.

Groping in the darkness he found his old rifle, and he was just rising to his feet when Scotty spoke.

"Brother, what is it that you think to do?"

"I go to the council fire yonder, where perhaps I will shoot old Peeagament."

Scotty's intake of breath was loud and clear. "*Wagh,* my brother, that is a very big thing—"

Posey snorted. "It was a joke, that is all. But in spite of *Shin-op's* hunger I do not wish to see us surrender to the whites, to the meri-cats. The old fool Peeagament needs to keep his silence about this thing, for he has nothing to say about it. He was never a part of our big raid."

"That is so," Scotty admitted.

"Listen, brother, that is the voice of Wash coming from over yonder. And that is the voice of Captain Jack. Do you hear? They are both telling Peeagament to be silent. Come, let us join our voices with theirs. Those horses belong to us now, and it is time we make a fleeing with them into these mountains!"

"But . . . what of *Shin-op?* What of his hunger?"

"He is not eating us, is he?" Posey laughed scornfully. "Now come, brother, for there will be much to do before *Shin-op* coughs back the moon—"

———o—o—o———

In the moonlight Jimmy Heaton found himself wide awake, staring upward to where most of the Ute fires had burned low. The eclipse had been a remarkable thing to see, and Jimmy could only imagine how the superstitious people on the flat above him might have felt. But now it was over, most of the men of the posse had fallen asleep, and Jimmy was wishing that he could also get some rest.

The trouble was, somebody had mentioned that they were only a few miles southeast of Moab, and from that moment on, all Jimmy had been able to think about was his friends Isadore and Alfred Wilson.

Would they be at home, he wondered, sleeping in the loft Isadore had described for him? Or would they be out on their range, wherever that was, riding herd on their father's cows? Jimmy didn't know, of course, but of a sudden he was filled with a terrible longing to ride into Moab and find out.

Maybe that was exactly what he should do—saddle the horse Bill Ball had given him, say nothing to anybody, and just ride out. He could most likely be in town by daylight or a little after, and then he and Ise would have a fine time discussing all the amazing things he had been reading in the Book of Mormon.

Yes sir, Jimmy thought with a wry grin, that was exactly what he should do. But he wouldn't—not now, not ever. He just wasn't the sort of man to run out on his neighbors, especially when there might be desperate need of his help come daylight. His pa had taught him that, and he would stand by it and expect others to do the same.

Still, he thought as his eyes slowly closed, in spite of what he had told Isadore about coming to visit, he had never expected to get this close to Moab. Maybe when this whole unpleasant affair was over, the captain would release him, and he and Ise could spend a day or so together. Yes sir, and maybe they could even take a ride down into Bluff to see Billy and Eliza Foreman, and to find out how the Lord had healed little Willy—

28

Thursday, May 12, 1881

Bluff Fort

"Eliza, did you see what that horse just did?"

Turning in surprise at the tone of Annie Lyman's voice, Eliza nodded. "I did. Wasn't it the cutest thing the way that animal kissed little Willy's cheek? He does seem to have his father's way with animals—"

"Get him over here to the well, quick! We must wash those fluids off immediately!"

"Why, whatever for?" Eliza responded with a laugh. She had already picked her son up and was dabbing at his face with her dainty kerchief.

"Because he could die from it!"

"What? Annie, be serious."

"I'm more serious than you could ever know!" Annie was so intense that Eliza followed her to the well, where Annie drew a bucket of fresh water and began vigorously scrubbing the protesting Willy's face. "There," she breathed when she was finished and Willy was wailing his resentment, "I just hope we got it in time."

"Annie, I have no idea what you are talking about."

"I'm talking about a most horrible disease called glanders."

"Glanders? I've never heard of such a thing."

"Then my dear Eliza, you're not well enough read. Come to my home this minute, and I'll read for you what I learned from *Ballou's Dollar Monthly Magazine,* which, as you no doubt know, is published in the great city of Boston and is well respected both in the United States and abroad."

"You have that magazine here?" Eliza asked in surprise as she followed Annie to her cabin. After all, there was little reading matter in the entire fort, and almost none of it was anywhere near current.

"I have several old issues that were lent to me by Mother Lyman. I read them at night when I'm lonely and unable to sleep." Entering her home, Annie took a small stack of magazines from a shelf, leafed through them, and stopped.

"Very well, Eliza, listen to this article, published under the title 'Remarkable death.' The editor writes, 'The awful death of Madame Palesikoff, one of the most charming amongst all that bevy of charming Russian ladies who sometimes gladdened the winters of Paris, has created a terrible shock in the circles she embellished. The unhappy lady left Paris but a short time ago on a summer tour to Germany. While stepping from the door of the opera-house, at Berlin to gain her carriage, she let fall one of her bracelets close to the pavement. Stooping to pick it up, she noticed at the time laughingly, that one of the horses belonging to a carriage standing at hand had dropped his head so close to her face that he had touched her, and left a moist kiss upon her cheek.' You see, Eliza? It was just as that horse yonder did to little Willy! A moist kiss! Allow me to continue: 'In a few days the unfortunate lady was taken ill with that most horrible disease, glanders, and in a few days more breathed her last, in spite of her attendance by the best physicians in Berlin, and every resource to be obtained by wealth, or by ceaseless vigilance of friends.'"

"But . . . what is glanders? Do you know, Annie?"

"I know only that it's a terrible disease spread to humans by contaminated horses and mules. It causes the glands to swell horribly, originates a burning fever, and by inflammation destroys the mucous membranes in the nose and throat. I don't know if that animal outside was contaminated. But given Willy's history of poor health, and given that we're a hundred miles from the nearest settlement and two or three times that from the nearest competent physician, I can see no reason to take chances."

Eliza smiled. "Of course you're right, Annie, and both Willy and I thank you for your concern."

Annie was immediately embarrassed. "I . . . uh . . . well, I'm sorry I was so abrupt with you. But your dear child is precious to me. Besides which, both you and Billy have given me of your time, and I . . . well, I swan if I know what I'm trying to say."

"Annie, you're such a dear!" Reaching out, Eliza embraced her friend. "It's remarkable the way you reach out to others, trying in every way to make yourself useful to them. I mean it when I say that you're a wonderful woman."

Together the two women stepped outside, little Willy running ahead.

"Between tending babies, Annie, reseeding our fields and trying to redig that frightful ditch, you and I haven't had much opportunity for conversation. Are you . . . doing any better? I mean, since you spoke with Billy?"

"To tell the truth, Eliza, I don't think so." Annie smiled, trying to mask other emotions. "I . . . I'm still more lonely than I can say. I feel utterly without value or purpose in my life. I'm terrified of what our future in this place may hold, and I feel helpless to do anything about it. Does that sound as though I'm doing better?"

"Not much, it doesn't." Eliza gazed into her friend's moist eyes. "You still feel nothing from prayer?"

Silently the woman shook her head.

"And you're doing all the things Billy suggested?"

"Without fail. I study the scriptures, I pray, I ponder—and nothing! I'm simply not able to feel the Holy Ghost! I'm even fasting in behalf of our crops today, Eliza, just as the bishop asked, though I'm as certain as I can be that our miserable ditch is destined for another failure. I suppose that isn't exercising faith, but I can't help feeling as I do."

Eliza smiled sadly. "That's two of us, then, for I can't feel any confidence in it either. To be candid, Mary feels the same, though she applies her feelings much more broadly than just the ditch. Yet when I pray, about the ditch or anything else concerning this mission, I feel a peaceful assurance that all will be well."

"But . . . how can that be? If the ditch fails, or if the river floods us again—"

"I can't answer your questions, Annie, for I don't know any answers. I know only that the Lord has finally filled my heart with peace, and it's a wonderful feeling." Eliza wiped away sudden tears. "Like you, I had prayed for months without getting any response from the Lord, at least that I could discern. And then when the response came, it didn't start out as a spiritual thing at all."

"Really?"

Eliza nodded. "I think it started when the Lord sent those four boys to visit with Billy and me. I felt such a closeness to them, and especially to the two younger ones, Jimmy and Isadore. There was such hope and joy in them, their discussions about the gospel were so enlightening, and they were so willing to comfort Willy and poke delightful fun at my sad tales of woe—that I quickly realized the Lord had sent them to rekindle my hope.

"Then he sent Hádapa to Willy and me. She's a remarkable woman, and although that we were never able to speak with each other, I love her as my own sister."

"Has she been back since she left the goats?"

"Not once." Eliza's voice was filled with sadness. "I . . . I don't know what happened, but I pray God to bless her every day. The strangest thing, Annie, is that I no longer even think of her as Navajo. I look at her, and I see Hádapa—and that's all! Surely that's how the Lord must want us all to feel about each other.

"Anyway, Annie, that feeling of love has expanded in my heart until I feel peaceful practically all the time. I haven't received a revelation or anything like that. But when I pray I find myself weeping with love and gratitude, and I know that the Holy Spirit is bearing witness of God's love and concern."

"And yet," Annie asked in wonder, "you still feel as though the ditch may fail and our crops perish?"

"Ludicrous, isn't it." Eliza chuckled. "Of course, I may be wrong. This time the fool thing may carry water like a charm, and the community will end up with a harvest more than sufficient for our needs and to repay the debt in Colorado. I suppose we'll know by tomorrow sometime, won't we."

Soberly Annie nodded. "Yes, I suppose we will. I just wish I could feel as much peace about the outcome as you do!"

"It'll come, I promise. See you at meeting?"

Annie smiled bravely. "I'll be there, Eliza. Hold a seat for me if you get there first, and I'll do the same for you and your family."

"Thank you. And sometime, if it isn't a bother, I'd love to borrow those magazines."

"My word, Eliza, those old things were published in 1858—twenty-three years ago!"

"In this howling wilderness," Eliza laughed as she scooped up Willy, "such material can still be newsworthy! Or life-saving. See you tonight "

———◇─◇─◇———

For some reason Annie was suddenly having difficulty breathing. Yet the room wasn't excessively warm, and the testimony meeting wasn't so crowded that she felt squeezed between Eliza and Frederick Jones, a newer member of the community who was seated on her other side.

At the moment Mary Mackelprang Jones, Frederick's wife, was bearing testimony of the truthfulness of the gospel, restored in the latter days through the Prophet Joseph Smith. Already Mary had described her birth and early days in Cedar City, her call to the San Juan shortly after her marriage to Frederick, and their journey a few months before through the treacherous Hole-in-the-Rock and on to Bluff.

Annie shuddered at the enforced memory of some of those former scenes and suddenly found herself becoming emotional. Surely Brother Lyman and the rest of them had been blessed and protected during their solitary journey of the winter before. There were simply too many things that might have gone wrong—too many dangerous situations that might so easily have destroyed them. That none had, and that they had traveled alone across that awful wilderness without incident, was a testimony to Annie that she could not deny. So she had given prayerful thanks for those blessings dozens of times. Perhaps hundreds! Yet never, so far as she knew, had she felt the Lord's acknowledgement for those expressions of gratitude. Never could she remember having felt the Holy Spirit as Billy had described.

Now though, as she fought to control her tears and regain her breath, Annie realized abruptly that she was feeling the effects of the Holy Ghost upon her body! These feelings were the Holy Spirit's way of communicating with her, informing her that the Lord loved her and that he wanted her to testify of that love!

Her mouth feeling dry with the fear of what she knew she was about to do, Annie nervously smoothed her dress. How could she say such powerful things? she worried. How could she possibly put into words such sacred feelings and experiences as were suddenly coursing through her mind? How could she tell those present that the Lord's arm had not been shortened, and that he could just as easily protect them here on the San Juan as he could on that frightening road—

Suddenly the new Mary Jones was concluding and sitting down, and lest her fear cause her to waver or shrink, Annie Lyman arose and began—for the first time in her life—to bear her testimony according to the recognizable and undeniable impressions of the Holy Ghost.

29

Friday, May 13, 1881

Bluff Fort

"Morning, Harriet. Morning, girls. Has there been any word on how the ditch is working?"

Harriet Barton smiled at Anna Decker while her two daughters played around her skirts. "Not that I've heard. But oh, how I hope that the dam will work and the ditch hold water! Then maybe our lives can become a little more normal."

"Don't plan on too much normalcy today," Elizabeth Stevens stated as she joined the others. "In case you've both forgotten, it's Friday the thirteenth. Sure as you're born, sisters, something is bound to go wrong before the day's out."

"Why Elizabeth, I had no idea you were superstitious."

The young woman smiled. "I'm not. But I'm wise enough to know there are usually reasons why folks pass along such beliefs. Did you hear that my brother-in-law David brought the mail in from the Mancos last night?"

"I didn't," Harriet Ann responded. "Was there anything for Joe or me, I wonder?"

"I couldn't say." Elizabeth was excited. "Sounds as though we're going to have some more recruits coming from the settlements, though; maybe a whole slew of them! David told us that Brother Lyman got the word, and Adelia told me only moments ago that two who have already been called are Samuel and Josephine Wood."

"Why, that's wonderful!" Now Harriet Ann was excited. "They're a fine family, and folks hereabouts are going to love Jody."

"Jody?" Anna Decker asked. "You mean we're going to have another Jody in the fort?"

Harriet Ann smiled. "Yes, just as we have three women named Eliza and two named Harriet and so forth. The difference this time, Anna, is that Josephine or Jody Wood is a woman while Jody Lyman isn't. How soon are they coming, Elizabeth?"

"Sometime this winter or next spring, I suppose. There's also word that Elder Orson Pratt is doing poorly and isn't expected to live much longer."

Separating her two daughters, who were now pinching each other, Harriet Ann was saddened. "Joe will be sorry to hear that. Elder Pratt has been one of his favorite thinkers for years. It'll be a blow to Billy Foreman, too, as he and Elder Pratt were close personal friends. Is the mail here in the meetinghouse?"

"It is," Elizabeth replied. "I hope you received something. And remember, Friday the thirteenth. Be careful, Harriet. Girls."

It was such a lovely country, Harriet Ann Barton thought as she gathered her two daughters and turned toward the meetinghouse. In spite of the fact that it was mid-May, the cottonwoods along the river were still bright green, contrasting wonderfully with the dark cliffs and startlingly blue sky. Yes, the days and even the nights were intolerably hot, but the air always smelled so fresh and clean, and—well, in spite of the problems that seemed always on the verge of destroying them and their mission, Harriet was more than thankful that she and Joseph had come to the San Juan. Now, if only that fool ditch would hold water for a change—

"Darn that Elizabeth Stevens anyway," she muttered as she led her girls into the dark interior of the meetinghouse, "reminding me of the date. Now she's started me in to worrying."

"Morning, Sister Harriet." Walter Lyman was his usual, happy self.

"Morning, Walter. Are you handing out the mail today?"

"Yes'm, but there's nothing for you or Joseph—or Amasa, either, for that matter. I'm right sorry."

"So am I, but maybe next time. Any word on how the new ditch is working?"

"Not much. Billy Foreman told me this morning that the river was dammed last night about dark, and they expected the water to be high enough to make the jump through the headgate and into the ditch along about daylight. If he's right, and if the ditch holds, we'll have water on our crops sometime this afternoon."

"Won't that be wonderful!"

Walter smiled. "Yes, ma'am. Of course, today is Friday the thirteenth—"

"Walter, I'll thank you not to repeat that awful superstition again today—to me or to anyone else. You do, and you'll soon have folks worrying themselves silly over everything imaginable—the ditch outlaws, Indian raiding parties, and goodness only knows what else, and there won't be a particle of truth to any of it! So please don't mention it again. You hear me?"

Walter bobbed his head, his eyes fixed to the window behind Harriet Ann. "Yes, ma'am, Sister Lyman, I hear you. Not a particle of truth." Now his expression turned deadly serious. "Thing is, ma'am, superstition or not, truth or not, here comes what might be a Navajo raiding party through the gate right now."

Spinning in surprise, Harriet Ann stepped to the door. "That's not much of a raiding party," she scoffed after a careful look. "It's only one old man on a burro and one young woman leading—Why, that's Hádapa! That's Eliza's Navajo friend! And . . . and . . . Oh, my goodness! The old fellow on the burro doesn't look well at all—

"Walter, go get Eliza Foreman! Quick! And if Mary Jones is home, get her, too!"

Darting out the door, the youthful Walter Lyman sprinted for Eliza's cabin. And as Harriet Ann Barton held her girls' hands and started through the rutted dirt toward Hádapa and her heavily loaded burro, all she could think of was Friday the thirteenth! Friday the thirteenth!

Upper Mill Creek, LaSal Mountains

"Keep after 'em, boys!" Captain William Dawson was excited. "We've got 'em running again!"

Grinning widely, young Jimmy Heaton spurred his horse, urging it through the thick brush that lined the steep hillside south of Mill Creek. It was already the second day of the battle, and he couldn't remember the last time he had had so much fun. With daylight the day before, they had launched their attack on the rapidly fleeing Indians, and all day long they had chased them over Black Ridge and down into Spanish Valley, shooting up a storm while they went. By nightfall both they and the Indians were in camp along Pack Creek maybe two miles apart, and the murderous, thieving Pahutes knew they were in a fight.

"You okay, Jimmy?"

"Never better." Jimmy grinned at Hard Tartar, who was riding just above him in the brush. "Think any of these redskins are going to try and cross this creek?"

"Not here." Hard glanced toward the bottom of the canyon, maybe fifty yards below them. "Cliffs down to the creek are too steep and the jump too wide. Happen you take a look, you'll see a forty-, maybe fifty-foot drop-off to the creek bed. There's no way they can cross it, not with horses. Same with this mesa we're on. John Galloway says the cap rock above us is too high for horses to get over it. So I say, kid, that we've got 'em boxed good."

"What if they keep going?"

"Country up ahead looks mighty steep, worse even than here, and you can see up yonder where the snow hasn't even started to melt yet. All they've got left since we took back May's and Thurman's horses are some mighty sorry-looking ponies, and I guarantee they'll never make it through those ten-foot drifts. So I don't think they'll keep going, at least not in this brush. But keep a sharp lookout, Jimmy. Any time now we'll be running into 'em again, and if they're as boxed as I think they are, they'll be madder'n a nest of baby rattlers on a hot skillet."

Jimmy grinned. "I'll be looking. Wasn't that shooting star last night something?"

"It was, at that—brightest one I ever saw. Captain Dawson took good advantage of it, too, having ol' Jack Galloway shout out some more nonsense about the Great Spirit burning up a star with his anger."

"You reckon they believed him?"

"Some, probably, but not enough to talk 'em all into surrendering. Still, it was mighty sweet how we got that whole herd of horses back this morning. There they were, grazing along that little creek, without even a single Pahute guard 'cept them squaws."

"Horse Creek, the captain's calling it." Jimmy was watching but so far could see nothing that seemed dangerous. "Seemed like we surprised 'em again, second morning in a row, though I can't hardly imagine how that could be."

"Strange doings, all right. Now we have our horses, a whole slew of their ponies, and a bunch of captured squaws. Not too bad for a morning's work."

Jimmy had to agree. So far they had experienced remarkable success, and even Captain Dawson was pleased. About the only thing that Jimmy wasn't pleased with was the shooting of an unarmed squaw first thing that morning. Thank goodness, he thought, it hadn't been him who had killed her! In fact, so far as he knew, he hadn't killed anybody—which in a way was too bad, because some of them certainly deserved it! Besides which, a man couldn't help wondering what it would feel like, gunning down a murderous Ute brave—

The explosion of rifles up ahead brought an end to Jimmy's reverie, and seconds later he saw a half-dozen ragtag Pahute ponies pounding through the brush ahead of them.

"Heyaah!" he screeched joyfully as he pulled his pistol and fired at their fleeing backs. "We're in the middle of 'em now, Hard! Let's go get 'em—"

Bluff Fort

"Oh, Hádapa, you've come back!" With Willy in one arm and her crutch under the other, Eliza was fairly flying toward where the Navajo woman was vainly trying to explain herself to Harriet Ann and her daughters.

The woman spun around at the sound of Eliza's voice, and a bright smile spread across her troubled countenance. "Ásdzáán nééz!" she cried as she dropped the rope to her burro and hurried toward Eliza.

In an instant the two were joyfully embracing, and when Willy scrambled into the arms of Hádapa a moment later, his hard hug brought not only the lovingly murmured *Haskéts óósi,* or Slender Warrior, but tears of joy as well.

"Are you all right?" Eliza demanded as they turned back to the patient burro and its slumped-over load. "Is something wro—Oh, is this your father? Mercy sakes, Hádapa, what's wrong with him?"

Carefully the small woman tried to explain the purpose of their visit, mixing her limited English with Navajo and coming up with less than satisfactory results.

"I don't know, Harriet Ann." Eliza was shaking her head. "I just can't tell what she's trying to say."

Harriet Ann shook her head. "Neither can I. It sounds . . . sort of like she's saying that this old man's her husband. But that can't be. Maybe she means—Well, I just don't know what she's trying to tell us, Eliza, beyond that this poor old fellow seems very ill. Look how Hádapa has tied him in place and propped him with blankets. He must be extremely weak. Too bad Maggie's over in Montezuma Fort caring for that poor little Davis girl. She'd know what to do, and her husband has taught her some Navajo, too."

"He's also taught Mary a little." Eliza looked back at the Jones cabin. "Walter said she wasn't home, but unless she's at the Jump with Kumen, I have no idea—"

"Where . . . Haskel?" the old Navajo on the burro asked weakly, interrupting Eliza. "M-Me see Haskel."

Stunned, Eliza and Harriet Ann stared at the old man. "Hádapa," Eliza finally responded, "why didn't you tell us your father spoke English? I would have—"

"Me see Haskel," the man repeated, quickly growing impatient.

"We haven't seen Haskel," Harriet Ann responded instantly, "not for two or three days. Most likely he's gone to Montezuma Fort."

For a moment the only sound was some chickens cackling down in the community pen, and neither Harriet nor Eliza knew what to do. Hádapa was now standing stoically, her eyes downcast, and the old man on the burro seemed content, at least for the moment, to simply suck in more air.

"Sister Eliza," Walter Lyman suddenly said as he hurried past them and into the meetinghouse, "there's a letter here for Billy. Came in last night with David Stevens." Stepping back outside, the young man handed the envelope to Eliza.

"Thank you, Walter." For an instant Eliza glanced at the envelope, wondering. "This is the letter from Brigham Young, Jr., that Billy's been waiting for—"

"Letter?" The old Navajo on the burro suddenly tried to look up. "Me see letter."

"This?" Eliza asked with surprise as she held up the envelope. "But . . . it's a message for my husband."

"Letter come mail, long . . . far off?" It was now obvious that the old fellow was trying to understand the concept of letters, not to obtain the one Eliza held.

"That's right. When we can't go somewhere we send letters through the mail. That way we talk to each other long far off."

Slowly the old man nodded his head, showing that he understood. "Me s-see Haskel," he then repeated, looking away. "Haskel write . . . letter, send *Shin-op. Hacoon!* Come on!"

"Hádapa," Eliza pleaded, "don't let him go! It's a long ride to Montezuma Fort, and your father seems very tired, very sick—"

"*Kanaagháii*," Hádapa said quietly. "Long . . . time sick."

"Yes," Eliza exclaimed, delighted that Hádapa had finally been able to communicate something to her. "Your father has been sick a long time. No more riding, at least today. Tonight he can rest in my home—"

"He not f-father to . . . to Hádapa," the Navajo woman responded haltingly as she started the old burro toward the eastern gate, ignoring Eliza's fervent invitation. "He . . . husband. His name Natanii nééz . . . but called Frank. Haskel . . . words of power, kill Natanii nééz—"

Thunderstruck, the two silent women were still staring after the departing Navajo couple when the pounding of hoofbeats interrupted their reverie.

"Water's broken out of the ditch a couple of miles up!" Hanson Bayless shouted anxiously as he slid his mount to a halt near the two women. "Get your shovels, everybody—women and big kids, too—

and come a-running! This ain't no little bitty break, folks! We need all the help we can get, and even that might not be enough!"

And in the pandemonium that followed, Eliza hobbled to the log bench in front of the meetinghouse and lowered herself onto it, her heart pounding fearfully in her chest. That was Navajo Frank on that burro! That was the evil tall one, the man Kumen had encountered, the worst of all the raiders on the reservation! Oh, glory be! And Eliza's dear friend, who had spent so much time in her home and with her loved ones, was the notorious raider's wife!

30

○─○─○

Saturday, May 14, 1881

Head of Mason Draw, LaSal Mountains

His eyes wide with amazement, Posey stared off down the apparently empty slope. Twice bullets from the white man's guns had come so close to him that he had actually felt them fly past. Or at least he had felt the wind their passing had caused. He also had fired twice—at brief and fleeting targets. But he knew he had missed, and he could not understand why that was so. And now he could see no sign of these *mericats,* no sign of movement whatsoever.

In his mind now, Posey was trying to recall the events that had transpired since *Shin-op* had eaten *mat-oits* the moon and then coughed it back up, just as the white man's voice had promised. It had been a frightening thing for all the People, and many, including Henry and old Peeagament, had argued in favor of the voice, urging surrender. But not himself, Posey thought with pride. He, Mike, Wash, Poke and his brothers, Captain Jack, and certain others had advocated fighting, just as they had planned since the day the horses had first been taken. Their voices had prevailed, and with the dawn they had been driving their animals up the impossibly steep mesas that comprised the southwestern slope of the LaSal Mountains, fighting a running battle through the day, and finally going into camp on a flat above Pack Creek.

There *Shin-op* had again done a bad thing to the People, burning up a *poo-chits* or star in the northern sky. Shortly thereafter the same white man's voice had called to the frightened Pahutes, reminding

363

them of these wonders in the night sky and once again saying that *Shin-op* demanded their complete surrender.

Long had the council fires burned as warriors debated the issue. In the darkness some of the squaws had been weeping in fear, the massive herd of animals had been restless and difficult to hold, and more of the warriors had grown weak and were supporting Henry and the old fool Peeagament. Yet to Posey's relief, their ideas were rebuffed, and the decision was made to continue into the mountains, seeking another good place for an ambush.

Early the next morning the mericats had again attacked, shooting an old squaw who had stopped at a spring of water to rest and capturing many other squaws as well as most of the now nearly sixteen hundred head of stolen horses. At least, Posey had thought with relief, Too-rah had not been among the captured.

But that had been the young warrior's only relief. His heart filled with bitter disappointment, Posey and the others had fled across what would become known as Horse Creek and up the south side of the cliff-walled gorge of Mill Creek under Haystack Mountain and the north slope of Boren Mesa, firing at the despised whites as they could and hoping some of their bullets would hit home.

Finally able to cross Mill Creek where Shafer Creek emptied into it, the rattled Pahutes had stopped in the oak brush to rest their few remaining ponies, which were utterly exhausted. Suddenly the hills to the west had erupted in gunfire, Posey and several others had nearly been killed, and in a panic the whole ragtag horde had either run or beaten their exhausted ponies northward, up the steep Shafer Creek gorge. And there, Posey thought, something good had finally happened.

Just as he had been about to throw himself onto the back of his spavined pony to make a last, desperate fleeing, a small, soft hand had taken hold of his. Turning in surprise, Posey had been amazed to see the large, luminous eyes of Too-rah looking up into his own.

"I am afraid," she had said simply. "Will you help me up the mountain?"

Up until that moment exhausted himself, Posey had been instantly rejuvenated. In fact, he had not even climbed onto his sorry mount, but with almost no effort at all he had led both of them—the stumbling horse and the comely maiden whose hand seemed perfectly designed to fit into his own—up the steep and rocky gorge.

They had taken advantage, during their fleeing, of the thick stands of aspen, maple, and other trees that had hidden the way of their passing and so had not been fired upon again. With Bald Mesa to their left and Mount Waas and Horse Mountain to their right, they had crossed the narrow saddle above the head of Shafer Creek, and there they had stopped. While most had continued north down Mason Draw, with the panoramic view of Castle Valley and the desert spread out far below, Posey and Too-rah had spent long moments holding each other's hands and saying little. There was still snow where they had stopped, and though the trees at this elevation had not yet leafed out, they were thick, and the two had little fear of being seen.

For Posey it had been a precious time—a portent of things he was certain would be in his future. Never had he felt anything like he was feeling; never had he imagined how wonderful it might be to actually touch the hand of a maiden such as Too-rah. Why, with her nearby, counting on his strength and wisdom, there was nothing he could not do! *Wagh!* Show him the mericats! Without assistance he could put all of them under the grass! Without the aid of anyone else he—

Abruptly Too-rah had pulled away, taking her hand from his, lingering with her eyes gazing into his for just an instant, no longer, and then slipping with whispering feet through the snow and down the north slope of Mason Draw. But before she had disappeared into the trees and brush, she had looked back up at him and smiled.

With his heart large in his chest, Posey had turned back toward the saddle he and Too-rah had just crossed, hiding himself and intending to sell his life to the suddenly relentless whites as dearly as possible. In that way he could protect her. *Oo-ah,* yes! And when it was known to her what a great warrior he had been—

Downslope Posey could once again see the whites moving through the trees, making their way almost heedlessly up the mountain. They were shouting back and forth, their voices filled with joy, and it was that joyful noise that finally drove thoughts of Too-rah from Posey's heart, from his mind. In fact, he was beginning to wonder as he crouched with suddenly dried mouth, sweaty palms, and pounding heart, at the frightening difference between these Colorado mericats, who showed no hesitation whatsoever to kill, and the weak-kneed mormonee from down on the big river who, though they might easily have killed many of the Pahutes a few sleeps before, had never fired their guns at all.

Hesitantly he lifted his big gun and sighted along the barrel, hoping to find a target that he might destroy. But there was never a clear shot. Not once did any of the mericats expose themselves for long enough for Posey to take aim. It was as if they knew he was there, waiting—

And then, to Posey's great joy, one of the mericat posse rode out of the trees directly toward him, completely separating himself from the others. Yet he was looking in another direction, distracted by something, and so did not see the hidden warrior.

"*Wagh*," Posey breathed excitedly as he checked his percussion cap and then aimed squarely at the approaching rider, "now Too-rah will see what a great warrior Posey has become!" And with no hesitation whatsoever, he fired.

Montezuma Fort

"Me . . . see Haskel," the old man who had been the strong and youthful Natanii nééz pleaded from the back of his burro. He had been riding three days now and was more exhausted than he had ever been before in his short life. "Heap . . . hurry—"

Fearfully the white child turned and ran into the small group of cottonwood-log cabins that were being called Montezuma Fort, and a little later the thin old Indian missionary and interpreter who was becoming known throughout *Diné-tah* strode toward them. Pausing near where Hádapa sat under some willows, still holding the burro but with her eyes continually downcast, he also sank to the earth.

"I am called Haskel," he declared after a short time of polite silence, speaking in Navajo. "You have sent for me, my father?"

The old man on the back of the burro looked pained. "I am . . . not your father," he murmured weakly. "I . . . am called Natanii nééz—"

Haskel grunted but otherwise showed no surprise. "There has been a great change in you, Natanii nééz."

Making the sign of agreement, the Navajo pushed on. "Your words w-were filled with power, Haskel—great power. I was a strong raider, also filled with power, perhaps more than any other of the *Diné*. But my power was as sand before the wind in the face of your words. Can you see what you and the one called *Shin-op* have done to me?"

Thales Haskel made the sign that he could see, knowing that the Navajo was using the Pahute word for God simply because his people had no one god of their own with which he could identify. "Yes, Natanii nééz, you were a great thief. But for many seasons your heart has been bad, and you have lost your *hózhó*, your balance in the world. You have stolen from your true friends, the mormonee, and you have taught others to do the same. When you were warned that *Shin-op* was not pleased with your ways because you had become selfish and were hurting the mormonee, you laughed and scorned. When you were told that the mormonee were the true friends of *Shin-op* as well as the *Diné,* you laughed and scorned and stole even more. And when, at last, words of power were spoken against you so that your evil days would end, you laughed and scorned for the last time."

Weakly Natanii nééz made the sign of agreement. "All y-you say is true," he admitted quietly.

"Yes, and now you are dying."

With a sharp intake of breath the young woman holding the burro turned her head away, her body racked with silent sobs.

"Is this your woman?"

"Her name is Hádapa."

For a moment Thales wondered at the woman's name, knowing he had heard it before but not immediately recalling where.

"Does Hádapa understand this thing that you have brought upon yourself?" he finally asked.

"She does not wish . . . her man to die."

Thales Haskel said nothing but stared at the earth between his moccasined feet. Though he did not look at Hádapa, he could feel the greatness of her sorrow, her pain. And there was also something else, another sort of goodness that he could not even begin to define. Yet in spite of the woman's downcast eyes, it was there—

And then in a rush it came to him. Hádapa! This was the woman who had brought the goat's milk to nourish and strengthen the Foreman child! Day after day she had made the journey from wherever her *hogan* was all the way to the river and then across it to the fort. Maggie had spoken of her with high praise, both Mary and Kumen Jones had spoken of her with deep admiration, and he had intended for some time to seek her out and have a visit. But something or other had always come up—

Abruptly Thales Haskel also knew something else. Hádapa was sorrowing not *for* Natanii nééz but because of him. Yet, his mind argued, how could that possibly be? She was this man's wife, and so how—

"Haskel," Natanii nééz muttered, "this is the thing I . . . would have you . . . to do. It is . . . why I have come . . . to this place. I would like you to . . . write a letter to *Shin-op.* Say to him that . . . Natanii nééz is a thief no more. Say to him that Natanii nééz is now a true friend of the mormonee. S-Say to him that it will be so always. Say to h-him that the woman Hádapa is without child, and that is why she does not wish Natanii nééz to die."

"Write a letter?" Thales Haskel asked as he looked up, too surprised to remember all of what this former enemy was saying.

"Yes. Put it . . . mail . . . go far off. Say these words to *Shin-op* so that Natanii nééz may live."

"I'll say the words," the old interpreter said as he unfolded his long legs and rose to his feet. "But know this, O tall one. *Shin-op* is *Shin-op,* the greatest Holy One of all. Haskel does not tell *Shin-op* what to do; *Shin-op* tells Haskel. I will give your words to *Shin-op,* but he will do with Natanii nééz as he wishes."

And without another word, or even a backward glance at the stricken Natanii nééz or the deeply mourning Hádapa, who had been pulled so abruptly and so permanently from the arms of those she had come to love, Thales Haskel turned and walked back toward the small fort in the riverbottoms of Montezuma Creek.

Head of Mason Draw, LaSal Mountains

In the last of the daylight Jimmy Heaton held his borrowed copy of the Book of Mormon and a partially completed letter on his lap. As he fingered the sore spot on his neck where the second Ute bullet had taken away the skin but done no other harm, he was thinking deeply, wondering at both what he had read and what he had written. At the moment, his whole mind seemed in turmoil, and although he had borrowed a pencil and a couple of pages of foolscap from Harg Eskridge on which to write his letter, he could think of nothing more to say.

For two days now he and the Rico posse had fought a running, sporadic battle in which, to the best of Jimmy's knowledge, no one had been killed but that old squaw, and she had died only that morning. Of course, that morning the posse had also captured the massive herd of horses and a bunch of squaws who had been guarding them. But then, and Jimmy grinned as he thought of it, the captured squaws had turned the tables and tricked the thirteen boys who had been left to guard them, stampeded every last one of the horses into the timber, and then escaped themselves, leaving the guards (and who was the sorry soul who had decided on leaving an unlucky thirteen of them as guards? And on Friday the 13th, no less?) with nothing to do but take a hike down to Moab, some eighteen miles off, to pick up new mounts and whatever else they needed and then hopefully rejoin the fray.

Jimmy shook his head, wondering for the hundredth time why he hadn't been one of the lucky ones who'd had to walk into Moab. It would have been so good to be out of this mess for good, and to maybe spend a little time with Isadore Wilson and his family. Oh, the fellows who'd left had been given the raspberries, all right, but they'd all taken it in good fun, promising to hurry back and save the boys once the real battle began. And Jimmy, who had watched them go, had felt such a powerful longing—

Of course, most of the posse didn't think there'd be the kind of battle Jimmy was expecting, the Utes showing too much disposition to run. But they hadn't had such a narrow escape as he had, and besides, they were ignorant of some precious, important facts.

Well, Jimmy thought with a grin, at least they'd seen some beautiful country, places he knew he would never forget as long as he lived. Take these LaSal Mountains, for instance. He'd never seen such mountains for steepness, but likewise he had never seen such surpassing beauty. And wildlife? Mercy, mercy! Deer were everywhere, and over on Bald Mesa he'd watched two different herds of elk, mostly cows and new calves and a few bulls scattered about, the cows and calves talking back and forth to each other as if they knew what they were saying, and one old bull bugling so near it had made Jimmy shiver clean to his toes it was so beautiful.

Jimmy had also seen a couple of bears that afternoon as he had approached the saddle where they were now camped, a sow and her new cub. He had been watching them instead of paying attention to what he should have been when that first bullet had come whistling through his coat—

Seemingly of its own accord, Jimmy's mind came back to the passage of scripture he had read just moments before he had started his letter: "And when ye shall receive these things," it had said, "I would exhort you that ye would ask God, the Eternal Father, in the name of Christ, if these things are not true . . ."

It was interesting, Jimmy found himself thinking, how Isadore had told him to pray about the book, and now the book itself was telling him to pray. The thing was, it had been so long since he had knelt beside his mother that he wasn't actually sure he knew how. Of course, Isadore had made it sound simple enough, and maybe that was what the book was doing, too. Ask God, the Eternal Father, in the name of Christ. Of a truth, he thought with a wry grin, that didn't seem so hard. And the book had certainly raised a host of doubts and questions in his mind that needed to be asked of somebody! It was just that . . . well, he felt sort of silly even thinking about praying—

"You still reading that fool book, Jimmy-boy?"

Jimmy didn't even need to look up to identify the gravelly voice of John Galloway. "As a matter of fact, Jack, I've just about finished it."

"And what good has it done you?" The man's voice was filled with sarcasm and ridicule. "Oh, that's right! Reckon I forgot you're all interested in marriage, and that book's taught you all about old Brigham's spiritual wifery. Right?"

Now Jimmy looked up at the man. "You know, Jack, I've always thought of you as a friend, and in some ways I reckon you're a good man. But if I ever even thought of being as rude to someone as you're being right now, my ma'd tan my hide—but good! Too bad your mother ain't around to do the same."

"Now, see here—"

"No," Jimmy said as he rose to his feet, his book and unfinished letter in his hand, "*you* see here, Jack Galloway! For your information there ain't a particle of information in this book about the Mormons or their church. What it is—and you can read it for yourself—is a record of some ancient people and their dealings with the Lord. Fact is, Jesus came to see those folks after he was resurrected. He came right down out of the sky—scared 'em practically to death!"

"And you believe that Mormon tommyrot?"

"Whether I believe it or not doesn't have a thing to do with whether it's true. I don't know yet if it is, but rather than remaining an ignorant fool like some folks I know, I aim to find out."

John Galloway snickered disdainfully. "And how you going to do that, you young pup? Ask your Mormon friends? You know good and well they'll just lie to you!"

"No," Jimmy responded, his voice suddenly calm, "I will not be asking them. Instead I'm going to ask God, who will not deceive. Now, if you'll excuse me?"

And without a backward glance Jimmy walked away from the staring, angry man.

—o—o—o—

In the flickering firelight Jimmy Heaton turned a little so he could better see the letter he was nearly through composing. He'd been writing now for an hour, maybe more, and he wasn't certain at all that he'd said what he was feeling. Thing was, with daylight they'd be riding again, and he didn't know when he'd get another chance—

"Well, boys, we've got 'em routed." Captain William Dawson

took up a burning stick and lit his pipe, which he felt was the most impressive way to start a smoke. And one of his biggest concerns, everyone understood, was creating the right impression. "I reckon by tomorrow it'll be all over but the shouting! We had no casualties today, and from the amount of blood we found, we probably killed five, maybe six of them."

"Afore it's over we'll make it another twenty-five or thirty," John Galloway growled. "They ain't never dealt with a real posse afore, so I reckon this'll settle their milk some."

"Amen," Wiley Tartar agreed. "And good riddance to 'em. I say we take no prisoners, either. Far as I'm concerned, they all die!"

"Women and kids, too? I thought we already decided against that."

"Then we've changed our minds! Women can shoot as well as men, and like they always say, nits make lice. Kill 'em now and they won't cause trouble later!"

"Well, one of 'em like to have caused some real problems today. Whoever that was who was shooting from up here in the saddle this afternoon—well, for an Injun shooter he wasn't too shabby. He like to have parted Jimmy's hair permanent-like—twice."

"That's no fooling," Wiley's brother Hard agreed soberly. "How he missed the kid I'll never know. Speaking of which—Jimmy, what in deuce you doing over there all alone? You still reading that fool book them Mormons gave you?"

"Nope. I'm trying to write a letter," Jimmy Heaton mumbled from where he sat on a rock a few yards away, his stub of pencil in his hand and the two small sheets of paper on his knee.

"Is that a love letter to the famous Miss Sally?" George Taylor teased.

"Or would that be the infamous Miss Sally?" Tom Click added merrily.

Jimmy sighed audibly, letting them know that their jokes were getting tiresome. "As a matter of fact, boys, it isn't to Miss Sally at all."

"Your ma, then?" Hiram Melvin chipped in. "Them near misses make you a little nervous today, Jimmy?"

Looking up so that the firelight illuminated his face, Jimmy's serious expression sobered the men. "They did, Hi, and that's a fact! Like the rest of you fellers, I don't know how that Injun missed me. His first ball went through my coat, but I was turned and couldn't tell where he was hid up. So when I dove off my hoss and hunkered down to try and find him, he could see me plain and had me dead to rights."

"Yeah, from twenty feet away."

"That's right, George." Reaching up, Jimmy again rubbed the front of his neck. "His second shot went right under my chin—took off a little skin is all—and then he skedaddled."

"You was lucky, all right."

Jimmy's eyes were bright. "That wasn't luck, Hard. The good Lord protected me from that Injun kid—"

"Kid?" Captain William Dawson was dubious.

"Yeah, I got me a good look at him, Captain. He was a kid, all right, younger even than me, and his hair was all sort of greenish. He was also surprised that he'd missed. I could tell that by the way he looked from me to his rifle and then back at me. By all rights I should have been dead, and he knew it as well as I did."

"But you figure the Lord protected you?"

Jimmy finally grinned. "Yeah, Hard, I do. Thing is, I can't figure why."

"What're you talking about? We're in the right, is why!"

"Maybe, Dave." Jimmy was looking at Davis Willis but not really seeing him. "And maybe not. According to Billy Foreman and some of the other Mormons, the Lord ain't pleased when we start thirsting after the blood of the Indians."

"That ain't nothing but Mormon talk," John Galloway scoffed. "If it ain't downright evil, it's at least foolishness!"

"Not when you recollect that the good Lord created everybody," Jimmy replied quietly, "including these Utes we've been chasing the past two weeks."

"Now you're going to tell us you believe that Mormon claptrap about the Injuns being the blood of Israel, too?"

Jimmy grinned. "Maybe I do, Hi. Which is part of why I'm confused about not getting killed this afternoon. Boys, despite that I was warned not to do it by a Mormon bishop, I've been thirsting after the blood of these folks for days."

"That's because they're murderers, Jimmy, and don't you forget it!"

"Some of the men, maybe. But the women, Captain Dawson? Or the little kids? I don't hardly think so. That's why I keep speaking out against killing 'em. And even if the men are murderers, hadn't we ought to be taking them back to trial instead of just killing them outright?"

Captain William Dawson blustered to his feet. "Now see here, young man! I'm a legally elected sheriff, and out here I am the law. Them Injuns is murderers, and we're executioners! And there's a mighty big difference between the two."

"That's fine, Captain. I'll accept that and stick with you boys to the end, no matter. Thing is, I can't help thinking the good Lord might see things a little different than we do. That's what I've been trying to clear up in my mind."

"How's that?" someone cackled. "By writing a letter to the Lord?"

"Naw! He's written a letter to that fool Mormon bishop!"

Jimmy sighed again, wondering that he had ever considered these men so highly. "Wrong on all counts," he declared quietly. "It's to a couple of friends of mine, including a young feller name of Isadore Wilson from down to Moab. When all this is over, I aim to pay him a visit."

"Unless the Lord strikes you dead first for being so wicked," someone snickered.

"Or can't protect me on account of my stupid disobedience," Jimmy breathed sadly as he folded the finally-finished letter and slipped it into his shirt pocket. "That's my big worry—"

31

Pinhook Draw

"Hear these words, my brother. Soon the whites will be coming, and you will see that Mike and the others have set a good trap."

Posey, who sat crouched with his brother on a steep hillside overlooking a small, sloping valley, snarled disdainfully. "Perhaps. But it is more likely that I will see another great losing of face for the warriors of the People."

Vigorously the larger but younger Scotty made the sign that he disagreed. "It will not be so!" he hissed, his voice growing louder. "Have we not taken many fine horses for our people, more even than a man can count? Have we not put *piuni,* four whites under the grass? Are we not now waiting with our rifles *to-wudg-ka,* loaded for the ones who are following?"

"We will see if this last thing is so," Posey replied angrily. "But the horses we lost to the mormonee are big in my mind, my brother. Yes, and so is the shame that covers me like a wet blanket each time I remember that we were as squaws and *to-wats-en,* children, before them!"

"Yes," Scotty admitted, "that was a strange thing, one I do not understand. Nevertheless, my brother, we have taken many other horses—"

"Those, too, have been lost to the mericats!" Posey snarled angrily.

"That is also true. But think of the mericats we have already put under the grass. There is much glory in that, just as there is much glory in what is about to happen in this place."

"*Pe-nun-ko,* there is no glory in what has not yet happened," Posey snarled as he looked in vain for sign of movement up the canyon. "Only *e-tish,* in the proud deeds already done by our warriors in the days before this one. *Wagh!* You will see that I—"

"And there will be no glory for either of you," their father Chee interrupted from where he lay concealed in the rocks and brush a few yards from his sons, "if you do not stop chattering like little girls."

Instantly chastened, the boys grew still. But Posey's active mind would not leave the matter of this big raid. If he had not been completely convinced the day before, his mind was now firmly settled on it. From start to finish the raid had been poorly planned, poorly executed, and even a young warrior such as himself could see this. Already he had mentally cataloged and examined the previous mistakes—except, of course, those made by himself. Those he was still considering. But this . . . this ambush, would no doubt turn into the biggest mistake of all.

The day before, not long after Posey's two carefully aimed shots had somehow missed that young mericat posse member, the Ute warriors had gathered in the north-facing Mason Draw where the aspen, fir, and other denizens of an alpine forest had been thick enough to offer decent cover. There Wash, Mike, and the others had begun to plan this current ambush as a final retaliation. And it had definitely been time to retaliate, Posey knew, for their riding ponies had been spavined and exhausted, the People were tired and hungry, the mericats with their laughter and big guns were close behind, and the warriors of the People must not get too far from the horses that the mericats had stolen back.

Tragically, at least in Posey's mind, one of the warriors had remembered this place where he and the others were now crouched and waiting and had suggested it as a proper place for an ambush, a trap. From the height of Mason Draw it had not looked too bad, either. A flat, sloping valley of perhaps a thousand yards in width, the draw, which was already being called Pinhook by the whites on account of a rocky escarpment that reminded them of one of the protruding bones of a cow's pelvis, was flanked to the east by the steep slope of Harpole Mesa and to the immediate west by a short, abruptly steep ridge called Porcupine Rim. Beyond that, less than a mile farther to the west, were the almost impassable cliffs of Wilson Mesa and the Castle Valley Rim.

If the Pahutes would but hide themselves along the steep sides of Harpole Mesa and Porcupine Rim above this long, brush-filled draw, it had been argued, they could easily put under the grass this mericat posse who had so brazenly restolen the horses and turned the Pahutes' raid into a rout.

To Posey, such a place for an ambush hadn't looked likely, and now that he was hidden with his brother, his father, and some others under the edge of Harpole Mesa, their rifles facing west down into the draw, it looked less promising than ever. For one thing, the range was great, especially for weapons such as his. For another, the brush across the bottom was thick, and Posey was certain the whites could use it as cover and easily escape the ambush. Finally, and this to Posey was the biggest problem, it simply did not look like the place for an ambush. It was too open, too innocuous-looking. It would have been the last place Posey himself would have selected—

"*Ungh!*" Old Chee suddenly grunted, causing the youth's head to swivel in surprise. "Here they come, my sons. Now we will show these white devils the way of the true warriors of the People. Now we will show them that they can never *in-e-to-ah*, they can never get away from our guns!"

Pinhook Draw

Young Jimmy Heaton shifted his rifle to his left hand with his horse's reins and then wiped his sweaty right palm on his jeans. It was a warm morning, all right, but he knew the sweat was from nervousness, not the weather.

"Ain't this living?" Hard Tartar growled from nearby, no doubt in response to Jimmy's apprehension. "A good horse to ride, a comfortable saddle, a straight-shooting rifle, fine companions, and a chance to help put a stop to the thieving Injuns who've made life so miserable for us white folks the past few years. What more could a man ask than that, Jimmy?" The man grinned widely. "Of course I'll allow that if Miss Sally were here on her little bay mare, holding your hand and letting you steal a kiss now and then, well, that would make life more than better, wouldn't it! I allow it would make it practically perfect."

Jimmy smiled at the man's attempt to ease his mind, but he did not reply. Instead he was thinking again of the warning he had been given that recent night in Bluff, worrying about it even while his eyes were scouring the brush-covered slopes on either side of where he and the others were riding. He'd lusted after blood, all right, and done it a-plenty! Now he was fairly trapped, so that even if he wasn't lusting and the Utes happened to attack, he'd have no choice but to fight back—

Earlier, coming down over the snowbanks scattered through Mason Draw, they'd flushed out three more bears that were just out from hibernation, two blacks and a blond. Normally bears were great sport for the men, but they had had to let them go without a roping party because the Indians were escaping pell-mell down Pinhook Draw toward the Castle Valley Desert. And now they were in that same silent Pinhook Draw, riding slow and wary because a couple of the scouts had claimed to see movement on one of these side hills. But it was about as unlikely a place for an ambush as Jimmy Heaton had ever seen. In fact, it looked so innocent that he had volunteered to ride ahead with a bunch of his neighbors to see if they could decoy anything out from cover. But so far there'd been no sign of life but chipmunks and lizards skittering about; them and a shrieking red-tailed hawk sailing off above Harpole Mesa to the northeast. Still, Jimmy felt nervous about this place—

"Watch that prickly pear," Davis Willis said conversationally as he rode a few yards away. "Them spines don't do much for a horse's hocks."

"Country's looking more and more like desert, all right," Jordan Bean commented. "Yonder's some catclaw, and that stuff's good to stay shy of too. The way we're dropping in elevation, boys, by the time we get to the bottom of Pinhook we'll be in the desert for sure."

"So will Bill May and the boys he took with him," Hard Tartar agreed as he scanned the apparently empty hills. "By the time they get off that Castle Valley Rim and head these poor, scared Utes, we'll have to be hunting waterholes again."

"I hope he can get down." Wiley Tartar lifted his hat and scratched his head. "That rimrock looks steep, and the way we're being divided up, seems like we're running low on men."

"What's the matter, Wiley? These redskins got you spooked?"

Wiley grinned at the speaker, Tom Click. "Maybe a little, Tom. What with thirty of our sixty men off riding that rim somewheres and thirteen more gone afoot to Moab, I know there's a sight more of them than there are of us."

"Maybe we ought to go into camp and send somebody back to Rico for reinforcements!" Jimmy suggested.

"What's the matter, kid?" Harg Enkridge sounded as sarcastic as John Galloway, although Jimmy was no longer surprised by it. "You getting yellow fever?"

"That would be very unseemly," Captain Dawson declared somberly. "Besides, Rico's more'n a hundred miles, one way. Then too, you all know the army at Fort Lewis is sending out troops to assist us should there be need. No, sir, boys, with the world watching, we have no choice but to go ahead!"

Jimmy nodded, never taking his eyes off the innocuous-looking hillside they were riding under.

"The trouble is," the captain suddenly continued, his voice a great deal more quiet, "we have no good idea of where the troops are or how many they brung. Where in tarnation is Bill May? After all, it's his brother's death we're trying to avenge!"

"You know doggone well he's trying to head the Indians by dropping off that rim," someone responded. "You sent him there."

"I know *where* he is!" the captain growled irritably. "I want to know why he hasn't arrived! Or why we haven't heard firing down valley where he's caught them Utes. Or where, by thunderation, Spud Hudson's posse is!"

"You feeling antsy, Captain?"

"I am, Hard, and that's a fact! Something sure as sin don't feel right. Besides, I've been studying on it, and tell the truth I haven't ever seen a better place than this draw for an ambush."

"Here?" Jimmy Heaton was astounded.

"As ever, kid. First off, it don't look like a good spot, which is always important. Second, see how Porcupine Rim here bulges out into them two knolls with about a hundred yards between 'em? Was it me, I'd put shooters on them little hills and wait till we was between them, which is about where we are. That's easy shooting, Jimmy—plumb easy. Finally, we got no cover out here for hundreds of yards but a few juniper and piñon and this useless scrub oak."

"There's a wash up ahead," Dick Baumgartner piped in helpfully. "Looks like a good hide-up to me."

"Maybe. But we can't see where it goes or how deep it is, so it might offer no cover at all. Of course, they ain't a'going to attack on account of they're natural-born cowards, but if I was leading these Ute buzzards, I'd—"

The sudden crash of rifle fire was deafening. Davis Willis cried out and tumbled from his horse, which plunged away into the oak, and Jimmy Heaton knew instantly that the man was dead. There was another cry, Jordan Bean flew from the saddle to land in a heap in the rocks, and from the blood on his head Jimmy was certain that he, too, was gone. And the rifle fire from the two knolls did not let up.

"I'm hit!" Harg Eskridge shrieked as he reached down to grab for his ankle, at the same time trying to control his terrified mount. The rest of the horses by then were also plunging and screaming. Gunfire continued to echo from everywhere above them; bullets were splattering into the rocks and dirt all about, some ricocheting away with vicious whines; and Jim Hall's horse went down screaming with the same bullet that had just put a hole through the calf of Jim Hall's leg.

"The ravine, boys!" the elderly Tim Jenkins shouted into the melee. "Head for the ravine! It's the only cover we've got!"

In a panic Jimmy Heaton slapped spurs and yanked his horse's head in the direction of the ravine, which when he got to it proved too shallow even for himself, let alone his horse. But since there was nothing else even close, and since the continuing gunfire sounded like popcorn popping on both sides of the draw, and finally since his companions who could were piling into the same shallow wash and doing their best to hunker down out of sight and still find something to shoot back at, Jimmy hurriedly abandoned his horse and dove for shelter.

And immediately wished with all his heart that he hadn't!

Pinhook Draw

In open-mouthed amazement Posey stared down off the hill. It had come to pass! The ambush had actually worked! Mike and those other old fools had set a proper trap, and now these mericats were caught in the open of the valley floor and were *e-iqueay,* they were dying!

Oo-ah, yes, they were trying to hide in that shallow wash. But it offered no cover whatsoever, and so without difficulty Posey could see every one of them. And though the whites were *to-edg-mae,* a great way off from his own place of hiding, Posey could also hear their voices clearly. Some were shouting, some were crying and screaming in fear and pain, three had escaped back up the draw on the only three horses that had remained afoot, and even as he watched, Posey saw three and then one more of the mericat cowboys sprawl out and grow still like the two who had been first shot from their ponies. Thus Posey was certain that they were all *e-i,* dead.

The firing from Porcupine Rim was practically continuous, and the warriors hidden there were growing more and more bold, dashing out toward the draw, firing almost at point-blank range, and then darting back into cover. And Wash, who now appeared to consider himself invincible, kept strutting out onto a large boulder in full view of the whites and shouting encouragement and instructions to the men of the People.

Without hesitation Posey lifted his own rifle, sighted it toward one of the men in the ravine—the same, it looked like, who had somehow escaped his rifle balls the day before—and pulled the trigger. Through the powder smoke he saw clearly where his ball struck the earth—at least thirty yards short of the man.

"That gun is no good," Scotty declared with an innocent look, his eyes also on the spot where Posey's spent bullet had raised a puff of dust.

"*Ungh,*" Posey grunted as he hurriedly poured more powder into the muzzle of the old rifle. "I will lift the muzzle with this round, and then we will see—"

When the second ball hit in almost the same spot as the previous shot, Scotty couldn't help but chuckle. "Perhaps the one you shoot at is mormonee, my brother. Remember the words of the man Haskel?"

With a snarl Posey loaded again, raised his rifle muzzle even higher, and fired. And for the third time he watched in amazement as his ball fell in exactly the same place—thirty yards short of the very mericat who Posey was now certain had escaped his fire the day before.

"Haskel said that gun was no good," Scotty breathed, now as amazed as Posey and no longer trying to make a joke. "He also said Posey would never kill a mormonee. Scotty thinks Haskel's words had power in them—great power."

"Scotty doesn't think at all!" Posey growled angrily as the battle raged before him. But though he reloaded he did not fire again, and he did not attempt to crawl any closer. Instead he simply remained on his belly, watching.

And thinking.

For now, as he studied out the great victory unfolding below him, Posey was certain he knew the best way to take power from these cursed whites. *Oo-ah,* yes, and next time it would most assuredly work against the cowardly mormonee who had encamped on the bank of the big river!

Pinhook Draw

"Hard? Hard Tartar?"

"He ain't a'goin to answer you, kid. Hard's dead—has been for an hour or more."

Numbly Jimmy Heaton pressed himself farther into the rocky bank of the shallow arroyo. Hard Tartar dead? Somehow he couldn't comprehend that. Not Hard Tartar. He was too good a man, too strong. How could he have allowed himself to be killed by these rag-tag Utes?

Licking his lips, Jimmy glanced at the sky. Two hours, he thought. Maybe three. Three hours since the Indians had attacked and he and the others had tumbled pell-mell into the shallow ravine.

Somehow Captain Dawson, Dick Baumgartner, and old Tim Jenkins had kept hold of their horses, and after a few minutes in the deadly ravine they had thrown themselves aboard their mounts and escaped back up the draw to where the others were hiding and waiting. But Jimmy's horse had run a few yards and then been shot dead, as had several of the others, and so he had been trapped good.

Tim Jenkins had fought Indians before, he had said, and in the first few terrible minutes in the ravine he had directed the men to move down it until they had come to a little cul-de-sac where the ravine ended. It seemed like the best place to hole up, and that's where most of them had stayed— except for old man Jenkins and the other two, who had ridden through a hail of bullets and escaped. Shortly thereafter Tom Click and Hiram Melvin had been killed within minutes of each other, and Wiley Tartar had had his leg busted. Tom Click's body was only a few feet from Jimmy, in the full sun, and although the young man couldn't smell him, the flies apparently could, for they had become almost unbearable. Fact is, because he couldn't wave them away without attracting more fire from the hidden Indians, Jimmy had to keep his eyes and mouth closed just to protect his own body against invasion.

Two bullets thudded into the earth nearby, one after the other, and Jimmy's entire body cringed as he tried to make himself smaller, less visible. Somehow he hadn't been hit, although he couldn't imagine how he had escaped. There had been hundreds of rounds fired into the arroyo by the Utes, many hundreds, it seemed, and to Jimmy it was a miracle that any of them were still alive. Yet even with that knowledge, he still found the whole situation incomprehensible.

How could he and the others have gotten themselves into such a fix? With more than sixty men in the posse, they had taken the fight to the Utes from Kane Springs all the way up and across the west side of the LaSals and down to here, and now the posse were the ones being killed? It made no sense to Jimmy Heaton, no sense at all. Where were Bill May and his boys? Where were the fellows who had gone into Moab after fresh horses and supplies? Where was Spud Hudson's outfit that they had been expecting? Where was the army out of Fort Lewis? And why the double deuce hadn't Captain Dawson opened up an attack from his position back up the draw?

Surely he could get a few of the boys into position to at least make things a little warm for the Indians. Even a little fire from another direction would help!

Of course, some time earlier Pat McKinney had come sprinting down the draw and into the ravine, sent by Captain Dawson to encourage the men to run the gauntlet of rifle fire and escape back up the draw. Jimmy and most of the others had been willing, but one man had begun to plead with them not to leave him, sobbing that he couldn't attempt an escape, for he knew he would be killed if he tried.

Poor Pat McKinney, who had stripped to his socks and long-handles to make the daring rescue attempt, had about argued his fool head off for at least some of the boys to follow him back to safety. But when the Tartar brothers, Jimmy, and the rest had said they'd stick it out with their terrified comrade, Pat McKinney had been forced to begin his erratic race back up the draw alone. The wonder to Jimmy was that he had made it—both ways. And though McKinney's feet had been torn to shreds and filled with thorns just from the run down, and had no doubt suffered even worse damage going back, he was at least alive. The frightened man they had all stayed behind for wasn't. And neither were any of the others but himself, Jack Galloway, and Wiley Tartar. Of course, he didn't know about Harg Eskridge and Jim Hall, who had both fallen in the brush and never made it to the ravine. Probably, Jimmy thought, they were dead too—just like Dave Willis and Jordan Bean, both of whom he had seen shot off their mounts in the opening fusillade from the ambush.

Three of them left alive in the ravine, Jimmy thought as he licked his lips again—three out of more than two handfuls of men who had lusted after the blood of these people that the Book of Mormon called Lamanites—

Castle Creek

"Ise, you hear that?"

It was a little past noon on a quiet, boring Sabbath, and Alfred Wilson was lounging with his younger brother beside their dead fire near Castle Creek on the east side of Harpole Mesa, playing a friendly game of poker. Of course, officially he and Isadore didn't hold with gambling, and their folks back in Moab didn't approve of owning face cards at all. Tools of the devil, their mother called them, used only by the lazy and indolent. Idle bodies and idle minds, their father usually added, were nothing more than the devil's workshop. And the Lord couldn't bless or protect people who worked with the devil!

But neither of their parents understood how boring it was sitting around a campfire with nothing to do but stare at the sky or watch the cows chewing their cud all day long. Besides which, not that Alfred didn't believe in it, but Mormonism was starting to seem like sort of a stuffy old religion anyway, not at all like the philosophies and beliefs of the cowboys and rustlers and other ringtailed buckaroos who occasionally stopped at their fire. And it didn't take too much, he thought with a grin, to get Isadore to go along with him—

Unfortunately, during the past week no such dashing *companeros* had dropped by to liven things up. Instead, the two youths had been alone with their father's cows every day from dark to dark and then some. Their only excitement had been to rope and drag to the pole corral beyond their fire every old mossyback troublemaker that seemed bent on leading the others into forbidden paths, as their father would have put it, meaning the poison jimson weed that seemed to be growing everywhere that spring.

"I heard it, Alf." Isadore was sitting up and straining his neck, trying to pinpoint the sound. "Gunfire. Lots of it!"

"As ever," Alfred agreed, rising quickly to his feet. "Sounds like it's coming from west of here, toward Pinhook or maybe beyond."

"You reckon it's Brother Burkholder and the boys?"

"Well," Alfred responded, thinking quickly, "I don't know anybody else over that way. Glory be, Ise. What if the McCartys and some of them other owlhoots are finally giving old Burkholder a real shooting war? I know he sure don't hold much with rustlers, and if he or some of the others caught those boys with a few of his cows— well, there'll be the devil to pay if that's the case!"

Instantly Isadore was consumed with guilt. All along he'd known it was wrong to be consorting with such men, spinning yarns and laughing and gambling with them, even if it was only for matchsticks around their nighttime campfires. Such things were contrary to everything he'd ever been taught, and Isadore now felt bad about it.

Why, what would his new friends Billy and Eliza Foreman think after they had set such store by him and taken him in the way they'd done? And Jimmy Heaton! What in tarnation would he think, especially now that Isadore had got him to reading the Book of Mormon and studying on the truthfulness of the gospel? If Jimmy happened to drop by Moab and saw that it meant so little to Isadore, after having heard so much of Isadore's preaching and explaining and testifying, why, he probably wouldn't even be interested anymore. And Isadore wouldn't blame him—not after the kind of example he had been setting!

There were also his parents—wonderful folks who had done their level best for Isadore all his life. Never once had either of them let him down, yet here he was, playing with these fool cards on the Lord's day and wishing right along that the McCarty brothers and Matt Warner would drop by and enliven the day a little. Lawsy, lawsy! Could a son have ever gone more wrong or let his folks down any harder? No wonder his father had felt compelled to warn him and Alf about losing the Lord's protection through disobedience—

"Ise, you listening to me?"

Isadore blinked. "I . . . uh . . . I'm listening, Alf. What do you reckon we should do?"

"Well, we're not going off half-cocked and riding for help, that's for sure—not at least until we've made certain it's them that's under attack. Come on, little brother! Let's go find out!"

"But . . . we aren't armed! And Pa said we shouldn't leave the stock."

Alfred grinned as he loosed his horse from the empty pole corral and leaped onto the animal's bare back. "We ain't on the attack, Ise, and we ain't abandoning Pa's precious cows. We're just riding to the far edge of Harpole to take a quick look-see. Besides, those shots are far enough off we'll never be in range, and we probably won't be seen, either. Now let's go! I don't want to miss any of the excitement."

For a moment only, Isadore hesitated. Something was nagging at him, dragging his mind away from his bareback horse—away from the distant sound of gunfire. What was it? he wondered. Was he being warned about something? And why the dickens was he all of a sudden thinking so much on his new friend Jimmy Heaton? For off and on through the morning he had been, wondering where he was, what he was up to, and especially how he was feeling about the Church. It was almost as if he was actually nearby, maybe even coming to get Isadore's father to baptize him—

"Ise," Alfred shouted from thirty yards up the hill, "get the lead out! Somebody may need our help! Bad!"

Gulping and then taking a deep breath to calm his pounding heart, Isadore Wilson loosed his pony, threw himself aboard, jammed spurs to bare pony flanks, and hung on hard as his mount squealed, lunged, and then began pounding after his older and wiser brother. After all, he thought, they'd only be gone a few moments.

And it was in that instant, when he could no longer do anything about it, that Isadore Wilson remembered his horrifying dream—

Harpole Mesa

"*Shan-neech,* my brother. Go slow. I hear something coming up through those trees."

Posey, knowing that his younger brother's ears were better than his own, instantly focused on the clump of oak Scotty had indicated. The two of them, as well as several others of the Pahute warriors, had finally grown tired of the well-planned ambush. There was no joy in listening to the distant booming of guns but of seeing nothing but a few dead horses and one or two dead white men. And for Posey, there was absolutely no joy in seeing every ball fall short of the exposed mericat no matter how he tried to adjust his aim.

In boredom he, Scotty, and several others had left their positions and wandered up and onto the relatively flat top of Harpole Mesa, looking for they knew not what but hoping to run into other members of the posse. But until the sharp-eared Scotty had heard the noise—

"*Poon-ny-won-y,*" Scotty suddenly breathed. "Look!"

At once alert, Posey lowered himself into the brush, at the same time keeping his eyes on the large stand of scrub oak. He had no idea what the others of the warriors were doing. He didn't even know if they had heard Scotty's warning. All he knew was that except for the explosions of distant gunfire, the afternoon was still; his old rifle was once again *to-wudg-ka,* loaded; and there was definitely something coming up the slope toward them through the oak.

"Do you see?" Scotty muttered as he ducked even lower and notched an arrow to his bow. "Mericats!"

And then at last Posey saw them, two white men heedlessly urging their mounts through the thick-growing trees.

"Wagh!" he breathed as he pulled back the hammer on the old cap-and-ball musket. These two were coming straight for him and Scotty. *Oo-ah,* yes, just as the mericat had done the day before! In another moment, perhaps two, they would be out of the trees and directly under the sights of his rifle, and this time he would not miss!

With a look of fierce determination Posey steadied his weapon through the sagebrush and waited. This was a good thing, very good. Perhaps his rifle had misfired when he had thought to kill the small mormonee with the glass before his eyes at Boiling Springs. Yes, and perhaps some strange thing had caused him to miss the mericat yesterday on top of the pass or kept his rifle balls from reaching the same mericat today—the one lying quietly in the bottom of the draw called Pinhook. Yet these were small things, Posey now decided, of no consequence whatever. And certainly they had nothing to do with the foolish words of the mormonee Haskel—the foolish words his younger brother kept repeating. Before him now came two more mericats, no doubt members of the posse, and in another moment Scotty would see that those words had no power. Yes, he would see what a big gun such as Posey used so well could do.

Drawing his breath Posey held for an instant, saw the first rider's chest appear beyond his sights at a distance of no more than forty yards, and then he gently squeezed the trigger.

Click.

Stunned that the old rifle had again misfired, Posey hastily pulled back the hammer and tried again. And again the weapon misfired.

In anguished amazement he rose to his feet while the thunder of exploding guns echoed from all around him. In an instant the two white men were on the ground, along with one of the horses, which had also been wounded. And in another instant Posey, who was nearest, had rushed forward and was glowering at the two downed men.

They were young, he noted as he quickly snatched up the fine new hat one of the two mericats had been wearing, and they looked a great deal alike. Brothers—almost certainly they were brothers. The first one was dead, and jamming the hat onto his head and thrusting a new cap onto the nipple of his rifle, Posey stepped to where the other one lay.

Though the young man was neither moving nor speaking, his eyes were wide and frightened, and Posey could tell he was silently pleading for mercy—for life. The thought made Posey laugh, and as Scotty and the others came up around him, Posey coolly thrust forward his rifle, placed the muzzle against the wide-eyed youth's forehead, and pulled the trigger.

Click!

Astounded, Posey set the hammer and pulled the trigger again, and when it failed to fire for the fourth time he stood slack-jawed and irresolute, not knowing what to do. A sudden explosion from directly beside him emptied the wide, frightened eyes of the youth, leaving them vacant and staring, and in wonder Posey looked from them, once again, to his beloved gun.

"Mormonee," Scotty said quietly, his voice filled almost with reverence. "Mormonee everywhere."

"You are a fool!" Posey snarled. "They are mericat, not mormonee!"

"No, my brother," Scotty declared, his attitude both sad and defiant. "These two are mormonee. See? No weapons, no guns. Like the mormonee on the big river, they did not come to fight. Haskel's words have power, great power. That gun is no good. It will not kill the mormonee—not ever."

After Scotty had walked away from his stunned brother, Posey turned with the others to more carefully examine the dead brothers. The two indeed had no weapons, and neither was there anything of value on the wounded, barebacked horse. And so like a frenzied horde Posey and the several warriors stripped the bodies and then bounded down the backtrail of the two brothers, seeking the other horse and perhaps their encampment.

Soon that too was found and raided of the small bag of flour and other basic foodstuffs. But other than the two bedrolls, the camp yielded the warriors nothing, nothing at all.

But it was there, standing with his rifle in his hand and staring about the empty camp, that Posey finally admitted to himself that for once the foolish Scotty had been right—not about Haskel and his words of power, for Posey scoffed at that. Such things were for children to believe in, not warriors.

No, what he now admitted was that his big gun had betrayed him—not once, not twice, but *piuni,* four times on this day alone, and maybe three more times if he were to count the shots into the draw that had fallen so short of their mark. Yes, and there were also those two misses yesterday, and the two times it had misfired back at Boiling Springs! Surely the gun was cursed! Surely it had a devil that kept him from becoming the warrior he was destined to become, the warrior he already knew himself to be!

"*Pikey!*" he snarled to the other warriors as he threw the useless weapon onto the cold ashes of the white man's fire. "*Pikey—tooish apane!* Come on—hurry up! We must get back to the ambush, brothers. Perhaps there is a weapon there among the dead mericats that is worthy of a great warrior such as myself. *Oo-ah,* yes," Posey said as his face broke into a grin, "and if not among them, then it should be a simple matter to find a fine big gun among the mormonee who have made a camp along the big river."

Pinhook Draw

For a few minutes, at least, Jimmy Heaton had finally felt a little hope. Moments before, he had heard a pile of shooting from up on Harpole Mesa. None of the posse that he knew of should have been in that country, but maybe some of the boys had sneaked around, trying to lend a hand. Doggone! Maybe it had even been Bill May and his boys, who had finally found a way down off the Castle Valley Rim and were riding to help.

But that whole idea hadn't washed, Jimmy now sadly admitted.

If it had been Bill May and his posse, then the Utes would surely have been skedaddling by now. That they weren't, and that he and Wiley Tartar and John Galloway were still pinned down, was evidenced by the continual thudding of bullets into the arroyo around him.

"Jack," he called hoarsely, "how's Wiley doing?"

"I don't hardly know, kid. He took a hard one ten, fifteen minutes ago, and he hasn't answered me since. I hate to say it, but I reckon he's a goner. You got any water?"

"Naw." Without thinking, Jimmy licked his lips again. "Like a fool I left my canteen on my saddle. You?"

John Galloway cursed softly. "Not anymore. Some Injun plugged my canteen square, and I couldn't do nothing but watch it drain dry. Where do you think Bill May is?"

"I don't rightly know." Jimmy was squinting up through the oak brush that lined the arroyo, trying to see something to shoot at. All the hours he'd lain there, he hadn't fired a single round. Fact is, he hadn't even seen anything to shoot at. "When all that shooting started up on top of Harpole a little bit ago, I thought maybe it was him."

"At first, so did I. But now I don't think so. The way it sounded to me, there were too many rifles, not any handguns. It was the Indians that surprised somebody, and not the other way around. That's why I don't think it was any of our boys. You . . . ah . . . you wish you'd gone with Pat McKinney?"

"Sort of," Jimmy answered. "What I really wish, though, was that Miss Sally had been awake before we left Rico so I could have said good-bye."

"Yeah." John Galloway's deep voice softened. "I'll bet you do. To my way of thinking, Jimmy Heaton, you're a lucky son-of-a-gun. I ain't never seen a purtier gal in my life than Miss Sally, and she's just as sweet as she is purty."

"She is that, Jack. Why, I allow—"

"Jimmy," the man interrupted, his voice again intense, "I sure am sorry I was rude to you the way I been."

Surprised, Jimmy smiled. "No problem, Jack. It didn't hurt me none."

"You . . . uh . . . you really believe in that Mormon stuff?"

"I reckon so."

"You a Mormon, then?"

"No, but lately I've been wishing I was. Ise Wilson once told me his pa'd baptize me if I wanted—"

John Galloway grunted. "I ain't never been baptized either. That's on account of I ain't never believed. You figure if we die we're going to meet up with the Lord Jesus?"

"I believe so—yes."

The man sighed deeply. "Then he'll likely send us both to hell, won't he—on account of neither of us has been baptized, I mean."

Jimmy started to shake his head and then remembered that he had to keep still if he expected to live. "No, Jack," he said, "that just ain't so. According to Billy Foreman, Mormons do the baptizing for lots of folks after they've died. It's even in the Bible. He showed it to me."

"You believe in that?"

"Reckon I do, Jack. I read it."

Again John Galloway sighed deeply. "Wish I'd listened more to Billy and them two other fellers this past winter. Thing was, I didn't want the boys from home thinking I was turning into a gol-durned Mormon sky-pilot. They'd of laughed at me something fierce, and I couldn't have stood it! But now you done it, Jimmy—become a true believer, I mean, and it don't seem bad at all. No sir, besides being lucky with Miss Sally, you're a mighty good man, Jimmy Heaton, terrible brave when we was making fun of you this past couple of weeks, and I wish to heaven I was more like you—"

A close, booming explosion echoed in Jimmy's ears, followed by a rattle of stones near John Galloway.

"Jack?" Jimmy whispered frantically. "Jack Galloway, you all right?"

Jimmy's ears were greeted with silence. There was no firing of enemy rifles, near or far. Nor was there any sound in the arroyo but the buzzing of hundreds of flies. And that was when it struck Jimmy, with all the force of a mule kick, that he was alone. Everyone else he had tumbled into the ravine with three hours before was dead. Every one!

"Oh, dear Lord above," he breathed as he did his best to control his racing heart, "what are you doing here, Jimmy Heaton? You didn't even tell your Ma or Pa good-bye, or your big brother Henry W. either! What sort of a durn-fool trick was that? Not even Miss Sally knows where you are. You'd have sure been better off staying in Rico and courting her, which would have beaten by a mile laying all alone in this fool ravine trying to dodge Ute bullets."

Blinking his eyes, Jimmy squinted against the sun glaring through the oak brush, trying to see. "Or even quitting this bunch when you thought about it a couple of nights ago and riding on down into Moab," he continued, squeezing his eyes shut once again. "Now that would have been the smartest thing to do, Jimmy Heaton! Smarter even than courting Miss Sally. Yes, sir, you could have had a proper visit with Ise and his folks, learned a bunch more stuff, and then ridden back to Rico when things with the Utes had quieted some. Then you could have told Miss Sally about the Mormons and all the things you've been considering the past few weeks. She'd have believed you sure, and then you and her could have —"

Something made Jimmy open his eyes and look upward just then, and as he did so he realized that a Ute brave—a man with the widest, most cruel-looking mouth Jimmy had ever seen—was standing directly above him in the oak brush, outlined against the afternoon sun. Not more than six feet separated them, and for a fraction of a second Jimmy wondered when the man had come to be there, or how he had, without making any noise. Then he wondered briefly if his rifle had a bullet in the chamber and if he could get it raised before the Ute fired, and he was still wondering that when something slammed hard against his head, causing a terrible noise and a blinding flash of light.

In almost that same instant Jimmy thought again of Miss Sally and of her kisses, which he had never once actually tasted—and of the fact that he'd never even dared speak to her, at least not directly. Fact is, his incredibly alert mind reminded him even as darkness gathered, despite what he'd told Billy and Eliza and all the others, he wasn't engaged to Miss Sally at all. Worse, he'd never even learned her last name!

But . . . he was going to speak with her and find it out! his mind continued peacefully as the darkness continued to grow. Sure as shooting he was! First thing after he'd talked to Ise and his pa a little more about religion—and after he'd figured out what that beautiful, bright light was that seemed to be calling out to him from off in the distance . . .

32

Wednesday, May 18, 1881

Bluff Fields

Billy was holding his son in his arms, and Eliza was standing next to him, but it seemed like they were clinging to each other, using each other for support. So were the Waltons, the Redds, both families of Perkinses and Joneses, the Rowleys, the Lillywhites, the Stevens, the Nielsons, the Deckers, the Mackelprangs, the Lymans— in short, practically every soul who was a citizen of Bluff. They were all together but standing apart from each other in small groups of families, staring mostly eastward. And none of them, including the children, was saying much at all.

Above them a large black crow soared through the morning air, its raucous cry somehow magnifying the silence, the tension. Another crow, perched on top of one of the looming sandstone cliffs that had given the community its name, cried out in distant reply, and then the silence returned. In fact, it was so quiet that the murmuring river, nearly half a mile away to the south, could be heard clearly. And so could the gentle lapping of water that was gathered practically at the feet of the subdued populace.

"How did it happen, Ma?" young Caroline Perkins asked.

"It's a flood," her younger sister Katherine responded simply.

"I know that, dum-dum! I was asking how the flood happened!"

"Girls, girls, be nice to each other—"

"I want to know how it happened too." Youthful Elizabeth

Stevens did not look up at her husband Joshua. "I mean, it hasn't even been storming!"

"Betcha it was storming somewhere upriver though," young Charlie Eugene Walton ventured.

"Either that," Samuel Mackelprang agreed, remembering his recent conversation with Billy Foreman, "or the heat's been melting the winter snows off yonder in the San Juan Mountains."

"Or the La Garita Hills," ten-year-old Benjamin Lillywhite ventured.

"They're the same thing," his older brother Joseph snapped. "Ain't that so, Pa."

"The La Garita Hills are part of the San Juans, yes." Joseph Lillywhite's voice was subdued. "That's where John C. Fremont lost so many men and mules a few years ago when he was exploring a railroad route. But this isn't the time for that, or for arguing."

"It's never a time for arguing," their younger sister Mary Eleanor declared piously.

"I'd sure like to know where all that blue clay comes from." Ann Rowley was still shaking her head in disbelief at the devastation spread before the community.

"Or how to get it to go back there," Rachel Perkins said. "Lem, is the ditch as buried this time as it was a few weeks ago?"

Lemuel Redd's shoulders were slumped with discouragement— a condition that applied to nearly every adult present. "I reckon it is," he replied without looking at his neighbor.

"Well, did it just overflow real bad during the night, or what?" At the moment, Jane Walton was being the most inquisitive. "I can't see how the ditch could have carried this much water and clay."

"It didn't." Billy Foreman's voice was quiet. "Bill Ball warned us that the river was subject to sudden surges and floods, and that's what happened during the night. Whatever happened upstream, the water rose quickly and formed a crest. When it hit our cribs and dam during the night, it overflowed and followed the easiest path, over the jump and along our ditch, covering everything with silt and clay just like before."

"So, why isn't it flowing now? Has the fool river gone down already?"

"Most likely, at least if it was just a crest. I don't—"

"Dam's gone!" George Lewis shouted as he splashed his horse through the water and mud toward the group. "The middle cribs are washed away entire!"

"How about de cribs dat ver protecting de yump?" Bishop Nielson called.

"They're still there, Bishop. So's the headgate. But the ditch is full of silt all the way from there to here, and the water's back down to four, maybe five feet below the Jump. It doesn't look too promising. How thick is the clay and silt over our fields?"

"Half an inch, maybe three quarters," Knmen answered. "But the crops did get a good soaking, which should germinate them. Still, if this clay hardens up like the last time, the plants won't be able to push through it."

"Can't we work it with rakes? Break it up?"

"We could if we knew where the furrows were, and where the new plants were trying to sprout. Even if we could do all that, we've still lost that doggone ditch again! Without it, even if we could get the crops up through the dry hardpan this mud'll turn into by tomorrow, we couldn't keep 'em watered!"

"Den by yimminy," Bishop Nielson growled, "ve vill yust haff to dig out de ditch again und start ofer!"

"Come on, Bishop, give it up! The river's licked us good, and you know it!"

"No, I do not know it! I yust know dat ve haff been called to dis place by de Lord, und vith a little sticky-to-ity ve can—"

"Platte, tell him! You're the stake president. This whole thing's a bust, as everyone here will admit! I say we abandon this miserable place and go home."

"I second the motion! All in favor—"

"Now, hold on a minute," Platte said as he stepped in front of the group. "Maybe some of you have forgotten, but this church isn't a democracy and never was."

"We all vote on things, Platte."

"No, we either sustain or do not sustain, but we do not vote. If a vote fails, an issue or decision is dropped. If one fails to sustain, the issue or decision goes forward while the one who failed to sustain it is dropped. It's called a theocracy, brothers and sisters. God rules through inspiration to his mortal leaders, and we each have the choice of whether or not to follow them. That's our agency. But we're never given the choice about whether to silence the Lord. He rules, and he will not allow us to vote him out of office."

"Well, I still say we should abandon this mission."

"That's right, before we all starve to death!"

"You have that right," Platte Lyman replied quietly. "But neither I nor the bishop has the authority to release you, so if you go it won't be with the Lord's blessing."

"Elder Snow told us we could go if we wanted!"

"Yes, he did, and that was an official offer to be released and to leave with the Lord's blessing. But it was also issued last fall, not now. By staying, you again accepted your call, and though I will once again write the Brethren in Salt Lake to ask for a general release for all of us, it will be sometime in the fall before we receive a response. So, to obtain the Lord's blessings we must exercise Bishop Nielson's sticky-to-ity and persevere, washed-out ditches, flooded crops, and all."

In the silence that followed, Eliza squeezed Billy's hand, and he knew she was saying that she was willing to stay. So was he, but there were still some things—

"Besides which," Platte concluded, his voice noticeably softer, "as both Paul and the Prophet Joseph taught, we are all members of the same body—the church or body of Christ. All members of the natural body are not the eye, the ear, the head, or the hand. We're spread all over. Yet the eye can't say to the ear, I have no need of thee, nor the head to the foot. And if one member suffers, all the members suffer with it; if one member rejoices, so do all the rest.

"So it is with us, you Saints of the San Juan. All of us are united in eternal bonds of fellowship and love, and each of us is dependent upon the rest of us for our very survival. Our numbers are now so few that if any of us leaves, the rest of us may not be strong enough to make it. As the Lord said in the Doctrine and Covenants, 'Without the feet how shall the body be able to stand?' Every one of us is part of that body, helping it to stand rather than fall, and we're all needed here more than we can know!"

"President Lyman iss right!" Bishop Nielson limped forward to stand beside the shorter man. "All in favor off trusting in de Lord und staying to help us vork true dis difficulty, vill you please make it known by raising de right hands?"

A few responded immediately; others were more reluctant. But soon all the settlers had raised their hands.

"Ya, dat iss goot!" the old bishop said. "Any opposed? Ya! President Lyman, I belief de sustaining iss unanimous in de affirmative!"

Platte smiled. "Thank you, Bishop. Now, what to do? We'll need to redig the ditch, of course, and rebuild the lost cribs. We'll also need more seed, so somebody will have to make a quick trip to Colorado. I'd also recommend that somebody return to Escalante for a couple of wagonloads of Charlie Hall's barrels. Except for the ditch, that's the only way I can think of to get water to our crops, and it's a stopgap at best. But I believe it'll be better than nothing."

"President, we're closing in on the end of May. It'll be June before we can get anything replanted, and you know what the June heat is like down here in these bottoms."

"I do, Josh. So starting today we'll be praying for the Lord to temper the elements to our needs. Any other suggestions, folks? Or volunteers?"

"I'll head back to Escalante for the barrels," Lem Redd declared as he raised his hand. "I've still got a couple of good teams that ain't been stolen—"

"Rider coming!" someone called, interrupting the proceedings.

"That's Bill Ball," Kumen declared, and he wasn't the only one to notice the sorrowful look on the man's face.

———o–o–o———

"Howdy, folks. Lem; Platte; Bishop Nielson. Looks like I caught you all at a bad time."

"Yeah, the river's done about what you told us it would," Samuel Mackelprang declared without much rancor.

Bill Ball gazed for a moment at the muddy devastation. "That's too dad-burned bad," he said sincerely. "Treacherous stream's a real monster, all right. You figure on packing it in?"

"We'll be staying," Platte replied firmly, speaking for the community.

"Good for you! I can send a couple of hands down to help out—maybe three or four. Just give me the word."

"Thank you, Bill. They'd be much appreciated."

"Then you'll have 'em!" For a moment Bill Ball grew as silent as his mule, which had moved hardly a muscle since its rider had pulled rein. Quietly he adjusted his hat, then adjusted it again, and no one could help but notice the bleakness of his expression or feel nervous because of it.

"Well," he finally drawled as he shifted a little in his saddle, "this sure seems like a bad time for it, but I don't reckon I've got me much of a choice."

"Something else we should know?" Platte asked.

"I reckon so. Few weeks ago a couple of young fellers from up to Moab bought some cows from me—for their pa. We talked about 'em a little, last time I was down this way."

"We did. Alfred and Isadore Wilson."

"That's right, Platte. They said they'd spent time here and got real close to you folks, especially Billy and Eliza Foreman."

"That's them," Platte replied, nodding toward where Billy and Eliza were suddenly clinging to each other more tightly.

Bill Ball nodded. "Pleased to meet you, folks. I just wished it hadn't come this way."

"What . . . is it?" Eliza asked as she fought the sudden fear that felt as though it were crushing her very soul—

"One of my riders came in from Moab last night, filled to the gills with news of a big Injun battle over in the LaSals—place called Pinhook Draw. Lots of folks was shot, white and Injun both, and it seems that two of the white folks were Alfred and Isadore Wilson."

Her hand over her mouth and her eyes wide, Eliza could not speak. She could hardly even breathe! Ise and Alf both shot? But . . . how could that be? her mind screamed. They didn't even carry guns—

"Were . . . were they—" Billy started to ask. But he didn't finish, for there was no need. As plain as day, he could read the answer in Bill Ball's eyes.

"I'm right sorry," the tall foreman of the LC said as he removed his hat and held it at his side. "Both were killed within a few feet of each other, or at least that's what I was told. By Injuns—Utes or Pahutes, I reckon. Seems the boys weren't armed and were shot from ambush, so it was sure-enough murder. The way the sign laid out, folks in Moab figure they heard the shooting over in Pinhook and were on their way to see if maybe they could lend a hand."

"That sounds like them, all right," Billy said quietly as he held his now-sleeping son and tried to support his grieving wife, who was sobbing quietly and still trying to comprehend. "I know they were more than willing to help us when we needed it."

"Ya," Bishop Nielson added as he stepped to the other side of Eliza and put his arm around her, buoying her up with his compassion as much as his strength. "Yesus said, 'Greater love hass no man dan dis, dat a man lay down hiss life for hiss friends.'"

"Amen," Platte said solemnly.

"Amen," others repeated.

The morning's silence now broken by quiet sobs, Bill Ball did not know what else to say. Neither could he bring himself to look directly at the Foreman couple, who seemed the hardest hit.

"I'm right sorry," he breathed again, knowing it was not enough and that no matter what he said, it never would be. "I sure-enough am! In some ways, I reckon, this is a mighty tough country to grow old in!"

And without another word he placed his hat back on his head, turned his mule, and rode slowly away.

EPILOGUE

Saturday, July 30, 1881

Bluff Fort

"Joseph Nielson, what are you doing sitting on the ground?"

With a start Joseph Nielson looked up from behind the newspaper he had been reading, and he was immediately embarrassed. "Sorry, Sister Eliza, I didn't even see you come in. I . . . uh . . . I was just reading how the outlaw Billy the Kid was shot dead in Fort Sumner, New Mexico Territory, just two weeks ago."

"Then that must be a new paper!"

"Yes, ma'am. Brother Lyman brought it in last night. From Colorado. The date on it is just a few days ago." The young man's attention returned to the paper in his hand. "I just can't believe that the famous Billy the Kid is dead."

Eliza shook her head in disgust. "We do live in a bloodthirsty country hereabouts. By the by, Mary told me we had some mail here."

"Oh, that's right!" Embarrassed, Joseph scrambled to his feet and hurried behind the plank, stretched over two barrels, that served as a counter. "I'm just spelling Walter off this afternoon, so I ain't . . . I mean, I'm not used to running this new co-op. Let's see—Yeah, here it is, unsealed and addressed to Billy. It's a thick one, too, from a feller name of Henry W. Heat—" Joseph paused in surprise. "Eliza, this is from Henry W.! Jimmy Heaton's brother!"

"What a pleasant surprise," Eliza said, beaming as she took the proffered letter. "We haven't heard from them since they left last spring."

"Well, once you've read it, Sister Eliza, be sure and tell me how they're doing."

"Since it's addressed to Billy," Eliza said, "I'll have him read it and make the report. How does that sound?"

"Dandy." Joseph grinned. "Just dandy." And by the time Eliza was out the door, little Willy scampering after her, the son of Bishop Nielson was already absorbed again in the death of Billy the Kid.

"I'll tell you what, hon-bun," Billy declared with a wide yawn. "Henry W. didn't write much of a letter. Mostly this is just a bunch of newspaper clippings from some Colorado papers."

It was late evening, although because of the longer days of summer it was still quite light outdoors. But the chores were done, the Saturday-night baths were behind them, and Billy, his muscles still aching because of the hard labor on the infamous ditch that he and every other able-bodied individual in the fort was putting forth, could hardly hold his eyes open.

Eliza was seated in her rocker before the fireplace, keeping her hands busy darning holes that seemed to appear daily in her husband's well-worn socks. Of course, with boots that were worn out and didn't fit him properly otherwise, she thought, it was no wonder the woolen socks were so ravaged. Sadly, his feet were in much the same condition.

Out of habit she glanced toward the small pallet where little Willy was sleeping, making certain of the boy's well-being. It was amazing what he could sleep through, she thought, and what he couldn't. She hadn't noticed those things before his illness. But now that he was doing so much better, she was seeing all sorts of little things about her son—things that drew her heart to him more than ever.

"What does Henry W. have to say?" she asked as her hands continued their work.

"Not much. 'Dear Billy and Eliza and little Willy, Hope all is well with you. All is as well here as can be expected. I think of you often, with many fond remembrances. I thought perhaps you might be interested in reading about the band of Utes what caused us all so much grief and sorrow this past spring. Hopefully they won't do it again. I have included a note from Jimmy. Your friend always, Henry W. Heaton.'"

Eliza smiled. "Henry W. was a man of few words, all right. What does the more loquacious Jimmy have to say?"

Billy shuffled through the papers. "I don't know. Henry W. must have forgotten to include it, because there's nothing else in this envelope but the news articles."

"Oh, dear! The envelope was open when I picked it up this afternoon. I do hope Jimmy's note hasn't been lost somewhere by the carrier."

"Well, if it was, we'll just write Jimmy and request another one. What do you think? I'm sure Henry W. is sending these accounts on account of the Wilson boys who were killed in the Pinhook fight, so they'll likely be mentioned. Are you up to listening to such a tragedy?"

Laying her head back against her wooden rocker, Eliza closed her eyes for a moment. "I don't know, Billy," she finally admitted. "The deaths of those boys hit me mighty hard."

"I know they did. I also know that you're no more than a month and a half away from delivering your second child. I don't want to read you anything that might upset you."

"Thank you, darling." Eliza sighed. "Still, I'm feeling a great deal more peace about their deaths than I first did."

"Time does that, doesn't it." Billy was smoothing the folded articles beneath his hands.

"Why don't you go ahead, darling. If need be, I'll stop you."

"Very well." Billy smiled. "Here goes. The *Dolores News* of June 25, 1881, says, 'War! with the Indians—Rico's Boys Who Went to Recover the Property of Unprotected Settlers Have Met a Sad Fate.'"

"Rico?" Eliza asked. "Weren't those fellows you worked with from Rico?"

"They were." Billy was now reading silently. "Apparently the Indians killed some ranchers named May, Smith, and Thurman," he explained as he read, "stole their horses, and headed west toward the Blue Mountains. They killed another man at Piute Springs, stole Spud Hudson's herd of horses, and then at least some of them came here to Bluff and stole ours. Their hands were already stained red with blood when we met up with them to get our horses back, and more and more the miracle of our safety becomes obvious. Even now I can't imagine that no blood was spilled there at Boiling Springs. Why, the way those Pahutes were yelling and shrieking and poking their guns into folks was a caution."

"I've never doubted that the Lord protected you."

Billy nodded. "This article says, 'The eighteen brave boys of Rico fought nobly, and compelled the copper-colored hell-hounds to leave behind them one hundred head of horses and a large number of sheep and goats.'" Billy paused, again looking up. "Platte says the number of horses was actually closer to fifteen hundred head, which after Spud Hudson and his posse rounded them up off the LaSals and cut their hundred out, the army boys drove back to Colorado."

"That's a frightful lot of horses."

Billy nodded. "It is. I . . . Oh, goodness! I do know these fellows! Listen to this: 'On the first day, J. H. Eskridge, James Hall and Dave Willis were almost surrounded by Indians, and instead of retreating, these three of the world's bravest men stepped in and fought hand to hand with more than ten times their number, killing several Indians. Here Willis was riddled with bullets; Eskridge, whom it is supposed the Indians believed to be captain (as he had a large, gaudy chihuahua hat), had the hat riddled with bullets so it cannot be worn, and his hair was nearly all cut off with scalp wounds and grazing bullets. Hall was wounded in one knee, one shoulder, and the ribs of one side were seriously injured. Here the Indians retreated, and soon afterwards fired upon the boys again, wounding Eskridge in the ankle so seriously that amputation will be necessary if he lives until that aid can be rendered. He laughs most all of the time with his suffering, and when forbearance of pain ceases to be a virtue, he shrieks as loud as his lungs will permit and at last account wanted to fight. Hall bears his suffering bravely too. Both are unfit for battle. Eight of the eighteen were missing on the eve of the first day. Jordan Bean of the missing ones, alone, was found on the second day, shot through the head, but conscious and able to talk, saying that he did not know that one of the remaining seven was dead, but felt positive that they were *all* dead. The names of these are: Jack Galloway, H. H. Melvin, Tom Click, T. C. Taylor, the two Tartar brothers, and a young man unknown.

Billy looked stricken as he put down the paper. "Oh, Eliza, every single one of those fellows was on my crew—dead and wounded alike!"

"Billy, I'm sorry—"

"I can't hardly believe this! The Wilsons and now them? No wonder Henry W. sent these papers to us. I need to get word to Dick and George—"

"Who do you think the unidentified young man was?"

Billy shook his head. "I don't know," he responded sadly. "I'm just glad it wasn't Henry W. or Jimmy! That would have been more than I could take!"

"I feel the same. Is there more?"

Billy nodded. "Here's another article, dated July 2. 'Last Version of the Grand Valley Indian Battle,' it's called. Maybe they'll identify the young man. 'The first day's fight began on a small creek near Mill Creek, the Indians firing and retreating for a distance of seven miles, into Little Castle Valley, which is about eight hundred yards wide, walled in with steep cliffs on both sides. The Indians took shelter or protection in the rocks at noon, from where they kept up a continual firing for about an hour and a half, when they divided their forces, sending mounted, to the valley, sixteen Indians armed with Winchester rifles. Captain W. H. Dawson had with him in his engagement, eighteen men, whom he says were brave without an exception. The party of eight which were killed, together with the Wilson brothers—'"

"Oh, Billy," Eliza breathed, stopping her husband, "this is so hard to hear! Just imagine what their dear parents have had to live with!"

"I . . . I can't even begin to." Billy paused for a moment to keep the emotion from his voice. "Perhaps they've taken some comfort in knowing that their sons were true heroes. I certainly hope so!"

"But how could you possibly deal with your loneliness? With

knowing that your children, who are supposed to outlive you and who still have their whole lives in front of them, will never be coming home again? will never on this earth be able to fulfill any of their dreams!"

Soberly Billy shook his head. "I don't know, Eliza. I truly don't. If that was little Willy who had been in that battle, then . . . then— well, like I said, I just don't think I could bear it!"

For a moment the two sat in silence, the only sounds the ticking of the Regulator clock and the distant barking of dogs. Finally Billy spoke again: "Speaking of Alfred and Isadore, Platte told me that a Brother Joseph Burkholder of Moab was one of those who found their bodies. According to Platte, he backtracked from where they lay to their camp, which the Utes had looted as expected, taking everything. But there on the cold ashes of their campfire was a perfectly good cap-and-ball Indian rifle, which fired the instant one of the searchers touched the trigger. Why do you suppose the Indians would have left behind a treasured weapon like that?"

"Maybe they forgot it?"

Billy shook his head. "Maybe, but not likely, at least to my way of thinking. But I don't have a better reason, unless maybe it got in the way of one of their customs or beliefs. Posey has an old rifle like that, one that I know for a fact doesn't work too well. It'd be something if it turned out to be his.

"Let's see," Billy continued when Eliza didn't respond, "I was . . . here: 'The killed, it is supposed, fought for about seven hours where they were killed. They had been engaged in a running fight from 10:00 A.M. and fought till sunset; several had been wounded before being killed; Jack Galloway had one hand neatly bound and tied with a handkerchief, when found.

"'On the next day a detachment was sent out in search of the killed and wounded, coming in conflict with the Indians again. Here the Indians would have prevented their finding the lost, and the party wisely retreated four miles, hotly pursued by the Indians, where the white party having a little advantage, killed several Indians.

"'It is estimated from all seen and known that eighteen Indians were killed. The white party fought in every conceivable manner, the Indians having a great advantage the first day. The dead bodies were found on the fourth day and were so decomposed that it was almost impossible to bury them at all, but they were buried about where they fell. Five were buried in one grave and three in another.

"'To say that our friends were faultless, who have gone from us, would be untrue, for they were men. Who has not a fault? They were our friends and comrades. Mothers, sisters, fathers, and brothers, and bereaved wives and children, will weep for those who are no more. They are gone, and who will measure the time of their leave? They loved and were loved. The tender chords have been severed and cannot be forgotten, and when the news breaks the silence of their absence at home, do you think tenderly, or do you realize that they are gone? The dear ones at home hoped that they might sometime return, but alas! they are now gone forever.'"

Again Billy looked at Eliza. "You know, as badly as I feel for those fellows from Rico, I can't help but wondering who will weep or call for sorrow at the loss of the Utes, some of whom were women and possibly children. Platte says this battle is being called a massacre of white folks, but what does that mean it was for the Indians, who lost nearly twice as many?"

Shocked, Eliza looked at her husband. "Are you truly serious? You know very well the Utes deserved what they got, and probably a whole lot more. They murdered those men in Colorado, stole their horses, nearly stole ours, and would have killed you and the other brethren but for the direct intervention of God! Merciful heavens, Billy! It's fine to feel sympathy, especially for women and children accidentally killed. But I can't imagine that you would feel sympathy for those murdering savages!"

For a long moment Billy was silent, thinking. Then he smiled. "I reckon that's the mothering instinct in you, Eliza, feeling protective of little Willy and me. It's the same emotion that causes you to suffer for that unknown boy. That's part of why I love you so much, and why I count my blessings every day that the Lord brought you into my life."

"Billy," Eliza declared in frustration, "it's more than that! I'm telling you, it is! I . . . I think I'm okay with the Navajos, or at least most of them. But as for the Pahutes, I absolutely loathe them!"

"No you don't, hon-bun," Billy argued, his expression now

serious. "I know you too well. I know your heart, your spirit, your faith! I've watched you grow in the Spirit until you were ready for this harsh land, ready for the peace mission we've been called to fulfill. We've been called to it by the Lord's anointed, both before we left Cedar and since. But that doesn't mean we're here on the San Juan to enjoy peace. No, not yet, at least. Instead, we've been sent here to proclaim it, and to do our best to live it so that our wild and woolly neighbors can clearly see the benefits of it in our lives. As Platte says, we can do that best by practicing the Golden Rule—treating these souls as we hope and pray they will learn to treat us. If we'll do that, never thirsting after their blood no matter what they do to us—if we'll just turn their wickedness over to God and nurture the love of Christ in our hearts toward them, then our peace will be in the Lord God of Israel. He will go before and after us and leave his angels to stand guard round about us like they did that day at Boiling Springs, and we will truly have nothing to fear."

Billy smiled again. "You know all that, hon-bun, for you're filled with more natural love than any other human being I know—"

His attention diverted by the newspaper clippings in his hands, Billy began reading again, and Eliza was left to herself, wondering. Could it really be so simple, she thought? So pie-in-the-sky—

"Oh, no!" Billy suddenly exclaimed as he rose to his feet. "Oh, dear God in heaven! Not him too!"

"Billy, what is it? What on earth's wrong?"

His expression now truly bleak, Billy laid the papers on the table.

"Billy—"

"The young man they . . . they couldn't identify?" Billy was weeping as he rose and went to his wife, drawing her up to him. "Eliza, darling, it . . . it *was* Jimmy! Our Jimmy Heaton!"

Once again Eliza was speechless. This couldn't be happening! It just couldn't! "Are . . . you certain?" she asked in a forced whisper. "How do they know it was Jimmy?"

"It's here in an Extra I just read," Billy replied as he wiped his eyes and then blew his nose. "It says . . . that Henry W. went to the site and identified him. Apparently he was lying with the seven others in a small ravine, so close together that a thirty-foot rope would have reached across all of them."

Elixa's eyes were boring into her husband. "What . . . what else does it say?"

"Eliza, I don't think—"

"Billy, what else does it say? I want to hear it all! Now!"

Surprised at his wife's sudden anger, Billy helped her back to the rocker. "Very well," he said as he returned to the table, where he once again wiped his face, "this next account, dated July 9, says, 'The second rescue party crossed over into a wide, open valley and it was the battleground. To the right of the trail, about fifty yards, completely hidden by brush, lay the body of a squaw. She was probably fatally wounded in the early part of the fight and crawled away to die. The head was uphill and the blanket was drawn lightly around the shoulders. Shortly afterward we found where an Indian pack had been cut loose. The saddles which had been ridden by Jack Galloway and Wiley Tartar were thrown upon the bushes, being very poorly rigged. On the field was found the pocketbook of young Jimmy Heaton, one of the murdered. All that was in it when picked up was a photograph of his brother, one of himself, and a letter—'"

Eliza's eyes were wide and moist. "Oh, Billy, do you think that was our letter?"

"I reckon so. Only somehow it got lost—" Again choked up, Billy returned to the article and somehow finished it: 'A letter to one of the Tartar boys was found and several coats left. Some few Indian trinkets were picked up, including a comb, some arrows, and several jing bobs to ornament bridles.'"

Eliza, her darning forgotten in her lap, closed her eyes. "Does it . . . ever say that they caught the Indians? Or punished them?"

His eyes scanning the rest of the clippings, Billy slowly shook his head. "Not here. According to this, the army trailed them back to the reservation in Colorado and then returned to the Blue Mountains to establish a permanent post. From the bloody rags found along the way, they do believe there were many wounded."

"Oh, Billy, it's all so unfair!" For a moment Eliza's anger held. But finally grief washed over her, and she dissolved into body-wracking sobs.

———◇—◇—◇———

"Billy? Eliza? You folks at home?"

Billy, who had just lit the lantern, stepped to the door. "We're home, Platte," he responded heavily. "Will you come in?"

Platte Lyman smiled. "Not tonight, thank you. I still have another meeting before morning, and I'm tired. But Delia was going through my saddlebags and found this letter addressed to you. It isn't in an envelope, and it looks like it's seen some rough—Billy, what on earth is the matter?"

Ignoring the question, Billy reached hesitantly for the letter. "Do . . . you know who it's from?"

"I didn't look. Your name is on the outside, so I just brought it over. Billy, what is it?"

"This is . . . from Jimmy Heaton." Billy was struggling again with his emotions and could hardly control his voice. "He . . . he was one of the Colorado posse killed in that Pinhook battle—"

"Oh, no! Billy, I'm right sorry to hear that. The Wilson boys and now Jimmy. I just didn't know!"

"We . . . didn't, either—not until today. Thank you, Platte. This means more than I can say!"

Inside again, Billy sat at the table and simply looked at the two crumpled, soiled sheets of foolscap paper. Eliza, her eyes bright but no longer tearful, did not speak, and so after a few moments Billy took a deep breath, unfolded the pages, and began:

"'My dear Friends Billy Eliza and Ise:

"'I was going to write you separate but this is all my paper and I had to burrow it. I am here chasing Injuns with the boys from Rico and had one close shave and not much else but am feeling worse all the time on account of I bin lusting after the blood of the Lamanites which the bishp says is a turrible sin and I admit I am guilty. I bin reading the Book of Mormon and have purty much done it up proper but I still have a great many questions I think too many and I wish I had gone to Moab insted of here so I could ask your pa Ise but I didn't. I would also ask you Billy and Eliza as I know you would say the truth but I'm not nowhere near Bluff so I can't.

"'I'm back now and the light is poor at best and getting worse as the fire dies and the boys are starting in to pester me again which

412

seems to be their fun so this will be short. The thing I just done a little bit ago I suppose on account of my sorrowful feelings and not being able to get you Ise off my mind I reckon on account of you are close by in Moab was to go off into the trees and ask the Lord as the Book of Mormon says about my questions. Nothing much happened except that while I was fixing to finish this letter I was thinking about it and it come to me that I couldn't recollect my questions any more and I wasn't worried any more neither which was some surprise I can tell you because I bin terrible worried about some lies I have told you and others about me and Miss Sally which are really wishes but which weren't right nohow and I knew it all the while.

"'Now I have me the feeling that I won't be leaving this mountain alive which is fearsome but ok as I think God is saying I've cleared things up and have learnt the truth about things which is important. Course I am probably just being a little kid worrying over nothing but if not I am glad you are all my friends and will maybe think of me from time to time. I haven't ever kilt anyone even Injuns and I am glad of it as I think it is wrong no matter. I also heard Miss Sally was going away with a Misisipy riverboat gambler but I didn't tell no one on account of I was being a little kid that way too and I am sorry but now I feel happy and think all will work out for the best for her. Only thing is I wish I could say adios to the 3 of you and my folks and Henry W. who I expect will feel bad but other than that all I want is for you to see that I am baptised and whatever else you need to do after I am kilt so I can be with the Lord insted of some wheres else where I wouldn't want to be if you know what I mean.

"'Like all of you tolt me about a thousand times the gospel of Jesus is true and I am certin of it at last. I reckon that means I am a Mormon like you the thought of which gives me good feelings all over and makes me glad to say it to others too. Your friend forever James Heaton.

"'P.S. I hope you keep calling me Jimmy.'"

———◦—◦—◦———

"Billy, are you awake?"

Rolling onto his back, Billy stared up into the darkness. "I am," he breathed. "Somehow I can't seem to stop thinking about those boys. I've never felt quite this lonely, this empty."

"I feel the same. My memories are dim, of course, but this seems harder to bear than the separation from my family when I set sail for America." Eliza sighed deeply. "Who'd have supposed that we could get that close to those youngsters in such a short time?"

"Who indeed?"

For a moment the two were silent, the ticking of the clock the only sound in the stillness of the night. Next to their bed, Willy breathed softly and regularly, and abruptly the unborn child in Eliza's womb began to kick.

"Billy, we've both been praying for a girl, haven't we."

"Well, I have, mostly because I keep having the feeling that's what you're going to have."

"If you're wrong—if I'm wrong—" Eliza's voice suddenly broke. "W-would you mind very much if we named the child J-Jimmy? Jimmy Isadore?"

"Jimmy Isadore Foreman," Billy said as a smile spread slowly across his face. "Hon-bun, I can't think of a better name on the face of this wide green earth!" And in the darkness Billy reached out and tenderly pulled his grieving wife nearer to his heart.

Soon to be released: *Heart's Afire: Book Three—Curly Bill's Christmas,* continues the dangers and experiences of the various inhabitants of the San Juan country through the rest of 1881. In addition, the author's *To Soar with the Eagle,* previously released by Deseret Book, is a prequel to the *Heart's Afire* series.

AUTHOR'S NOTE

Because various aspects of the preceding story seem to beg a historical explanation, I offer the following. The San Juan River was called by the settlers the Grim Monster as it defied, time and time again, all their efforts to tame it. Twice in the spring of 1881 it flooded, both times destroying all their previous labors. To supplement their nonexistent agricultural income and to put food on their tables, nearly all the men drifted far afield in the winter months, seeking employment. Most ended up working for the railroad in Colorado and becoming at least acquainted, and often friends with, the citizens there. They also referred to their riverbank home as the "Fort on the Firing Line," and all who left records wrote that life seemed a continual battle for their very existence, with enemies every direction they turned.

Natanii nééz, after defying several dire warnings from Thales Haskel, was cursed as described in the story and endured about twenty more years in that condition. The same sort of curse was pronounced upon Posey and his big gun, though what ultimately happened to him took much longer to play out. Dah nishuánt was the father of Peokon, who perished of unknown causes after a curse was pronounced upon him (see *Hearts Afire: Book One—At All Hazards*). The elderly Navajo was always friendly to the Mormon settlers and used his influence at all times to foster good relations between them and his Navajo people. Bitseel, on the other hand, was not friendly to the Saints and apparently hated Posey and the Pahutes just as fervently.

As I explained in the preface, the Navajo woman Hádapa, who

brought daily rations of goat's milk to save the life of a starving Mormon child, is a historical character with a fictional name. The Bluff Saints quickly accepted her, as they did all others of both tribes who returned their friendship and love.

The words of the Navajo and Ute/Pahute languages used in this story have been included in order to show the reality—and true diversity—of the two cultures. Though the spellings may be slightly off, the words are real, and I have made every effort to use them in their proper context.

The Ute/Pahute raid on the horse herd of the Colorado ranchers is well documented, as is the subsequent chase by the posses of Spud Hudson, Captain William Dawson, and Bill May. The news articles quoted in the epilogue are the actual articles printed in area newspapers at the time of the Pinhook battle. The way the Mormons of Bluff became involved in this raid is also historical, as is their miraculous deliverance.

My friend Karl Barton was kind enough to conduct me to the Pinhook Draw on the Castle Valley side of the LaSal Mountains, where we gazed at the weather-worn grave markers of the slain members of the Rico posse and looked down from the positions the Indians held when they opened fire. We also saw the site (unmarked, sadly) where several of the Indians were slain a day later. It was truly a sobering experience on all counts!

But despite the fact that the Big Raid was life-changing for a large number of people, the Mormon settlers on the San Juan were dealing with so many threats and crises, both before and after the raid, that their records attach no more importance to it than, say, another failure of their recalcitrant but essential ditch, or the loss of a few more horses to the thieves of whatever culture happened upon them.

Any connection between Alfred and Isadore Wilson and Henry W. and Jimmy Heaton, or between them and the Bluff Saints, is entirely speculative on my part and has been written fictitiously. The ideas for these associations, however, came from accounts of actual interactions between the Bluff Saints, the Moab settlers, and the more established citizens of southwestern Colorado.

That said, I had the feeling as I did my research and put this book together, that the story my characters were in fact playing out was one of survival amid grueling, unending hardship, with an ever-increasing faith the lubricant that enabled all the groups to reach toward a frictionless future together. Book three will finish this aspect of the story.